THE
CHILLING

'Rug up for this icy survivalist thriller: *Touching the Void*
by way of John Carpenter's *The Thing*.'
**Benjamin Stevenson, author of *Everyone on
This Train is a Suspect***

'Riley James is one to watch: stoke the fire and lock the windows,
you're in for one hell of a ride.'
Margaret Hickey, author of *Cutters End*

'Drier than a Jane Harper novel, more snow than a shelf of Scandi
noir, *The Chilling* is a white-knuckle thrill ride from the first page.
One of the best crime debuts of the year. I couldn't stop reading.'
Aoife Clifford, author of *It Takes a Town*

'*The Chilling* is an atmospheric thriller with a wild setting and
a fast-paced plot—you won't be able to put it down.'
Christian White, author of *Wild Place*

THE
CHILLING

RILEY JAMES

ALLEN&UNWIN
SYDNEY•MELBOURNE•AUCKLAND•LONDON

First published in 2024

Allen & Unwin
Cammeraygal Country
83 Alexander Street
Crows Nest NSW 2065
Australia
Phone: (61 2) 8425 0100
Email: info@allenandunwin.com
Web: www.allenandunwin.com

Allen & Unwin acknowledges the Traditional Owners of the Country on which we live and work. We pay our respects to all Aboriginal and Torres Strait Islander Elders, past and present.

A catalogue record for this book is available from the National Library of Australia

ISBN 978 1 76147 087 5

Set in 12/17 pt Minion Pro by Midland Typesetters, Australia
Printed and bound in Australia by the Opus Group

10 9 8 7 6 5 4 3 2 1

The paper in this book is FSC® certified. FSC® promotes environmentally responsible, socially beneficial and economically viable management of the world's forests.

A Serpent when he is benummed with cold, hath poyson within him, though he do not exert it; 'Tis the same in us, whom only weakness keeps innocent, and a kind of Winter in our Fortunes.

—Justus Lipsius

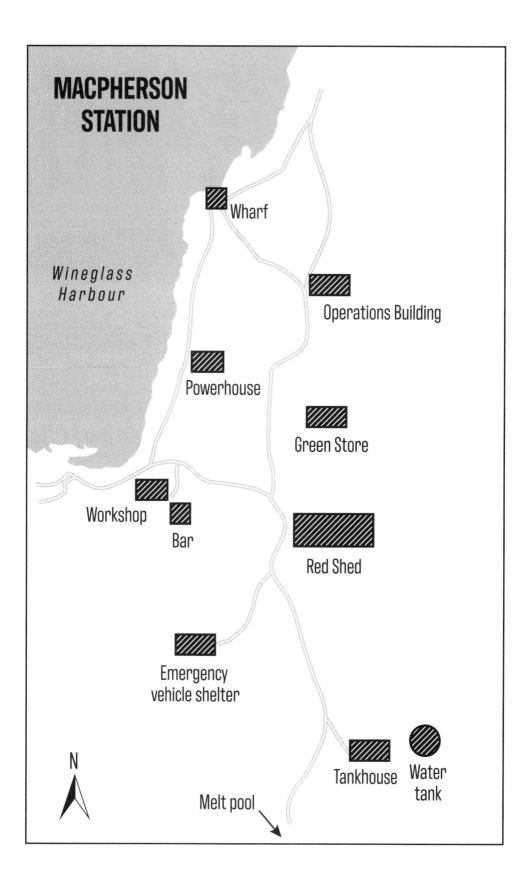

PROLOGUE

It was a bird that lived on carrion—a bird that ate the dead.

Arindam heard the skua gull before he'd fully regained consciousness. He was still strapped into his plane seat and had no idea how long he'd been there. The impact of the landing must have knocked him out. As he came to, the bird's repetitive burr echoed over the empty white valley.

There was usually no life in this godforsaken place, nothing that could eat or breathe or even make a background noise—no trees, no dogs, no trilling insects. But now there was this one bird somewhere outside his window. It had to be a skua, didn't it? The predatory creature was known for scavenging the carcasses of seals and penguins. It also chased, robbed and pirated the food of other birds, and it gorged on their fledgling young. But mostly, it ate the dead.

Oh great, thought Arindam in despair.

He knew his injuries were not catastrophic: there was only a cruel throbbing in his head and a stiffness in his neck—he'd been in worse pain with a dislocated shoulder last summer. But he couldn't ignore the sickening dizziness and the furious pounding of his heart. He was suffering from severe shock and he wasn't dressed for minus eight degrees Celsius. A search-and-rescue team wouldn't make it in time. As an ice driller, he'd done too many field-training exercises to fool himself otherwise: he would soon be carrion.

Prior to the crash, their twin-engine aircraft had been lost, technically speaking. On any other day, the captain would have handled the weather with ease. An experienced pilot and a fellow Brit, Noah was used to flying in snow-covered terrain. He'd flown the same interior route to East Antarctica dozens of times—he'd already transported Arindam's field research group twice that season—and he knew what to do in a whiteout. But today, when the aircraft had reverted to flying by instruments, something hadn't been right. Noah suspected the altimeter was broken.

'We're not where we're supposed to be,' he said, an edge of concern to his voice. 'I don't think we're in position. I'm just going to duck under this cloud bank.'

He was speaking to his co-pilot Roger, but Arindam heard everything from the first row. He'd learnt they'd been in the air too long and should've been approaching the runway by now.

'If I could find the horizon,' muttered Noah, 'I'd have a visual reference.'

In an Antarctic whiteout there was no way of telling the difference between the sky and the ground. There was no contrast between the clouds, the great sheet of ice on the water and the snow coating the surface—everything was a uniform shade of white. Usually, the pilot could catch a glimpse of shadow or a jagged peak. But in the current conditions, he was having trouble finding even the landing aids.

'I don't like this,' said Noah, glancing back at his three passengers. 'This just doesn't look right.'

His voice had been calm, but when Arindam saw the captain's face, his stomach plunged. There'd been a flicker in Noah's eyes, a flash of panic.

Arindam couldn't remember much after that. There was the deafening roar of the engines as Noah tried to turn the plane, and there was Roger's frantic mayday call to base. Arindam clung to his seat, the aircraft rocking, his muscles aching with the strain. When he glanced at the window, a blur of white sped past before a grey ridge loomed into view.

Now the plane was still and quiet. There was a pile of snow where the cockpit had been. On top, a pale arm stuck out at an odd angle, stiff and frozen. Arindam registered that it was wearing Noah's watch before a wave of nausea pulled him under.

When he woke again, a cold wind was blowing through the fuselage. His head felt worse than before. He slowly turned and saw that the tail section was gone. A gaping hole exposed the wreckage to the drift outside. It was still daylight, but the sky had turned a dishwater grey.

'Hello?' he croaked into the void. His throat felt dry, like he'd been shouting.

No one replied. No one else was on board. It occurred to him he was going to die alone. Unless there was someone in the tail section? Someone still strapped to their seat? Outside?

As he went to unbuckle himself, pain shot through his hand, a burning pins-and-needles sensation. He groaned and looked down to see a fine crystalline layer of ice had formed on the exposed flesh of his forearm. It extended from his elbow to his wrist, covering the friendship band his daughter Aisha had made for him. With a shock, he realised his skin looked like frozen meat. His body was being devoured by the cold. Soon the blood in his veins would be frozen too. He imagined tendrils of ice stretching up his neck and into his scalp.

3

The skua sounded its alarm again outside the window. Arindam hunched forward to get a better look. The powerful brown-grey bird was perched on a plane seat a few feet away from the fuselage. It kept bobbing up and down, its pointed wings drawn back like a Viking helmet. It was yanking at something with its frightful beak.

The bird filled Arindam with fear. He moaned into the silence, his heart still pounding. This is no way to die, he thought, with that creature out there waiting for him. He recalled eight-year-old Aisha presenting her gift bracelet, begging him to remember her. For his daughter's sake, he could get up and stomp his feet; he could get his blood pumping and generate some warmth. Perhaps the feeling would come back to his fingers and he could write a note. Then he could find one of his colleagues—Pete or Barry—and they could shelter together and make a plan.

With fumbling hands, he unclicked the seatbelt. He slid out of the chair onto his knees. His seat was broken and bent, almost ripped from the flooring. His yellow coat rustled as he inched into the aisle and crawled towards the back of the aircraft, panting and moaning. Unable to feel his hands and feet, his limbs got caught in the scattered bags and equipment on the way. When he got to the opening, he tumbled towards the ground below. With a soft crunch and a puff of snow like smoke, he landed on his back. Somewhere in his sluggish brain, he could feel his Polartec trousers grow cold and wet.

Breathing heavily, he struggled to his knees, and looked over the crash site. There was a dirty streak like a driveway scorched into the ground, and several patches of debris across a field of crevasses. Most of the wreckage was submerged in snow. He could make out the shape of a wing to his left and something that might have been the tail section further off. His heart sank when he realised there was no sign of other people, dead or alive. The lonely part of him would have preferred carnage to this desolate wasteland.

Then he spotted the skua, still on the back of the seat.

He lurched towards the bird, ploughing through the snow on his knees. 'Shoo!' he called out hoarsely, as he stumbled forward. 'Shoo!'

His voice sounded weak to his own ears, but it startled the bird, which hopped to the ground, beating its wings impatiently.

As Arindam rose behind the seat, he spotted an arm thrown over the side. 'Hello?' he called, peering around the front.

His heart stalled in his chest.

The broken, twisted corpse was slumped into the cushions. Its head was bent at a sickening angle, with its neck elongated and one cheek resting on its shoulder. The face was livid white, and instead of eyeballs there were only two bloodied holes.

Before he could look away, he noticed that the sockets were framed by torn pieces of flesh and bare patches of skull where the skua had been feasting. On one side of the corpse's mouth, a row of stained teeth was exposed; on the other, a piece of frozen drool trailed down a white beard.

He had found Pete.

On the flight, the lead scientist had been sitting behind Arindam. A long-limbed man, he kept pushing the back of the chair, until Arindam turned around and glared at him. 'Sorry, buddy,' said Pete, who was simply uncrossing his legs. He sounded sincere and Arindam felt bad for being so prickly. It had been a long day: they'd been cutting trenches in the ice since early morning. As a courtesy, Pete moved to one of the empty rows in the tail.

Arindam collapsed against the side of Pete's chair, his breath coming in great heaving sobs. When the bird returned to its feast, Arindam jerked his head away and staggered backwards. He'd taken only a few steps when his boot plunged through the dusty surface of a snow bridge. He dropped into the crevasse as if through a trap door.

With a hard jolt, he landed upright on a platform hardly wider than a window ledge. The crevasse walls glowed pale blue, and the caverns below appeared eerily lit from within. The sudden fall in temperature was shocking. His lungs gasped for air, and he could no longer feel any part of his body. He was beyond cold, beyond breath and beyond pain.

Barely conscious, he heard a low rumbling in the distance. To his surprise, he realised it was a motor engine: a Hägglunds.

The vehicle stopped, and a door creaked open. There was a flurry of human movement and the crunch of feet on snow. It seemed to go on for some time.

Then a man began talking only a few yards away, his soft Australian twang rising and falling in the wind. 'There's no survivors,' he said. 'They're all dead.'

1

'He's an arsehole,' said Daphne.

Kit Bitterfeld glanced up warily from her Sunday newspaper. She'd never heard her mother swear before. Even now, despite the dementia, the word didn't sound like it should be in Daphne's vocabulary.

Reluctantly, Kit peered at her mother's face and took in her confused watery-eyed expression. The elderly woman was seated upright against the pillows on a narrow single bed. Her electric blanket was on even though it was a hot summer's day, and her cheeks were flushed pink. Her ancient eyes darted about the room.

'I beg your pardon?' said Kit, her voice tired and neutral.

'That man,' said Daphne, her gaze coming to rest on Kit's face, 'your husband.'

'My ex-husband,' corrected Kit.

'Yes, that man. He's a castle.'

'A *castle*?' said Kit, a little surprised.

Daphne nodded, and Kit nodded back with encouragement. She was relieved to find that it was just a nonsense word, a random firing from her mother's brain. Kit hadn't the energy to cope with another outburst, not today.

'I told you,' continued Daphne, 'when you introduced me to him. I warned you about him. I said, "He's a remarkably handsome man", didn't I? We were in the kitchen at the old house, and you said, "We're going to get married." And that's when I warned you. I said, "There's such a thing as being too good-looking, Kitty." And that man is *too* good-looking.'

Kit frowned and shifted uncomfortably. She was disturbed that Daphne had remembered.

That day, the two of them had been alone in the kitchen. Elliot had just gone to the bathroom, and they were waiting for him to come back. They'd been discussing Kit's new hairdo, a self-styled pixie cut. Her mother was complimenting her, even though Kit had cut the fringe too short and severe. Daphne said she liked it, that Kit looked like a pretty Joan of Arc. Kit was pleased.

That was why the veiled insult took her by surprise.

'You should be careful, Kitty,' Daphne said suddenly. 'A handsome man is like a castle.'

The boiling jug gurgled on the bench, and the teacups rattled ominously. Kit felt a weight in her stomach. *Here it comes*, she thought. Trust her mother to cut her to the quick with a he-can-do-better-than-you, just when Kit felt so stupid about her hair—and when she already knew Elliot was out of her league.

'You know the old saying,' said Daphne. 'A handsome man is like a castle, and a castle much assaulted will eventually yield. Women will look at him on the street, they'll make suggestions, they'll throw themselves at him.' Her eyes narrowed. 'And being a man, he'll like it. He'll like the attention and the suggestions, just you wait and see—he'll give in to them.'

In that instant, an image of Elliot from the night before came to Kit's mind. He was standing at the picnic table in the backyard, talking to boring Lucia from the bushwalking club. He was smiling politely, throwing in a line here and there, helping the conversation along, his square jaw moving and his eyes working their charm. Lucia looked animated for once.

But from where Kit sat inside, she could see Elliot subtly incline his head to the right, to where Melody stood not more than a few metres away.

Melody was wearing a short one-piece jumpsuit, the kind you had to take off completely to go to the bathroom. It made her look even more childlike than her petite frame suggested, despite her tattoos. She was tottering on a steep pair of heels. Earlier in the night, when Kit had made some biting comment about them, Melody drunkenly declared that she could go out dancing in her shoes all night *backwards*, if she had to. To prove her point, she'd come up to Kit and gyrated her hips. Next to Melody, Kit had felt tall and awkward; she'd moved away and gone into the house.

It was through the living-room window that Kit noticed Melody walk casually up to Elliot and touch his arm. He greeted her as if he'd known she was there all along, had been waiting for her to come over. His smile finally looked genuine.

And so, Daphne had ended up being right: Elliot had been assaulted, and he had yielded. But it had taken some time for Kit to discover the deception. Ten years, in fact. The problem, she now realised, was that his love was a refrigerator light—whenever she saw him, the light was on. His love was a glowing, bright yellow beam. And like an infant she'd assumed the light was on whenever she wasn't there.

'Yes, Mum,' she said. 'There is such a thing as being too good-looking.' She gave her newspaper a satisfying flick. 'Thankfully, *I* will never have to worry about it.'

'Yes, I know, I know,' said Daphne carelessly, and Kit chuckled. But her mother's next question came like a blow to the chest. 'Has that woman had her baby yet?'

Kit took a ragged breath and stared intently at the newsprint. The words blurred, but she kept her voice neutral. 'No, she hasn't, Mum. Melody's not due till August.'

Kit's thoughts flashed back to the week before, the first anniversary of their separation, when Elliot's best friend Grey had come to her office at the university. She worked there as a researcher in the dental school. 'Come in,' she'd said, her mind reeling. She hadn't seen or spoken to Grey for at least six months, and his visit was unexpected. 'What brings you here?'

'Sorry to drop by without calling.' He failed to look her in the eye. 'Do you have a moment to chat?' Without waiting for a response, he came in and sat on the stool by her desk. As he looked down at her, she could see his nasal hairs and a fine sheen of sweat above his lip. He placed his hands on his knees and drew a breath. 'I wanted—'

Kit leapt up and gestured towards a small landscape painting behind him. It was part of the university furnishings; a colleague had brought it to her office the day before. Bland and soulless, the watercolour wasn't something Kit would have chosen, but she liked her colleague and didn't want to offend him. 'You know,' she said to Grey, her eyes fixed on the picture. 'I think that painting is crooked. Could you . . .?'

Grey obligingly stood up. He raised his arm and used a finger to tilt the edge of the frame to the left. He appraised the picture, then sat back down, taking a moment to pull out a handkerchief and wipe his nose.

But she couldn't resist an opportunity to needle him. 'No, I'm afraid it's still crooked.' She directed him, pointing to the right. 'No, more to the left.' She frowned. 'No, I think that's made it worse.' As he tried again, she held her breath. 'Oh, okay,' she said finally, 'that'll do. For now.'

10

He resumed his seat, his legs now wide apart on the stool. He looked her in the eye and then looked away, clearly annoyed. 'Kit, I'm here because Elliot has asked me to come about the settlement, and because you and I are friends—'

'Are we?' she asked in a quiet voice.

'Yes,' he said. 'And I know this is a terrible business, and I don't want to take sides, sweetheart—I'm just as much Team Kit as Team Elliot, I swear to God. I love you like my own family.' He paused, his fist clutching the hanky.

'Well, thank you,' murmured Kit, with a small serve of sarcasm. She doubted he'd notice the mild derision—he was a man who possessed both a supreme self-confidence and a supreme insensitivity. Even before the split with Elliot, Grey had been known to walk away from Kit mid-conversation, without a word of explanation. It had happened at least twice while she was speaking. Once she'd been asking Grey a question at a party when his eyes started to roam the crowded room. He'd given a two-fingered wave to someone else, then promptly sauntered off. The unexpected snub had left her confused and humiliated. It also made her doubt his current professions of love and loyalty.

He was obviously there as Elliot's emissary, and he was now gearing up to deliver a prepared speech. 'I'm here to ask you to bring the settlement date forward,' he announced.

She cleared her throat. 'You might have saved yourself the trouble and called me, you know. I'm getting ready to go away.'

'Yes, I know.' He glanced at the desk, where Kit's passport sat on a pile of papers. 'In fact, that's why Elliot asked me to come and see you.' Grey looked her in the eye. 'You haven't been answering his calls, and he needs to get this thing sorted as soon as possible—before you leave.'

With a sigh, she slumped back into her chair. 'I haven't been answering his calls, that's true. But it's because the lawyers are handling everything now. There's nothing more I can do personally. It's out of my hands. We did try to sort things out informally, you know, but it just didn't work.' They'd tried to divide the apartment, car, furniture and super; the negotiations hadn't ended well. Elliot's face appeared in her mind, red and blotchy, distorted with rage. She blinked to make the image disappear. 'It's better to have a mediator for these things.'

But why had Elliot sent Grey as his representative? The man was hardly a diplomat.

'I've come to tell you something,' he said, as though answering her unspoken question. 'I don't know if you've heard.' He hesitated. 'Elliot and Melody are expecting a baby—in August. A little girl.'

His words hit her like a punch to the stomach. 'No, I didn't know.'

He struggled to look sympathetic. 'I realise this must be painful for you,' he said, without a skerrick of compassion. 'I know that you and Elliot tried for a baby, so hearing this must be really, *really* hard.' He softened his voice. 'But now Elliot has a chance for happiness with Melody, and they just want everything to be ready for when the baby comes. If you have any love left in you, any scrap of feeling for him, can you please, please just ask your people to hurry things along a bit? Maybe ask them to drop the superannuation thing . . .?'

Kit waited two heartbeats, then flashed him a grim smile. Grey had clearly gone off-script now, because Elliot would never have appealed to her feelings. He would have kicked her in the guts, but he wouldn't have done so with such a complete lack of grace.

'Just give him *something*,' said Grey, mistaking her smile for benevolence.

She leaned back in the chair, crossed her arms and tilted her head. The pose gave her an unflattering double chin, but she didn't care. She was tired. 'I'll be away from next week, and I'm busy packing,' she told Grey, ignoring everything he'd said. 'Elliot will have to contact the lawyers. It'll be difficult for them to get in touch with me over the Antarctic winter, and I won't be able to phone them directly. I'll be there from March till November, working the whole time. But the lawyers should be able to email me if the need arises.' She sighed. 'And I might reply.'

'So you're not going to agree to an earlier date?'

'No.'

'And there isn't anything I can say to change your mind?'

'No.'

He stared long and hard at her desk. When he spoke again, his voice held a note of warning. 'If you don't cooperate, Elliot will destroy you. He'll leave you with nothing. *Nothing*, Kit. You'll be glad if you never have any children, because you'll be raising them in poverty—I can promise you that.'

Taking a short breath, she counted to ten in her head. She wished that she could just walk away from Grey, as he'd done to her in the past. But this was her office, and he was taking up her space. 'I think you should leave now,' she said.

He frowned and coughed into his handkerchief. 'Okay,' he conceded. 'Well, I think that's everything I had to say anyway.' He tucked the hanky into his jacket.

As he approached the door, she had an idea and spoke again. 'You know, on second thoughts, I will give Elliot something, as a token of my feelings.'

Grey looked back in surprise.

She rose from her chair and pulled the unwanted painting off the wall. With a smile, she pushed it into his arms. 'Here, give him this.'

When Grey slammed the door, she was still smiling.

•

At her mother's side, Kit smoothed the covers on the overheated bed. She stood up and placed the newspaper back on the bedside table. She then leant over and gently rubbed Daphne's knee. 'I have to go now, Mum,' she said.

'Where are you off to, dear?'

'I'm going away, Mum. I won't be able to visit for a while. I told you about it before.'

'Did you, dear? Oh, well, never mind, that's no bother. You go and do what you have to do. I've got Maude here to keep me company.'

Maude was her mother's older sister, an object of inveterate hatred since childhood. But it now seemed that Daphne had forgiven her. It helped that Maude had been dead for thirty years.

'I'm glad to hear that,' said Kit. 'Because I may be some time.'

2

Kit stood on the docks, gazing up at the gigantic orange ship moored at Hobart's Macquarie Wharf. The *Southern Star*, an Antarctic icebreaker and supply vessel, loomed almost three storeys above the pier. It had the tough and rugged appearance of a tank, ready to smash through anything, and boasted two helicopters, a trawl deck and multiple research labs. The ship would be her home for the next sixteen days or so, as she travelled 5500 kilometres from Tasmania to Macpherson Station in the Australian Antarctic Territory.

In the *Star*'s mighty shadow, several people were engaged in earnest farewells. One man was slowly ascending the gangway, turning at intervals to wave like one of the Beatles. Another man was dramatically shaking a bottle of champagne in the midst of a small throng.

Two young children, a boy and a girl, were happily playing with paper streamers, the girl standing rigid while her brother wrapped her like a mummy. It had once been tradition for departing expeditioners to share each end of a streamer with loved ones on the ground. As the ship pulled away, the streamers would stretch and stretch until finally they ripped in two. Kit was disappointed the ritual was no longer permitted. The children had found something different to do with streamers, but Kit liked the symbolism of tearing people apart: so brutal and final.

She'd joined the expedition primarily to get away from people. She'd never been to Antarctica, but when her friend Sally Ann Rivers had offered her a job, she'd jumped at the chance. She yearned to be someplace where nobody knew her, among strangers who had no idea about the pain and degradation she'd been through. She needed a break from the emotional fallout of the divorce. So she'd applied for unpaid leave, and her supervisor had approved it. Now she was an official expeditioner of the Australian Antarctic Division. She'd 'pulled a geographic', as Sally said, in the irrational belief that changing location would solve her problems.

'Hey!' a familiar voice shouted cheerily from above.

Kit looked up and spied Sally waving to her from the first deck of the *Star*. She waved back. They'd been friends since their final years of high school. Back then, Sally had been a good-time party girl with long dark hair. She'd worn light-coloured floral dresses and patterned blouses, while Kit had been the quiet studious type, invariably cloaked in a duffel coat and heavy boots. Over the years, some of their differences had evened out. Sally now wore her hair short, and was more likely to be attired in a tracksuit and puffer jacket. Kit still had cropped blonde hair, and mostly wore the jeans and black turtleneck she was wearing now. They remained close.

'Come on up!' called Sally. 'What are you doing down there?'

'Making my way to the gangplank.'

'Gang*way*!' Sally shot back, laughing.

Before moving forward, Kit went through a mental checklist. Her wallet and her passport were in the daypack slung over her shoulder. Her important cargo—her research tools, her red survival bag, and her extreme cold weather gear—were already on the ship. These were her essentials as Sally's assistant out in the field. While the sun still shone, Kit would be working in the freezing katabatic winds of East Antarctica. Her expertise in forensic dentistry would be put to use by inspecting the teeth of Weddell seals in the wild. She would help Sally capture the seals, monitor their health and collect their scat; basically, she would be going to the ends of the earth to pick up poo, Sally had joked. As a trained dentist, Kit would also have some light medical duties in the surgery.

When the sun stopped shining altogether in about mid-June, she would be mired in darkness on the base with twenty or so others. The last plane was scheduled to leave Wilkins Aerodrome in early March and would be unable to return till spring, so there would be no escape from the isolation, not even in an emergency.

The forecast this coming winter was especially grim. Despite the warming effects of climate change, this February had been unexpectedly frosty. At the start of the month, tourist ships had been turned back from the Antarctic Peninsula due to unseasonal pack ice. It was now mid-February and conditions had deteriorated even further. There had even been talk of closing the aerodrome early and cancelling the last of the intercontinental flights. If that happened, once the *Southern Star* had finished its resupply voyage and dropped off the winter expeditioners, there would be no way home. Kit would be stuck there.

She could hardly wait. With a lightness in her step, she headed up the gangway.

On deck, she recognised a few familiar faces from the pre-departure training sessions. One of the helicopter pilots was standing across the way, his back to the docks, engrossed in taking photos of kunanyi, or Mount Wellington. He was clean-shaven and wearing a bulky coat with a camouflage-print scarf. When they'd first met, a few weeks earlier, he'd been sporting Wolverine sideburns and a T-shirt that read *The Man*, with an arrow pointing to his head, and *The Legend*, with an arrow pointing to his crotch. His name was Kurt Wilder. Predictably Sally had nicknamed him 'the Legend'.

Kit also noticed Dustin Witherall, the medical practitioner, greeting another winter expeditioner in a bear hug. When she wasn't out in the field, she would assist Dustin if anyone needed dental care on base. An affable man in his forties, the doctor had a receding hairline and the bulging eyes of an overactive thyroid. He'd been a warm and reassuring presence at their training sessions, well liked by the other expeditioners. She was looking forward to working with him, but couldn't help but notice his passion for health and safety bordered on the fanatical. At the last session, he'd given everyone a half-hour lecture on the merits of taking vitamin D supplements for twelve months prior to departure. Preferring to get her vitamins the natural way, Kit had secretly binned her pre-scribed dose as soon as she'd received it. Dustin now spotted her and waved enthusiastically, and she waved back with a twinge of guilt. She knew he meant well—it was his job to keep everyone safe in one of the most inhospitable places on Earth. A little fanaticism was understandable.

She sidled up to Sally, who was still leaning against the rail and looking down below. 'Hey,' said Kit.

'Hey.' Sally turned to give her a one-armed hug.

From the ground, the children waved up at the ship with their heads thrown back. The two friends smiled, their arms around each other's shoulders.

'Ready for lift-off to another planet?' asked Sally.

'Ready as I'll ever be.'

They could hear the rumbling of the ship's engines and feel it beneath their feet. It wasn't long till departure.

Sally's gaze drifted to the lines under Kit's eyes. 'Do you think he'll come to say goodbye?'

Kit frowned. 'Definitely not. Elliot's not even speaking to me. I think I've well and truly pissed him off.'

'Good.' Sally held up her water bottle in a mock toast. 'Here's to pissing Elliot off.'

Kit joined in the toast. 'And here's to pulling the mother of all geographics.'

They laughed as the ship's horn blared over the docks.

•

Twelve days into the journey, Kit was seated in the ship's mess, looking worriedly at seven pairs of disembodied legs. The communal area was furnished with several grey tables fastened to the floor, and a motley assortment of plastic chairs. In front of one wall, seven men held a single white sheet above their heads, disguising their identities as they proudly displayed their naked calves. Kit and several other women were seated in a row before them. Their task was to guess the owners of the calves in a competition named 'Find Your Sea Legs'.

The men had agreed with surprising speed to take off their pants. Some of them had even taken off their socks and shirts. A sign behind the line-up read, *Please keep this area clean*, but no one had paid it any heed. One man behind the sheet wanted to know if any woman had a longing to see his third leg under a sheet later that night. Only the men laughed; the women just rolled their eyes.

A small crowd had come to the event, hoping for something more entertaining than the usual quiz night. There was only a smattering of the seventy people on board, ranging from permanent *Star* crew—including the first and second mates, a helicopter mechanic, and the cooks—to the passengers, including a journalist, a few scientists, and half-a-dozen expeditioners bound for Macpherson.

19

For the last couple of days, the ship had been sixty degrees south and the weather had turned unkind. The temperature outside was a frosty minus twelve degrees Celsius, or minus twenty with the wind chill factor. The oceanography work that day had been undertaken in difficult conditions before it was finally called off. A group of CSIRO scientists had sent down a sensor to record salinisation and oxygen levels, but the line had been pulled off course by the current.

Several tired crew members were looking for some light relief. At home this would have been a visit to the local pub, but here it had to take the form of a 1950s parlour game. The consumption of alcohol aboard ship was strictly forbidden by the Australian Antarctic Division. For the winner of that night's game, the coveted prize was a packet of contraband anti-nausea pills from New Zealand.

It was fair to say that Kit hadn't yet found her sea legs. After a long day of gale-force winds and nine-metre swells, she had instead found her dinner all over her bed. Despite its tank-like structure, the ship had been rising and falling ceaselessly. She wasn't the only one who had experienced some queasiness. Sally reported that she'd thrown up her cereal in a bag at the breakfast table and no one blinked an eye. Only the most hardened sea-dogs had been spared. This night, Kit hoped, would be calmer.

Sally had lured her out of her cabin to partake in the fun. As they walked down the corridor, the swell rolled them against the wall. They lurched into the mess like drunkards on a pub crawl. 'Now, now, girls—curb your enthusiasm,' a helicopter mechanic intoned from a nearby table.

Kit sat down clumsily, and an English expeditioner called Alessandra brought her a piece of paper and a pencil. A thin, elegant woman with grey hair, Alessandra somehow made a thermal top and waterproof trousers look stylish. Sally and Kit had met her several months earlier in the pre-departure training sessions, and they'd become good friends. 'The weather's supposed to get better this evening,' she assured them with a smile. Alessandra would know—she'd be their meteorologist at Macpherson this winter.

She'd suggested that night's game, and she had an advantage: her husband Gareth would provide one set of legs.

'Do you think Alessandra will recognise Gareth's shins?' mused Kit when the woman had walked away.

'Oh, I wouldn't count on it,' replied Sally. 'Somehow I doubt that married life for Alessandra is one long carnival of bare naked pleasure.'

Gareth was a cold, uncommunicative scientist-type who rarely looked anyone in the eye. Tall and thin, with a stooped head, he'd frequently passed Kit and Sally in the narrow passageway without so much as a chin tilt. Alessandra was the opposite—extroverted and outgoing. They would both be monitoring the weather station this season to ensure it sent automated data back to Australia.

After a brief introduction to the parlour game, the men came out, shuffling like crabs and carefully keeping the sheet over their heads. For several minutes, Kit's mind and answer sheet were blank. She chewed the end of the pencil as she strained her eyes to guess the hair colour of the furthest leg on the left. The thick calf was lacking in muscle tone. It appeared to be hairless, but when the leg was raised to the light—in a half-hearted effort at burlesque—there was a glimpse of ginger-red stubble and freckles. She believed that leg belonged to the red-haired electrician named Blondie Richmond.

Kit had got to know Blondie a bit better a few days into the voyage. A veteran from other expeditions, he'd singled her out as a first-timer and urged her to join him at the bow for some alba-tross spotting. With his large ruddy face and wide roguish smile, he reminded Kit of her criminal cousin from Bendigo. At fifty, Blondie was fifteen years older than her—still young enough to think he might stand a chance. She'd caught him looking sideways at her in the mess, so she insisted that Sally come outside too.

For at least half an hour, the three of them stood on deck in their polar fleeces and polarised sunglasses. It was windy, and the sea spray dampened their hair and faces. The rail was freezing to touch, but the day was bright and sunny, the sky a brilliant blue expanse.

They stood dumbstruck before the gently rolling Southern Ocean. When they did speak, they engaged in minimal chitchat and casual observations. They snapped photos and wandered aimlessly about the deck. The whole time, they saw only a single albatross: a lonesome white cross in the sky that circled the ship thirteen times.

Sally was counting. 'Is that unlucky?' she asked, taking the camera from her face and squinting at the sky.

'Nah,' replied Blondie, 'only if ya shoot 'em with a crossbow.'

Sally laughed at the unexpected Coleridge reference.

'I think they're actually a sign of good luck,' Kit chimed in. 'Something about the cross formation of their silhouette. If you're religious or superstitious, the sign of the crucifix is a blessing.' The all-embracing arms of Jesus, she thought, providing succour and comfort to the afflicted. Or something like that. She held out her arms in demonstration.

'A blessing?' asked Sally.

'Yeah,' said Blondie, 'a blessing. Like the green flash—have you heard of the green flash?' Kit and Sally shook their heads. 'When conditions are right on a clear night at sea, you can see a green flash as the sun sinks beneath the horizon. According to Scottish legend, those who see the flash will be blessed—they will never again be deceived in matters of the heart. They will be able to see clearly into their own hearts and to read the thoughts of others.' Blondie gazed sagely at the horizon.

'Oh my God,' responded Sally. 'That's not a blessing, that's a curse! I don't want to hear what other people are thinking.'

'Me neither,' said Kit. 'It's bad enough that millions of people are shouting their every thought on social media. Why would you want to hear anything more?' On this voyage, they had no TV, no radio and no internet; at Macpherson, they would have only limited access to emails and the restricted use of a satellite phone. Kit was more than happy to be liberated from her inbox.

'Yeah, shut the fuck up already!' shouted Blondie at the sky. The women laughed in surprise. 'But the green flash is real,' he added. 'I've seen it with my own eyes. It's just an optical phenomenon, a refraction of light in the atmosphere. But it does happen, blessing or no blessing.'

'Knowing the dour Scots,' mused Kit, 'it's probably a portent of tragedy or disaster. You know, the evil spirits sending us a message. I doubt it's a good thing.'

'Hey,' said Blondie with mock indignation. He arched his eyebrows, pointing to his Celtic red hair and freckled complexion. 'Don't knock the Scots.'

Kit hadn't seen Blondie's bare legs that day. He'd been wearing bright red wet-weather overalls that she thought were overkill—until she got back to her cabin and found her trousers uncomfortably cold and damp.

Now she reappraised the naked legs in the line-up. If those belonged to Blondie, then he was probably standing next to his best friend, a fellow tradie named Warren.

The men on the left kept elbowing and nudging each other, trying to make their mate laugh and drop the sheet.

That would be a good guess, she thought. On her piece of paper, in small cramped handwriting, she wrote: *1. Blondie. 2. Warren.*

Sally leaned over to peek at Kit's answers. 'And that's gotta be *the Legend*,' she whispered, pointing to the far right.

Those legs were tanned and toned—and possibly shaven. They looked like they belonged to a cyclist who enjoyed getting decked out in lycra on the weekends. When it was his turn to flaunt his legs in the air, he kicked so high that the crowd could glimpse his red underpants. A woman behind Kit gave an ear-piercing shriek.

She winced. Truth be told, her heart wasn't in it, and her stomach was protesting. The swell tugged at her insides again. Leaning forward, she surreptitiously glanced at her wristwatch: she'd been in the mess for only twenty minutes. Jesus, how the night dragged on.

At that moment, she noticed a bearded man looking at her from across the room: Jamie Betterworth, the first mate. It was odd to see him in the mess. He was usually perched on a comfortable seat at the bridge, overlooking a set of charts and an oversized computer screen. A serious, hard-working man, he'd been friendly and welcoming at their first meeting, but had never followed up on his offer of a bridge tour. He now raised a cup of tea in greeting. Kit held up her piece of paper. He smiled and came over to where she was sitting with Sally.

When he knelt beside her, a sudden rough movement of the ship made him grab the back of her chair. His arm brushed against her, a surge of human warmth on her shoulder blade. 'Whoa,' he said. 'Wanna come up for that tour now?'

'Hey,' said Sally plaintively, 'why does *she* get to go to the bridge?' Sally was still looking straight ahead, her eyes fixed on the legs.

'Because you ladies are having fun, while this lady looks like she could do with a distraction,' said Jamie.

'Distraction!' Sally gestured towards the display of burly limbs. 'What more distraction could a woman want?'

'True. I can think of few diversions better than these pale, hairy legs. But at the start of the trip, I did promise this lady a tour of the bridge, and it's now day twelve—the voyage is almost over.'

'Yeah, yeah,' said Sally with mock resentment. 'Go on, play bridge. See if I care.'

With Jamie's assistance, Kit stood up. 'Here, take my guesses,' she said to Sally, inching away from her seat. 'Do me proud.'

Out in the corridor, Kit smiled at Jamie. 'Thank you. I had no idea who those men were.'

'You looked like you could do with an excuse to leave.' His grin was wide beneath his bushy beard. 'Looking a bit green about the gills.'

'Yes,' said Kit.

There was a companionable silence as they negotiated the narrow stairwell to the wheelhouse deck. Beneath their feet, the engine emitted a low peal of thunder. The walls on either side of them vibrated.

'And what brought you down for the festivities?' asked Kit.

'A bite to eat, actually. Foolishly thought I could hold something down.'

'Oh.' She was surprised. 'I thought you would have been one of the lucky few.'

'Nah, not me, mate.' He laughed. 'When it's this rough for this long, there's hardly anyone who doesn't chuck up their guts.'

'Oh, lovely.'

'Still, we've been pretty lucky. Could be worse. *Snow Petrel*'s been beset in ice now for three weeks. At least we're going somewhere.'

The *Snow Petrel* was a polar supply vessel. It had been heading home to Hobart from Casey Station and the Amery Ice Shelf when it had become stuck in heavy pack ice in Prydz Bay. Despite its own icebreaking capability, the *Petrel* was suspended in an Antarctic nightmare, surrounded by a wall of ice and with complete loss of helm control. The ship had drifted for some distance towards the coastline, helpless to alter its course. Meanwhile, its twenty-four crew and passengers just had to wait for the ice to break up.

From a distance of several hundred kilometres, the *Southern Star* had been following their plight. This wasn't the first time a ship had become trapped in the bay during summer. In 2001–02, a resupply vessel called the *Polar Bird* had spent a whole month in the frozen sea until another icebreaker had come to its rescue. The *Star* was waiting to hear further news in case it was needed this time.

If a strong south-easterly blew in, according to Jamie, the wind might loosen up the ice enough for the *Petrel* to get free. But coffee rations were already dwindling to dangerously low levels—in a few weeks, the crew might have to start drinking instant. 'There'll be a mutiny, I'm tellin' ya.' He shook his head.

'Gosh. Will they need our help then?' said Kit, panting. She was struggling to keep up with Jamie as he marched down the narrow passageways.

'Dunno.' He shrugged. 'If conditions are really that bad, we don't want to risk it. But we might get close enough to send out a heli-copter and shuttle back some of the crew. We could also restock supplies, if need be.' The *Star* carried emergency food rations for a full nine months, just in case.

'Could save them from a fate worse than granulated coffee,' said Kit.

'Depends on the weather. A helicopter mission could be more dangerous than an icebreaking attempt. We'll wait and see. Might be best for us to smash a path through and then tow them out.'

'Tow?'

'Yeah, with a cable. It worked with the *Polar Bird*. Not as difficult as it sounds. We'll wait till we get word from the captain. There's really no hurry. They'll be okay for a while yet.'

Kit and Jamie arrived at the bridge. He held open the door, and she entered first. Though it was early evening, the room was bathed in clear natural light. Through the window, she could see several immense flat-topped icebergs in the distance. Mackerel clouds hung in the sky above them, while white-crested waves lapped at their sides.

The captain, Richard King, was seated in his comfy chair at the controls with a cup of coffee in hand. He was a thin, grey-haired man of about fifty, dressed in jeans, thermals and a navy-blue top. His appearance was in casual contrast to the two navigation officers, who wore bright orange coveralls.

'Hi there,' said Jamie. 'Brought Kit in for an impromptu tour. We've just been discussing the *Petrel*.'

'Oh, right.' The captain shook his head. 'Just got off the phone to them an hour ago. Sounds like things are coming unstuck.'

'The ice?' asked Jamie.

'No,' he replied grimly, 'the crew.' Then he reassured them with a smile. 'Nothing serious, just a bit of cabin fever. The captain reported hostilities on the helideck today.'

'Hostilities . . .?' said Kit.

'A fight between two men—two scientists, apparently.'

'Brawling *scientists*?' asked Jamie. 'Jesus. Sounds like it might be time to evacuate.'

Richard laughed. 'Well . . .' He hesitated. Then he looked at Kit and spoke a little more formally. 'The director of expeditions is advising us to do nothing but stand by at this stage. The weather might come good. It is February, after all, so we might still see some change. The voyage leader is going to do up a program of recreational activities—you know, try to get people working in teams. Maybe do some refresher training courses, quiz nights, group cooking exercises, karaoke or something.'

'Oh, yeah. Karaoke. That'll sort them out.' Jamie gave a snort. In one swift manoeuvre, he jumped into his high seat.

Kit stood silently at his side and looked out the panoramic windows to the rolling grey sea. The glass was sprayed with mist.

'Yeah, or a party might do it,' said the captain, sipping from his cup. 'There seem to be some tensions that need resolving.' His brow wrinkled as he examined his coffee. After a short while, he asked them, 'Do either of you know your Bible at all?'

'Nah,' responded Jamie.

There was a brief silence. The engine grumbled and groaned under their feet. The navigation officers played with their instruments.

'I know a bit,' offered Kit. A lapsed Anglican, she'd attended Sunday school as a child.

'It's just something the captain mentioned before we got cut off,' said Richard. 'Something that sounded like it came from the Bible. He kind of mumbled it, like a prayer. Said it over and over again. Not sure what it means.'

'I'll tell you what it means,' muttered Jamie. 'Poor man's losing his mind, that's what it means. Too much pressure. All that ice. So lonely out there, nothing to look at but stark flamin' white. No freedom of movement either. Would drive me nuts too.'

The captain ignored Jamie. 'He said they'd done many things to help the situation but neglected the one thing needful. *The one thing needful.* He said it again and again.' Richard looked at Kit. 'Have you heard that phrase before?'

'Oh, yes.' She remembered her mother's stern face bearing over hers, enunciating every word as though it had been written for her. 'It's from the New Testament. When Jesus visits the sisters of Lazarus, he chides one of them—Martha, I think—for fussing over him and troubling herself about everything, everything except "the one thing needful".'

'And what's that?' asked Jamie.

Kit frowned, feeling perplexed. 'Oh, I think there are different interpretations about what he meant. But most think that he was referring to the salvation of the soul. "The one thing needful" is redemption or the saving of the soul from destruction.'

The three of them looked at each other. Kit kept her face neutral, while Jamie's eyebrows were raised in surprise and bemusement.

Richard frowned, then shook his head. 'It's probably nothing, then. He's just a bit of a religious nut.'

'What do you mean it's nothing?' Jamie laughed with a cheeky glint in his eye. 'Clearly he was sending an SOS! A strange and cryptic SOS, obviously, but an SOS. Basically, his words meant: "Save our souls".' Jamie held out his hands in humorous supplication.

One of the navigation officers looked up in mild alarm.

The captain grinned and continued shaking his head. 'It's okay, I don't think we need to send out the cavalry just yet.'

The navigation officer went back to work.

'If the *Petrel* captain wants to send an SOS,' added Richard, 'he can use a proper distress signal like everyone else. He doesn't need to quote his Bible at a bunch of atheists.'

The captain and first mate chuckled good-naturedly.

Kit smiled at their easy banter. Inwardly, she wondered if tensions on the *Petrel* would escalate. It couldn't be easy being trapped on board, not knowing when the ordeal would end. It would be even worse being trapped with someone you loathed.

After a brief tour of the instruments, Jamie offered to show Kit around outside. He wanted to take her to the deck above, known as Mandrill Island, the highest point on ship. It provided the best views on board, and they would be able to see the sunset from there. But first they'd have to change into their cold weather gear. The seas had grown calmer, but balaclavas and bright yellow-and-red overalls were still compulsory fashion items on deck.

Back in her private cabin, Kit sat on her bed and held her face in her hands. Rubbing her cheeks, she stared at the floor. It was in moments by herself that the heartache would return. Every thought about her life in Hobart—the adultery, the failed settlement, the pregnancy—was a sting of misery. Once again she pictured Elliot's face the last time she'd seen it: angry and pained, spitting out words like so many blow-darts to her heart. She despised him for what he'd done, and she resented being abandoned. She would never forgive him for leaving her just as Daphne's mental state had deteriorated.

Soon, not even her own mother would remember her. She hated the thought of being so alone and unloved.

Kit contemplated lying down on the scratchy carpet, curling up in foetal position, and letting the ship push her body backward and forward across the cabin. But the ship was no longer dramatically rising and falling, exhaling and inhaling, with the swell: it was relatively, mercifully, still. And she was due out on deck.

Kit shook herself out of her melancholy and changed into her gear.

Feeling bulky in her layers, she left the cabin and headed outside. In the dimly lit corridor, she saw a man she didn't know lurking in the doorway to the stairwell up ahead. He was leaning against the wall as though he was waiting for someone, and when he heard her approaching, he glanced up with apparent interest. His hair was collar-length and greasy, and there was dirty stubble on his chin. He was painfully thin, almost emaciated. He looked like he might work in the engine room, as he wore a navy-blue windbreaker and blue trousers.

As Kit went to pass him, he held the stairwell door open with a gap-toothed smile.

'Thanks,' she said.

'No problem,' he replied before letting go.

Just before the door closed, she heard him whisper something. The low hiss was almost lost in the vibrations of the ship's walls. She couldn't make out the words, but the intonation was creepy. He might have been commenting on her outfit. He might have said 'great duds'. Or he might have been offering her drugs.

She turned to stare at the closed door. *What the hell? Was I just propositioned?* But then she shook her head—it was possible her mind was playing tricks on her.

Frowning, she laboriously climbed the steps to Mandrill Island. Outside, the cold wind stole her breath away. With her balaclava on and her head down, she took the few painful steps to the sheltered observation deck. When her lungs had recovered from the shock, she sat down and pulled her balaclava off. Her breath emerged as a frosty white cloud.

She cursed Jamie and his wretched idea. The first mate was nowhere to be seen. He'd probably been held up with work. It was just her and the emerging stars and the setting sun that glowed orange-red on the horizon. Despite its reassuring presence, she shivered violently inside her padded cold weather gear. Hugging her knees to her chest, she leaned her back against the cold steel wall. She gazed trance-like at the sun's reflection on the ocean, wishing she had someone there to share the glorious moment.

Gradually the sun disappeared, piece by piece, slipping towards the horizon.

When it was almost gone, she heard the door to the observation deck rattling. She stared in the direction of the noise. Whoever was there pulled at the handle a few times but didn't come out.

'Hello?' she called. 'Jamie? Do you need some help?' It could be difficult to open the ship's doors with cold or gloved hands.

But no one responded. And still the door didn't open. The ship creaked and groaned, and a few lazy waves lapped at the hull.

Kit shifted from her seat and stood upright. Her legs and shoulders were tense. Her heart thudded in her chest.

The door stayed closed and the rattling stopped.

It's nothing, she told herself. *Someone just changed their mind and decided to go back to their cabin. It's too cold out here.*

When she relaxed and finally turned back to the horizon, her eyes fell on the crest of the sun. For one brief moment, a breathtaking pulse of green light appeared at the rim of the solar disc.

The flash washed a hazy green glow over the sun's surface, just before it disappeared beneath the horizon.

Kit laughed in joyful astonishment. She'd glimpsed the legendary green flash.

When she recovered from her surprise, she tried to remember what Blondie had told her about the phenomenon. She couldn't recall his exact words; she could remember only what she had said.

She'd dismissed it as a portent of doom and disaster.

3

Kit had grown used to the continual noise of the ship. At night-time, the disturbances were more noticeable than during the day. The walls rattled and hummed, the floors shook, and rumbling and groaning could be heard from the bowels of the engine room, deep down below.

In the first week, the night-time hammering kept Kit awake; some nights, it almost drove her mad. But by the second week, she found it comforting. She would imagine herself inside a great big womb, listening to her mother's heartbeat, the soft gurgling of her stomach and the pounding of her blood. It would lull Kit to sleep.

Sometimes, the ship would lift and surge and roll as it broke through ice on the water. The vessel didn't just ram the pack ice but gracefully rose on top and crushed it. Usually when this happened, Kit would be startled into consciousness by a terrible cracking noise, like artillery fire. Or a short sharp bang, like the sound of metal striking rock. She knew it was just the ice being crunched and broken underneath. She would go back to sleep.

That morning, Kit wasn't sure why she'd woken so suddenly.

She lay there in the grey light, waiting for whatever had disturbed her to repeat itself. But there were no terrible cracks or bangs. The engines simply sounded different. She could hear the propeller struggling to manoeuvre the vessel and the engines roaring in protest.

After a few minutes, she heard soft footsteps out in the corridor. When someone knocked on her cabin door, she leapt out of bed and grabbed for the handle.

Sally looked as though she had just gotten out of bed herself. Her hair was knotted and tangled, and she was dressed shabbily in her day clothes and a loose-fitting coat. 'Did I wake you?'

'No.' Kit wondered what time it was. She had probably missed breakfast, but the thought of tepid scrambled eggs pained her stomach anyway. She'd stayed up late, too excited to sleep after the green flash.

'We're taking a detour,' announced Sally with raised eyebrows. 'You'd better come in.'

Sally moved inside the tiny cabin, turned around and sat on the side of the bed. 'It's the *Snow Petrel*. The captain received an automated distress signal at about eight this morning. We're heading there now.'

'A distress signal?' asked Kit with quiet concern. 'What's happened?'

'We don't know.' Sally shook her head. 'It seems all their communication systems are down—radio, satellite phone, internet . . . No one can contact them. Our bridge received the mayday call by radio signal and then heard nothing by voice. Someone must have hit the distress button at the other end.'

'Could it be a mistake? Something set off by . . . a blizzard, perhaps . . . ?' Blizzards had been known to occur in Prydz Bay this time of year.

'Doubt it,' said Sally. 'These signals are meant to be activated only when there's serious, life-threatening circumstances. I don't reckon it would just go off. Plus, it seems to have remained on. No one has *de*activated it, if you get what I mean.'

'Jesus,' breathed Kit. 'Does our captain have any inkling what's wrong? Could they be sinking or taking on water?'

Sally screwed up her face. 'Does it smell like vomit in here?'

Kit ignored her. 'Could the ship have broken apart?' she asked.

'No one knows!' said Sally in exasperation. 'But it seems unlikely that the ship would break up. Unless . . . I suppose if several tonnes of ice were to crush it in the middle of a storm . . . maybe then. If the wind were particularly fierce.'

They stared at each other in the dim light of the cabin. Sally's eyes were lined with tiredness.

'Jesus . . .' repeated Kit, biting her lip. 'Will we have to . . .?'

'I doubt it,' replied Sally, with the assurance of a two-time Antarctic veteran. 'I don't think they'll need you and me to be part of the rescue operation.'

As winterers at Macpherson Station for the coming year, they'd undergone intensive search-and-rescue or SAR training. They'd learnt first aid, crevasse rescue techniques and firefighting skills, among other things. But neither of them had thought they'd have to use that training so soon.

'They'll have experienced crew on board here who'll form an Incident Management Team and deal with the rescue part of things. I'm sure of it.' But Sally now sounded uncertain. 'They'll send the helicopters out ahead to see what's happened. The choppers will transfer people here, if necessary.'

Kit hugged her arms against her chest. 'How long till we get to the *Petrel*?'

'I don't know. There's going to be a briefing.'

•

That afternoon, the mess was crowded with curious people. Some were seated on chairs, others were perched on benches and table-tops, some were leaning against the walls. It seemed that everyone on board was there—everyone wanted to know about the fate of the *Petrel*.

The captain entered the room, accompanied by Jamie, who threw her a quick apologetic look, as well as the ship's doctor, a man that Kit knew only as Dr Sidebottom. Also present was Dustin, the friendly Antarctic medical practitioner, and several tech support people, including the Legend and his fellow pilots. In a far corner she spied the thin man who'd spoken to her in the stairwell.

Richard began by announcing what they all knew: they'd received a radio distress call from the *Snow Petrel* only a few hours earlier. He didn't know what kind of damage the *Petrel* had sustained, or what kind of danger the crew were in. He couldn't establish any verbal or written communications with the ship. He knew only what a distress signal of any kind would tell him: there was grave and imminent danger to life on board the vessel.

By virtue of the beacon, he also knew the precise coordinates of the icebound ship. There were other icebreakers in the area, includ-ing a research vessel from China, but the *Southern Star* was by far the closest. The Australian Antarctic Division had instructed them to lead the rescue effort until other parties could arrive.

At this point, the captain handed the briefing over to their voyage leader, Henry 'Hank' Lederman, the head of the emergency management team. He would be their search master, the man who would coordinate the search-and-rescue mission.

Hank was an imposing individual with a bald, bullet-shaped head, a thick neck and wide, hefty shoulders. He had a small black-and-yellow tattoo of a light bulb behind his right ear and the hint of several other—less innocent—tattoos beneath his shirtsleeves. It was rumoured that he had a secret military background.

'As the only vessel in a five hundred-kilometre radius, we're going to the aid of the *Petrel* as quickly as possible.' Hank spoke in rapid-fire sentences. 'We've radioed to let them know that we're making SAR preparations. We've not heard back from them, but we've been heading there since 8 a.m. We expect to be close by within a day or two, but this will depend on the weather and the ice. We anticipate that we'll have to break through at least eight kilometres of heavy pack ice to reach the ship. This could take some time. But we'll send the choppers ahead to find the *Petrel* and map out the best route. Once the *Petrel* is in our sights, we'll attempt to establish communications the old-fashioned way.'

Kit had no idea what that meant. She envisaged Hank hanging out of a helicopter, his large hands cupped to his mouth as he shouted, *Can you hear me?*

'There are many variables that must be taken into account. We may or may not proceed to evacuate the crew of twenty-four via helicopter shuttle.'

Hank nodded in the direction of the Legend, who was leaning against the wall. He had his arms folded across his chest, ready for action.

'He seems rather *cock*sure,' mumbled Sally, standing beside her.

'I'd expect nothing less,' whispered Kit. They exchanged amused looks.

'Above all,' continued Hank, 'we'll have to assess the danger to our rescue team. Obviously, if boarding the vessel poses any potential risk to life and limb, then we'll be proceeding very cautiously.'

Kit liked the sound of 'very cautiously'—it was reassuring. Though Hank was uncertain about what they would find and what they would do, he exuded quiet confidence. *A good person in a crisis*, she thought. He was neither excitable nor anxious and despairing. His words were precise. There was a formal procedure to be followed in these circumstances, and he would follow it.

'Next, we'll want to determine that all on-board personnel are unharmed and safe and comfortable.' Again, his words were measured. 'If someone does require medical treatment, then we'll aim to treat them with the *Petrel*'s own facilities. But if that isn't possible, and if the weather permits an evacuation, then we'll bring them to the *Star*.'

All eyes fell on Dustin and Dr Sidebottom. They looked down at the floor and nodded. When Dustin glanced up, he caught Kit's eye and smiled kindly.

'Finally,' Hank said with a sigh, 'we might be facing the possibility of there being serious structural damage to the *Petrel*. She could have a breach to the fuel tank, or she could have a damaged hull—we don't know. Once we get there, we'll have to determine the extent of the damage and whether it warrants us evacuating personnel. Again, in the cold and the wind, it might be better and safer to keep all crew on board while we assess and repair the damage. Or, we may want to bring them all here. The *Star* would be at full capacity.'

All eyes fell on the kitchen staff, three women standing near the galley entrance. They would be the ones taking on the extra burden of feeding and cleaning up after the unexpected guests.

Kit's stomach rumbled in the silence, while Hank scratched his light-bulb tattoo and searched his notes. At this unexpected break in proceedings, the crowd began to talk among themselves. A low chattering hum emanated through the room.

'Okay.' Hank clapped his hands and spoke louder. 'I would now like to talk to the rescue team. If you're not part of the team, then you don't need to be here. I'll repeat: if you're not part of this operation, then go back to your cabin. We'll let you know what's happening once we receive word from the *Petrel*.'

With some relief, Kit turned to face the door. But before she could join the orderly queue at the exit, a hand touched her shoulder.

It was Dustin. 'Kit,' he said, 'could you stay for a minute?' He looked grave.

She reluctantly sat back down.

Sally threw her a puzzled look as she disappeared through the door with the other crew members.

Dustin waited for Dr Sidebottom and another man to come over before he began talking. 'Right. Hank wants us to get together a stand-by medical team and to prep some emergency rooms, just in case. Kit, I'd like you to be part of that team.'

Years before, as part of her degree in dentistry, Kit had undergone basic medical training. It was a key reason the Antarctic Division had approved her job as Sally's assistant. When Dustin had discovered this information, he'd asked her to become his medical assistant for the duration of the winter. For Kit, leading up to the voyage, this role had involved a refresher first-aid course and a long session on the finer points of telemedicine. For Dustin, this meant that he didn't need to do a two-week intensive training course at dental school—a usual requirement for Antarctic medical practitioners. Kit would also provide back-up support for Dustin, the sole doctor on station, if he became sick or incapacitated.

Although Kit was happy to help, she hadn't been a practising dentist for more than a decade. She'd specialised in forensic odontology, the analysis of animal bite marks and other dental evidence in the context of criminal investigations.

Now Kit was in mild shock to find herself part of an emergency medical team. The two doctors were discussing triage, stretchers, and the possible conversion of the lounge space into a temporary hospital.

At one stage, Hank came over for a brief chat. He emphasised that the team were to do *nothing* without his prior arrangement or knowledge. His broad shoulders shook as he stressed the point with a chopping motion. Everyone nodded vigorously.

Kit nodded too, shuddering inwardly. She'd hate to let Hank down.

4

The next morning, Kit found herself standing next to Dustin, gazing out of a porthole in the sick bay. On Hank's orders, they'd been running an inventory of medical supplies as the ship headed towards the *Petrel*. Their task completed, they were now having a cup of tea.

The ocean was unusually calm, though there were a tremendous number of icefloes littering the seascape. Some left a trail of white petal-like fragments. An occasional glacial berg shone luminescent in the sunlight, a hulking blue mass on the water. As Kit watched the scene, one of them calved, splitting apart as the waves lashed at its side.

'Icebergs,' said Dustin, pointing to a distant specimen, 'come from frozen fresh water on land—also known as glaciers—which calves off from the ice shelf into the ocean.'

Aware that Kit was a first-timer, he'd taken it upon himself to explain the different kinds of ice: icebergs, icefloes, sea ice, fast ice, frazil, greasy, nilas, pancake, pack ice—he was leaving no ice unexplained.

'And sea ice is made when the ocean freezes,' he continued, sipping his tea.

She recalled why she'd found him so longwinded at their pre-departure sessions. 'But the sea doesn't freeze completely, right?' she asked, a smile tugging at the corners of her mouth. 'There's still water underneath . . .?'

'That's right—the ice just forms a layer on the surface. During winter, the sea ice in Antarctica forms an impenetrable wall around the continent, doubling its size and preventing access by ship. The ice has usually receded back to the coastline by summer.' He paused to take another sip.

'With climate change,' she mused into the silence, 'I wonder if there'll be any sea ice left in the years to come. It'll be devastating for those creatures who depend on the barrier as a habitat and breeding ground. Creatures such as seals, for example . . .' She cocked her head to peer at him.

'Yes, that's true.' He continued to stare out the porthole, oblivious to her quizzical look.

Another smile played at her lips. He seemed to have forgotten she studied fast ice as part of her research on Weddell seals. The animals used their specially adapted teeth to create breathing holes in the ice during winter. Few studies had investigated their dental health in light of climate change—that was the point of her research.

'Mind you,' he piped up, 'this February is bucking the trend. In East Antarctica, at least, the ice barrier seems to be expanding early, and there's a large amount of pack ice for this time of year.'

'Yes. I was reading an article about why climate model simulations failed to account for this year's ice. The authors are speculating that spring winds may have had a cooling effect on sea surface temperatures, enhancing sea ice formation.'

He blinked at her mention of the scientific literature. 'Yes, uh . . .' he stammered, then emitted a quiet chuckle. 'I guess I must be teaching you how to suck eggs.' He threw her an apologetic look.

She regretted making him feel foolish. In their training sessions, she'd already asked her fair share of thorny questions. To assist the crew's wellbeing, he'd prepared both a pre-departure and winter-over regime of daily supplements and light treatments. For several months, the expeditioners had been expected to monitor their supplemental intake via an app he'd designed. He'd set it up to send notifications whenever anyone forgot to check in. She found the incessant pings infuriating, but couldn't turn them off. When she questioned him about the app, he'd become flustered and embarrassed.

Now wondering if she made him nervous, she changed the topic. 'We must be almost halfway to the *Petrel* by now.'

'Almost,' he agreed. 'We should reach them by tomorrow night.'

She paused. 'I heard that there were tensions on board the ship, between two scientists.'

'Yes, I heard that too.' They still had no idea why the automated signal had been activated. While the transmission had now ceased, they'd failed to make any direct contact with the *Petrel* crew. A helicopter crew had gone on ahead to find out what had happened.

'It can't be easy being thrown together like that, for days on end.' To soothe Dustin's pride, she steered the conversation towards his own research interest: the effects of long-term isolation on polar expeditioners.

'You're right,' he said. 'Close confinement can bring out the worst in people.'

'If you were on the *Petrel* now, what would you recommend?'

'Well . . .' He blew the air out of his cheeks. 'Prevention is always the best cure. It's important to select the right type of people in advance, to have the best mix of character.'

For their own expedition, she knew, he'd taken precautions to safeguard the welfare of the winter crew. With the help of colleagues at the Antarctic Division, he'd screened for personality traits and selected out for conditions such as neuroticism and alcoholism.

He'd assessed for the risk of mental disturbances because they could turn into physical threats, and it would be impossible to evacuate anyone who needed help.

'But is the screening process foolproof?' she wondered. 'Isn't human interaction more of a vague art than a science? I know I haven't yet found an algorithm for building successful relationships.'

'Yes,' he agreed, 'but we still have some sense of what works well and what doesn't. I like to follow Sir Ran's advice about having good-natured people on expeditions.' He referred to Ranulph Fiennes, the famous English polar explorer and adventurer. 'He warned that you don't want to be in close confines with anyone who turns malicious under pressure. You want to avoid expeditions with anyone who's quick to anger or becomes sarcastic in moments of vital negotiation. You want someone who's always even-tempered and who'll maintain group morale; someone who doesn't get too excited when things go well, or too depressed when things fall apart.'

'Gosh, did he ever find anyone to accompany him?'

Dustin burst out laughing, his eyes gleaming. 'I think it was an aspirational goal, not something he always attained. Expeditioners are only human, after all: tensions arise, people get depressed, people get pissed off.'

'Are you speaking from personal experience?'

He looked taken aback.

If she'd known him better, she would've pushed further. Instead, she retreated. 'I'm sorry, that was a bit rude.'

'No, no, it's fine.' He looked pensive and continued in a low voice. 'By the end of my first winter, ten years ago, I was actually in a bad way. We were locked up indoors for at least two months: I had no privacy, no sensory stimulation, and little contact with family or friends. By September, I just felt . . . *empty*. There's no other way to put it. There was nothing I took pleasure in, nothing I looked forward to.' He shook his head at the memory. 'It wasn't boredom:

it was something more sinister. In theory, I knew winter-over syndrome was a common phenomenon—Jesus, I'd written a thesis about it—I wasn't the first to discover that isolation did peculiar things to a man. But it really got to me.' His mouth thinned to a line.

'All those gruesome tales of nineteenth-century explorers should've warned you,' she joked, to lighten the mood. 'There's a reason those early polar expeditions ended in madness and cannibalism.'

'Absolutely!' He grinned. 'And those were just the tales of survivors.' He paused for a moment, lost in thought. 'My friend Eddy used to call it "the chilling point". If a boiling point is when people can't control their anger, the chilling is when they can't suppress their hostility or lack of sympathy. It's that stage of winter when the smallest tic starts to get on everyone's nerves, and people lose their sense of fellowship.' He closed his eyes and rubbed his forehead. 'Luckily, I didn't develop any lasting mental health issues. When I got back home, I was fine, I snapped out of it.'

She knew that other polar expeditioners weren't so lucky—they couldn't shake the gloom so easily.

'It's not all bad,' he added in haste, 'don't get me wrong. The flipside is that isolation can forge the best of friendships. That first winter was when I met Eddy. He was younger than me and we didn't really have that much in common. He was a plumber, I was a doctor; he was public school, I was private; he drank whisky, I drank beer.' His face held the ghost of a smile. 'But he was the only other chess enthusiast on base. When that bleak curtain of winter fell, we played game after game after game. He could see that I wasn't coping. To keep me distracted, he told stories about his family and his life back home. His mother was Fortunata Sandman—you've probably heard of her—she was a well-known mountaineer and polar explorer in the seventies. She once climbed Everest without oxygen, and was the first woman to fly a hot air balloon over the

North Pole. She met Eddy's dad while pulling him out of white-water rapids in Chile.'

'I'm picturing her as a brawny Amazonian queen with legs like tree trunks.'

'You're spot on. That's exactly how I picture her too.' He snorted in amusement, then sighed. 'Eddy became one of my closest friends.'

Kit watched Dustin with curiosity. When engaged, as he was now, he was more likeable and less of a bore. His shoulders were relaxed and his voice had lost its formality. She could see why others had warmed to him.

But his levity didn't last for long. Once they stopped chatting, a sadness passed over his features like a cloud. Studying his reflection in the porthole, she saw his face turn slack. It hadn't skipped her notice that he referred to Eddy in the past tense.

'What about me?' she asked in a bright tone. 'Do you think I'll cope over the winter?'

'Yes, you'll be fine. I'm glad you're coming along.'

'Why's that?'

'Because, with your help in the surgery, I'll be free to conduct surveys and interviews. This year, come what may, I plan to complete my project on mood and cognitive performance in winter-over residents.'

During training, he'd told them he wanted to build on Lawrence Palinkas's famous study of the effects of combined supplements and exposure to bright light. He hoped his research would be beneficial for long-duration space travel—maybe even a trip to Mars.

'So, you're determined we're all going to have a good time?'

'Oh yes. Everyone *will* have a good time—even if it kills me.'

While his words were humorous, his expression remained impassive. She shivered as she caught sight of him again in the window.

'Look there.' He pointed to a bird hovering in the sky. 'It's a diving petrel.'

She gazed at the graceful bird floating effortlessly outstretched on the breeze.

'They're also known as firebirds,' he added. 'They're apparently drawn to fire or light.'

'It's magnificent.'

The ship began to slow its pace. They were entering an icefield, an extensive area of unbroken pack ice. As the *Star* crunched its way into the solid mass, there was an appalling grating noise. The sound was unnerving, almost alien.

'Would you like to take this to Hank on the bridge?' Dustin held up a printout of their completed inventory.

'Sure,' she said. Lord knew, she could do with the distraction.

•

The bridge was a scene of quiet, serious activity. On the starboard side, several men stood with binoculars in hand. Outside, there was nothing but a white expanse, seemingly for miles.

No one seemed to notice Kit's presence, and she didn't want to interrupt Hank, who was deep in conversation with Richard. Around the console, a strip of red carpet designated the crew's work zone; the blue carpet areas indicated where spectators could stand. Kit lingered in the blue near the windows and contemplated leaving the sheet of paper on a bench.

But then Hank received a call from one of the search helicopters. She couldn't hear the message, but she could see his knuckles turn white as he gripped the radio. 'Oh shit,' he cursed into the mouthpiece.

The crew on the bridge snapped to attention. There was a collective intake of breath.

'Jesusss,' hissed Hank, his face turned to stone. 'Okay, let me know what you see when you get closer.'

'What is it?' the captain asked.

'Smoke—the choppers can see thick black smoke coming from the *Petrel*.'

'A distress signal?'

'It's too massive,' said Hank. 'It's an enormous black cloud over the ship. They think it might be on fire, but they aren't close enough yet.'

The hair stood up on the back of Kit's neck. Anxiety rippled through the bridge. Everyone turned in the imagined direction of the *Petrel*. Those with binoculars clambered for a position at the windows hanging over the water; those without squinted at the horizon.

From his own vantage point, Richard stood silently and peered at the ocean, his mouth a grim line. 'Okay,' he said in a calm voice, 'I need to know the fastest route through the ice.'

A murmured response came from others in the room.

Kit felt conspicuously in the way. Her mind was numb with the reality and the horror of the *Petrel*'s predicament. She inched towards the door.

'Kit,' said Hank without looking at her.

She stopped moving. A shiver of dread went through her. She was surprised that he'd noticed her.

His voice was flat and expressionless, and he never once took his eyes off the pack ice. 'Tell your team to prepare for burns.'

5

Kit and Sally heard the Legend's update later that day. They spoke to him in the passageway as he waited for the choppers to be refuelled. He'd lost some of his usual swagger.

'Oh man, it was terrifying,' he said, taking a swig of water. 'I could see a wall of orange flames all around the deck equipment.' He gestured with a gloved hand. 'It was burning the rubber rafts, the shipping containers, the side cranes—you name it, if it was on the deck, it was on fire. We couldn't get close because flames would shoot in the air every time a fuel tank ruptured. It was a nightmare, a complete nightmare.' He shook his head.

'Could you see any of the crew?' asked Sally.

'Nah, not a living soul. But they wouldn't have been on deck anyway, that's for sure. There was just too much smoke—wouldn't have been safe.' He looked up as if he could still see the scene. 'It was just this tower of black clouds over the ship,' he said, sweeping his arm into an arc.

Kit and Sally exchanged worried looks.

On the third day following the distress signal, they were able to view the stricken vessel for themselves. The *Southern Star*'s arrival had been delayed by the maze of dense pack ice. Frustratingly, once they found the *Petrel*, they couldn't risk getting closer in case their ship, too, became entrapped. The *Star* had to keep moving to-and-fro, to avoid being stuck, and they had to be content to view the *Petrel* from a distance.

It was clear that even if they'd arrived sooner, they couldn't have fought the fire. Any up-close attempt to salvage the *Petrel* could have endangered the lives of the *Star* crew, and any attempt to extinguish the flames from a distance would have been useless and potentially disastrous. The Antarctic winds were fierce and unpredictable. Even if the crew could have prepared a flowing water supply in time—a rather remote possibility in sub-zero conditions—it couldn't have been directed at the vessel with any accuracy. The winds would have either blown the water off course or fanned the flames back to life.

Everyone desperately scanned the horizon for the *Petrel*'s crew and passengers. No one could be seen aboard, yet no one could be spotted wandering or stranded—or lying dead—on the pack ice. Two helicopters searched the ice in the surrounding area. But with low cloud and occasional snow showers, visibility was poor. The pilots kept looking until the wind picked up and they were forced to return due to safety concerns.

Hours ticked by. The whereabouts of the crew remained unknown and utterly mysterious.

'Perhaps they're in their rooms, in lockdown, till the fire dies out,' mused Sally to Kit. 'There's still smoke coming from the ship. That's probably why we haven't heard from them. They're sensible.'

'Yes,' said Kit, wanting to believe her. In her mind's eye, she envisaged people lying stiff and lifeless in their cabins, their faces ashen, asphyxiated by smoke and toxic fumes. 'But the emergency procedure would have been to abandon ship, especially if the fire was out of control. They should be on the ice somewhere.'

'But if they couldn't get on deck due to the intensity of the fire, perhaps the best thing to do would've been to stay below, don't you think?'

'I don't know.' She didn't want to tell Sally there had been other, whispered, speculations about the fate of the crew. Earlier Kit had overheard an engineer saying that the *Petrel* had a temperature-controlled 'double skin' for both the engine room and the cargo holds; to maintain a constant temperature, preheated fuel was continuously circulated around the ship. 'If something ignited that fuel,' said the engineer, shaking his head, 'the entire inner ship would have erupted.'

Desperate to find survivors, Hank called a meeting of the SAR team at midday. As everyone gathered in the mess, Kit held her breath. Earlier she'd been told that if the ship were safe enough to enter, she and Dustin would represent the medical staff in an on-board rescue operation. Meanwhile, Dr Sidebottom and his assistant would prep the sick bay in anticipation of casualties.

In an instant, all her fears were realised. 'We're going to board the ship,' said Hank. 'The engineers have spoken to the chopper crews, and the hull looks sound.'

Kit exhaled. She made eye contact with Dustin, who smiled in sympathy. It wasn't enough to calm her buzzing nerves.

'There appears to be no major structural damage,' continued Hank. 'Helicopter surveillance has detected no cracks in the hull, nothing to suggest the ship's going to break apart anytime soon— the pack ice has hemmed it in again. We think that with oxygen tanks and firefighting equipment, we should be able to enter the vessel without unduly compromising safety. Time is of the essence. If anyone's injured on board, they'll need our immediate assistance. You should keep in mind, however . . .'

Hank counselled everyone about what they could expect, about how they might be traumatised by scenes aboard the *Petrel*.

Kit was reminded of the first body she had seen, in her first job as a forensic dentist for the coroner. It was the charred body of a teenager; he'd been killed in a house fire in a neighbouring suburb. The authorities suspected that he and a friend had ignited a homemade bomb. She was required to identify the body from dental records. It smelt of smoke and barbecued meat and something else, something sweet, like scorched hair. The flesh was black and flaky, and the skull gleamed grey through the seared scalp. When she realised she'd have to wrench open the boy's jaws, panic engulfed her. She turned away before the dry-retching began, surging upwards from the pit of her stomach and wrenching her throat.

Her mentor, a fatherly man in his sixties with a black sense of humour, gripped her shoulders as she leaned over, heaving, with her hands on her knees. 'After the first body,' he said, 'there is no other. Take it in, girl, take it in. This'll be the only time.'

She took it all in, but he'd been wrong. Body after body, the panic and the nausea never left her. Eventually she'd quit the job, resolving to work with animals alone.

Now, in the mess hall, Kit was in difficulty again. Her breath was coming in short, sharp gasps; her arms felt weak and tingly, and there was acid in her throat. She stared at the floor, trying to regain her composure. Discreetly, she placed a hand over her mouth and pressed a finger against one nostril.

After a while, with some effort and concentration, her normal breathing pattern resumed.

Hank's voice came back to her. 'There will be two search parties. We're going to divide the *Petrel* into two search zones and allocate each party to check those zones thoroughly. Here's the layout . . .' He held up a large sheet of paper. 'You'll each have a smaller one of these.' His voice boomed with authority. 'Now, you'll see we've numbered each subsection of the ship. Once you've completed searching a numbered section, the party leader will report back to me, to let me know the area is clear—or not. Each party will have a nominated deadline for reporting back. You'll all be kitted out with oxygen, torches, ropes, whistles and radios. There will be one medic per search group.'

Hank looked at Kit. She looked back at him without blinking. Her face became a mask, calm and composed. Once he looked away, she swallowed in discomfort.

'If there are any injured parties,' he continued, 'the medic will administer immediate first aid. If anyone has life-threatening injuries, they will be transferred here via helicopter as soon as possible.' He paused and then emphasised, 'Everyone in the individual rescue parties is to *stay together*. The party leader should do periodic checks of names and numbers in the group. We don't want to lose anyone. So, what are you going to do? Repeat after me— stay together.'

'Stay together,' repeated everyone.

Alessandra the meteorologist entered the mess. She came up close to Hank and whispered in his ear. He looked at the ground in dismay.

After a while, he spoke up. 'Okay, everyone. Some bad news.'

The room fell quiet.

'A storm's on its way. We're expecting snow and hurricane winds in a few hours.'

There was a brief period of stunned silence.

'This shouldn't affect our mission,' said Hank. 'We have maybe two hours till the storm hits. So you go to the flight deck now, you get on board, you do your job promptly, you do it *thoroughly*, and you get out.'

•

Inside the helicopter, Kit stared out the window. She couldn't look at her companions. Whenever she glanced in Blondie's direction, all she could see were the whites of his eyes. One man's knee kept jiggling up and down. No one spoke. There were five rescuers in total, and they all wore goggles, face masks and gloves. Everyone was dressed in extreme cold weather gear. Jamie, their team leader, stood out in a fluorescent yellow safety vest.

Within minutes, they reached the *Petrel*. The helicopter hovered above the blackened deck, while each rescuer was winched carefully on board. The helideck wasn't yet considered safe enough, and they didn't want to improvise a landing pad on the ice.

Following a preliminary safety check, Kit was lowered out of the chopper. When her boots touched the metal of the deck, she detached the yellow rescue strop from her waist and let it fall to her feet. She deftly stepped aside and gave the helicopter crew a thumbs up. The strop was winched back to the cabin.

Kit took a deep breath. The scene was shocking but also unreal. The fire had left its mark on everything, reducing every piece of equipment to a blackened skeleton or husk. The walls of the deck were shades of grey and black. The entire superstructure of the ship looked haggard and old. *Like a ghost ship,* thought Kit. She wondered again why there was no sign of the *Petrel* crew. Was it possible they hadn't survived?

Jamie called the party to attention. 'Right, everyone,' he said. 'We've already spent half an hour getting on board. Let's go—we've got to move quickly. Our team will start with the bridge.'

At his instruction, everyone turned on their oxygen tanks. As a safety precaution, he warned them not to take their masks off till they had re-emerged in the open air. Two of them also had fire extinguishers specially equipped with a charge of nitrogen to propel a fire-retardant powder at flames. One man carried a forcible-entry tool for wrenching open locked doors and breaking into cabins.

The first door they prised open led to the stairwell. Inside, they were relieved to find the stairs intact and unobstructed. The fire-resistant door and its steel frame had withstood the blaze. A little further up, by ghostly torchlight, they could see a fine dewy frost glistening on the steps. Though it seemed the fire had been confined to the deck, it appeared there was no power or warmth anywhere aboard the ship. Its engines were dead. Once the fire had died, the ice had stretched its tentacles to every corner. Soon the interior would be the same temperature as outside.

The group moved upwards. Within moments, a rescuer slipped a few steps and landed awkwardly ahead of Kit.

She darted to his aid. 'Are you okay?' she asked, a hand on his arm.

Using the handrail, the man pulled himself to his feet. He held the small of his back and grimaced but gave a thumbs up. Jamie nodded encouragement, and the group resumed their progress to the bridge.

On the way, Kit keenly observed her surrounds. The walls, the fixtures and the flooring were eerily untouched and undisturbed. There were no signs of panic or emergency. Someone shone their torch at a pristine fire extinguisher on the wall, its fasteners attached. There was an occasional creaking or scraping noise—the ice against the hull—but the ship itself was quiet. The only other noise they could hear was their own breathing. It came in a chorus of loud mechanical rasps as they climbed the stairs.

The door to the bridge refused to open. Jamie signalled that one man should come forward with his forcible-entry tool. Kit moved out of the way. The man heaved his weight against the instrument. The two other men came to help.

Finally the door sprung open. The glare from the bridge shone like a lighthouse beacon into the interior of the ship. Their torches were redundant.

Jamie entered the room first, then stopped.

Everything—the navigation equipment, the radio, the radar, the gyro—was blackened beyond recognition. The floor was littered with fresh snow and glass and pieces of crumpled metal. Kit could see that the heat or an explosion had shattered the high windows and destroyed everything. The captain's chair was a bare distorted frame, creaking as it swung in the wind.

After a moment, Jamie ripped off his oxygen mask and pulled out his radio. Kit kept her mask on. The tank was keeping her breathing nice and regular; she was afraid that without it, she might start over-breathing. The destruction of the bridge was unnerving. The ship had lost its command.

Blondie stood next to her. He removed his mask, exposing the soft red stubble on his chin. 'Someone must have had time to set off the distress beacon before this fire took hold. Where are they now? Why aren't they here?'

'The crew must've known they couldn't fight it,' replied Kit. 'Everyone knows it's impossible to fight a fire in the Antarctic wind.'

'Perhaps they tried and then had to abandon ship . . .?' said Blondie.

'Okay,' Jamie spoke up, addressing Kit and Blondie in particular. 'Let's just keep doing our job and find the crew as quickly as possible. I want us to leave here in less than an hour. If the storm hits while we're here, the choppers will be grounded.'

A healthy gust of wind blew into the bridge. The bad weather front was rolling in, reminding them that hurricane-force gales were on the way.

Jamie held up a fluttering sheet of paper and pointed. 'Our next destination is the mess and the galley, and we'll proceed from there to the cabins on the C deck and the hospital room. Okay? The other party will be inspecting the engine room, the cargo holds and the laundry.'

As he spoke, a chopper could be heard hovering overhead: the second rescue team was being delivered.

Kit's group filed out of the bridge. Before she left, she turned to look one more time at the console of blackened knobs, buttons and dials. She shook her head and followed the others.

•

The mess was quiet and empty. Plates and bowls lay abandoned on the tables. Coats and jackets were thrown over the backs of chairs. Magazines were spread out, their crosswords and Sudoku puzzles only half-finished. There was a lot of frost-covered Weet-Bix and Vegemite on toast—the crew had left their breakfast in a hurry.

Kit's group moved into the galley, where the cooking area was in disarray. Frying pans and their contents littered the floor, pots and pans were strewn over the bench, onions and apples had rolled out of their boxes. Yet the ship should have been relatively still, trapped in the ice.

Clearly something had happened in the kitchen area. It looked as if someone had gone on a rampage. Kit shivered despite her cold weather gear. The scene in the mess had been concerning enough, suggesting a hurried exit, but this was chilling—this suggested violence.

Scanning the galley, Kit spotted a dark brown streak on the floor in one corner. She moved in closer and knelt down. Her gloved hand wiped at the smear, brushing up against something hard and jagged, a pebble-like fragment. She pressed the piece between her thumb and forefinger, and squinted in the torchlight.

When she finally realised what it was, she almost laughed: it was part of a tooth. Here she was, a dentist, and she'd found a tooth. She took off her oxygen mask. 'Blondie,' she called.

He came over. 'What is it?'

'It's part of a tooth. And I think there's blood.' She pointed at the streak on the floor. Her disquiet mounted as she noticed the dark brown streak continued across the galley. It reminded her of a crime scene she'd seen in her previous job. 'Look,' she said, gesturing. 'They're drag marks. They go from under the sink to the coolroom. And look—' she pointed beneath the sink '—one of the black slip mats is missing.' The galley floor was covered in black rubber slip mats, the industrial kind with textured tessellated holes, but not in that part of the room.

Blondie tried the coolroom door, but it wouldn't open. 'I think it's locked,' he said, shaking the handle.

The coolroom was a large stainless steel walk-in cupboard that housed all the fresh fruit and vegetables aboard the ship. It was equipped with an ozone generator to help the produce ripen. At the start of a trip, a coolroom was typically overcrowded; by the end, it was almost empty. After several days of besetment in Prydz Bay, it might have been necessary to lock up the *Petrel*'s remaining food. That made sense.

Kit tried the coolroom door for herself. It wouldn't budge. Blondie tried again.

Jamie interrupted their efforts. 'We have to speed this up,' he said from the doorway. In the dim light, his face looked serious and unnaturally grey. 'Our job is to search for survivors. And we don't have much time. Come on, we've got to get to the cabins.'

'We think something could be in the coolroom,' said Kit. 'It's locked, and we can't get it open.'

'Forget about that. We have less than forty minutes, and if there are going to be people anywhere, they'll be in the cabins, not in the food store.'

'Okay,' agreed Kit with some reluctance. 'But if there's time, we should come back.'

At the doorway to the first cabin, she steeled herself for the potential horror. She'd seen dead bodies before, so she knew what to expect. It was easier if you didn't look at their faces, but it was even better if you didn't look at all.

With her foot, she inched the door open and peered inside.

To her relief, the cabin was empty.

After a quick inspection, they moved on to the other rooms. Each one had an unlocked door, an unmade bed, and a pile of clothes and toiletries. But after a while, Kit noticed what was *not* there—each room was missing its crew member's survival kit. The red bags contained immersion suits, thermal clothing, socks, balaclavas, gloves, and various crucial items such as whistles and drinking cups.

At the end of their search, Kit mentioned the bags to Jamie.

'Good.' He rubbed the back of his neck. 'This is good—this is really good. There's obviously no one here. I think everyone got out. Let's check the sick bay and the last few stairwells on our list, then get the hell out too. We have less than thirty minutes.'

•

On deck, they waited for the helicopter to return from scouting the bay. The rescue parties had found nothing and no one. In the meantime, the temperature outside had become shockingly cold. The wind whipped about their heads.

Near the ship's rail, Kit stood with gloved hands on hips. When Jamie joined her, she asked him, 'Where are the lifeboats kept?'

'Usually different places on both starboard and port side,' he said, panting heavily. It took some effort to speak in the cold air.

'One of the lifeboats isn't there,' she said pointing.

The *Star* had been facing the *Petrel*'s starboard side, unable to see the missing lifeboat on the left. Jamie now took a closer look. 'There's a slim chance that during the firestorm it was burnt loose from the launcher and crashed through the ice. But I reckon someone's cut the line.'

Kit squinted hopefully into the distance, looking for tracks or ridges. All she could see was white expanse and grey sky. Wherever the orange lifeboat had gone, it was now out of sight or covered by snow. 'Could a group of people drag one of those boats across the ice?'

'I don't see why not.' Jamie pulled out his radio and asked to speak to the Legend.

The news from the pilot was disappointing. In a crackling voice, he reported that he'd searched the surrounding area until the ice began to thin out. Due to fog, visibility had been reduced to twenty metres in some places. It was possible the crew were on an icefloe heading out to sea, he said. The currents in that part of the bay were strong, making the pack ice fragmented and unstable. But the Legend hadn't been able to spot them. And without knowing the precise direction of the current, any further search would use up valuable time and fuel. He would have to resume once visibility improved.

The Legend was on his way back to get the rescue teams. The storm was due to arrive in less than twenty minutes.

While Kit's group waited, the other rescue party emerged on deck, looking cold and miserable. The team leaders swapped notes and spoke in grave hushed tones, while the other rescuers milled about, stamping their feet and trying to keep warm.

Kit sat with Blondie in a sheltered part of the razed deck. She kept thinking of the smear of blood and the tooth fragment in the galley. Kicking restlessly at the ground, she scanned the deck with a suspicious eye. Again she was reminded of crime scenes from her work in forensics. 'Does this look deliberately lit to you?' she asked Blondie.

'I don't know,' he said, taking a cursory glance around.

'It just seems hard to believe that so much of this could be burnt to a crisp. Look at it—it's all made of steel.'

'Perhaps there was an accident, a fuel spill . . .? Over there.' He pointed to a dangerous patch of deck near starboard, where the flooring had burnt away.

'Yes, a fuel spill. An accidental fuel spill that accidentally ignited in the Antarctic.'

Blondie raised a brow in response to Kit's tone.

'Someone was bleeding in that galley,' she ruminated. 'And someone jammed the coolroom door. Perhaps to hide whatever they had put in there.' She looked at the ground and tapped out a nervous rhythm on her knee.

'All right. So what exactly are you getting at?'

She made eye contact. 'We should go back and look in that coolroom.'

He laughed. 'I'm not sure that's a good idea. Do you want to spend the night out on this boat? We have less than twenty minutes.'

'That's enough. The helicopter has to take the rescue parties back one at a time, anyway. We'll be sitting out here, freezing our tits off, until they return. Don't you want to find out what's in that coolroom? We searched *everywhere*, we found nothing and no one, and we couldn't get inside that bloody fridge.'

'We should tell someone.'

Kit jumped up and called to Jamie, who was still talking into his radio. 'We're going back to the galley,' she said, the cold piercing her lungs.

He held the radio to his chest and cupped a hand to his ear. 'What?'

She gestured at the door. 'We're going back!'

'No, you're not,' he said, pointing to the flooring of the deck. 'Sit back down.' He turned his head again to speak into the radio.

The wind was growing fierce. Flecks of snow darted back and forth in the air. When the Legend returned, the groups would have a narrow window to get back to the *Star*.

Kit recalled Hank's stern face and thick tattooed neck. She trembled inwardly at the thought of him looking at her with disapproval. Could she really disobey a direct command?

Don't do anything without telling me. Stay together.

But somehow she found the courage to stand up. 'Come and get me if I'm not back in fifteen minutes,' she said to Blondie. She headed below deck.

•

Kit knelt beside the coolroom door. She had her torch in her mouth, and she was poking and prodding at the lock with tweezers and a sickle-shaped dental probe. Her heart was thudding wildly in her chest. She tried to calm herself by listening to her own breath, but it came in a heaving pant. Her mind was filled with the horror of possibly being left behind.

When Blondie rushed in wielding a fire axe, she jumped back in alarm.

'Out of the way,' he instructed.

'Jesus!'

Dramatically, he swung the axe at the handle of the coolroom door. Upon impact, the knob sprang off, almost hitting him in the head. He swore, but was undeterred. He swung again.

Finally, something went click. The sliding door opened by itself, just a few millimetres.

Kit pushed, but it wouldn't open any further. Something was obstructing the entrance. She squeezed her head in and shone her torch on the ground.

At first, she couldn't comprehend what she was seeing. It looked like a leg of lamb, something you might see hanging in the butcher's front window. It was bluish-white and cadaverous. She shone the light further in.

It was the leg of a man—a large man, lying naked and curled up on his side.

'What is it?' asked Blondie impatiently from the galley.

Kit glanced back at him, barely registering the question. 'Can you shine this into here?' she said, handing him her torch and dropping her bag. She pressed her weight against the door, forcing the man's knee off the sliding track. She sucked in her stomach and eased herself through the narrow opening.

'What's in there?' asked Blondie, a rising note of concern in his voice. He wedged his large head into the gap and peered awkwardly around. 'Jesus,' he breathed.

Kit knelt before the unmoving figure and grabbed at his frigid hand, pressing two fingers against his wrist. She held up a finger to Blondie, warning him to be silent. She had to concentrate for at least a minute. The body was cold, but perhaps not fatally cold—not yet.

'I think he's got a pulse,' she said. 'Throw me the first-aid kit.'

Blondie did as he was told.

She pulled out her stethoscope and listened for a heartbeat. After half a minute, she was sure: she heard a faint palpation. 'He's alive,' she said. 'Quick, go get help.'

Once Blondie was gone, Kit unfurled the first-aid blanket and threw it over the man. He was tall and muscular. In the confines of the room, he seemed gigantic. The crumpled silver throw barely covered his legs. She patted and rubbed his shoulder. Then she curled up behind him and hugged his back.

They had to get him off the *Petrel*. Soon the storm would bear down on them. The ship wasn't a stable place to be in a snowstorm. If they stayed aboard, this man would die.

Leaning on her elbow, Kit scanned the coolroom with her torch. The cold air contained the faint stench of vomit and faeces and blood. Clothing had been scattered about the shelves and the floor. Some of it looked like extreme cold weather gear, turned inside out and roughly torn at the seams. There was a smear of blood on the ground next to the man's head.

Sitting upright, she shone the torch full on his face.

The man looked to be in his thirties. He had lank dark brown hair and a full reddish-brown beard. His skin was unnaturally blue and puffy, and his eyes were closed as if he were asleep. His lips were slightly apart and barely discernible beneath his whiskers. There were obvious signs of trauma. Around his eyes, there was grey and purple bruising, and there was a faint trickle of blood from his nose. His beard was soaked in blood from his bottom lip to his chin. On his forehead, there was an ugly black and red gash: a head injury.

Kit cocked her head towards the door—she could hear the clanging of boots in the stairwell. She patted the man's shoulder and looked down at his face. Then the blood froze in her veins.

The man was looking back at her with cold black eyes.

6

As the storm descended, they wrapped the injured man in two space blankets, then airlifted him from the deck of the *Petrel*; they placed two strops around his torso and winched his body into the helicopter. The wind had picked up.

Terrified, Kit waited on deck, her legs trembling. When her goggles frosted over, she pulled them off. The cold assaulted her eyes. She squeezed them shut and tried to reposition her goggles with clumsy gloved hands. Once she could see again, the scene before her was a blur of red and white: the red of the remaining rescuers' cold weather suits and the white of the swirling snow.

When it was her turn to be winched up, the chopper leaned dangerously, struggling against a gust of wind. On board, she could breathe again, but her legs still trembled. Next to her, the unconscious man started to shiver as his body temperature rose. The chopper vibrated.

As soon as they landed on the helipad of the *Star*, the Legend blasted the rescue crew. She couldn't understand a word, but she gathered that the delay had placed their lives in peril, that if the chopper had crashed and burned, it would've been their fault, and that he would've reminded them of that in hell. As he turned away, Kit noticed that his hands were shaking.

In the sick bay, Dustin used a controlled dose of barbiturates to place the rescued man in an induced coma. He had a head injury, and his condition was critical. When they'd found him, his core body temperature had been thirty-two degrees Celsius, a full five degrees below normal. That meant he had severe hypothermia and was at grave risk of death.

They would care for him till the ship reached Macpherson Station in four or five days. A flight was scheduled to take him from the ski landing area to Wilkins Aerodrome. From there, he was expected to take an intercontinental flight to Hobart for proper medical treatment. The same aircraft would bring in members of the Australian Antarctic Division, the Australian Maritime Safety Authority and their Research Coordination Centre to secure the *Petrel* and search for its crew.

Technically, the *Star* could have headed straight to Macpherson and been there the next day. But they chose to remain in Prydz Bay in the hope of finding survivors. After the storm, they once again sent out choppers, with no luck. It appeared that the beacon on the *Petrel* lifeboat had been either destroyed or accidentally switched off. The search conditions had been worse than unkind; a low weather system had lingered for days, leaving an impenetrable fog over the terrain. Despite expert analysis of the wind and the currents, it had been impossible to determine the lifeboat's probable location. In response, nearby ships from China and the United States were on their way—the hunt for the crew had become a multinational endeavour.

•

One day after the man's rescue, Dustin visited Kit in her cabin. She was lying on the bed and had just opened her aching eyes to the late morning light. He cracked open the door, his eyebrows crooked and his smile apologetic. 'Sorry to bother you.'

'Do they know who he is yet?' she asked straight away.

'Haven't a clue. But we do know something's wrong with his teeth.' He looked rueful. 'Think you'd better come and have a look.'

'Okay,' she said, sitting up with a frown.

'Don't worry,' he assured her, 'the guy's out cold. You won't have to talk to him.' Dustin's laugh was hollow.

●

In the sick bay, Kit positioned a metal stool and a powerful lamp close to the unconscious man's face. Dustin had lowered the top of the retractable bed so the man's head was leaning backwards, his chin pointed to the ceiling. Her instruments had been sterilised, their handles wrapped in plastic.

A small crowd was loitering outside the room, and Dustin went to tell them to go away. The *Petrel* story had received extensive media coverage back home; everyone on board was eager to find out more to tell their loved ones. The journalist on board had been regularly feeding information to the *Herald Sun*. Today the paper's headline read, 'Naked man found on Antarctic *Marie Celeste*', and the story mentioned half-eaten bowls of Weet-Bix. Other news outlets hinted darkly at a major terrorist incident, while some conspiracy sites had already linked the crew's disappearance to Malaysia Airlines Flight 370. The world waited to hear more.

While Dustin cleared the hallway, Kit pulled on a pair of blue latex gloves and positioned her face mask. Perched on the stool, she took a sickle probe in one hand and a mouth mirror in the other. She leaned in and, with two fingers, softly applied pressure to the man's upper lip, revealing his front teeth. His incisors were strong and straight and white. His smile, she thought, must be warm and engaging.

Dustin came back into the room.

'Okay, I'm ready,' she said, drawing a deep breath. 'You can open his mouth.'

Dustin tilted the man's chin forward with one hand on his jaw and, with the other, placed a wooden depressor on his tongue. Kit recoiled at the foul stench of the man's breath but didn't show any other signs of disgust—her frown simply deepened.

An expert first glance revealed that the man's back teeth had been badly damaged. If she had to guess, she would say he'd been whacked in the side of the head with a cast-iron skillet from the galley. The bruising on his cheek matched the injury to his jaw. The lower right-hand molars were shattered; the second molar was almost missing, with only a few remaining shards and splinters. That tooth had taken the brunt of the attack. The surrounding two teeth had been knocked and chipped but could possibly be salvaged with onlays or crowns. The noxious smell emanating from the man's mouth was a combination of natural halitosis and old dried blood that had pooled in the open wound of his broken tooth.

Kit made eye contact with Dustin, who looked questioningly back at her and relaxed his grip on the man's chin. 'He needs emergency dental treatment,' she said, 'to prevent an infection and to dull the pain of damaged nerves and blood vessels. If he were awake, he'd be in agony.'

With a grimace, Dustin let his hands fall loose. He gave a low whistle through his teeth.

'We'll have to extract the shards and put him on antibiotics. I'll need to make an incision, because there look to be some splinters below the gum line. They'll have to be cut out.'

Dustin broke off eye contact and stared at the floor, while Kit contemplated the difficulties of performing surgery on a moving ship at sea.

Outside the porthole, the wind continued to hiss and howl.

'Could it wait?' Dustin asked. 'Till he got home . . .?'

'Maybe.' She shrugged. 'But he'll be in a lot of pain when he wakes up, and an infection could take hold—if it hasn't already.'

Dustin looked reflective before he spoke again. 'Okay, we should do it. Let's get on the phone to the telemedicine people. We could do with their help.'

•

They performed the procedure the next day, once the wind had abated and the man's condition had stabilised.

Afterwards, Kit sat with the unconscious figure alone for more than an hour, studying his face. It was various shades of aubergine and yellow from bruising to his forehead and cheek. Otherwise his skin had returned to its normal colour, his beard had been washed of blood, and he looked peaceful. His dry lips were slightly parted, and when he breathed out, he made a faint wheeze. He smelt like toothpaste.

As Kit sat there, she thought of the streak of blood in the galley. During the operation, she'd regarded the man as nothing more than a disembodied head. She noticed that he'd done a better job of cleaning the molars on his right side, that there were signs of wear and tear to the enamel on his upper teeth, probably as a result of grinding them in bed, and that his jaw clicked when it was moved up and down. She knew from this that he was right-handed and possibly prone to stress.

Now it was impossible to ignore the rest of him—his gigantic sleeping frame. Even lying down, it was apparent that he was unusually tall. His body dwarfed the flimsy single bed. Standing upright, he would have a formidable physical presence. She'd seen his powerful limbs in the raw flesh. If he woke up insane or aggressive or even just frightened, Dustin and the others would have difficulty controlling him. She glanced at the cupboard containing the sedatives and wondered if there were any restraints on board.

Hopefully he wouldn't regain full strength before they found out exactly what had happened in the galley—and what kind of person he was. Something violent had taken place on the *Petrel*, and this man had been locked away.

Dustin came into the sick bay, cleaning his hands with sanitiser. 'How's our patient?'

'Fine,' she said, brushing a wisp of hair from the man's injured forehead. She frowned at the gash, thinking again of the bloodstain and of the scattered pots and pans. 'He's been in a fight.'

'That's possible,' said Dustin. 'But then again, quite a few people in the final stages of hypothermia are found with bruising on the head and limbs. I think it's part of the mental confusion that comes with the condition. People stumble around, knock into things, knock themselves out. They can't use their hands and legs properly—their muscle coordination goes out the window. They can also become confrontational and aggressive. I've seen it on mountain expeditions—people throwing their packs off cliffs, and stupid stuff like that. He probably fell and knocked his own teeth out.'

Kit wasn't satisfied. 'Sure, but his face is so battered and bruised nobody has recognised him. The injuries don't seem self-inflicted. And he was locked in that coolroom for a reason. I think someone left him there to die . . .'

Looking mildly surprised by her remarks, Dustin wiped his hands, collecting his thoughts. 'It's not obvious he was left there to die. It might have been a hide-and-die response, him being in that coolroom. It's most likely he took all his own clothes off, one of the last things that people with severe hypothermia do. The experts aren't sure why. One theory is that in the final stages, the vital organs send blood back to the extremities, and this causes a hot flush or a burning sensation. In their confusion, the victims remove their clothes, even though this accelerates death by freezing. It's called "paradoxical undressing" and—'

'Sure, but why lock himself in a coolroom to do it?' She'd grown tired of Dustin's propensity to explain everything in elaborate detail.

'Well, like I said, the undressing comes in the final stages before death. This can be accompanied by terminal burrowing behaviour, where the victim instinctively hides under a bed or in a cupboard. Was he curled up?'

'Yes . . . on his side, right in front of the door.'

Dustin nodded. 'It's likely he shut himself away in the coolroom—to die.'

Kit pressed her lips together. Dustin was determined to see the best side of people. In the pre-departure sessions, he'd always been the first to defend someone or to sympathise with someone else's point of view, even when they were getting up everyone's noses. In his eagerness to keep the peace, she'd never heard him say a bad thing about anyone. It was exasperating.

'Dustin, that's a nice theory. But I was there, and I witnessed how difficult it was to enter that coolroom. The door had been locked from the outside, its handle deliberately damaged. Someone had trapped him in there.' Someone had hit him with a skillet and imprisoned him—she was sure of it. Meanwhile, it bothered her that there were no clues to his identity. 'Are we any closer to finding out who he is?'

Apart from a puffer jacket propped under his head, the man had come aboard the *Star* with no personal possessions. The jacket pocket had contained a scrap of paper with a possible allergy warning in spidery handwriting:

6753   Shouldn't
6247   eat!

'No one has recognised him yet,' said Dustin. 'Hank spoke to the station leader at Casey, who said three men fit his basic description—tall, dark-haired, bearded men are quite common in Antarctica. The candidates are Kendall Thorn, Michael Renfold and Nicholas Coltheart.'

'Really?' Kit glanced at the hulking form beneath the blanket; she couldn't believe all three men were that tall. 'Why don't we do a search of his measurements?'

Before departure, every expeditioner in Antarctica was required to enter their details into a personal profile, in order to get kitted out with special clothing. They had to fill in their height, weight, shoe size and other measurements.

With a plastic tape measure, Dustin took the man's height and shoe size. To assist, Kit pulled back the blankets and straightened his legs. He was 194 centimetres and had a size thirteen shoe.

The database came back with a result. 'He's Nick Coltheart,' said Dustin. 'Nicholas James Coltheart, age thirty-five.'

A geophysicist, he'd been stationed at Casey for three months. He was a veteran of other expeditions; it was his third summer in Antarctica. He held both American and Australian passports. And his profile noted that he'd been recently divorced from a woman named Anna Nelson.

Still listed as next of kin, she was the first person officially notified of his rescue. In the absence of any other contacts, the Crisis Management and Recovery Team at headquarters were keeping her updated.

For Kit, it was some relief to know who the man was. But she needed to know more.

7

Two days later, Dustin came to tell Kit that Nick was awake. He'd been brought out of the induced coma.

'How is he?' she asked, zipping her polar fleece up to her neck.

They walked down the passageway.

'Well, he has a sore jaw,' said Dustin, 'so I offered to get you to come and look at his teeth straight away. It's probably just residual pain from the operation, but—'

'Yes, but *how is he*?' asked Kit, feeling impatient. 'Is he upset? Disoriented? What does he remember?'

'Oh, it's hard to say. We've only spoken to him a few times. Didn't want to wear him out. From what I can gather, he seems to have acute post-traumatic retrograde amnesia.'

'He has *what* exactly?'

'He has no backward-looking memories, for the time being. He can't remember who he is, where he came from, or why he was on the *Petrel*. He certainly doesn't remember what happened aboard, or anything about the fire. But there don't seem to be any signs of permanent brain damage. He should get over it pretty soon.'

'How can you tell all that without a proper scan?'

'An educated guess, I suppose. As far as I can tell, there doesn't appear to be any catastrophic neurological damage, and his cognitive abilities are unimpaired. He's moving slowly but with good coordination. His language skills are unaffected. He can speak in full sentences. I think his prospects for recovering his memories are good.'

'Will he remember how he got the bump on the head?'

'Well, no, probably not,' conceded Dustin. 'It's common for people who have undergone severe trauma to lose all immediate memory of the event itself.'

'What about his name? Can he at least remember his own name?'

'No, he can't.'

Kit was shocked. 'Is that normal for . . . what did you call it, severe post-traumatic amnesia?'

Dustin paused in the stairwell, placing a steadying hand against the wall. 'I don't know,' he admitted. He looked like he could do with a good night's sleep; his brow was creased, and his eyes were bloodshot. She knew he'd been up till 4 a.m. speaking to a head injuries expert from the Royal Hobart Hospital. He ran a hand through his thinning hair. 'I'm just learning this as I go along. It's beyond my everyday expertise. I don't know what's normal.' He searched her frowning face for some understanding.

'No one's expecting you to have all the answers,' said Kit quickly. She didn't know what to say or do. She didn't want to offer him a reassuring pat on the shoulder—that felt too condescending. But he looked rather forlorn. 'I just want to know what happened on the *Petrel*,' she said in an apologetic tone. 'I saw the damage, and it's been days and the crew are still missing. A lot of loved ones are in an agony of suspense. Nick might have the answers.'

With the help of passing ships, the coordinated search effort had intensified and the authorities remained hopeful, even though there had been no sightings of either the lifeboat or its passengers.

To the public, however, it now seemed doubtful anyone would be found alive. The media were speculating about the crew's meagre resources and their slim chances of surviving hypothermia, dehydration and starvation in extreme weather. If they hadn't already drowned, they'd soon run out of fresh water. They'd have to use fuel stoves to melt the snow, and when they ran out of fuel, their thirst would be unbearable. A few pundits predicted the corpses wouldn't be found till next summer, once the ice had thawed, if they were ever found at all.

Dustin straightened his shoulders. 'I know things look pretty grim. But Nick might remember something over the next few days.'

They walked together up the stairs.

'I'm no neurologist,' he added, 'but from what I gather, autobiographical amnesia can sometimes be a result of diminished blood flow to the brain.'

'So the hypothermia might have reduced the blood flow and contributed to his memory loss?'

'Yes, that's right,' said Dustin, apparently warming to the idea. 'He's also quite sedated, so he's rather foggy headed. But I've reduced the dose of painkillers, so he should be more like himself soon. He'll be headachy, but he might recall something.'

They came to the door of the sick bay.

When Kit entered the room, she saw a large man sitting upright on the edge of a bed. At first, she didn't recognise him. He was clean-shaven, and his brown hair was partly hanging over his face. He wore blue jeans and a black thermal top that accentuated his broad chest and shoulders. His size thirteen feet were bare. Only the ugly gash on his forehead and the bruising on his cheeks gave him away.

Kit moved cautiously towards him. Up close, Nick Coltheart was abnormally pale, like a fresh corpse raised from the dead. He didn't speak but stared ahead with the cloudy red eyes of someone under sedation. The skin beneath his eyes was dark, his lips were dry and his shoulders hunched.

'This is Dr Kit Bitterfeld, our dentist,' said Dustin. 'She's come to check on you.'

Swallowing, Nick shifted his gaze to the floor. 'I don't like dentists,' he said in a quiet voice.

Kit laughed mirthlessly through her nose. 'Well, that's okay. I don't like patients.'

When he heard her voice, his arms tightened around his chest. 'Perfect.'

'Okay to leave you two alone for a few minutes?' said Dustin. 'I want to have a word with Dr Sidebottom.'

Kit nodded, but she was ambivalent. She almost wished that Dustin would stay. Nick had spoken like a near-comatose drunk, and she was wary of him still. She could hear a vague whisper of caution in her head but couldn't make out the precise words. Turning to say something to Dustin, she found that he was already gone.

'Okay,' she said, shaking the whispers out of her head. She turned to Nick again. 'Why don't you lie back down on the bed, and we'll take a look at your teeth.' When he failed to respond, she moved in closer and peered beneath his fringe. 'You okay?' she asked, smiling.

For the first time, he looked up at her. As their eyes met, his lips parted and he breathed in. A light appeared in his face as if he'd only just emerged into full awareness—as if he'd only just realised she was in the room. He didn't speak but looked at her so intently she felt a thrill of electricity in her veins. His dark-brown eyes gleamed in the fluorescent light. They seemed to hold a question for her, but its precise wording was difficult to discern.

She squeezed his hand, the impulse to touch him coming without any conscious thought or reflection. His skin was surprisingly soft and warm. 'You've been through an ordeal,' she murmured, rubbing his thumb.

Finally, he shifted his unnerving gaze and smiled at her, flashing a hint of perfect incisors. 'I'll be fine,' he said, his lips forming a smile that quickened her pulse.

Her cheeks reddening, she smiled again. 'Why don't you just lie down,' she repeated, 'and we'll take a look at your teeth.'

Moving slowly, he lay down but continued to look at her.

As she gathered her instruments and flicked on gloves, it took all her concentration to focus on the task at hand. She didn't know why she felt so unsettled. She'd seen Nick twice before—the first time naked—and neither time had sparked any attraction. On both occasions, of course, he'd been more of an object than a person. Now his intense animal presence was difficult to ignore.

After a deep breath, she sat next to the bed and positioned the lamp close to his face. 'Okay—open, please,' she said, taking the mirror from her tray of instruments.

At first, his gums looked fine. But when the light reflected from the mirror, she spotted some redness and swelling near the incision point. She pressed her index finger to the spot. 'How's the gum there?' she asked, frowning and squinting.

His tongue nudged her finger as he tried to reply, and, as she pulled back, her knuckle brushed his lips.

'There's some inflammation,' she said, her blush deepening. She didn't dare look him in the eye. 'Let's give your mouth a good rinse, and we'll see if more antibiotics can clear it up over the next few days. You can sit up if you like.' She held out her hand to help him. He was still weak, she thought.

But his grip was strong and firm. He sat up and swung his legs over the side of the bed. She helped to steady him, then moved over to the bench to prepare the rinse. The hiss of running water resounded in the silence. When she turned off the tap, she realised he was asking something.

'. . . become a dentist?'

'What was that?'

'So if you don't like patients, why become a dentist?' he repeated, his eyes holding a subtle challenge.

'I'm not a *dentist*-dentist,' said Kit, turning her back to him. She prepared the saline solution in a plastic cup. 'I'm a forensic dentist, and I'm more of a research scientist these days. My subjects are usually dead, I'm afraid.'

'Dead?' He sounded mildly alarmed. 'Christ. I hadn't realised dental problems were that bad in Antarctica.' When he said 'Antarctica', he emphasised the 'Ant' like an American, but otherwise his accent was Australian.

'They're not—not in humans, anyway. I'm here to assist someone studying a colony of Weddell seals near Macpherson Station.'

'Oh. So you're a . . . sealologist?'

'I think you mean "seal biologist". And no, that's the team leader. I'm going to be examining the teeth in live seals and their carcasses, as a research assistant.'

'Right. And this is because . . .?'

She paused at the bench and faced him. He peered at her from over his shoulder. 'You ask a lot of questions for someone newly raised from the dead,' she said, her eyes narrowing. 'You should be resting. Your body and your brain are exhausted from the effort it took to keep you alive. You almost died, you know—it was only your physical fitness that saved you.'

'I'm nervous.' He sighed. 'Did I happen to mention I don't like dentists?'

'You did.' She turned back to the bench, blinking furiously.

'So who are you running away from, Kit?' His tone was casual, but the question was unsettling.

'Excuse me?'

'Or should I say *what*? What are you running away from?'

Inclining her head at him, she frowned. He reminded her of her mother when her memory first started to fade. Daphne's conversation had become unnatural and erratic, difficult to predict; she'd masked her awkwardness with a fixed smile.

Nick smiled pleasantly. 'Isn't everyone in Antarctica running away from something?' he asked, gesturing with one spade-like hand.

She responded in a serious tone. 'I'm here to do research. The Weddell teeth are a kind of bellwether for climate change. During the winter, the seals bite through sea ice to get to the surface. This means their teeth deteriorate, so they can't eat anymore and they die. But our research suggests their teeth are improving yet their mortality rates are increasing. We think it's because the sea ice is thinning and so isn't as tough on their teeth, but at the same time they're losing their natural habitat. I'm here to do data collection.'

'So you and I,' he said, 'we research similar things . . .?'

'Do we?'

'I measure and document the thickness of sea ice.'

'Oh, that's right, you're a geophysicist.'

'So I've been told.' A shadow crossed his brow, and his face stiffened.

She brought him the cup for rinsing. He took it from her and slowly lifted it to his mouth. But instead of drinking, he gripped the sides and squeezed the plastic till it cracked. Some of the solution spilt onto his wrist, but he didn't seem to notice.

Standing before him, Kit waited for him to say something or rinse his mouth. Instead, he stared straight ahead. After a while, he lowered the cup to his lap as tears trailed down his cheeks.

The cup dropped to the floor and landed with a splash.

She bent to pick it up, her eyes fixed on his grief-stricken face. 'Are you okay?'

'What happened?' he asked. 'No one . . . *no one* will tell me.'

Confused and alarmed, she said, 'I'm not sure it's best that I—'

'Just tell me,' he said, suddenly grabbing her by the shoulders. His eyes were dark and fierce. Then it seemed he registered her worried expression, because he relaxed his grip. 'Just tell me,' he whispered, smoothing her sleeve. With his mottled cheeks, he looked like a child. 'What happened to the people on that ship?'

She proceeded with care, wanting to reassure him but reluctant to say too much. 'We don't know.'

'Are they all dead?'

'I . . . I think you need to rest.' She frowned and busied herself finding tissues on the bench. There was a heaviness in her heart— it was difficult to see someone in so much pain. She went back and handed him a tissue.

'Oh my God,' he cried. 'They're all dead, aren't they?'

'No, no,' she reassured him. 'We don't know that.' She couldn't think what else to say.

He wiped his face with the tissue, his distress mounting, and she could offer no solace or comfort.

'They haven't been found,' she said quickly. 'They're missing on the sea ice. But there's a helicopter search party out looking for them right now.'

His shoulders relaxed, and he sighed a ragged breath. 'Why am I here, then?' he whispered.

'You were found unconscious on the ship.'

He seemed puzzled. 'But why wasn't I with the others?'

'We don't know.'

He was silent.

A thought occurred to her. 'We found a note in your pocket,' she said. 'It says that you shouldn't eat either 6753 or 6247. Are those numbers codes for sulphites or something you might be allergic to? We couldn't find them on a list of additives—the closest number was for monosodium glutamate and the code matches a modified maize starch. Could you be allergic to MSG or maize?'

He shrugged. 'I don't know.'

She went to the bench and remixed the solution. She brought it over in a glass tumbler. 'Here, rinse,' she said, touching his shoulder. He swished it about in his mouth. After she fetched a stainless-steel bowl, he dutifully spat into it. 'Thank you,' she said, as he leaned back and laid his head on the pillow.

At the sink, she cleaned out the glass and the bowl. Once she'd finished, she ran a hand through her hair, breathing deeply, and watched the water swirl down the drain.

Her heart was hammering. 'You should rinse every four hours,' she said.

He didn't respond.

'Every four hours . . .' she repeated in a louder voice, turning around. She was startled to hear a noise coming from the bed.

Nick's eyes were closed, and his head was thrown back, his mouth open. He was snoring.

8

Marion Lovall lay inside the sodden bivouac, miserable and gazing at the roof. The sun shone through the thin layer of polyester, tormenting her with its lack of heat and comfort. The wind sucked at the tent walls, expanding them to full stretch and then billowing them in again, whistling and hissing as it did so. In her sleeping bag, her toes were numb, and her skin felt pruny and wrinkly. Her damp brown hair had escaped from her beanie and was clinging to her face. Her spine was a frozen rod.

She rolled to her side and her hip came up against a hard object. It was the gun, wrapped inside a tea towel. When she'd first awoken, she'd been lying on top of it.

Rolling the other way, she could smell her socks and mukluks, the fetid odour of wet sheepskin permeating the tent. It was impossible to get comfortable.

This is hell, she thought.

Each passing hour brought a fresh source of misery. Four days earlier, their ordeal on the *Petrel* had begun with fire and heat, it had escalated with the rising of the wind, and it had now reached the point that they were lost in the fog. They had no idea how to get back to the ship.

Once the flames had taken hold, the alarm had sounded: one short blast followed by one long resounding blast, then repeated twice more. Most of the crew had been eating breakfast in the mess and as a collective they knew what to do.

Alone in the passageway, Marion had been paralysed with fear and incomprehension. What did the siren mean? When she smelt smoke and saw people spilling out of exits, she exclaimed once she realised they were being told to abandon ship. But she couldn't join the others straight away. There was something she had to do . . .

Her task completed, she rushed to her cabin. Shaken and panicked, she stuffed the gun into her survival kit. The naturally pessimistic part of her already envisaged a scenario in which their short-term evacuation turned into a long-term battle for survival. In such a scenario, the gun would come in handy. If things became desperate, as they surely would, she could walk away from the crew, out onto the sea ice, and make her escape on foot. Sometimes pessimism was just pragmatism.

She soon joined the rest of the crew mustered at a safe distance from the burning ship. They hunched together in the cold, clutching their survival kits, some laughing nervously, others gaping and shaking their heads.

In an act of heroism, four crew members went back to release the lifeboat. They dragged it across the ice, depositing it about three hundred metres from the ship. With a signal from Thorn, their voyage leader, everyone picked up their bags and went to shelter near the orange vessel.

Marion couldn't recall Thorn's first name. Everyone just called him Thorn, and the voyage leader himself addressed everyone by their last name.

Thorn had ensured that the crew took enough food supplies, bivvies, sleeping bags and fuel stoves to camp out on the bay for several days. At the time, those provisions seemed unnecessary— even overkill, as one cynic put it. But when the fuel tanks exploded, and the deck was consumed by flames, even that cynic said a prayer of thanks for Thorn's foresight. They wouldn't be returning to the *Petrel* in a hurry. A conflagration of flames and smoke swirled and eddied in the air as the fire fed on the fuel. All they could do was stand by and watch the ship burn.

When the wind changed direction and toxic smoke besieged their camp, the crew moved further afield, a kilometre or so away. Even then, the greying clouds reached out to them with long slender fingers, beckoning them to return. If they dared to remove their goggles or masks, the smoke stung their eyes and assaulted their lungs. Without being told, they silently prepared to spend the night on the ice.

Everyone knew their situation was precarious. Occasionally, the rolling waves from some distant wind would rise beneath them, making the sea ice swell underfoot. There was a chance that the same wind would loosen the pack and create fissures in the surface. But they had no choice, and no one expected them to be there for long. They calculated that it would take two to three days for the *Southern Star* to break through and get to them. They would likely spend a few cold nights out on the bay with hardly any sleep, but they wouldn't come to any real harm.

Marion was grateful to be sharing a bivvy with Curly Hollow, one of her closest colleagues for three years. They'd been on Antarctic expeditions before. At the muster, they'd gravitated towards each another, and Curly had held her hand when it was confirmed that her boyfriend Jason Weathers and their friend Nick Coltheart were missing. Thorn had said that Jason and Nick were most likely taking shelter on board, and no one should worry.

Overcome by trauma, Marion had barely spoken a word to Curly for several hours. But she was glad to have his calming presence by her side. In their working life, he just got on with the job despite inevitable difficulties. While she was an atmospheric physicist and worked on theoretical models, Curly was a mechanical engineer and thought a lot about earthly practicalities. She couldn't think of a better colleague to have with her right now. Conditions were cramped in their bivvy—they were much closer physically than they'd ever been before—but she didn't care, provided she could stay warm.

Once they were alone in the shelter that first night, Marion had turned to him. 'What happened?' she asked, her voice cracking. 'What happened on board?'

'What do you mean?' he said, momentarily confused. He half rolled over to face her. 'The ship was on fire, so—'

'What about *Jason*?' she whispered in an urgent tone. 'Did you see him?'

Curly hesitated. 'No one was able to find him. No one knows what happened to him.'

She fell silent. The wind was picking up, and the bivvy rustled with a dry flapping sound.

'What about Nick?' asked Curly quietly. 'What happened to him?'

Marion rolled away and stared off into space. 'I don't know,' she said, shutting her eyes.

The next day, they awoke to discover that an oppressive fog had surrounded the camp, casting a hazy yellow glow over the bivvies alongside the lifeboat. With some unease, the crew realised the fog was obscuring their vision of the *Petrel*.

'Where's the ship gone?' asked the second mate, peering into the vapour. The garish red vessel was nowhere to be seen.

'Don't worry, cobber,' said Thorn. 'She'll show her face once the fog has cleared.'

'Why don't we go back now?' asked Curly. 'The fire seems to have died down.'

'We could give it a shot,' suggested Thorn, rubbing his chin, 'but I'd feel better if we could actually see where we're headed. The last thing I'd want is for us to be wandering lost in the mist.'

As if on cue, somewhere in the fog, a fuel tank exploded.

'That settles it,' said Thorn, with some satisfaction. 'It's too dangerous to go back right now. We'll stay here until this pea souper moves on.'

Less than an hour later, the group heard a helicopter hovering above their heads. They scrambled out of their shelters and craned their necks. Some waved their arms, shouting, 'Hey! Over here!' Thorn even hurried to set off a flare.

But they could barely see the sun through the mist, let alone a helicopter. It was unlikely the chopper crew could see them.

The group paced back and forth in the gloom as the rotor noise faded.

'We should've gone back to the boat,' muttered Curly, kicking at the ground.

'I know,' said Marion. 'The search-and-rescue team will be headed straight there.'

'And we'll be left out here, to freeze to death.'

'No.' She shook her head.

He glanced at her, looking surprised by her optimism.

'No,' she repeated. 'We'll die of thirst before then.'

•

On day three, the *Petrel* crew knew they were in trouble when the wind finally picked up. At first, it made its presence felt as a continuous rolling swell beneath the ice. They could see and feel the swell of the waves, rising and falling in gigantic breaths.

Then the realisation dawned: the ice was coming apart.

When the blow finally came, the group was blindsided. The crack appeared in an instant.

Marion and Curly had been standing near a fuel stove, huddled together with steaming cups in their hands, when a cry went up. Marion looked over and watched, dumbstruck, as the sea ice parted, separating one man and the lifeboat from the main party. The bulk of the group were on the stable ice and stayed where they were. But the free-floating segment was drawn away by the current, leaving a widening gap.

With a start, Marion realised that the man on the isolated floe was Tom Priestley, the captain of the *Petrel*. He was wearing goggles and a balaclava, but his black-and-white scarf gave him away. Tom had worn the same Collingwood Magpies scarf when she first met him in January. It seemed like only yesterday when he'd greeted her together with Curly, Jason and Nick, as the four of them boarded the *Petrel*. Tom had been proudly displaying his team colours, and Nick had made some quip about the ship giving him the collywobbles. Tom had chuckled and shaken his hand.

When Tom realised that his floe was moving away from the group, he panicked and tried to leap across the divide. He stepped back, then launched himself into the air. He landed heavily against the side of the ice and slid into the water.

Flinging his cup to the ground, Curly scrambled to the edge. On his stomach, he spread his body flat over the icy surface and reached down to the water. Tom tried to grab his hand, lunging and splashing about. But then he vanished, the current pulling him under.

The group reacted with mute anguish and disbelief. Curly remained lying on the edge of the ice for a full five minutes until someone went over and helped him up. Some people clutched at their beanies in shock, while Marion covered her face with gloved hands.

Only Thorn was calm and collected. 'We have to move,' he said. 'We have to move people, now. We can't stay here. Strong winds are headed our way, probably a storm, and we don't have much time— we need to aim for the coast, where the ice is stronger and thicker.'

They knew they weren't far from the fast ice, the frozen sea water attached to the coastline. Unlike pack ice, it didn't move with the currents and the wind. In winter, it provided a breeding ground for penguins and seals. It was stable and trustworthy.

Yet there were murmurs of protest among the group. The second mate suggested a return to the ship.

'You don't get it,' insisted Thorn, stuffing gear into a bag. 'The ice is coming apart. Even if we can find the ship in this fog, it isn't safe. It isn't safe inside, and it isn't safe outside. We need to move to firmer ground, and we need to move now.'

They packed up and headed towards the coastline, praying the ice would harden the closer they came to land. It was no comfort that Thorn had been right: a great snowstorm arrived that very afternoon.

•

In the bivvy, Marion tucked the gun away as Curly stirred beside her. They had stayed awake all night as the wind moaned and groaned outside, tugging at their shelter.

'Hey,' he said in a hoarse voice, 'how are you?'

'Not good.'

He let out a weary breath. 'Yeah, me neither.'

'I keep thinking about Tom—I just don't know why he jumped,' she said, shaking her head. 'He had the lifeboat, so he would have been fine. The raft would have provided him with shelter and protection. He might have even got the emergency beacon to work. It could have been spotted by a SAR team.'

Curly didn't reply.

'Perhaps Tom thought his chances of surviving were greater if he stayed with the group . . .?' she speculated, glancing at Curly's profile against the light.

Still, he remained silent.

'I guess it was just a split-second decision—'

'I want to go back to that moment,' interjected Curly. 'You know, the moment when Tom fell in the sea.' He looked wild-eyed at the sky, an arm flung over his head. 'I can see myself grabbing the collar of his immersion suit. I can even feel myself hauling him up onto the ice. It wouldn't have been a big deal. Tom would've been grateful, and we would've laughed about it later. But instead, he's dead, and it's the biggest deal in the world.'

'You did everything you could,' she said with tenderness.

'Yes, but my everything meant nothing.'

'That's not true.' She patted his sleeping bag. But she understood how he felt.

Jason's beaming face emerged in her mind, his handsome features not yet blurred to memory. He gazed at her with love and amusement, his tanned skin and honey-coloured curls radiating youth and good health. He'd always looked more at home on a surf-board than a Ski-Doo.

Oh, my darling, she thought in despair. *My everything meant nothing. There was nothing I could do.*

9

Using ski poles, Kit gingerly walked away from the wharf area, looking up at Macpherson Station's gigantic Lego-block buildings. The primary colours of red, yellow and blue were reassuring. In the midst of so much white—white sky, white sea, white land— there was no doubt where her new home stood. The station was on the stony hill at the curved part of Wineglass Harbour, a dumping ground for the katabatic winds that incessantly roared down the slopes from the ice plateau.

The *Star* had arrived at base a full five days after discovering Nick on the *Petrel* and a tardy twenty-one days after leaving Hobart. For Kit, it was a relief to be on firm ground. The wind had immediately come to greet her, a stream of dense cold air raging past the buildings and out into the bay. It roared past her hooded head now like a low-flying jet. Then it quietened down for a bit, before coming back as a throng of demonic lovers, each one wanting to embrace her. They pulled her this way and that, fighting to hold on to her coat. She'd been told the weather could stay like this for days.

The ship was being unburdened of its cargo before heading back to Prydz Bay, to resume the search for survivors. The *Star* crew were about to complete the last run to the Green Store, the main supplies shed, and a few straggling members were standing about waiting, hugging their chests.

Kit had returned to the wharf to retrieve Dustin's medical supplies—a few replacement drugs and fluids—to ensure they went straight to the surgery. The goods now tucked in her backpack, she nodded and waved to Blondie, who was securing a crate to a trailer up ahead. From a distance he was indistinguishable from the others, but when he turned to steady the crate, she could see 'Blondie' in black marker pen on the back of his vest.

She drew near him, her legs dragging like lead weights. 'Hi there,' she called out, breathing heavily.

Blondie swung around. 'Hi there yourself,' he said with a broad smile.

'Can I hitch a ride with you?'

'Sure, hop on board.'

He secured his load, and they climbed into an enormous Hägglunds, the favoured mode of taxi on the Antarctic continent. Resembling army trucks, Häggs were box-shaped vehicles with rubber-track wheels that could be relied upon to traverse both hardened sea ice and soft loose snow. This one would take them to the largest Lego-style building, known as the Red Shed, where the winter expeditioners had each been allocated a bedroom or 'donga'.

The Red Shed dominated the station landscape like the towering citadel of an ancient city. The heart of domestic life on the base, the scarlet building was the size of a small factory and situated at the highest point above the harbour. It housed the dining room, the kitchen, the lounge area, the sleeping quarters, and all the medical facilities on base.

The gravel roads leading from the wharf fanned out like lines on the palm of a hand. The main lifeline went straight past the Green Store, while an orthogonal headline led to the tradies' workshop in the west. At the forked point where those two roads met was a single heart line trailing up the hill to the Red Shed. Various smaller structures—including the operations building, the water tanks, and the emergency vehicle shelter—were scattered around the rocky outcrop, amid a swathe of dirt and snow.

Nick would be joining them in the Red Shed later that day.

'Has Nick been told?' asked Blondie, staring ahead at the road.

'Yes, he knows about the change of plan,' said Kit with a frown.

The original plan had been to take Nick via helicopter to the ski landing area near Macpherson, then to Wilkins Aerodrome and back to Hobart, where he would undergo proper medical treatment. They'd expected him to be back in Tasmania in less than forty-eight hours.

That morning, however, the Antarctic Division had made a difficult call. They had cancelled Nick's flight.

'The decision wasn't made lightly,' said Kit, echoing Dustin's announcement only a few hours earlier.

Prior to finding Nick, the Division had already shut down the aerodrome for the winter season. The runway was typically open only in the summer months. His evacuation had been planned as a special one-off trip, but that plan had always been dependent on the weather, and the weather didn't want to cooperate.

Kit continued. 'The authorities felt that conditions were too dangerous, and they refused to let the evacuation flight leave Hobart. Dustin said they weren't willing to risk the lives of multiple employees to airlift one passenger who doesn't have life-threatening injuries.'

'S'pose that's understandable. But what's gonna happen to Nick?'

'Well, the long-term weather report indicates that things will be better next week. So, fingers crossed, the plan is to send an evacuation flight then.'

'Why aren't they just shipping him back with the *Star*?'

Kit shook her head. 'It'll take too long. The ship's services are needed in Prydz Bay for the SAR effort. And even a delayed flight will be quicker than returning with the ship—the *Star* might not be back in Hobart for another three weeks.'

With the ice closing in, it was imperative to find the *Petrel* crew as soon as possible. The SAR team were still hopeful, despite dire speculation in the media. In breaking news the day before, a Chinese helicopter had discovered the orange lifeboat to the east of the bay. No one had been on board, but it was anticipated the crew would be found on a larger icefloe nearby. Choppers were out searching scattered floes in the area.

•

At lunch that day, their first meal at Macpherson, everyone was discussing the lifeboat news. In high spirits, a noisy group of new arrivals and existing expeditioners swapped stories of Antarctic survival. They recounted epic tales of the Heroic Age of Antarctic Exploration in the early twentieth century, during which stranded men with crude equipment and rudimentary clothing had endured months on the ice, surviving everything from food poisoning and crevasse falls to frostbite and scurvy. The conversation was intended to raise everyone's hopes for the *Petrel* crew. But to Kit's mind, the tales only unscored how insanely easy it was to die in Antarctica. Only one thing had to go wrong, one misplaced step or miscalculation, and the ice would take you.

She wasn't surprised when the conversation turned to bleaker subjects. With sadness, Alessandra recalled the fate of five British men who'd gone missing in East Antarctica only a few summers before. Their Twin Otter had gone down in relatively accessible terrain not far from Macpherson, but despite an extensive search by air, the plane couldn't be found. Eventually, the weather had become so horrible—the winds so strong and visibility so poor—that the search had to be called off. Then winter had settled in, and all thoughts of a recovery operation had been abandoned. There'd been multiple follow-ups since, but the wreckage had never been located.

With each passing day, everyone on base was aware that the *Petrel* crew potentially faced a similar fate to that of the British expeditioners. If a SAR team didn't find them in the next few weeks, there would be little chance of finding them in the next seven and a half months. Come the dead of winter, the continent would be enclosed in ice and blanketed in darkness.

Kit was glad that Nick wasn't at that first meal to hear the speculations about his colleagues. Physically speaking, he'd regained much of his strength. His heartbeat was regular, his lungs were fine, and he was no longer experiencing jaw pain. But he still had no memory of preceding events or of his identity before he'd been found in the coolroom. In his own words, it was like 'a bloody big ice sheet' in his head.

To Kit, the prolonged memory loss was strange and a little suspicious. Again, at the back of her mind, she could hear a crackling, hissing note of caution. She was reminded of when her mother first became ill. She'd heard similar alarm bells, but had dismissed Daphne's personality changes, bizarre comments and memory lapses as the effects of old age. Later she'd learnt about why dementia often went undiagnosed in the early stages: the sufferer and their family were complicit in explaining away the symptoms. Kit now wondered if she and Dustin might be explaining away Nick's symptoms. She didn't suspect him of harbouring an illness or a cognitive disorder; but still, something didn't seem right.

After lunch and their first briefing on daily routines and station rules, Kit took Dustin aside in the mess. A sprawling communal area, its main feature was an industrial-size dining table in the centre. On one side, the room opened into the stainless-steel kitchen; on the other, it hosted a line of lounge chairs facing floor-to-ceiling windows. Moving to one of the chairs, Kit sat down, and Dustin joined her next to a formica coffee table. She waited till the others had left before airing her thoughts.

'Aren't you surprised that Nick is still showing such profound memory loss?' she asked in a quiet voice. 'You're right that he doesn't appear to have a severe brain injury—he's communicating well. I would have thought a period of rest would have helped his recovery by now.'

'Well, I don't know about that.' Dustin shrugged. 'It's early days yet. Let's see if being on the ground jogs his memory.'

'If he's still showing symptoms of post-traumatic amnesia in a few days,' said Kit, 'we may have to consider other reasons for his loss—his apparent loss—of memory.'

'Well, yes, you're right. There might be *psychogenic* reasons for the loss. There might be emotional or psychological explanations for the brain's inhibition of certain memories. As in, he might be repressing something traumatic or distressing. That's entirely plausible.'

Kit was impatient with Dustin. She stared at his bright, unsuspecting eyes. 'There is another explanation, though, isn't there?'

'What do you mean?'

'Oh, come on, Dustin,' she said in disbelief. 'Has it really not occurred to you that he might be faking it?'

Dustin's surprise looked genuine. He blew air into his cheeks and exhaled loudly. 'I suppose that's a possibility. But his disorientation and confusion seem pretty real to me. Don't they seem real to you?' He searched her eyes for some agreement. 'And why would he fake it? What possible reason could he have?'

'I don't know,' she admitted. 'But I would've thought he'd at least remember who he is by now.'

'Oh, but Kit,' Dustin's brow creased, 'keep in mind the effect of all those painkillers. He's been on a rather high dose—he was in an induced coma only a few days ago.'

'Okay. So why don't we try taking him off the drugs?'

'Yes, yes, we will . . . eventually. A complete withdrawal isn't advisable, not just yet. He's lucky not to have a broken jaw, and—'

'It might not be advisable, Dustin, but it might be *necessary* if we want to find out the truth sooner rather than later. This man might be able to tell us something that helps the SAR team find the *Petrel* crew.'

Bowing his head, Dustin looked at the floor. When he spoke, his tone was wearier. 'Everything suggests Nick's just some poor bloke who got left behind and shut himself away to die. Kit, has it occurred to you there might be nothing to tell?'

Though she knew the doctor might be right, she couldn't shake her doubts. 'There are twenty-three people out there in the freezing cold, Dustin. I think we should take Nick off his meds and see if his memory clears. If it doesn't, we should seriously consider the fact that he may have something to hide. You and I should see if we can get him to tell us what happened. We might even think about contacting the federal police.'

Dustin's manner softened, and a smile played at the corners of his mouth. He clearly thought she was overreacting. 'Okay, okay,' he said, holding up his hands. 'Let's not get the police involved just yet, shall we? Let's try a gentler approach and see how he responds to a teleconference with his ex-wife. Perhaps seeing her and speaking with her might jog his memory. We might also start reducing his meds.'

Kit was satisfied. The teleconference and the meds would be a good start. At least they wouldn't be waiting around for something to change.

10

Once Kit had left, Dustin tossed his ballpoint pen on the coffee table. It bounced a few times and then rolled off the edge, landing with a satisfying clatter. He crossed his arms in frustration. Nick needed more recovery time. People with severe hypothermia could go on to have serious difficulties—an irregular heartbeat wasn't uncommon and could even be fatal. Dustin wanted to err on the side of caution.

Plus, if Nick stayed on the base, he might make a good control subject for Dustin's research project. Nick hadn't been a participant in the pre-departure regime, and he hadn't had any supplements or light therapy—not that Dustin knew of, anyway.

It seemed strange that Kit suspected Nick of lying. Once again, Dustin found himself wondering how she'd get on with the other expeditioners during their stay. Only an hour earlier, she'd questioned him at their communal lunch. It was the first meal among the Macpherson winter team, but the last with key members of the Star—including Richard, Hank, Jamie, Dr Sidebottom and the helicopter pilots—who were heading back to help in the search. In front of their fellow expeditioners, Kit queried Dustin's request that everyone take the vitamin supplement as part of a daily toast, now that the phone apps were disabled. 'Do we really need one every day?' she asked, frowning as he poured tumblers of juice.

'Yes,' he said, handing out the glasses. Ignoring Kit's sigh, he then proposed a toast. 'To good health,' he said, standing up and raising his glass, 'and to fair weather for our *Petrel* friends. May they soon be found.'

'Hear, hear,' replied the group.

From his seat at the end of the table, Dustin saw Kit position her pill next to her bowl. It remained there for the entire lunch, much to his frustration. As he ploughed through his rice and lentils, he kept looking up under his brows to see if she'd taken it. Each time he spied the tablet, it made him more irritable. He mechanically shovelled the food into his mouth, spoonful after bitter spoonful.

When Kit stood up to take her bowl to the kitchen, he abruptly stood too. 'Kit,' he said, trying to conceal his annoyance, 'are you going to take that?' He gestured to the oval capsule she'd left behind.

'Oh,' she said, apparently surprised. 'Of course.' She picked it up.

'Of course,' echoed Dustin, mustering a fake smile.

Now, alone in the lounge area, he took a deep breath. It was just the beginning of their stay, and he was having trouble keeping his irritability in check. He worried that things were only going to get worse.

11

It would have been better, thought Kit, if Nick had been stretchered from the ship to the shore. But when the medical team considered his size and weight, and the hazards of carrying him across the ice, they abandoned all thoughts of a stretcher. Instead, he was asked to get off the Zodiac dinghy and walk across the harbour with the assistance of Dustin and Dr Sidebottom. Kit offered to meet them at the wharf in case she was needed—in case Nick collapsed and someone had to run for help, she thought.

When she arrived, the doctors were already flanking the stooped giant. As the taller of the two, Dustin took most of Nick's weight. The doctor's face was contorted with effort, the strain showing in his eyes. Despite the blowing gust and the cold, he was sweating.

Nick's few belongings—some donated clothes and toiletries— were packed into a nylon gym bag lying open and exposed in the snow. Kit did her best to zip it up with gloved hands.

He looked excitedly about him, peering over Dustin's head. His face was bathed in a euphoric light. 'Hey, Kit!' he yelled, struggling to make himself heard over the wind. 'Hey, is this the ice of the bay? Is there water underneath us?'

'Yes,' she called back, smiling and hoisting his bag over her shoulder. 'This is Wineglass Harbour. But you needn't worry—the ice is pretty thick, I'm told.' They were standing on the fast ice of the bay, a few metres from land.

'Oh, I'm not worried.'

'Just don't walk on any cracks, okay?'

'No, I won't.'

'Good,' she said, 'because if you fall in, I won't come and rescue you.'

Nick laughed, oblivious to her seriousness.

'We're trained not to,' she responded, deadpan.

When the doctors stopped to reposition Nick's weight, she stopped with them. He beamed at her. He was resting against Dustin's shoulder, seemingly unaware of the burden he was placing on the smaller man.

Nick reminded Kit of a drunken Elvis impersonator. His unwashed hair was slicked back extravagantly from his forehead, his large sunglasses had dipped down his nose, and his eyes were shining. 'How are you?' he asked her.

The wind momentarily abated, and all went quiet. He locked eyes with her, and her traitorous heart skipped a beat.

'I'm fine,' she said, pleased to see he'd recovered from his anguish.

'How are the seals?' he asked. 'Still chipping away?'

'Yes, still chipping, as far as I know. We're going to see them tomorrow.'

Dustin threw her an inquisitive look. She looked down, her cheeks warming.

Once Nick felt ready, they headed to the waiting Hägglunds. It took them back to the Red Shed, where Nick would be free to wander within the confines of the main sleeping and living quarters, from the kitchen to the mess to the entertainment area, and also a little way outdoors, depending on the weather.

Kit had suggested that like all station members, Nick should be allocated light roster duties such as cleaning the floors and peeling vegetables. That way, provided he wasn't too weak and unwell, he'd be kept occupied for the next week, until the evacuation flight arrived.

Now she accompanied him and the doctors to the door of his donga. Without seeing inside, she knew it would be like every other bedroom in the elaborate maze of the upstairs sleeping quarters: a narrow cave, with a single bed, a bookcase, a wardrobe and a desk all crammed into a space no bigger than a public toilet. The furnishings would be in blonde wood and chrome metal, and the colour scheme would be bland and relatively inoffensive—with the likely exception of the quilt cover. Hers was a landscape of paint vomit in garish green, yellow and red.

Kit deposited Nick's half-empty bag on the ground and started to bid the men farewell.

Nick nudged her elbow and leaned down to speak to her. 'Thanks for all your help,' he said, flashing his charming smile. 'I really appreciate it.'

She glanced up at him, and their eyes met. A look passed between them. It was gone in an instant, but it was definitely a look, thought Kit. She didn't know what it meant, but she knew one thing: it made her uncomfortable.

12

Marion found it difficult to sleep with the noise of the cracking, the continual grinding and groaning of the ice beneath her. Several times in the night, she had woken in panic, the memory of Tom's death still vivid. There was always someone on watch, but she'd scramble out of the bivvy anyway, especially if a crack sounded nearby. The irony wasn't lost on her. They'd been stuck in pack ice on the *Petrel* for three weeks, praying for it to break up; now that they needed it to remain compacted, any fragmentation was looked upon with dread.

Thankfully, for almost a week they hadn't experienced anything like the shocking blow of that day when the ice split apart. Regardless, a sense of hopelessness had spread among the crew. Since then, there had been no sign of helicopters or SAR teams despite the clearing of the fog and the release of flares. Morale was at an all-time low. No one wanted to speak to anyone anymore. In the morning, most of them stayed in their bivvies. A few wandered around with slumped shoulders or sat listlessly on the ground, their eyes dull and staring.

Curly, Marion and Thorn agreed to convene an emergency council of war around a fuel stove on the ice. Thorn had asked to meet with them because they were senior personnel and veterans of Antarctic expeditions.

They needed a longer-term plan. Their supplies were almost gone; they hadn't been extravagant with food, but in anticipation of a speedy rescue, each person had consumed at least three small rations a day. They were also running dangerously low on fuel to light the stoves to melt snow. Soon, things would be desperate. Good hydration was essential, and regular meals had helped to keep the crew warm and energised. The effort required to light the stoves and fix a cup of tea had also kept them focused and in the moment. Now they needed to think ahead—and strategically. It was becoming clear that they might not be found for several more days or even weeks. They might not be found at all—but no one wanted to say that out loud.

Thorn had been their voyage leader on the *Petrel* and had remained their leader on the ice. During the evacuation, he was the one who'd barked orders to bring the bivvies, sleeping bags and supplies. A tall man with a red beanie and a black beard, he was easy to spot doing the daily rounds in the campsite and talking to despondent crew members. He oversaw the rationing of food—mainly biscuits, chocolate and pemmican, a blend of dried meat and fat—and he made sure everyone was keeping hydrated.

Marion knew that Thorn was starting to get on Curly's nerves. As they waited for the meeting to begin, he asked, 'Have you noticed how Thorn refers to everyone by their last names?'

'Yes,' she replied, 'what of it?'

They were seated outside on their packs, enjoying a rare moment of respite from the wind.

'He reminds me of an engineer I used to know in the mining industry in America. He used his fists to settle arguments. Thorn's just a bit too dictatorial for my liking.'

Marion murmured something noncommittal. She liked Thorn and got on well with him.

'Technically,' continued Curly, 'he isn't even our voyage leader anymore. When we left the *Petrel*, the voyage officially ended.'

'Sure,' said Marion, spying Thorn emerging from his shelter. 'Here he comes. Why don't you tell him that?'

Curly snorted, prodding at the ice with his boot.

'Lovall, Hollow,' Thorn greeted them.

As Marion moved over to make room, he sat next to her, placing a gloved hand on her shoulder. She pretended not to see the annoyed glance Curly flicked at him.

'Okay,' said Thorn, getting down to business, 'we have to talk about the food situation. It's clear that we need to keep moving.' The wind picked up and lashed at their heads, underscoring his point.

Marion nodded. From the corner of her eye, she saw that Curly was clenching his fists inside his pockets. 'I'm open to suggestions,' she said.

Thorn cleared his throat. 'We should keep moving along the firmer ice, along the Lars Christensen Coast,' he said.

It occurred to her that Thorn didn't want to give them a chance to speak—he didn't want to hear any of their ideas. He was keen to get his own thoughts out on the table, to determine the direction of conversation. Marion knew what could happen when other people voiced their suggestions first: it tended to have a bandwagon effect in which everyone jumped on board and blocked off other possibilities. It had happened with Nick and Jason many times. The friends always stuck together, thick as thieves, and backed one another up.

A long-time colleague, Curly was adept at dealing with Nick and Jason in difficult work situations. The trick, he said, was to divide and conquer. If he needed the team to think outside the box, he would introduce an idea separately to one of them—usually to Jason, who tended to be more pliable—but make him think it was his own idea.

She was interested to see how Curly would deal with Thorn now that the other man had taken the lead.

'Are you sure?' countered Curly reasonably. 'Won't that take us too far from the *Petrel*? Will anyone be looking for us out along the coast? It could be risky.'

'The risk,' said Thorn in clipped tones, 'is staying here.'

Curly pushed his fists deeper in his pockets and straightened his back. If they'd been standing up, Thorn would have towered over him by at least a head. But perched on the ground, they were on a level. Marion suspected that Curly was sitting up straight to make himself look bigger.

'I know,' he said, 'but I am just wondering about the wisdom of straying too far from the ship.'

Thorn made a derisive noise in the back of his throat. He smiled in disbelief and shook his head.

'What's wrong with staying put?' asked Marion. 'Or even heading back to the *Petrel*?'

'What *isn't* wrong with it?' Thorn started counting off a list on his fingers. 'We don't know precisely where the ship is, for starters. And if we try to find it, we'll be in danger of the ice coming apart or thinning out, as it did before. In the meantime, we won't have a reliable food source—'

'It's not like we'll be trekking hundreds of miles,' said Curly, 'we just have to head back in the direction we came—'

'It will be like finding a needle in a haystack.' Thorn's voice was mildly belligerent. 'The compasses won't help us if we get lost in a blizzard. We could hit a whiteout, or the sun could be hidden from us for days, and we won't know where we are—we'll either freeze to death or starve.' The expression on his face was pure contempt, a look heightened by his bloodshot eyes and deathly pallor. In less than a week, he'd aged about ten years.

'Okay, so what would you like to do then?' said Curly, making his classic move. Marion knew they could sit there offering counter-suggestions to Thorn all day, only to have them knocked back again and again. The best way to stop the cycle was to get him to make a suggestion of his own.

With barely concealed irritation, he said, 'We should use the compasses to keep moving along the fast ice attached to the coast.'

Marion could see that Curly was considering this option. The great thing about Curly was that he liked to weigh up every side of a proposal before proceeding. His mantra was something British Prime Minister Harold Macmillan had once said: 'quiet, calm deliberation disentangles every knot'. There would always be a solution, Curly would say—he just needed time to find it.

But time, unfortunately, was something they didn't have. They'd already stayed put for almost a week in the hope the SAR team would return. Their food supplies were nearly gone. And Thorn now awaited a response.

'In the Arctic,' suggested Marion in the silence, 'the Indigenous peoples would use fast ice for hunting and travelling. We could do the same here. We're likely to find colonies of seals and penguins scattered along the shoreline, and we can eat them and use their blubber as oil—we'll need both the food and the fuel.'

'But no one will be searching for us along the coast.' Curly looked straight at Thorn. 'Do you want to spend the winter out on the ice? Because that's what we're facing.'

Thorn shut his eyes and breathed in impatiently, as if he couldn't believe Curly was being so stupid. With his eyes closed, he said, 'The coastline here runs towards the Mawson Coast, a couple of hundred kilometres away.' He opened his eyes. 'No one is coming here for us—we're God-knows-how-many miles from the *Petrel* by now. If they can, they'll be tracking that fucking lifeboat anyway.' He gestured dramatically into the distance. 'This way, we'll hedge our bets. We could eventually end up at Wineglass Harbour and Macpherson. It's better than trekking back across the bay to find the *Petrel*, where we'll just end up hopelessly lost and starving, if we don't drown first.'

'But the weather's been unpredictable from hour to hour,' said Curly, 'and from day to day. How do we know the ice will remain fast along the coast? How do we know it will be safer than staying put?'

'I'm not suggesting it's going to be easy. I'm just suggesting we navigate our way along the stable ice towards Macpherson, as best we can.'

'Whatever plan we decide on, we need to put it into action as soon as possible,' said Marion with diplomacy. 'Now that we're on starvation rations, in just a few days we won't have the energy to go anywhere.'

Thorn and Curly nodded, finally agreeing about something.

'We should go where we know the food will be,' said Thorn.

Curly took a ragged breath. 'All right,' he said in resignation. 'Let's head for Macpherson.'

Clearly revelling in the triumph, Thorn straightened his neck and turned to Marion for approval, but she looked away. The conversation was over. She tightened the hood of her coat and struggled to her feet.

As Curly stood up too, Thorn spoke suddenly and pointed at him. 'You're the first one I'm eating,' he joked.

Curly gave a short laugh. But as he walked away, Marion heard him mutter, 'Not if I eat you first, you prick.'

13

The teleconference session with Nick's ex-wife, Anna, was scheduled for his second night on the station. Everyone agreed that sooner was better than later. It was hoped that the face-to-face meeting would have therapeutic value—or shock value, at least—for Nick. They arranged to place the call via satellite just after dinner. With some help from the communications team, Kit set up a computer with a large screen and a portable webcam in the library.

As a formality, Dustin asked Nick to remain in his donga at first, while the station medical team—namely Dustin and Kit—spoke to Anna alone. The doctor told Nick that they wanted to prepare her, so that Nick's complete memory loss didn't come as a surprise. Kit knew this was disingenuous, because she'd seen Dustin's long-winded email to Anna about the amnesia. He'd persuaded her to participate by suggesting she could be the key to her ex-husband's recovery: Nick might be prompted to remember particular events and feelings by talking with someone who knew him well.

The true purpose of the preliminary chat with Anna was to ask some rather delicate questions about Nick's state of mind before he came to Antarctica. Dustin was convinced that there were pre-existing psychogenic reasons for the prolonged amnesia.

Kit and Dustin seated themselves in front of the monitor. They were perched on two white plastic chairs with the cluttered bookshelves of the library as a backdrop. When Anna appeared on screen, her forehead loomed large and shiny, and her eyes were huge and alien-like. She was leaning over her computer, adjusting the webcam. Kit could see down her top, where a gold necklace swung to-and-fro, and her breasts shook gently in the dark recesses of an apricot silk shirt. Her first impression was of a stylish woman with expensive taste in jewellery.

Kit cleared her throat. 'Anna, can you hear us?'

The woman sat down and brushed a lock of hair from her forehead. 'Yes,' she said. The audio made her voice thin and tinny. 'I can hear you.'

'Hi, Anna, I'm Dustin, the medical practitioner here at Macpherson,' he half-shouted, waving at the screen. 'And this is Dr Kit Bitterfeld, my medical assistant.'

Feeling rather silly, Kit waved wordlessly into the webcam. They'd agreed that Dustin would lead the conversation and she'd jump in if needed.

'I know you received our email,' continued Dustin, 'but we wanted to talk to you in person, to ask you a few questions about Nick.'

'Okay,' said Anna.

'As you know, we have some concerns about his psychological wellbeing, both now and before the *Petrel*, uh, incident . . . and we're hoping you can fill in some gaps. Is it okay if we get started? I'm just not sure how long the satellite link will hold out.'

Anna shrugged, looking somewhat nonplussed. 'Sure.' She smoothed her collar and sat straight in the chair. She was stunning, with round hazel eyes, high cheekbones and a heart-shaped face.

Her dark brown hair was in a ponytail, with a centre parting at the front. The stray lock was now tucked behind one ear. She wasn't smiling, but her manner was open and relaxed. 'Does he remember me now?' she asked with an English lilt to her Australian accent.

'Uh, no,' said Dustin. 'No, he doesn't.'

She nodded, her emotions apparently neutral.

'Okay, great,' said Dustin. 'I suppose the first question is, what was he like when you lived together? Uh, can you tell us something about him? Or something about his state of mind the last time you saw or spoke to him.'

Anna laughed quietly, a low husky chuckle. 'Oh, all right,' she said, smoothing her hair and looking at the ceiling. 'Well,' she began, 'things were not good for us towards the end. We haven't really spoken since the divorce came through last year—'

'Perhaps you could just begin by telling us something more general, like what kind of person he was? What was he like when you first met?'

'Oh, right. When I first met him, about six years ago, Nick was funny and sweet. We met in a crowded pub, and a friend of mine knew a friend of his, so we got a table together. He said he was just heading off to Antarctica for nine months, and his pick-up line that night was, "Let's make hay while the sun shines," or something really corny like that. He's a corny kind of guy. He *was* corny, back then, I should say.'

Next to Kit, Dustin was busy taking down every keyword in a notebook propped in his lap, using a ballpoint pen. He underlined 'corny'.

'But we hit it off,' continued Anna, 'and we went out on a date when he came back from Casey the next summer. Got married pretty quick, I suppose, about six months after that. We went to Canada for our honeymoon. That was pretty good. But he was away a lot following that. He would go to America for work and, you know, he went to Antarctica again—to Macpherson—for the winter, about two years after we got married.'

There was a glitch on the screen. Anna's image froze, and the audio echoed and hissed, making it difficult to understand her.

Just as suddenly, her voice became clear again. 'That was a really long winter for me, you know?' she said, her image jerking back into place. 'We kind of grew apart in that time, and we became different people. When he came back, I've got to say, he was a lot less fun. I thought maybe something had happened to him while he was away, but he didn't talk about it, didn't say anything. He just became quiet and withdrawn. I suggested marriage counselling, but he laughed it off. He said it would reflect badly on his mental health record, so he didn't want to do it . . .' Her voice trailed off into a low mumble. 'So it's difficult for me . . . um, it's difficult to say what was bothering him. But I got the feeling he just didn't want to be with me anymore. Like I said, we grew apart.'

'Can you tell us something about his state of mind in the later months, before your separation?' asked Dustin. 'I understand you parted just eight or nine months before he left for Casey.'

'Oh, sure, yeah.' She frowned in thought. 'Um, well, he smoked and drank a lot.' She gave a bitter laugh. 'He smoked up to forty cigarettes a day at one point. And he would drink whisky *every* night—even pour it over his ice-cream. So I don't think he was very happy.'

Dustin scrawled 'heavy smoker/drinker', 'unhappy'.

'He just—he just didn't talk to me anymore,' she said, her voice becoming quieter again. 'It was weird for me. He used to be such a nice guy, you know? But he said some pretty horrible things. Once he said that he didn't even *remotely* like me. He said that I talked too much. He said that living with me was like having an irritating voice-over in his head. I said I didn't talk *that* much . . . I just wanted some connection, you know? I wanted to communicate.' Her tone had become resentful and defensive.

On screen, a tanned masculine arm appeared next to Anna and sat a teacup on the desk. She reached out for the cup and gave a weak smile to the man off camera. Her eyes were red and glinting in the light.

'You say that Nick seemed unhappy,' commented Dustin. 'Did he do or say anything to make you think he was clinically depressed? Did he stop socialising? Did he stay at home a lot? Did he seem to lack motivation and enthusiasm for life?' To Kit, Dustin sounded like he was reading from a mental health manual.

'Oh, he went out all right,' said Anna drily, sipping her tea. 'He was kind of secretive about it, wouldn't say where he was going or who he was meeting with. I wondered if he was just walking around or drinking alone at the pub. He didn't really have any close friends at home, anyone he could talk to, you know.' She shook her head with a smile. 'I would have suspected an affair, except he'd let himself go and didn't really care about his appearance anymore. Besides, he just seemed so uninterested in sex.' When she said 'sex', the audio echoed and hissed. She grabbed at a tissue on her desk.

Dustin snapped to attention, and scrawled 'no sex'. 'So you would agree he might have been depressed?' he asked, waving the pen at the screen, pressing the point. 'Intimate relations between you two had completely stopped . . .?'

'Um.' Anna looked at the ceiling, struggling to gain control of her face. There was a pause, then tears came streaming down. 'You know,' she said, her voice quavering, 'I think this might have been a bad idea—I don't think I want to talk to Nick. He was such a callous bastard in the end. He didn't really care about how he made me feel, even though I was going through a lot. And so I'm not sure I want to help him now. I'm so sorry.' Her beautiful face crumpled.

Kit silently cursed Dustin for failing to read the room.

She leaned forward in her seat. 'Anna,' she said, tilting the webcam away from Dustin, 'I know this must be hard for you—I know it must be bringing up awful, painful memories—but please just listen to me for a moment.'

Anna drew a short breath. She wiped her cheek with her hand and nodded.

'I'm sure you've heard there are people lost out there on the ice,' said Kit, 'the crew and passengers on Nick's ship, and we think he might know what happened to them. If we can recover his memories, this might offer us clues about why they left and where they planned to go. He might not be able to tell us anything, but we need to try. We need all the help we can get, Anna, because the search-and-rescue teams haven't had any luck, and those people are out there alone, without enough food or proper shelter.' Kit's chest heaved. 'Please, would you please talk to him, for just five minutes? It could make all the difference.'

A barely audible crackle came over the audio, and Kit held her breath. Then at last, Anna nodded. 'Okay. For a bit.'

Leaving Dustin to chat with Anna, Kit jogged down the rabbit-warren corridors to fetch Nick. She didn't want to leave Dustin alone with Anna any longer than necessary—his insensitivity could blow the whole thing.

•

When Kit peered through the doorway, Nick jumped up from the bed, his eyes gleaming. He'd become livelier once they lowered his dosage.

'Are you ready?' she said gruffly.

'Yes.'

'Well, come on then.' She held out her hand.

She beckoned to him and, when he came to the door, took his elbow. He let her steer him down the corridor. They passed through a series of identical doors, then marched through a maze of hallways. Kit prayed she was going in the right direction.

When they reached the library, she stopped and looked him full in the face. 'Are you all right about this?' she said.

He breathed out, his brow creased. 'Well, I'm a bit nervous actually.' He dropped his voice to a whisper and pointed at the door. 'What's Anna like?' he asked, leaning closer.

Kit became conscious she was still touching his arm. She withdrew her hand.

'Oh, she seems n-nice,' she stammered. 'Quite nice, actually.' She looked away before he could catch her eye. He'd been told he'd be meeting his ex-wife, but they'd avoided giving too many details.

Nick smoothed his hair. 'I wonder what she'll make of me now? Do you think she'll like me?' he inquired with a shy smile.

Kit wanted to tell him the truth; she wanted to tell him that this woman harboured a fair amount of residual anger and resentment towards him. Anna had been quick to badmouth him and call him a bastard—she wasn't going to be his friend in a hurry. But surely he must expect some ill feelings . . .? People didn't get divorced because they had harmonious relationships.

'Just be yourself,' said Kit, then steered Nick into the library.

Dustin announced, 'Here he is!' and stood up, gesturing for Nick to take the seat in front of the webcam.

Nick sat down. His face, bright-eyed and hopeful, popped up in a corner of the large screen. 'Hello,' he said, showing no sign of recollection.

'Hi, Nick,' said Anna. 'How are you?'

'Oh, I'm good, thank you,' he replied in a neutral voice. 'How are you?'

'I'm fine.'

'Great. That's great . . .'

A painful silence filled the room. Nick fidgeted and looked over at Kit and Dustin, who had moved off screen into a corner. Kit nodded encouragement, and Nick turned back to the monitor. 'Do I look any different to you?' he asked Anna.

'You've shaved off your beard,' she offered, pulling at a thread on her shirt.

Nick looked surprised. 'Do I usually have one?'

'Yes,' she said, as if the answer should be obvious, 'as a rule— a big bushranger's beard. It was your disguise, you said, so people couldn't see what you were thinking.'

'Oh, really?'

She paused. 'I've changed my hair,' she said, pulling the lock from behind her ear and inspecting it.

'What does it normally look like?'

She looked taken aback. 'Well, I was blonde when we were married.'

'Oh!' he said, brightening. He glanced fleetingly at Kit.

'And it's longer now.'

'Oh.' He smiled. 'It looks good.'

'Do you remember anything about me? Anything at all?' Her tone held a hint of irritation.

He shook his head and threw up his hands. 'No,' he said, looking uncertainly at Kit again. 'I'm sorry. I don't know you.'

At that remark, Anna took some offence. She flared her nostrils. 'You mean you don't *want* to know me,' she muttered under her breath. She pressed her lips together.

'Sorry?' asked Nick. He clearly hadn't heard her remark.

Dustin moved in closer to the mic. 'Anna, perhaps you could tell Nick a few things about your married life . . .?'

'Like what?' she asked with a frown.

Kit jumped in, afraid that Dustin was going to pry into their intimate relations again. 'Something memorable, like when you got married and went on your honeymoon. You mentioned that you had a honeymoon in Canada.'

'Oh right,' said Anna. 'We went to Niagara Falls. Do you remember that?'

Nick shook his head again.

'We stayed in a really expensive hotel, really close to the falls, and we were supposed to be able to see the whole thing from our window, but we could have been anywhere. It was very disappointing. All we could see was *mist*, all through the day and night after night—different coloured mist.'

'Oh,' said Nick. 'I'm sorry to hear that.'

'You got me a burrito from an outer suburb, because the room service was so terrible. It was just terrible. You got a taxi to the best Mexican place around, and it cost you four times more than the burritos did. But mine tasted like cardboard and salsa. You had to finish it for me.'

'Lucky me,' said Nick with a shrug.

'Then we went on a boat ride under the falls and got absolutely soaked. They didn't warn us about that when we got on the boat. The water destroyed my best shoes—my Manolos. I was so annoyed. We spent ages trying to lodge a complaint at the service desk. You don't remember that . . .?'

'No,' he said, a smile twitching in the corners of his mouth. 'Gosh, they didn't warn you that you'd get wet? Going under the waterfall? At Niagara?'

'No,' she said, straight-faced. 'We intended to go back there a few years later. Do you remember? I'd booked our flights, I'd paid for the tickets, and I'd even arranged for us to have the same room in the hotel. But at the last minute, you had to cancel because you'd agreed to go back to Antarctica for a season. You didn't consult with me about it—you just said you had to go again, to earn some extra cash with your friend Curly. And then somehow, we never did get back to Niagara.'

'Gosh, I'm sorry.' Nick shook his head, looking bemused and concerned.

'You don't remember *any* of those things?' Anna demanded. 'Nothing at all . . .?'

'No. I'm afraid I'm drawing a blank.'

'I don't know what else to say,' she replied sulkily. 'If you can't remember our honeymoon, what can you remember?'

Dustin spoke up. 'Nick, even if you can't remember anything exactly, are you getting an impression or an emotion, or something like that?'

'Yeah,' said Nick, barely suppressing his amusement. He gestured towards Anna. 'I'm getting the impression she's a complete *bitch.*'

'Excuse me?' she said, her eyes widening.

Now he started laughing. 'I'm sorry, but you sound like someone who's very hard to please.'

'*Excuse* me? Is this a joke? Is this just an elaborate practical joke? Because if it is, I'm not finding it very funny.' Her face looked grim—murderous, even.

Dustin had frozen in horror, his mouth open and his pen suspended in mid-air.

Kit stood up and grabbed the webcam, directing it towards herself. 'No, no, no,' she said in a calm voice, 'I can assure you, this isn't a joke, Anna. Your help has been very valuable to us. But, Anna, we're going to have to leave you now. I'm so sorry, but I think the satellite link is—' Her hands moved clumsily over the mouse, clicking on the hang-up button and disconnecting the call.

In stunned silence, Dustin and Kit shared wide-eyed looks of concern.

Dustin coughed into a closed fist. 'Yes,' he said to no one in particular, 'well, yes. I think I'd better send her a quick follow-up email, just to thank her. Just to follow up.'

He ambled out of the room, leaving Kit alone with Nick.

'Well,' he said. 'I think that went well, don't you?'

'No, Nick,' she said. 'I don't think it did.'

He leaned back in his flimsy plastic chair and languidly crossed one leg over the other, dangling a bare ankle. With his arms folded across his chest and his hands in his armpits, he gazed up into a corner of the library ceiling.

Kit shook her head at his nonchalance. She sighed and asked the first question that came to mind, even though she knew the answer. 'Did you remember her at all?'

'No.' His response was abrupt, the word echoing in the empty room.

'The sound of her voice, your honeymoon, the people she mentioned—' Kit couldn't keep the exasperation out of her voice.

'Nothing,' he said, still gazing at the ceiling. 'I remember nothing.'

The clock ticked loudly against the wall, and the chair creaked under his weight as he shifted position. Overhead the fluorescent light dimmed for a few seconds before it flickered back into brightness. The word 'nothing' resonated in the air.

While she stared at him in dismay, he became transfixed by his own foot. Taking a closer look, he bent his left leg and placed his ankle on his knee. He stared at a silky sickle-shaped scar above the bone; the scar was about six centimetres in length and as thick as a pencil. He pressed his finger against it and rubbed at the arc, as though trying to erase it. His brow was raised in wonder, as if he'd never seen it before.

Finally, he released his foot and let it drop to the floor. He frowned. 'How can a man not remember anything and still be sane?' he asked, his darkened eyes fixed on Kit. When she didn't reply, he returned his gaze to the ceiling. 'If I don't know what my upbringing was like, if I don't know anything about my starting point—the habits and principles instilled in me as a child—how do I know I'm not broken? For all I know, I'm just someone who does whatever he likes, whenever he likes, without any moral anchor.'

For some reason, Kit thought of Elliot the night before he'd announced he was leaving her. He was going out somewhere— probably to see Melody—and as he headed to the door, he leaned over the couch and nuzzled Kit's neck. His lips were warm, and his breath sent a shudder down her spine. 'Mm, you smell fantastic,' he murmured. 'Wish I could stay and snuggle with you on the couch.' He'd seemed so regretful. The next day she'd returned from work to find him waiting stony-faced in the hallway, his suitcases packed and his plans in motion. The preparation must have taken weeks. So why had Elliot engaged in that charade on the couch?

She studied Nick's troubled face in the fluorescent light. Was he performing for her benefit? Was he stringing her along till the truth was revealed? She was sick of performances. She was tired of being treated like a fool.

'You should remember by now, Nick,' she said. 'You're not suffering from any obvious brain damage, you've had a good rest, and your physical recovery is going well. You should remember.'

'Well,' he said, expressing mild disbelief at her remarks, 'I don't. There's not much I can do about that. Say what you like, it won't make me remember any quicker.'

'But why did you say those things if you didn't remember her?' She pressed the point. 'Why did you call her a bi—that word?'

'What word?'

'You know the word I mean,' she responded impatiently.

He shook his head. 'You'll have to remind me.'

She ignored his attempt to side-track her. 'I think a part of you remembers Anna, deep inside. I think that part was provoked, whether you realise it consciously or not. It's like they say—over a long period we don't always remember what people have said or done to us, but we remember how they made us feel.'

'They?' he asked with a nasty grin. 'Who are *they*, these people who say these things? Do you know these experts? Are you one of them? Because I thought you were an animal dentist.'

She recoiled as if he'd hit her.

But before she could respond, the door screeched open, and Dustin bustled back into the library. 'Think we should call it a night,' he muttered. 'Let's have a proper debrief in the morning.'

Stiff with tension, she left without another word. Inside, she felt a familiar bleakness rolling in.

14

Kit sat with her back to the afternoon sun, letting its warm glow seep into her spine. Over the past few days, the sun had been a rare visitor, one that was obviously in a hurry to be elsewhere. The mess was unusually quiet and empty. She was seated with Dustin at the main dining table, enjoying a rare break from her fieldwork with the Weddell seals.

She'd just spent three gruelling days in the biting wind, collecting seal faeces and checking the tracking equipment. The work had taken her and Sally to seven breeding sites near the shoreline. As they collected the data, the snow had blown about their knees and insinuated itself like sand into every seam and pocket. Once, when Kit had removed her outer layer of gloves, her liners became wet, and the wind started to freeze the skin. The pain had lasted for hours.

Today she was glad that her medical duties kept her inside for a change. She and Dustin would finally have a chance to discuss Nick's condition and a possible treatment plan. That morning, the station had received grim news about his evacuation flight. The conditions would be too treacherous for a plane to land at Wilkins and, with bad weather closing in, the Antarctic Division had been left with no choice: Nick would have to stay at Macpherson till October. Given his remarkable recovery and previous field training, there were few concerns for his physical health and wellbeing, and with ample resources on base, he could be accommodated among the winter expeditioners. In only four days there, he had endeared himself to the other inhabitants of the Red Shed. Alessandra was grateful that he'd volunteered to take her turn as kitchen assistant or 'slushy', Blondie had reported that Nick stayed up late talking with the tradies, and Sally had promised to knit him a beanie.

The poor weather also meant that hopes were fading for the *Petrel* crew. The station received regular updates about the search in Prydz Bay, but there'd been little to report since the discovery of the lifeboat. Meanwhile, the online rumour mills had been working overtime. There was still whispered speculation about a terrorist event on the *Petrel*: a deliberate explosion, a sabotaged engine, an abducted crew. Some commentators had even cast doubt on Nick's innocence as the lone survivor—why had he been so lucky, and why wasn't he talking? As the news cycle swirled, the expeditioners closed ranks around Nick. In unspoken agreement, to protect him, no one talked about the missing crew in his presence, and everyone did their best to get on with life as usual.

Across the dining table, Dustin's face was a dull landscape, his voice a relentless drone of information. Kit found herself almost nodding off, when finally he said something of interest. 'So, in my follow-up email I asked Anna if Nick had any allergies. Apparently he's not allergic to anything.' Dustin paused. 'Except reality, she said. She thinks he's allergic to reality.'

'Why do you think she said that?' asked Kit, a hint of mock-wonder in her voice.

'Well, I think, like you, she suspects him of faking the memory loss,' he said in a matter-of-fact tone, failing to detect the mockery.

'And you? Do you suspect him of faking it?'

'Look, Kit . . .' Laying his hands flat on the table, Dustin exhaled loudly. 'This is the problem.' He paused before declaring, 'I just can't see the incentive. If Nick's a potential terrorist or arsonist, as some online sources have suggested, then why fake *memory loss*? Why not just make up some plausible-sounding story about what happened on board? Plus, there's nothing in his background to suggest terrorist connections or serious psychological instability. Everyone here likes him—everyone thinks he's a really nice guy. *I* think he's a really nice guy.'

'All right, but perhaps we're not seeing the incentive,' suggested Kit, conceding the reasonableness of his main point. 'Perhaps there's some reason to keep quiet, and we just don't know it yet.'

'Okay.' Dustin crossed his arms and stared out the window. 'If that's the case, then what can we do? What plan of action can we possibly take in the here and now, with our limited resources?' He rubbed his chin meditatively.

'We could conduct a few simple neuropsychological tests,' she suggested.

'What kind of tests?' He sounded only mildly interested, his gaze still directed out the window. Kit noticed he seemed distracted that day, as if something was on his mind.

'I've been reading about short-term memory tests for faked amnesia,' she said, 'and I've found a few strategies for detection.' Her appointment at the university gave her unlimited access to library databases, and she was already familiar with the relevant literature. After her mother's dementia diagnosis, Kit had inadvertently become an expert on memory loss. A quick search had found some useful articles on amnesia in medical journals. 'They're not foolproof tests,' she added, 'but they might make a good start. If we can catch him out, we might be able to take further action. Mention it to the federal police, get them to interview him, perhaps.

Certainly he'd know we were onto him—it might make him think twice about keeping up the pretence. We might start to get somewhere.'

'Really?' said Dustin. 'The federal police? I thought we'd dismissed that idea. You sound like you really have it in for him, Kit.'

'I don't,' she said, somewhat chagrined. Perhaps she was being blinded by her suspicions, but she couldn't shake the sense that Nick had more to tell. 'I just don't like being taken for a fool.'

'Kit,' said Dustin, smiling with kindness, 'no one would take you for a fool.'

She was grateful for the sentiment, but an image of Elliot's charming face came to mind, and she knew it wasn't true.

15

Just this once, Dustin was willing to indulge Kit's scepticism. Today of all days, he didn't have the energy to challenge her. A few neuro-psychological tests wouldn't hurt, to rule out malingering. At the same time, he figured, he could prepare additional questions for Nick for his research project. Nick might not be able to answer any retrospective queries with accuracy, but Dustin would still enjoy having a control subject on base.

Before he could do anything, however, he needed a drink. He glanced at his watch and was disheartened to find it was only 3 p.m. *Probably a little early*, he thought.

At Macpherson, the consumption of alcohol was strictly rationed. All the booze was kept within the close confines of the old electricians' building, located away from the main living quarters of the Red Shed. Summer expeditioners were permitted to bring only a limited number of litres per person for the entire trip, while the winterers were permitted a little more. No doubt this privilege was intended to help them through the long months of seasonal affective disorder, when everyone needed something stronger than their daily dose of vitamin D.

Back home, there was once a time when midday had been Dustin's threshold for his first drink. He'd pulled back from that when ten had become the new twelve on weekends. On Saturdays, he would get out of bed and look hopefully at the clock: how soon could he start? If he wasn't careful, his old habit would creep up on him again. Every day felt like a weekend here, and despite his best intentions he'd been knocking back his daily ration of beers every night.

Dustin blamed the research project. Interviews, surveys, and health and fitness routines were only part of the job. As a researcher, he also needed to observe the expeditioners up close and get to know them, so that he could tell how they were coping. It was important that the group trusted him, that they could let their guard down and be frank with him about any emotional or psychological issues. So he'd been dropping into the station's bar on a semi-regular basis to socialise with Blondie, Nick and the boys. It would've been weird not to have a drink with them.

But if Dustin were honest with himself, he was also drinking because he was already finding it hard to cope. As the days got colder, he could feel that familiar winter emptiness and its depressive fog stealing up behind him. They were only four weeks into the expedition, yet he couldn't shake the feeling.

Earlier that day, he'd received an email about his old chess partner Eddy. It was a routine follow-up from the police. Because Eddy's death had occurred suddenly and without any obvious cause, the police had to prepare an inquest brief for the coroner. Their role was to provide a sense of what Eddy's life had been like in the lead-up to his death, by gathering information from his family, friends and colleagues.

No one had told Dustin explicitly, but he suspected he knew what had happened. Eddy had been one of the unlucky few who'd never recovered from his Antarctic winter. Instead of bouncing back and rediscovering the joy in life, he'd deteriorated further, until finally he'd withdrawn into himself and stopped socialising altogether.

The last time Dustin had been in touch, more than six months ago, Eddy had said that he didn't want to go out. Dustin got the impression he rarely spoke to anyone in person and did nothing but play online chess. When Dustin finally convinced Eddy to agree to come over for dinner, he cancelled at the last minute. He didn't send an excuse, only a text: 'Something's come up.' Dustin felt too annoyed to call him back.

He hadn't heard from Eddy again. A few months later, a mutual colleague had phoned to say that Eddy had been found dead in a luxury hotel room in the city. The family didn't know what had happened. They suspected he'd taken his own life, but they were puzzled. He hadn't left the house for months, he was basically a recluse, so why had he gone to a hotel room?

Dustin guessed that he'd done it so his mother wouldn't find him. Despite her unstinting bravery—her career climbing mountains, exploring the Arctic and conquering rapids—finding the body of her only child would have killed her. It would have been the one ordeal she couldn't have come back from. In a way, it was a classic Eddy move: he'd protected his queen.

The tragedy reminded Dustin of why his work was so important. He hadn't really wanted to return to the frozen continent at the age of forty-two. Even the cold weather in Hobart had started to leave a dull ache in his knees. But Eddy's death had spurred him on to take one last research trip, for the sake of future expeditioners. Although there were many signposted dangers in Antarctica, some of the worst were the hidden psychological ones—not enough people realised that.

While all Dustin wanted to do was drown his sorrows in beer, he opened his laptop and started to search the web. He needed to prepare those questions for Nick.

16

The following evening, Kit viewed the video footage of the tests alone in her donga. Outside the Red Shed, the wind howled and thumped at the walls like a gargantuan hound demanding to be let in. The sound and the fury were a welcome relief. Finally something was drowning out the noise of the station's generators. The perpetual buzz of the machine engines had started to drive her mad.

After starting her laptop and opening the video, she positioned herself against the pillows on her bed. Nick's handsome face and upper torso filled the screen. He was seated at a table in the library.

On the screen, a disembodied hand presented Nick with a sheet of paper. From the camera's viewpoint, the white paper shone blank under the fluorescent light, but Kit knew that it contained twelve series of more or less incomplete drawings of houses, trees, churches and various animals. The first image in each series was a geometrical outline, while the second contained fuller details of the first, and so on and so on, until the last image revealed the complete object. This was a simple check for visual recognition known as the Heilbronner Test; it was often given to primary school children. Dustin had downloaded it from the internet.

The doctor's voice crackled through the tiny speaker on Kit's laptop. 'As you know, we're going to conduct a few neuropsychological tests on you today—nothing too difficult or too stressful. Nothing to worry about. The first one involves these line drawings here. Tell me, what do you think this one is?'

Dustin's disembodied hands could be seen holding pieces of cardboard over portions of the sheet of paper, expertly revealing the first incomplete drawing in a series of trees: a crude vertical line with a few branches.

'Um, I guess that could be a tree—a pine tree,' said Nick. 'Don't see too many of those around here, do we?'

'Nope, that's right,' said Dustin in a neutral voice. His hands deftly shifted the cardboard to reveal another picture. 'And this one?'

For the next few minutes, Nick's responses were quick and reliable. He identified the images at first sight, in their incomplete forms. The test revealed that he didn't have an obvious impairment in his visual recognition skills. He could grasp the gist of a symbolic representation without additional information.

Next there was an attention test. Dustin gave Nick another shiny piece of paper and instructed him to circle every 'the' in the given piece of prose. It was a passage from *Jane Eyre* that Kit had photocopied. Nick circled forty-six out of fifty-three instances of the word, another perfectly normal performance.

The final test was for short-term memory. This promised to be more revealing—to Kit's mind, anyway.

'Right,' said Dustin, 'I'm going to read out a few series of numbers, and I'd like you to concentrate on what I say, then repeat the numbers back to me out loud in exactly the same order. Do you think you can do that?'

'I'll give it a try,' said Nick.

'Right, here goes. Let's begin with single digits. Nine, five, three, zero, three, zero, five, zero.' Dustin read them out slowly, with a slight singsong quality to his delivery.

'Nine, five . . .' Nick began. Then he faltered. He looked abashed. 'Oh damn, you got me. Zero? Completely lost the plot there. Better start again.'

Dustin continued reading out sequences at a slow pace, while Nick continued to repeat numbers in the same hesitant manner—sometimes doing better, sometimes worse. His best performance was four correct numbers in a row. On the last try, he stumbled after the first three, then added a number that hadn't even been in the series: forty-six.

Alarm bells rang in Kit's head. After hitting pause, she pulled up a journal article from her documents folder and scrolled to the relevant section. Zooming in, she read:

A healthy individual can memorise and immediately repeat a series of six to eight numbers. A failure to repeat at least three numbers is extremely rare. The fact that three numbers are not repeated should arouse suspicion of malingering. The inclusion of digits not presented by the examiner should also arouse suspicion.

Kit linked her hands over the back of her head and stretched out her elbows. More than once, Nick had only managed to repeat two numbers in a row; he'd also introduced a number that wasn't part of the original sequence. Her eyes narrowed as she stared at his face, frozen on the screen in an expression somewhere between embarrassment and bemusement.

'Gotcha,' she whispered.

•

Infuriatingly, Dustin couldn't be convinced that Nick had fudged the test. 'I think that the numbers test is much harder than you realise,' he said, when she voiced her concerns the next day. 'Why don't I read out a few lines to you and see if you can repeat them verbatim?'

'That won't be necessary,' said Kit, with obvious annoyance. 'I'm pretty sure I would remember more than two numbers, Dustin, even if I couldn't repeat an entire sequence. You don't need to test me on that.'

'But you do need more evidence before you start making wild and potentially time-wasting suggestions to the federal police. So Nick's failed one test in a suspicious manner—it's just *one*. There are other explanations for why he's flunked it. Perhaps he felt extremely tired and under great pressure. Perhaps he's no good with numbers. He might even have a kind of dyslexia when it comes to digits.'

'Dustin, he's a geophysicist. You're telling me he's no good with numbers . . .?'

The doctor laughed dismissively, a laugh so hearty that she wanted to kick him. 'You're not seeing this with clear eyes, Kit,' he said with a smile.

'And you're seeing this with *blinkered* ones,' she retorted, her neck hot with frustration.

'I tell you what . . .' His voice took a conciliatory tone, and his face relaxed into a serious expression. 'Bring me some further persuasive piece of evidence, and I'll mention this to somebody at the Division. I'll send a formal message in my capacity as medical practitioner. How about that? That's the best I can do at this stage.'

Kit was irritated he'd pulled rank, but she accepted the offer with good grace.

17

Dustin sat on a couch in the bar, listening to Blondie's mate Warren explain why there were frozen pizzas scattered at odd locations around the station. The story involved a runaway Hägg, a blizzard, and someone's slushy duties gone horribly wrong.

The bar at Macpherson was a rudimentary arrangement, a shed really, in the former electricians' building down the hill from the Red Shed. There was no bar as such, just an open bench space, a sink, and a few bottles on the shelves below. There were some scrappy misshapen couches, a few coffee tables, a karaoke machine, a TV, and loud country music blaring from well-positioned speakers. A few of the blokes had agreed to meet there before that night's festivities kicked off in the Shed. The evening was marked as a formal 'social event' on the Macpherson calendar.

Seated across from Dustin, Blondie was red-faced and slapping his leg, laughing uproariously, when Nick walked in. A huge bag of ice was flung over his shoulder. He was still wearing his coat, glistening and dusted with snow, and as he clomped into the room in his heavy snow boots, he looked like a Yeti.

As a rule, bar attendees were expected to take off their outdoor gear before coming inside, but everyone was willing to make an exception for Nick. He'd just laboriously fetched more ice from a far-flung part of the station, and he was well liked among the present night's company: Blondie, Warren, and the station chef Skelly Sullivan, who was semi-asleep in an armchair. After only eight days on base, they'd come to consider Nick one of the boys. He could pour a hell of a drink, and he could tell a joke as well as any of them. He was a good bloke.

'Where do you want me to put this?' asked Nick, panting under his hood.

'Ah, just stick it over there,' said Blondie, gesturing casually towards the bench. In the absence of any official employees, he'd assumed the role of bar manager. He was hopeless at mixing cocktails, but he could wire up speakers and fix the karaoke machine whenever it broke down—which happened with suspicious regularity. As their responsible server of alcohol, it was his job to monitor the patrons and check they weren't too tipsy to get home; he had to make sure that no one wandered out onto the sea ice or succumbed to hypothermia and frostbite on their way back to the Red Shed. It was only a short trek up the slope, but a few minutes in Antarctica could mean the difference between life and death.

Nick bustled about, taking off his gear and then making a fuss and bother as he got the ice ready for drinks. 'Right,' he announced at last, 'who wants a nip of the devil?' His eyes gleamed with mischief as he decanted ice into a plastic bucket. If Blondie was the unofficial manager, then Nick was the unofficial bartender. Much to everyone's delight, he'd discovered that he could mix a fine cocktail. 'Okay,' he said, rattling the shaker, 'who's gonna be the lucky guinea pig? This whisky's gonna taste so much better now, trust me.'

Warren extended his arm to hold out his empty glass, and Nick deftly poured the murky brown contents into it.

Sniffing at the glass, Warren mumbled, 'Smells like piss.'

'Come on, have a sip. Trust me. It's mixed with cinnamon, maple syrup, lemon juice and Antarctic ice as old as Jesus's nuts. It's gonna blow your mind.'

Warren eyed the glass with scepticism. 'This ice is thirty-three years old . . .?' he asked, screwing up his face in distaste and taking a reluctant sip.

Nick laughed. 'No, *two thousand* years old.'

Warren spat the liquid back into the glass, his face souring even more. He made an incoherent sound in his throat like the hiss of a possum.

'Oh, come on, Waggsy,' said Blondie, slapping Warren so roughly on the back that he coughed and spluttered, 'what do you think our everyday drinking water is made from, you bloody great idiot!'

They had fresh water at Macpherson due to a clever plumbing device known as the melt bell. A standard bore pump inside a bell-shaped copper case, the bell was designed to melt ice in order to form an underground well. To start with, the device was winched into a hole at the edge of the ice plateau. Hot water was then pumped through the bell, causing a melt lake to form beneath it. In turn, that water was pumped into large heated tanks connected to all the main buildings.

'It's not the water or the ice,' said Warren, rubbing his Adam's apple. 'This whisky still tastes like piss!' He coughed some more before blurting out, 'Christ, Blondie, couldn't ya have brought something better?' He squinted accusingly at his friend through watery eyes.

A strict teetotaller, Blondie had brought his regulation quantity of alcohol in the cargo, mainly in the form of whisky, to give to his mate. He now looked offended at Warren's lack of gratitude.

'Hey, come on,' Nick soothed. He took Warren's glass out of his hand and had a sip himself. 'I'll add a little more cola,' he offered, choking and grimacing. 'It'll be fine.'

Going back to the bench, Nick began another round.

From his seat on the couch, Dustin gazed thoughtfully at Nick.

It had been three days since Dustin had carried out the neuro-psychological tests for Kit. While he'd dismissed her concerns, he had to admit he was puzzled about how Nick could remember some things and not others. He marvelled that the man had such a sophisticated vocabulary, yet no recollection of where he'd learnt his words, or that he could engage in meaningful conversation without imparting any biographical information whatsoever.

And how can someone forget their Canadian honeymoon, but recall the ingredients for a Canadian Whisky Sour?

Dustin was now ambivalent about whether he should make a report to head office concerning Nick's continuing memory loss.

Thus far, the various members of the Macpherson group had worked together well. Alessandra had fulfilled the role of social leader by arranging dinner parties and role-playing games. Sally had acted as peacemaker among a few mildly hostile parties, Warren had become the storyteller, and Blondie was the trusty hard worker. Dustin saw himself in the role of counsellor and therapist: it was his job to ensure the mental and physical wellbeing of the group.

But he was aware that there were one or two personalities who could turn things around—Kit among them.

As the winter season dragged on, someone capable of providing comic relief would be essential to the group's harmony. Nick had shown himself to be a bit of a jester. He'd instigated a few activities that had helped to alleviate the boredom and stress on station. He was universally liked, a favourite among both the bar regulars and the quieter library clique. As far as Dustin was concerned, he posed no threat to others.

So Dustin was loath to make an alarmist report about Nick's malingering—if he were in fact malingering, as Kit suspected. Dustin felt that rather than make hostile allegations that could turn people against each other, he and Kit should support Nick during his time on base. He should be made to feel welcome.

If only she hadn't exerted such an influence over him, thought Dustin, he would have known perfectly well what to do: he would have done nothing. Instead there was this tugging at his conscience. He might have to say something, eventually.

18

On her way back to the Red Shed, Kit stopped to admire the setting sun. The sky was a swirling ice-cream mixture of pastel pinks and blues, with the sun resting low on the horizon like the tip of a golden cone. The entire west arm of the harbour was bathed in a soft pearly glow. Breathing in, she tried not to think about the breeze biting at her ears. *Here goes nothing*, she thought, inwardly cursing Alessandra for talking her into this.

Again indulging her enthusiasm for old-fashioned parlour games, Alessandra had proposed that that week's social event would be the Imitation Game from the 1920s. This classic game required three rooms. In one room, a man, Player A, tried to convince the players in another room that he was a woman, while a woman, Player B, tried to do the same in a third room. The group then had to ask questions designed to catch the man out. The first player who got voted 'a woman' for more than half the questions won the game.

Tonight, due to a logistical difficulty, Players A and B would be in the same room.

'It'll be great fun,' Alessandra had enthused, beaming maniacally in Kit's doorway that morning. 'You can be Player B, but don't tell anyone, will you? In any case, the rules will be that you can't give any answers that reveal your true identity, and you can't discuss your answers with Player A, who will be Nick. You guys will get the questions via my messages on a laptop, then you'll write your answers back to me, separately and without discussion. I'll have to trust you on this one!'

Kit wasn't sure how she felt about being thrown together with Nick. It'd been a week since their tense exchange in the library, and while they'd had occasional chitchat at communal meals, they hadn't really conversed.

In the porch, she removed her outdoor gear. She could hear voices inside, murmuring happily in conversation. She wasn't permitted to join them or even to show her face. But on her way to the designated room, through a cracked-open door, she saw people gathered around a table full of chips and Cheezels, with fizzy brown drinks in their hands. One of them was Sally, dressed in ripped jeans and a woollen jumper. She was talking to the station leader, a rotund man named Bill Goodall. Blondie and his mate Warren were there, and so were Dustin, Skelly, Alessandra's husband Gareth, and Prudence the comms technician, among others.

When Kit had first met Skelly, the day of her arrival, she'd given a slight start when they came face to face. He looked like the man she'd met in the ship's corridor—the one who'd whispered to her on her way to seeing the green flash. True to his name, the station chef was extremely thin, his shoulders were bony and brittle, and his face was gaunt and drawn. Yet he seemed to have supernatural reserves of energy. He worked long and hard, and he could cook up a mean frittata with only powdered eggs, hydroponic vegetables and a few dried herbs. He was a man of few words and a sedate personality, but his work was held in high regard.

Skelly was also the only person on base who thought he'd met Nick before. Neither Skelly nor Nick was in a position to verify the acquaintance, but Skelly thought they'd been intro-duced on a summer voyage to Antarctica several years ago. Both smokers, they might have met during a few brief puffs in the des-ignated area.

Kit darted into the corridor and headed for the medical suite, their meeting point. Alessandra was already there. When she saw Kit, she hurried forward with her face glowing and her hands flapping; she was trembling with excitement. 'You came! Come and sit down—sit down, that's it.' She seated her at Dustin's spacious desk, amid the clutter of his medical equipment, blood pressure monitors, and shelves full of surgical masks, bandages, and anti-biotics. 'Now, can I get you a drink? Here, have some Cheezels. You just get yourself comfortable, and I'll be back in a minute.' Alessandra hurried out, her heels scuttling on the linoleum.

A few moments later, Nick swept into the surgery, making the room seem suddenly small and cramped. He brought in a flurry of cold air and a breathless bonhomie. 'Hi there!' After pulling up a chair next to Kit, he threw a waterproof daypack on the desk, narrowly missing the bowl of Cheezels.

'Hi,' she said, crossing her legs.

She noticed that the bruises on his face were gone. A lank brown fringe hung over his forehead like a curtain, making him look much younger than his thirty-five years. His cheeks were rosy from the cold, and his eyes were shining. She observed that he was still clean-shaven, even though most men on station were growing their beards over winter. A competition for the most impressive beard had been drawn up on the whiteboard in the bar—Blondie was currently winning.

'Are you ready?' said Nick. 'Because I'm going to destroy you. I'm gonna be a great woman, I just know it.'

Kit couldn't help but smile. 'I think anyone would make a better woman than me.'

He looked disappointed. 'Well, that's no fun. You could at least *try* to give me a run for my money. Betcha know a thing or two that I don't.' He crammed a fistful of Cheezels into his mouth, munching loudly.

She relaxed and uncrossed her legs, finding his levity infectious.

Soon Alessandra came back in carrying two laptops and a bottle of red wine. 'Here you go,' she said, placing the items on the table. 'This should be everything you need.' She handed plastic cups to Nick and Kit, and they poured themselves drinks while she set up the computers. 'Right,' she declared, tapping the keyboards and peering hopefully at the screens. 'I think we're . . . almost . . . ready. Now, just to be clear, do *not* discuss your answers with each other. *Do* try to answer as quickly as possible—I'll be timing you for each answer. Do *not* use the internet to look stuff up—if you do, I'll know and I'll be cross. Okay? You can monitor each other's good behaviour. Got that?'

Alessandra looked stern, and Nick and Kit nodded like obedient schoolchildren.

'Right, good luck—may the best woman win!' She flew out the door to pester the others into coming up with clever questions.

Once she'd gone, there was an awkward silence. Kit folded and unfolded her arms, while Nick crunched Cheezels. 'So,' he said, 'what do we do now?'

'I guess we wait.'

A typed message appeared in the comments box on their laptops: *How would you describe your favourite hair style?* A ticking clock appeared in a corner of the screens.

Seized with the urgency of the matter, Kit and Nick turned away from each other and began typing their responses. Her mind drawing a complete blank, Kit wrote, *Anything simple and neat.* She hesitated. With time running out, she added, *Don't believe him, I'm the woman!* Then she relaxed her arms by her sides.

Soon Nick sent off his own response, laughing like a teenager. 'What did you write?' he said, looking at her sideways and peering at her screen.

'We're not supposed to discuss our answers,' she said, snatching her device away.

'Oh, come on, that's only while we're thinking them up. We can discuss them once we've sent them! It's going to be dead boring in here otherwise.'

'Okay,' she conceded, turning her screen to show him.

'Oh, you bitch!' he exclaimed with glee. 'I can see I'm gonna have to pull out a few tricks.'

'And you? What did you write?'

He showed her: *A classic long bob with feathered layers.*

'Feathered?' she asked incredulously. 'Is that even a thing?'

'Sure it is,' he said with a winning smile. 'Wispy locks in beautiful windswept layers.' He pretended to flick his hair at the sides.

Kit grinned despite herself, while Nick kept preening.

Seconds later, the next question appeared: *What comes first, toner or moisturiser?*

'Oh my God,' she moaned, flicking her own hair back and looking at the ceiling.

'That—that's really hard,' said Nick, gripping his laptop. But then he started typing, his fingers moving with agility over the keyboard.

She just typed, *Toner.*

He was still typing frantically, the time almost running out. Once he'd sent it, he turned his screen for her to read: *Well, I'm a natural woman. I use neither toner nor moisturiser but will get a facial, every now and then, to replenish moisture and help my skin feel smooth and sleek. Oh, and toner always comes first. LOL!*

'Now you're trying too hard.' She scowled in good humour. 'They're going to see through that. You've overdone it.'

'Well, you've *underdone* it, lady,' he said, glancing at her one-word response.

There was a pause, then she asked him, 'How do you remember gender norms, I wonder? Do they form part of your procedural memory?'

His face creased into a frown, as if the question disturbed him. 'I don't know,' he admitted. 'I just do.'

She gave a quick smile, to avoid ruining the mood. His face relaxed and he grinned back at her.

If he continues to feel at ease, she thought, *he might let down his guard*. His answers might show he remembered who he was—and, more importantly, that he recalled what had happened on the *Petrel*. The search for the crew had been scaled back only that morning—there was now no time to lose. Dustin would have to take her seriously if Nick's answers revealed him to be a liar and a fraud.

As his eyes fixed on hers, she held his gaze.

The laptop questions continued. *What should you always do before mopping the floors? Can you explain exactly what happens when you get your legs waxed? What would you rather do: parade naked in front of a man in a well-lit room or eat live insects? What's the worst thing you can say to someone after sex?*

They laughed and chatted through their answers, teasing each other in turn. Kit could see why Nick was so popular with the other expeditioners—there was something utterly charming about him. In some ways, he reminded her of Elliot. The men couldn't have looked more different, but to her they had the same charismatic appeal. Nick looked her in the eye, listened to her, and responded with apparent interest. He would often touch her wrist or grab her elbow when he made a point, causing her heart to race. His eyes were bright when he looked at her. Most attractive of all, he seemed to find her funny.

He was chuckling at her last response (*Was that your first time?*), when Alessandra burst in. 'All right, you two,' she said, like a harried parent, 'we're going to shake things up a bit. You're neck and neck. Someone has suggested that the woman should now pretend to be a man, while the man should be himself, just for a bit of a change.'

Later, Sally told Kit that out in the lounge area, their comms officer Prudence had complained about the questions: she'd said they implied that domestic chores were women's work and that women should be concerned with removing their hair follicles for the pleasure of men. Before Alessandra could rip out Prudence's hair follicles, Sally had suggested the alternative approach.

'So there will be a new series of questions,' announced Alessandra, 'then I'll tally up the party's guesses, and we'll see which of you has won overall. Okay?'

When they nodded, Alessandra grinned and ducked back out.

For a while they waited in silence for new questions to appear. Kit could hear the fluorescent light humming.

'So you're a man now?' asked Nick.

'I'm *the* man,' said Kit with a smirk.

The next question finally appeared: *What is a derailleur?*

He turned quizzical eyes on her, but she ignored him and typed her answer: *gear-changing mechanism on bike, controls chain and sprockets.*

'Oh, heck,' he breathed in dismay, watching her rapid-fire response. 'I'm gonna be no good as a man.'

They compared responses. He'd written, *Some French thing, don't believe her, I'm the man.*

'Yours smacks of desperation,' she pointed out.

'Well, yours smacks of too much . . . time on bikes.'

Then a comment, presumably from Prudence, popped up: *The following questions are mathematical, based on the sexist assumption*

144

that men are better at maths than women. Try to answer as quickly as possible.

Nick cracked his knuckles and shook himself awake. The bowl of Cheezels was empty, the wine bottle half drunk. It was the business end of the evening, and Kit suddenly felt weary—she wasn't sure she was up to a maths competition. But then an idea occurred to her, and her fingers hovered over the keyboard in readiness and anticipation. *This is the perfect test,* she thought.

The first question was subtraction: *6.11 minus 4.372 equals what?*

'Easy-peasy,' murmured Nick.

The next questions came almost too rapidly for Kit to keep up.

200 divided by 5?

5.76 plus 0.726?

801,825 divided by 15?

Kit and Nick compared their independent answers; each time, they'd both come up with the correct result, even for the tricky long division question.

A message told them that the competition was over and that soon the winner would be announced.

They relaxed into their chairs, and Nick grinned at her. 'You're very good,' he said warmly. 'Your math is really good.'

She smiled back with an ambivalent heart. She had to admit she liked him—too much for her own good—but she couldn't let things pass. Her mind flashed to the razed deck of the *Petrel* and to its abandoned mess area. In only a few days, all the search-and-rescue icebreakers would have to leave Prydz Bay, to avoid being trapped.

'You know, Nick, everyone here thinks you're a really nice guy . . .'

'Oh? Who's been spreading this malicious rumour?'

'I know you're a fraud,' she said bluntly.

For a second he looked crestfallen, but he soon recovered his smile. 'Well, even the most self-aware man doesn't know if he deserves to be well liked, does he? I just try to be friendly to everyone, to give everyone their due, till they convince me they don't deserve the effort.'

'That's not my point.'

He didn't seem to realise what he'd demonstrated. The inconsistency between his maths-quiz success and the failed memory test with Dustin was glaring. To complete the long division task alone, Nick would've needed to kept at least five numbers in his head. This was the evidence she needed.

'There's nothing wrong with your memory, Nick. You've just proved it to me in the clearest possible terms. Why do you keep pretending? This is ridiculous. Why don't you just tell us what happened on the *Petrel*?'

A dangerous silence descended over the suite. Her heart thumped heavily.

When Nick spoke, his voice was low and serious. 'You might find this hard to believe, but I have nothing to hide, because there's nothing in there to hide.' He tapped the side of his head. 'I remember *nothing* about what happened before you found me. Jesus, Kit, I don't even remember *you* finding me. So what if I remember my math? I can't tell you who my parents are, or where I grew up, or who my best friend was in high school. I don't know why that is—it just *is* . . .' He gave her an imploring look.

Before Kit could respond, Alessandra came in to announce the winner. 'The best woman *and* the best man . . . is Kit! Congratulations, Dr Bitterfeld!'

Leaning back in his chair, Nick clapped loud and long, then exclaimed graciously, 'Well done!'

For Kit, however, the victory felt hollow. All night, they'd been laughing and stuffing their faces. She'd enjoyed the competitive spirit and the friendly banter. But she wondered what kind of night the *Petrel* crew might be having out on the ice.

If Nick was hiding something that could help them, it would be obscene for him to be flirting with Kit, caressing her arm and trying to make her laugh—and it would be obscene for her to be enjoying it so much.

'Yes,' she murmured unhappily, 'well done me.'

19

The fine weather helped to raise Marion's spirits; the sun had dried some of her things and made life more bearable. She'd found it difficult to cope when her underwear, sleeping bag and jacket had been soaked through. Most mornings, she could barely force herself to put her arms through the sleeves of her sodden jacket—there was no misery quite like it. She was so cold, so unbelievably, bone-chillingly cold. But worst of all, she was unbelievably, painfully hungry. In place of her stomach, there was an aching pit. She'd barely eaten anything for fourteen days, and she could feel her body starting to cannibalise itself. She didn't know if it was willpower or mindless desperation that kept her going, but she couldn't stop thinking about food. When were they going to find food?

The *Petrel* crew had been out on the ice for three weeks, and their supplies were almost gone. It helped that they kept moving and had something to do each day: melt the snow, pack the bivvies, check the compass, walk for a few hours, look for a place to camp. The routine provided a diversion from the possibility of death by starvation. They'd made some progress along the coast but hadn't yet encountered penguins or seals. To compensate for the lack of food, they tried not to exert themselves; they also found that exercise produced layers of sweat that soon turned to ice. So, all in all, they were taking things slowly and trying to stretch their meagre supplies.

For some of them, this wasn't enough. Beatrice was in her bivvy and refusing to come out. The younger woman was shaking and sobbing, curled up in a ball in her sleeping bag.

Marion had been speaking to Beatrice most days. The only women among the crew, they stuck together out of sisterly solidarity. But lately they'd been running out of things to say, and neither of them had the energy for chitchat. Marion reproached herself for failing to notice how badly Beatrice was coping.

With trepidation, Marion approached the bivvy. She crouched low with a flask of hot tea in one hand, the other pressed to the ground. 'Bea,' she called gently.

Deep inside the sleeping bag, Beatrice stopped crying. 'Marion?' came a muffled voice.

'I've brought you some tea.' Marion inched forward, leaning on one knee.

'I don't want it,' wailed Beatrice, hiccupping.

'Come on, it'll make you feel better.'

'No, it won't.'

Marion sighed. 'You're right, it probably won't.' She leaned back on her haunches and stuck her free hand into her coat pocket, rustling about. 'But here's something that might.' She pulled out a crinkled packet.

After a moment, Beatrice's beanie-covered head peered out of the bag. Red-rimmed eyes shone watery-blue in the strange yellow light of the bivvy. 'What is it?'

Holding out a gloved hand, Marion opened it to reveal a small chocolate bar.

Beatrice frowned and stammered, 'Is that—is that a *Caramello Koala?*'

'It is,' said Marion with a smile. 'I'll give it to you if you come out.'

The younger woman's frown deepened. 'But I can't accept that,' she said, sitting up, her tears forgotten. 'That's your only meal today. I can't take that from you.' She sniffled, then wiped some snot across her face.

'It's okay, I had something earlier,' lied Marion.

There was a brief silence.

When Beatrice reached for the chocolate, she looked pained. 'I can't,' she said, pulling back.

'No, no, go on, take it.' Marion pushed the bar into her hand. 'I'll see you soon.'

Marion left before Beatrice could change her mind.

Her mother's favourite parenting technique was the time-honoured art of distraction. At home recently, she'd had the pleasure of seeing her mother practise this art on the next generation of Lovalls, the children of Marion's brother. But sometimes the distraction technique just didn't work, especially when the three kids were overwrought. When distraction failed, her mother deployed the arts of cajoling and bribery. Marion's brother and his wife opposed the bribery because they didn't like their children having sweets. But when Mum was in charge, she just did whatever worked. That was another classic trick in her bag: the art of whatever worked.

With Beatrice, Marion realised, she'd just exercised all the arts in one go. Her mother would be proud.

Marion could have done with her mother's peacemaking presence. The crew kept squabbling; they were irritable and impatient, unforgiving of foibles. Someone was creating too much condensation in the bivvy, another person was failing to carry his weight, and someone else was snoring too loudly. After twenty-one days on the ice, despair was killing any affection they once had for each other. The outer layers of benevolence were being stripped away by fear and self-interest. Some days, it seemed as though only a thin layer of civility prevented an act of violence.

Marion dealt with the inevitable disintegration the only way she knew how: by distracting, cajoling and bribing. But soon that wouldn't be enough.

Even Curly was becoming difficult—she didn't know what to do about him. While the two of them remained on friendly terms, he took every opportunity to question Thorn's decisions. When Marion spoke to Curly about it, he claimed he was just weighing up their options. But his tone and manner implied that he had some grievance with Thorn. Whenever the voyage leader suggested something, Curly saw a problem with it. The conflict wasn't helped by Thorn fighting back like a gamecock in a pit, but it was always Curly who started the fight.

Marion found it difficult to intervene, because neither man was prepared to listen to her. Her opinion didn't carry any weight or authority with any of the men, actually. For days she'd suggested the rotation of bivvy companions because it might help with morale; some people were feeding off each other's negativity, forming cliques and resentments. But only when Thorn suggested moving people around did the rotation finally began. Everyone was told to find a new bivvy partner *pronto*. She was relieved that Thorn had made it a command. She needed a break from Curly, but she didn't want to initiate it.

She'd worked with him for a long time. When they'd first met, on a voyage to Macquarie Island, they'd clicked straight away. They shared a mordant, sarcastic sense of humour and a love of amateur sea-life photography. In the whole time they'd known each other, though, the relationship had remained platonic. A couple of times early on, she caught him looking at her and wondered if he fancied her, but she never saw him as a potential partner. As much as she hated to be shallow, that was probably because he was shorter than her. While he had a lithe athletic build and beautiful sea-green eyes, he only came up to her chin. The spark of attraction just wasn't there.

Soon afterwards, she'd started going out with Jason. Curly's friend and colleague Nick had set up their blind date. The three men had worked together on a geoscience project during a summer expedition to Macpherson.

That Friday night, she stood inside a crowded pub in Hobart's Salamanca Place, waiting to meet Jason. She'd been given only a vague idea of what he looked like, but he'd texted to say he'd be wearing a turquoise hoodie. She kept smiling at strangers just in case he'd taken the hoodie off; it was summer, and the pub was stuffy and overcrowded. But then Jason texted to apologise for running late.

One of the men she'd smiled at came over and asked, 'Can I buy you a drink?' He seemed nice enough, but he had badly ironed clothes, and his face held a tincture of desperation.

'Ah no, I'm waiting for someone,' she said.

'Why don't I just buy you one while you're waiting?'

'Ah, no thanks, I'd rather wait.'

'No, no, we can't have that. I'll get you a drink.' To her quiet consternation, the man signalled to the bartender. 'Two pots, please.'

Oh God, she thought, *how am I going to get rid of him?*

Then Jason walked in. He was wearing the turquoise hoodie pulled down over his head; when he pulled it back, he revealed a mane of golden curls and a blond beard.

Marion could hardly believe her luck. Without thinking, she got on tiptoe and raised her right arm to attract his attention. He looked relieved to see she was still there. Heading towards the bar, he smiled apologetically. As he came closer, she exclaimed, 'Jason!' and opened her arms to embrace him as if it were the most natural thing in the world. He leaned in, appearing a little stunned, his whiskers against her cheek. She murmured close to his ear, 'Just go along with it, okay?'

'Okay,' he said.

Then she kissed him, just briefly but warm and full on the lips. When she pulled away, she berated him in a gentle tone. 'Where have you been?'

He looked stumped and embarrassed. 'Where have you been all my life?' he replied with a laugh as his gaze shifted to the badly ironed guy. The bartender set down two overflowing beers, and the guy shuffled away.

Funny and clever, with a broad Queensland accent, Jason won her over. They'd been going out for two and a half years before the *Petrel* voyage.

The day before the fire, Jason hadn't seemed like his usual relaxed self. She'd gone outside for some midday sun on the helideck, an open area flanked by shipping containers. She came around a corner and was dumbstruck to see him confronting Nick near the railing. Her boyfriend was on his toes to reach Nick's full height, leaning into his face. At a safe distance, she held her breath while the men exchanged words. She could only catch snippets of the argument, their voices brought to her on gusts of air.

'I can't live like this anymore,' said Nick. 'It's ruined my marriage, my health, my entire life . . . I've got to tell someone.'

Jason looked incredulous, his face reddening. He held out his hands in disbelief and spoke so loudly that he could be heard over the wind. 'There's nothing to tell, Nick. It's old news, it's forgotten now, and you should forget about it too . . . Fucking get on with your life—stop blaming others for your problems.'

Marion was shocked and puzzled that Jason was so angry at Nick. Jason had always looked on him as a brother, or so he'd said. Friendships forged in Antarctica weren't ordinary; there was a lot of time to get to know people in proximity, to become familiar with their true natures, and to see beyond the façades. If you remained friends through the winter, it was said, you would be friends for life.

Perhaps this was how true friends sometimes worked out their problems . . .? This was just Jason speaking his mind, telling Nick what he really thought—like a brother would tell a brother. She imagined that later they would joke around and clap each other on the back, with no hard feelings.

'How can you be so detached?' Nick yelled at Jason, stepping back and shaking his head. 'How can you not *think* about it?'

'Easy, mate.' Jason turned away. 'Just get on with your life. I have.' He started to walk off.

Nick stood still, the wind whipping his hair about his head. He called out to Jason, 'I'm going to tell the press!' He seemed to be steeling himself for his friend's response.

'What was that?' asked Jason, turning to scowl at Nick.

The words became hesitant. 'Gonna make an anonymous report . . . to the press,' he said, some of his bravado gone.

Jason moved as though catapulted by the wind. He grabbed Nick by the bib of his coveralls and pulled his face towards him so their beards were almost touching. Nick turned his head to the side. Jason spat at him, 'You fucking do that, mate, and as far as I'm concerned, you'll be fucking dead. You hear me?'

Marion saw Tom Priestley coming out of the hangar, his face alarmed. The *Petrel* captain had clearly heard the men fighting and wished to intervene.

Keeping his face turned away from Jason, Nick laughed harshly. 'I'm a dead man anyway. We're all dead men, Jase.' He grabbed Jason around the back and shoulders, embracing him in a bear hug. 'We're all dead men,' he repeated. He tightened his hug and kissed Jason on the cheek, before pulling out of his grip.

Jason turned on his heels and marched off before Tom could say anything. The captain gazed open-mouthed at his back, before he turned to Nick and asked if he was all right. Disturbed by what she'd seen, Marion remained behind the shipping container until the men had gone.

In her cabin that night, she asked Jason about the fight. He told her he thought there was something seriously wrong with Nick. 'He's got an idea in his head about the research team, some paranoid nonsense. He doesn't speak to me nowadays except to start a fight or to complain—if he talks to me at all, that is. Most of the time he's just giving me the silent treatment.'

'What's the matter with him?'

'I don't know.' Jason shrugged. 'He's become obsessed, paranoid. Suspicious of everyone.'

'But why?'

He hesitated. 'Something happened, something out in the field . . .'

'What?'

'We found something . . . It doesn't matter. It's confidential information. But Nick, he thinks we should tell the public. He's like a terrier with a bone.'

'Why not tell the public?'

'Because,' Jason said, his eyes flashing annoyance, 'it's an intellectual property matter. Okay?' Now he sounded angry at her too.

She was taken aback. There was a long silence. 'So, you've had a falling-out?' she clarified, hoping to veer the conversation in a safer direction.

'Yes and no.' Jason ran his hands through his hair. '*I* don't have a problem with *him*. He takes everything I say in a bad light. He mistrusts my motives, thinks I'm out to get him—he thinks Curly and I are both out to get him. We can't make a right move as far as he's concerned. He's suspicious of every decision we make, thinks we're leaving him out of important meetings. He takes everything to be a slight or even a threat.'

Marion opened her mouth to say something, then thought better of it. She'd just seen Jason threatening Nick. Everything else Jason said about Nick accorded with what she had heard—his unhappiness, his instability, his obsessive behaviour—but there was a discrepancy: it was Jason who'd lost his temper, not Nick. *You'll be fucking dead*, he'd said. But she'd only ever known him to be laid-back and even-tempered, so she had to suppose Nick had pushed him too far.

The next day, Marion had found Jason before the fire alarm sounded.

She shut her eyes as the painful memory came back.

She'd found Jason on the helideck, near the spot where he and Nick had been arguing. He was slumped behind one of the shipping containers, next to a fuel barrel. She knelt next to him, her body shaking. She was surprised by her certainty that he was dead—she knew he was gone straight away. She didn't need a doctor to check his signs or take his pulse. Half his skull was missing and there was a gun lying next to his head.

Marion knew that Nick was responsible.

Now, out here in the blinding snow, her mind was numb with these troubling thoughts. She regretted giving away the chocolate to Beatrice, now that her good mood had plummeted several degrees below zero.

With tears in her eyes, Marion observed the tired, hungry faces of her colleagues. She could see the cruel spectre of death everywhere. Some of the men had ice stalactites hanging from their scrappy beards. It was just as Nick had said—they were all dead men. The skin and the beards were only thin casings for the rot inside. Curiously, the crew seemed unaware of this fact.

Beatrice was wandering around and packing up her gear. She was even smiling at the others in a pathetic show of good spirits. Men were talking to her, patting her on the back.

She probably had the right idea earlier, thought Marion. It made sense to be sobbing in a sleeping bag, or even running about in the snow, shrieking. Marion was surprised that no one had thrown themselves off the fast ice. She felt like screaming, *We're all going to die out here, don't you know that?*

We're all going to die.

20

It had been two weeks since the night of the Imitation Game, and a full three weeks since they'd said goodbye to the *Southern Star* crew. The vessel was now on its way back to Hobart, its search for survivors called off ten days before. To distract themselves, the Macpherson expeditioners were looking for ways to wind down after a hard day's work. In the absence of cafes, restaurants and cinemas, pranks were high on the list of entertainment options. Kit preferred to read a book.

She could tell that Bill Goodall had had enough of the fun and games. Removing his beanie and smoothing down tufts of mad grey hair, the station leader stood before the expeditioners with a scowl of disapproval. It was clear that he hated this part of his job: the policing bit.

'Why can't they just be adults and regulate their own behaviour?' he'd said to Kit earlier. He especially hated the fact that his present task meant singling out the tradies—the electrician, mechanic and plumber—his 'own natural subgroup,' he'd told Kit, 'and not those bloody whingers, the scientists.'

There was no helping it, though: he had to put his foot down.

'All right, folks,' he began authoritatively, holding up his hands in a Pope-like gesture. 'Settle down. Let's have some peace and quiet, please.' He waited till a couple who were immersed in conversation gave him their full attention. 'As you might have guessed, I'm here to give you a bit of a talking-to.' Among the familiar faces in the crowd of twenty, there were a few smirks; Bill ignored their insubordination. 'Now, it's come to my attention that a few of you have been up late drinking in the bar . . .'

A chorus of boos went up, namely from Nick, Blondie, Warren and Skelly. They frowned at each other with pretended affront. The other expeditioners looked on, their arms crossed, while Kit just shook her head in bemusement.

'No, no, no,' said Bill, gesturing towards the men. 'It's okay. I'm not about to stop you drinking in the bar. You're entitled to your two standard drinks a day. But when it's a matter of personal safety, I have a duty to ensure that all station members are behaving responsibly and not putting anyone's life at risk. Now, I've learnt that some of you went for a little "jolly" in a Hägg on the weekend . . .'

Kit had heard about this incident. It had involved a fibreglass dog named Stay, a former Guide Dog collection box in the shape of a labrador.

According to urban legend, in the early 1990s some Antarctic expeditioners had covertly lifted the dog off the streets of Hobart the night before their departure. Since then, the dog had travelled far and wide across the frozen continent, even becoming a cult celebrity on Facebook. Those lucky enough to get her in their possession would post selfies of themselves and the dog: Stay and her owner on a fieldwork trip, Stay and her owner taking a midwinter swim, Stay and her friends going for a carpet ride down the slopes, and so on. Ownership, however, was precarious; it had become customary for expeditioners to stage daring dognappings, usually in the form of meticulously planned pranks. Stay never stayed in anyone's possession for long.

The past summer had been an exception: someone had kept Stay's whereabouts a closely guarded secret. But Skelly, who was well established among the old-boy slushy networks of Antarctica, had heard a recent rumour that the dog was hidden right under their noses at Macpherson. Following a cryptic tip-off from a contact in Hobart, Stay had been found in a plain cardboard box next to a crate of Weet-Bix in the Green Store supply shed. Everyone had whooped for joy, and the discovery had become station news.

That night, with Stay as guest of honour, there were riotous celebrations in the bar. Warren was on hand with a digital camera, and the expeditioners lined up to have their photo taken with the canine visitor.

Late in the evening, Nick suggested taking photos of Stay playing Stump with a nail positioned in the middle of her nose. Stump was a popular drinking game in which the participants sat around an old tree stump, each armed with a hammer, a nail and a full glass of beer. The game required players to toss their hammer in the air, flip it at least once and catch the handle with one hand, while holding their beer in the other. Upon each successful catch, players were required to slam a fellow player's nail into the stump. If a player didn't catch the hammer or failed to hit an opponent's nail, they had to scull their beer.

Blondie had the honour of hammering the nail into Stay's head for the photo. He'd intended for it to leave a neat, barely noticeable hole in one of her black nostrils. Much to everyone's horror, his hit split the fibreglass nose, making a jagged crack down the dog's head and neck. The crack exposed pale yellow fibres and threads, making Stay look like one of the monstrous, misshapen huskies from *The Thing*.

The bar patrons were aghast. In the past twenty years, Stay had been chipped, dented and scuffed, but no one had ever damaged her severely. After a panicked discussion, Blondie proposed they remove Stay to the carpentry workshop before word could get out. There they could fix her up with some glue and a touch of gelcoat, as good as new.

It would be hard, however, to get to the workshop in the darkness and the howling wind. Blondie bravely retrieved a nearby Hägg. A group piled on board, with Stay wrapped in a blanket, and went off to repair her. On the way back, they took a detour to snap pictures of Stay with the station silhouette in the background.

'Now I don't know if any of youse was over the limit,' said Bill, 'and let's just say for the record you weren't. It's hard to get over the limit on two standard drinks.' Kit knew that the teetotaller Blondie had in fact been sober. 'But we all know there are a hundred ways to die out there. Take a moment to think about it now: what are some of the terrible things that could happen? I can think of at least fifty things that could result in the loss of oxygen, loss of limbs, or loss of life.'

There was a chastened silence while everyone looked awkwardly at the floor. Kit had taken no part in the jaunt, so she didn't feel implicated, but she gazed at the floor in solidarity.

'Don't drink and drive,' said Bill flatly. 'Come on, folks, I really don't want anyone dying on my watch. From now on, as a safety precaution, no one will be permitted to drink in the bar after dark.'

With the sun setting progressively earlier as true winter approached, twilight was now ending at about 8 pm, but in only a week or two, darkness would fall in the afternoon. Bill had effectively shut down the bar after work.

There were murmurs of protest.

'No, I'm sorry,' he said, looking more annoyed than sorry. 'With the airstrip closed till the summer, we can't risk a major medical emergency. We have to look after each other and start being responsible. I think the doc will agree with me on that one.'

Dustin nodded vigorously.

As the crowd dispersed, Kit watched Nick approach Dustin and exchange a few words. The doctor looked pensive while Nick was talking, but then threw his head back and laughed. Nick gave him a light slap on the back and headed for the door. When she caught Nick's eye, he raised his chin with a smile. They'd not spoken since the evening of the Imitation Game, and she'd decided to wait before voicing her latest concerns to Dustin.

As fleeting as it was, Nick's smile kept her awake into the early hours. She wondered if it was a conciliatory gesture, a sign he was prepared to open up to her. Or perhaps a sign of gratitude that she hadn't yet told Dustin about his flawless maths skills?

But then, as she tossed and turned, it dawned on her: it might be a challenge. He might be signalling that Dustin was on his side.

21

The ice cliffs rose straight out of the water, complete with mock turrets at the top and lined ridges like brickwork. To Sally, they looked like the walls of an ancient burial place, a white sepulchral city. She had no doubt that this frozen piece of land had interred many a human body over the years, including a number of heroic early explorers and maybe some of the later ones too. It was like Bill had said the week before—there were a hundred ways to die out here.

Sally was in a hurry to affix a few more tracking devices before the weather set in. She'd sent Kit back to the station to start the data analysis. Only a few seals had hauled out at the study site that morning, so their work had been slow. Sally just needed to tidy up a few things before she joined her; she'd be done in five minutes.

The wind picked up her open coat from the bottom, flapping it noisily about her back and shoulders. She shivered and did her best to re-zip the coat with clumsy mittened hands. Grey clouds hung low in the sky, permitting only the thinnest strip of pale blue above the glaring white expanse. She tried to concentrate on the task at hand, but her mind kept returning to the conversation with Kit that morning.

'You sound really paranoid,' Sally had said, throwing a nervous side glance at her friend on the ice.

'Maybe.'

'No one else is worried about Nick being here, you know,' said Sally with a smile. 'You're the only one making a fuss.'

'I know, I know,' said Kit. 'It's like he's bewitched everyone somehow. No one has a bad word to say about him. Even Prudence was telling me the other day what a perfect gentleman he is— a "perfect gentleman", her exact words!'

'Wouldn't have thought that was a compliment, coming from Prudence,' muttered Sally, fiddling with a device.

'I just don't understand why everyone is so keen to embrace him, so intent on having a laugh with him, when twenty-three of his crewmates are possibly dead or dying out there on the ice. It seems macabre and cold-blooded. Am I the only one who thinks that? Why does everyone seem to have forgotten about the *Petrel* crew?'

Sally was aware that at Australian Antarctic Division head-quarters, finding the crew was the top priority. While there were no longer any icebreakers in the region, at Davis Station helicopter pilots were still carrying out search operations whenever the weather permitted. The media continued to speculate about what had happened to the ship and how so many people could have disappeared in an age of global satellite systems. But as far as topics of conversation at Macpherson went, people rarely mentioned the expeditioners, who'd been missing for thirty-nine days.

'They haven't forgotten them,' said Sally. 'It's just that it's not humanly possible to keep up that level of grief and concern for weeks on end, you know. Everyone has a natural aversion to unhappiness. They want to get back to happy, so they want to think the best, to hope for the best. Sure, the crew's been out there on the ice for weeks, but they have fair resources and good survival skills— there's reason to be hopeful, isn't there? Besides, would you prefer that we all just sat around getting depressed and anxious? Would you prefer that *no one* interacted with Nick, just in case he was in some way responsible for what happened?'

'No,' admitted Kit, but she clearly felt frustrated. 'I like Nick too. I just keep hearing . . .' She faltered, holding her head in her hands. 'I just keep hearing whispers in my mind, you know— whispers of warning, to be on my guard, to be mindful of him. He's faking his memory loss, I'm sure of it. And there can't be a good explanation for that, can there, Sal? I can't think of one.' She looked up questioningly.

Sally's worry deepened at Kit's mention of whisperings in her head. She looked at her friend with renewed concern, studying her for telltale signs of sleeplessness and anxiety.

She thought back to the night when Kit had rung her out of the blue. At first, all Sally could hear was breathing and intermittent sobbing. Sitting up in bed, her heart pounding, she thought, *Oh my God, someone has died.* In a panic, she asked, 'Kit? What's happened? What's wrong?'

'He's gone,' she whispered between gasping breaths. 'He's left me. He's left me for someone else.'

Oh Jesus, this is about Elliot, Sally realised with a jolt of relief. *All this emotion is being spent on that worthless man.* She hated him anew for what he was doing to her friend, but she was relieved it was only about him.

Elliot was neither a good person nor a good husband. At dinner parties, Sally had dreaded being sat next to him. His conversation was competitive, if not combative. He had an angry defensiveness that could come only from a deep consciousness of being inferior or having done something wrong. He was completely self-absorbed, though occasionally—she had to admit—capable of wit and charm.

Most disturbing was the effect that he seemed to have had on her best friend. Sally had known Kit since she was sixteen. The years with Elliot had turned a strong-willed and opinionated teenager into a quiet and reserved adult. Kit had grown dependent on him for her sense of self-worth. He also, apparently, required almost continual sexual gratification; Sally didn't imagine for one moment that Kit was the only object of that insatiable desire.

At one ludicrously drunk dinner party, shortly before Kit and Elliot's wedding, Sally had staggered into the bathroom. She was sitting on the toilet, gazing at a fleur-de-lis pattern on the wall, when Elliot opened the door. With one eyebrow cocked and her best sardonic expression, she drawled, 'Come on in, Elliot, join the wee party.'

He retreated, laughing. 'Uh no, Sal. Think I'll wait out here. Sorry.'

She took as long as she could, reapplying her make-up and even plaiting her hair, just to piss him off.

When she finally opened the door, Elliot stood in front of her, his body taking up the entire frame. His breath smelt of whisky and cigarettes. On any other man, Sally thought, she would find that a powerful aphrodisiac—but not on him.

She tried to sidle past, but he blocked her with his hips so that they were touching. He placed an arm around her waist, pressing himself warm and hard against her side. 'Where are you going?' he asked in a low voice.

'Ah, back to the party,' she replied, suddenly very sober. Avoiding eye contact with him, she brought her handbag up to her waist, forcing a barrier between herself and his hips.

'Come on,' he urged. 'Kiss me, Sal. Kiss me quick. Before anyone comes.' By anyone, he meant Kit.

Up close, his handsome face looked porous and sweaty, and his charismatic smile revealed an odd collection of crooked teeth.

Sally couldn't believe that he'd talked to her like that. As if he hadn't been sparring with her all night at the dinner table. As if she didn't find him repulsive. As if he were not engaged to marry her best friend.

So, Sally leaned in to kiss him.

As he swayed towards her, she brought her knee up to his groin, pushing him forcefully into the bathroom door and out of her way. Then she went back to the dining room.

Years later, standing in the snow, she felt immensely satisfied when she recalled the image of Elliot bent over in pain. She couldn't be glad that he was having a baby with another woman—Kit was hurting too much. But now she was rid of him. And about that, Sally was glad.

It was Sally who'd suggested that Kit come to Macpherson for the duration of the winter. She had convinced Kit that she needed to get a fresh perspective on her life in a radically new location— it had worked for Sally herself once. And Kit had jumped at the opportunity, with all the abandon and carelessness of someone who had nothing to lose.

But now Sally worried that cracks were beginning to show. Sometimes pulling a geographic wasn't the best idea if your worst problems were in your own head. From the beginning, Elliot had precipitated a shift in her friend's personality. Where once there had been light and reason in Kit's outlook, there was now darkness and suspicion. That was why she was having trouble accepting Nick at face value.

Distracted by these unpleasant thoughts, Sally dropped a test sample. Swearing like a trooper, she bent down to retrieve it. She sifted through loose clumps of snow and ice, but the small plastic container had disappeared.

That was how she failed to notice the Hägglunds on the horizon, heading towards her field camp. If Sally had noticed, she would have wondered what on earth it was doing there.

22

In the mess area of the Red Shed, Kit sat clutching a coffee and looking out the window, hoping to catch a glimpse of Sally's Ski-Doo speeding down the road. Kit had been there for an hour or so after cleaning up, and with each passing minute visibility had grown poorer. She felt uneasy. Sally should have been back by now.

In the first few days of April, the brutality of winter had made itself known, reminding everyone at Macpherson that the continent was now imprisoned in ice. Although the sun still shone occasionally, the daylight hours were shrinking. The average daily temperature was about minus eleven degrees Celsius, and the average wind speed 45 kilometres per hour.

That evening's dire forecast was for winds of up to 160 kilometres per hour. This would mean a complete lockdown for the station. Visibility would be at zero, and the katabatic gusts coming down from the plateau would be at their fiercest and most deadly. No one would be able to go outside, probably for days. To put her mind at ease, Kit was hoping to see Sally sooner rather than later.

'Have you seen Sal?' Kit asked Bill, as he wandered in for his regular afternoon tea, scratching his head.

'No. But I was just speaking to Dustin, who said he saw her earlier this afternoon.'

'Dustin?' asked Kit, puzzled.

She had left Sally doing fieldwork a few kilometres off station, while Dustin had told her at breakfast that he'd be in the surgery most of the day, doing a long-overdue stock inventory. He must have seen her on her return. Relief flooded Kit's body like oxygen.

'Where's Dustin?' she asked, standing up.

'He's gone to the bar before it closes,' said Bill, glancing at the clock.

On her way to the bar, the wind picked up and pelted loose gravel at her legs. She felt the breeze at her back all the way down the sloping path, past the side of the workshop to the bar in the old electricians' shed. Peering inside, she could see only Dustin and Warren. They were seated on opposite couches. Warren seemed engrossed in a magazine, and Dustin had a pint of beer propped up against his belly and was leaning back with his feet on the table.

It was unusual for Kit to see him like this. He liked to set certain standards of health and moderation for the rest of the station. When she heard he was frequenting the bar, she assumed he was merely keeping an eye on things. But he seemed to have had more than two standard drinks already—there were a few empty bottles on the table. His cheeks were flushed, and his eyes were fixed in a wide-eyed stare, gazing off into the distance. Veterans called it the Antarctic Stare.

'Dustin,' said Kit.

He started as if he'd just woken up. 'Oh, Kit,' he croaked. 'Hi there. Come join us.'

Warren looked up as if to say, *Who is 'us'?*

'Oh,' she said, 'I haven't come for a drink. I was just wondering . . . Bill said you'd seen Sal today. Is that right?'

'Oh, yes.' Dustin placed his feet on the floor and shook himself awake. 'Earlier this afternoon.'

'When? I was worried she was going to get stuck out there in the snow.'

'Oh, I think I saw her about one or two o'clock.'

'Really?' asked Kit with some surprise. It was almost six, the official closing time for the bar, and full night was about to descend. That would mean Sally had been back for at least four hours. It was odd that Kit hadn't seen her.

'She said she was going to come here, to the bar, later on,' added Dustin. 'What time is it now?' he asked with sudden concern, looking around.

'It's exactly . . .' Warren pulled up his sleeve to reveal a large watch. 'Five-forty.'

'Oh, Christ. I have to get to the store, to get those vitamin D supplements. We're completely out. And I have to get the Ski-Doo back to Blondie by six. Shit!' Though the Green Store was only five minutes from the Red Shed, the Ski-Doo was a handy vehicle for lugging small boxes of supply from building to building.

'Are you sure . . .?' asked Kit, watching him stand up rather shakily and spill some of his pint on the table.

'Yeah, yeah.' He waved a dismissive hand. 'It'll only take ten minutes. I'll be fine.'

She trusted him enough to let him go.

'Stay for a drink?' Warren asked her.

She knew the bar was about to close, but she expected Sally to turn up at any time, so she stayed.

She'd been there for half an hour, making polite chitchat with Warren, when they noticed a noise outside. It was a low rumbling in the sky, like a large aircraft flying overhead, accompanied by the sound of pebbles hitting the walls. Whatever the wind was blowing in, thought Kit, it was not good. Warren went back to his story about some frozen pizzas.

But soon the noise got louder and more frightening. Thumping and creaking came from above, as if an angry demon had landed on the roof and was trying to tear it off. The demon shook the building. A few minutes later, a battalion of witches joined him, screaming and whistling as they rode in on the clouds.

The snowstorm had arrived.

Kit eyed the ceiling, praying it would stay in place. 'Do you think we should make a run for the Red Shed?' she asked Warren anxiously.

'We'd better give it a shot,' he said, launching into action and reaching for his bag.

Together, they pulled on their extreme cold weather gear and their thick snow boots. When they opened the door, they were struck by a fierce blast of air. Kit instinctively turned her head.

She eventually peered out, but she could see only a metre or two in front of her—the rest was snow. In the darkness, the glow from the floodlights in the doorway made it look like a hardened, frozen wall of white.

As they stood there, a loose piece of corrugated iron flashed past in the light, twisting and screeching like an animal. She and Warren doubled back inside.

After they'd peeled off their gear and come back into the bar, the phone started ringing. It was Blondie, and he sounded pissed off. Stuck in the freezing powerhouse, he wanted to know why Dustin hadn't returned with his Ski-Doo.

Kit explained that Dustin had gone to the Green Store, and was probably still there, waiting for the storm to blow over.

'Jesus fucking Christ,' said Blondie.

She advised him to stay put until the worst of it had passed through. They would all have to be castaways for a little while, cut off from the rest of the world. But everything would be fine by morning.

Half an hour later, the noise died down. The thumping and banging on the roof ceased, and pebbles no longer drummed incessantly at the walls. The gale forces from hell had left—for now. In the bar, it was quiet and serene.

Warren offered to take a quick look outside. He came back to report that he could see several metres ahead with a torch; if they stuck to the gravel road, now under a thick coating of snow, they could be inside the Shed in five minutes. A row of thick ropes—blizzard lines—marked the way. He could even see the building's lights as a foggy glow in the distance. They should go now, he said.

'These little pockets of calm are what helicopter pilots like to call "sucker holes",' he explained as they zipped up their suits. 'You might think those azure-blue skies and gentle winds are a sign of better weather. But you get out there, and—wham!' He demonstrated with his hands, while his eyes widened. 'Suddenly, it blows up again. You're in the air surrounded by a shitload of trouble. So that's why we better go now.'

Once outside, however, Kit had an impulse to check on Dustin. She could see the blurry floodlights of the Green Store, up ahead to the left, and the faintest suggestion of a yellow object outside: the Ski-Doo. She was surprised that Dustin was still there.

'I'm going to see if Dustin's all right,' she called to Warren, her breath catching in the breeze.

'Are you sure?' he said, turning back in concern.

'I'll only be five minutes. You go—I'll be fine.'

Warren hesitated, then called out, 'Okay, just five minutes then. I'll see you back home.' He marched up the slope to the Shed.

Kit followed her own torchlight steadily along the other gravel road. When she got to the Store, she laboured up the steps and threw all of her weight against the door. It opened, and she stumbled inside.

Cavernous as a warehouse, the Store was on two levels. It was organised into rows laden with supplies—kitchen, scientific, medical, electrical and so on—much like a supermarket or a hardware store.

'Dustin!' she called. 'Dustin!' She didn't want to stay any longer than necessary. She could hear the light pitter-patter of gravel against the walls.

Without taking off her extreme weather gear, she ventured into the store itself, shuffling noisily in her thick boots. She knew where the medical supplies were kept, because during the changeover she'd delivered several boxes from the *Star*. When she located the correct aisle, she checked for boxes of vitamin D and found that their shelf was empty.

'Dustin!' she called again. But it appeared that he'd been and gone. He'd collected an entire winter's worth of vitamin supplements and then departed—without the Ski-Doo. She wondered what he could have been thinking. Perhaps shortly after his arrival, conditions had become so poor that he'd decided it would be foolhardy to ride a Ski-Doo up and down the slope. Possibly, he'd ventured back to the Red Shed on foot.

Kit located the phone and rang Bill.

The wind was tugging at the door as fierce gusts battered the walls. Just as Warren had predicted, the storm hadn't been dead but only resting. The Store shook with each fresh blast of air.

'Is Dustin with you?' she asked Bill, shouting over the bad line.

'No.' His voice was crackly and indistinct, as if coming from a great distance. 'Warren just told me you went to look for him in the Green Store.'

'He's not here. At least, I don't think he is—I didn't check the upstairs office,' she added, the thought just occurring to her. 'He might be having a nap. I'll go have a look and call you back if I can't find him.'

'Okay,' said Bill. 'You call me if you need me. Otherwise, hope to see you here as soon as possible. Don't think we've seen the last of it yet. You shouldn't be out there on your own.'

She agreed and hung up.

The upstairs office was empty. As she was shutting the door, the phone on the desk rang.

It was Bill again. This time the connection was good enough that she could detect the concern in his voice. 'Kit?' he said, breathing hard into the receiver. 'I've just spoken to Dustin. He's in the bar. He says he's been wandering around in the storm, and he's kinda disoriented. He wasn't making a whole lotta sense, to tell you the truth. He said he's bleeding quite badly from the leg. The line got cut off before I could get all the details. I need you to get over there to him and help him out, as quickly as possible, before the weather turns again. Can you do that?'

'Sure,' she said, with one ear cocked to the wind. She could hear a sinister change in the speed and frequency of gusts, but she calculated she still had a good ten minutes or so to fight her way back to the bar without being stuck in the blinding snow. She'd walked the path a hundred times—she could probably do it in her sleep. The bar was less than two hundred metres away. 'I'm leaving now,' she told Bill before she hung up.

After tucking a few bandages into the large pockets of her suit, she went to open the main door. As she pulled on the handle, it sprang inwards and pushed her against the wall with all its weight, knocking her off balance. A violent gust of snow blew into the entrance way.

Bending down on one knee, Kit huddled against the door, her shoulder to the wind, and readjusted her hood. She checked that her gloves were securely fastened around her wrists, her pockets were zipped up, and her suit legs were covering her boots; she didn't want any of that killer snow creeping through the cracks.

Clearly the blizzard had already returned with a vengeance. Her task was going to be hard enough without being frozen to the core. She would have to do this blind.

In the doorway, she pulled on her ski goggles and pointed her feeble torch, only to see a familiar wall of whiteness less than a metre in front of her. Visibility was zero, but she would have the assistance of the blizz lines strung between the buildings. As long as she had those, she reasoned, she could *feel* her way to the bar.

And so she proceeded down the Green Store steps, clinging to the rail as the wind slammed her into the wall. At the bottom of the steps, she lifted her torch to survey the path ahead. Once again, all she could see was a wall of snow. It was useless to point her torch anywhere but at the ground. The snow was so thick that she couldn't even see the floodlights behind her anymore. As she moved forward, however, the torch illuminated something bright yellow a few metres away—the Ski-Doo.

Struck with an idea, Kit struggled over to the snowmobile and turned it on with fumbling hands. But it was obvious the Ski-Doo would be of no help whatsoever. Though its engine had started with a lurch, its headlights were no use. All they did was illuminate an even greater expanse of snowy nothingness. If she got on board and set off down the slope, she could be out on the sea ice and hopelessly lost in the darkness before she even realised she'd gone the wrong way.

Kit switched off the engine and slowly placed one foot in front of the other, grasping the nearest blizz line. She leaned sideways into the blowing snow and inched forward, one hand on the rope, in what she thought must be the direction of the harbour and the main road. Under its snowy coat, she could feel the reassuring crunch of gravel on the path.

After toiling down the path for a few minutes, she suddenly felt an overwhelming fear and hopelessness. In addition to the deafening roar of the wind against her hood, she could hear an ominous whipping noise overhead. Her stomach flip-flopped as she realised that it must be some cables or cladding that had come loose. She dropped to her knees.

This is the height of stupidity, she told herself. If she lost the rope, she would be dead. Surely Dustin wasn't dying; surely he didn't require her assistance right that very minute. *I should go back.*

But when Kit tried to stand up and turn around, she couldn't do it. She had come so far and was so deep in the snowstorm that it was pointless to go back. It would be better to spend her energy going forward. Dustin was alone, and he was cold and bleeding. A combination of hypothermia and blood loss could kill him. She would never forgive herself if her lack of resolve led to his death—she had to get up and go on.

Ignoring the cracking whips in the sky, she continued with her torch trained on her feet and one gloved hand on the rope. *Keep moving, keep moving*, she repeated to herself. It was all she could do to keep on the road, to keep her balance, to keep her head in the midst of the swirling vortex.

Time dragged on. She seemed to be getting nowhere—but when the blowing snow lifted for a second, she recognised a familiar fork in the road. It was hard to believe that she'd stood there less than twenty minutes ago with Warren. The left-hand fork led back up the slope to the Shed, and the right-hand fork led down in the direction of the harbour, towards the bar.

Her steps would have to be even more careful now. The ground was relatively flat in this area, so if she got turned around or disoriented, she would have no idea where she was. And if she didn't keep a close eye on the side of the road and stay with the blizz line, she could miss the narrow footpath leading to the bar and end up out on the dreaded sea ice. With the wind shoving at her back, she positioned herself towards the right-hand shoulder of the road and kept moving. The walking came a little easier now.

But then Kit saw something that made her stop dead.

Out of the swirling whiteness in front of her, a man with a torch materialised. He was dressed in a partly open red coat, with a black balaclava on his head and woollen gloves on his hands.

Momentarily, she was numb with fright. Her breath caught in her throat, and her heart beat wildly.

It was only when the man stopped leaning into the driving wind and straightened up to his full height that Kit realised who he was—who he *had* to be.

It was Nick.

23

When Kit saw Nick emerge through the blinding snow wall, her first response was one of fear. Her second response was to rationalise it away and assume that, like Dustin, Nick had been caught unawares and was hopelessly lost. Or perhaps, she supposed, Nick had offered to come help her with Dustin. These thoughts flashed through her mind in seconds, enabling her to swallow her panic.

Lunging forward, she grabbed Nick's elbow and turned him around 180 degrees, so that he was facing in the direction of the bar. She couldn't stop, in case she lost her internal compass. For all she knew, Nick had no idea where he was heading. She needed to keep moving along the blizz line in order to hold on to her bearings.

Fortunately, he was prepared to comply with her guidance. He stumbled a little at first, but then he hooked his arm into hers. They lurched side by side down the line with the wind pummelling at their backs.

A few minutes later, with relief, Kit glanced up and caught sight of the foggy glow of the bar lights. After leaving the path, then stumbling over rock and snow, she and Nick were soon standing outside the building.

In the entrance way, Kit removed her gloves and goggles, while Nick pulled off his mittens and struggled to remove his sodden balaclava. His hands were trembling, and he was unsteady on his feet. 'Here,' she said, touching his cold fingers, 'let me do that.'

His face was a ghastly sight. His cheeks were deathly pale, his lips a deep shade of blue. His eyes were red-rimmed, and the ugly scar on his forehead was a vivid purple. On his collarbone there was a protruding white lump, like a piece of ice, where the cold air had stolen beneath his coat. But most alarming of all, his expression was dazed and open-mouthed. It looked as though he was going into hypothermic shock.

'We have to get you warm,' she said, gripping him by the shoulders and steering him inside.

As they entered the relative warmth of the bar, she noticed droplets of blood on the floor and a few bloodied footprints leading to the door. 'Dustin?' she called, scanning the room. He clearly wasn't there. She thought about phoning Bill, but decided to make Nick her priority. Wherever Dustin was, she hoped he was taking shelter.

Near the couches, she helped Nick to peel off his raincoat and instructed him to get out of his wet trousers, while she frantically searched the cupboards for sleeping bags. She knew they were kept there because a few of the regulars would get them out and sleep on the couches during the day. Like most of the gear at Macpherson, the bags were suited to extreme cold weather, made from the highest quality down for camping on ice and snow. She found two single sleeping bags of the same length, and started unzipping them to form a double.

She turned to look at Nick, who was seated awkwardly on the hard floor, still fully dressed and with only one boot off. 'We have to get you undressed,' she said sternly, forcing him to look her in the eye. 'You're cold, Nick—you could be going into hypothermic shock. Come on, you've got to help me.'

Finding a vestige of strength, he bent over and tugged off his second boot. He then started fumbling with his belt buckle, looking helplessly at his waist.

Kit had gone back to zipping up the sleeping bags. When she noticed him struggling, she instructed him to stop what he was doing and to stand up. Once he was upright, she went over and hooked her hands roughly under the front of his belt, loosening it enough to unbuckle it. Then she unzipped his trousers and tugged them down, urging him to take them off.

All this time, Nick was silent and passive. He did nothing unless instructed to. While Kit finished joining the bags together, he remained stiff and motionless, his pants still clinging to his knees.

'Okay,' she said, finishing her task and laying the conjoined bags over a rug on the floor. 'Come here.'

Standing in front of him, she used her foot to force the trousers down between his legs and onto the ground. She then gripped the bottom of his polar-fleece top and his undershirt, pulling them up over his chest. When they got caught under his chin, she yanked the clothing over his head and off his arms. With his damp hair standing on end, he looked even more dazed than before.

'There you go,' she said, 'now take those off and get into the sleeping bag.' She pointed at his boxers and then to the floor.

Out of politeness, she turned her back as she took off her own boots and her cold weather suit. When she faced Nick again, he was still standing there, shivering in his underpants, both arms hugging his naked chest.

'Nick, what are you doing?' she asked in annoyance. 'It's not like I haven't already seen you naked.' She pointed at the floor. 'Get in the friggin' sleeping bag!' In exasperation, she sprang forward and tugged his damp underpants off him. Gripping him by the arm, she then helped him clamber down into the bag. He nestled all the way in and pulled the top up to his chin.

Meanwhile, Kit stripped off her own clothing. She was bitterly cold, but she knew she was nowhere near as cold as Nick. He would benefit from her body warmth. That was the idea, anyway—it was a recommended first-aid technique.

She squeezed in next to him, then fully zipped and cinched the sleeping bag. With the two of them snug inside, their limbs were restricted. His bony knees were up against hers, his left elbow was sharp beneath her ribcage, and their faces were too close for comfort. She asked him to roll away onto his side. After some twisting and turning, she snaked her left arm over his waist and let her hand come to lie on his damp chest. She then pressed the rest of her body close to his. The soft skin on his back felt cold and clammy. His torso kept spasming and jerking as he fought off the urge to shiver.

She held him tightly. Against her face, his hair smelt like frying oil, and she remembered that he'd been on slushy duty the night before. She turned her face away and leaned against his shoulder, his muscles like marble beside her cheek.

After a while, his body stopped shivering. The wind persisted with its guttural moaning, and there was the occasional rifle crack in the sky or thunderous rumble under the floor. But it didn't seem as if the building would be ripped apart and consumed by the elements.

Once they were suitably warm, Kit took the opportunity to jump up and phone Bill, who would be waiting for an update. He was relieved to hear that she and Nick were fine but disturbed that Dustin couldn't be located. 'Let me know as soon as you hear anything,' said Bill.

Wondering where the doctor could be, she returned to the welcoming warmth of the sleeping bag. Now conscious of her nakedness, she shyly nestled back into Nick's side.

A few minutes later, he shifted his large body uneasily on the hard floor.

'Are you uncomfortable?' she asked, a glow rising in her cheeks.

'Um, think my hip's gone to sleep,' he murmured. 'Can we turn over for a bit, so that I'm spooning you?'

'Sure,' she breathed out, trying to turn around without tangling herself in the bag.

He rolled over, keeping his hips a respectful distance from her backside and his arms bundled close to his chest. Strangely disappointed she was no longer touching him, Kit distracted herself by talking.

'Why were you out in the storm?' she asked over her shoulder.

'I was supposed to be meeting Dustin at the bar.' His breath was warm against her neck. 'I was helping out one of the plumbers at the tankhouse and came over when the storm hit a lull. But I got caught out, big time. Looks like you did too, huh?'

'Yes, but I was better dressed for it.'

'Yeah, I was a bit complacent,' he admitted.

'Bit stupid, more like it.'

'Okaaaay.' He gave a soft chuckle. 'In my defence, the wind blew my coat open.'

'It should've been done up properly.'

'You're right. And why were you out in the storm?'

'I came to help Dustin.' She explained everything that had happened.

Nick whistled in surprise. '*Dustin* was outside in the storm . . .?'

They fell silent again as the wind hammered at the roof. When it stopped, Nick was so quiet that Kit wondered if he was still awake. It had been three weeks since her accusations at the parlour game, and she'd been hoping to ask him a few follow-up questions. When he coughed into the silence, she saw her chance.

'So, how've you been?' she probed.

'Fine, fine.'

'Has anything jogged your memory lately?'

'Pardon?' he asked, seemingly thrown.

'Has anything come back to you?'

'Oh, not really.' He paused. 'Except,' he added, 'for the past few days . . . I've gotta say, I've *really* felt like a cigarette.'

Her ears pricked up. 'You used to smoke, you know.'

'Did I?' he asked, sounding mildly surprised.

'What about when you're asleep? Do you see people in your dreams? I think dreams might tell you about what you've forgotten, in a mixed-up kind of way.'

'Yeah, well, my dreams are pretty mixed up, all right,' he drawled.

'What do you mean?'

There was another pause.

'I have a recurring dream,' he murmured. 'I'm sitting at the bottom of a great snow hill, and there are people on top, and they're moving in strange, contorted ways.' His voice was soft and wistful, as if coming from far away. 'Their movements are frightening and disturbing. Their heads are thrown back, and their legs are flying, with their arms waving about in the air.'

He raised his own arms to demonstrate, making the sleeping bag rustle about her face, and she batted it back down.

'I'm seeing them at a great distance,' he continued, 'and I always wonder what they're doing.' Then, sending a chill down her spine, he whispered in her ear, '*What are they doing? Why are they moving like that?* So I get closer, and I can hear music. It's this crazy, zany, big-band tune. All of a sudden, I realise . . . I realise what they're doing.' He paused again for effect. 'They're dancing. They're just dancing.'

'Oh,' she said. 'That all sounds very . . . metaphorical.'

'Yes, I suppose it is,' he admitted in his everyday voice. 'Except for the part when a bald man comes out at the end and tries to shoot me.'

'Oh, right. *Ha-ha.* Very funny.'

'No, I'm serious.' He laughed as though daring her to believe him. 'A bald man comes over with a gun, at the end.'

'Okay.' Feeling curious, she decided to go along with Nick. 'Do you see his face?'

'No, it's just a blank.'

'But he's bald?' she asked. 'Very bald or just a bit on top . . .?'

'Very bald—all over.'

'Sounds scary.'

'Mmmm.' A few seconds later, Nick was snoring.

Kit lay wide awake beside him, her mind busy. She thought about walking into the snowstorm and trying to get to Dustin, only to find Nick. She wondered if there was anything she should have done differently. Should she have turned back to the Green Store when she had the opportunity?

Finally she came to some peace when she realised that given a second chance, she would have done everything exactly the same. She was glad she'd found Nick; she would check on Dustin in the morning.

Kit drifted off to sleep.

24

When Nick opened his eyes in the morning light, the first thing he noticed was the resounding silence. There was no rattling, banging or cracking. The wind had gone.

The second thing he noticed was that he was lying naked beside Kit Bitterfeld. He was possibly the warmest he'd ever been in Antarctica.

They were tucked up in the double sleeping bag, their legs messily entwined, and he was spooning her from behind, leaning into the curve of her body. As she slept in his arms, he could feel the ebb and flow of her breath. His chest was pressed against her back, and his left arm encircled her waist. She had one arm lying over his, keeping him in place with a firm grip on his hand. When he became conscious of the silk of her skin, his body tingled, and he found himself growing hard against her.

He held his breath and wondered, *What would a gentleman do in this situation?*

Reluctantly, Nick loosened her grip and pushed himself back. He wanted her to think he was a good man, even if he wasn't. In his new position, he was less warm and comfortable, but he wasn't touching her intimately without her consent. It was the right thing to do.

Still asleep, she sighed and shifted her legs. With a lazy wriggle of her hips, she positioned herself right back into the warmth of his lap.

His breathing grew laboured, and he struggled to stay rational. It was true that she'd been the one to suggest they sleep naked together, and he'd anticipated that he might find the situation uncomfortable. But Christ, she'd only suggested it to raise his body temperature—it had been an emergency.

He reminded himself that a good man wouldn't just presume her nakedness gave him a licence to snuggle up to her. A morally upright man would get out of the sleeping bag and put his sodden clothes on. The storm was over. He'd recovered from the cold, and he really should be on his way.

But when Nick prepared to retreat, she gripped his arm even tighter and tucked it against her chest. With a heart-stopping thrill, he realised that he could feel the curve of her breast on his arm, and he grew harder, his breath uneven.

Trapped in her embrace, he pressed his nose to her neck, drawing in the scent of her hair. She smelt like coconut oil and vanilla, definitely not the regulation-issue shampoo. His lips brushed her skin.

He wasn't sure exactly when her breathing changed its rhythm, but her body was more alert than before, as though she were holding her breath.

'Kit?' he whispered.

Her response was to entwine her fingers with his. She exerted a gentle pressure on his hand, guiding it until his palm was cupping her breast, his thumb resting against her nipple. He moved his hips in closer, pressing himself to her and kissing her neck. With a sharp intake of breath, she tightened her grip on his thumb, then began stroking it back and forth across her nipple. Following her lead, he caressed her, breathing hard into her neck until she moaned softly.

That day in the sick bay, when they'd first met, it was as if she was the only woman he'd ever seen. He was struck by her glacial loveliness. With her clear blue eyes and short blonde hair, she looked Scandinavian, and there had been a rosy pink glow to her fine-boned features. He'd had to suppress an instinct to reach out and touch her, to feel the warmth of her skin. Now, as she arched under his caresses, he could hardly control himself again: he wanted nothing more than to immerse himself in her. 'Kit?' he said, his voice rough.

She released his teasing thumb and turned to face him. Her eyes were half closed, and her face was flushed. Again, she didn't respond in words—this time she gripped his head in her hands and brought his mouth down on hers. He smoothed a hand down her hips, slid it into the small of her back and pulled her closer. Licking her swollen lips, he parted them with his tongue. She matched his intensity, grabbing his hair and pressing her breasts against him.

As they kept kissing, he rolled her onto her back. She opened her legs and met his eyes with a smile. He rested in the cradle of her thighs, feeling the thrill of her heat against him, about to push forward—

Suddenly, she went rigid in his arms.

At first he was confused. Had she been asleep after all? Had she just woken up? Or . . . did she think he was someone else?

But when he looked at her face, he could see that something had distracted her. She raised her shoulders from the ground and cocked her head to the side. Her eyes were wide and alert—she was listening for something outside.

All he could hear was his ragged breathing and the pounding of his heart.

'Something's wrong.' She placed her hands on his bare chest and gently pushed him away, then scrambled out of the sleeping bag and reached for her clothes.

And then he could hear it too. A man was shouting, loud and panicked, from the direction of the harbour. 'It's the doc! It's Dustin!'

25

Dustin looked as though he were seated on a white throne, wearing a billowy cloak of crushed silk embroidered with ice crystals. He was sitting on a large cardboard box in the middle of Wineglass Harbour, about a hundred metres north-west of the bar. It seemed that he'd come to rest there in fatigue and despair, perhaps once he'd realised how lost he was, out on the sea ice with no lights or markers to give him any bearings. His back was straight and stiff, and he looked almost proud and dignified.

It wasn't a position in which Kit would have chosen to die. Lying down on the ice would be less uncomfortable.

A frozen shroud covered much of Dustin's head, leaving only one eye and the left side of his cheek visible. The eye was wide open and surrounded by fine ice-lashes. It seemed to be coolly watching the activity. Blondie had cleared a top layer of loose snow with his hands, while Warren was using a shovel to chip at the bottom layer of ice surrounding the legs. Closer to land, an idling Hägglunds was waiting to transport the body to the Red Shed.

Bill watched on in stony-faced silence, his arms crossed over his chest, his legs apart. He had instructed them to cut the body free and bring it inside, but the task was easier said than done. They were unsure where Dustin's limbs were positioned under the ice, and no one wanted to sever anything. Progress was slow.

At least it was a bright day with blue sky and fluffy white clouds, only disturbed by the occasional feisty gust of wind—a cruel contrast to the storm. In the distance, a mountainous pale blue iceberg sat majestically stationed at the edge of the sea ice.

When they were ready to lift Dustin off the box, Blondie, Warren and Skelly manoeuvred the corpse onto a stretcher. They didn't realise that the top of the box was stuck to the back of Dustin's freezer suit. When the men hoisted him, the cardboard ripped open. Half the contents of the box spilled out onto the ice, forming a tiny mountain of pristine pills. The men ignored the vitamins and threw a tarpaulin over Dustin's body, their faces stricken as they straightened the edges.

The Hägg headed back to the Shed.

Out on the bay, Kit watched the vitamins tumble about, feeling sick with misery. She was better equipped than most expeditioners to deal with the scene. But she was eaten up with regret. As she had told Bill, she wished she could have done something more to help Dustin. She regretted that she'd left the bar with Warren. If only she'd stayed put.

Her distress was compounded by the fact that no one had heard from Sally for at least twenty hours. She hadn't signed back in, and no one could confirm that she'd returned to station before the storm. Kit's anxiety grew exponentially every moment her friend failed to appear. Repeated efforts to reach Sally on the radio had been fruitless. Kit fervently hoped that instead of trying to come back in the storm, her friend had built a snow trench and bunkered down for the night.

Bill had organised a search-and-rescue with experienced colleagues for later that day, once they'd recovered Dustin's body and collected the right gear. It was no small thing to initiate a SAR response, and it had to be handled with care, to ensure that no one else was placed in danger. Kit knew that Bill was following strict procedure, but she was anxious that Sally might not be found in time—she might be stuck down a crevasse.

With that in mind, Kit was careful to follow the trail of footsteps back to shore and to avoid anything that looked remotely like a crack. The strong winds had broken up some of the ice further out to sea, making her nervous and mistrustful.

•

They made a rather grim party at dinner that night.

In difficult terrain, the SAR team had fought their way out to the Weddell seal breeding site where Sally had last been seen by Kit. Despite Dustin's reported sighting, they couldn't be sure she'd ever returned to base; her Ski-Doo was still missing and she hadn't signed back in. But the team—made up of Bill, Blondie and Gareth—could find no trace of her amid the great white expanse. They started to search the surrounding area before it began to snow heavily and they were forced to come back. Visibility was poor, and the blizzard had created hazards along the track.

Around the table, every face bore the strain of the day's events. Alessandra, in particular, looked as though she'd been crying all day: her nose was red, and her bloodshot eyes were swollen and puffy. She leaned her elbows on the table and held a tissue close to her cheek.

When Nick came in, he was bereft of his usual good cheer and avoided looking at anyone except Kit. As their eyes met, she put her head down. She wasn't sure how she felt about that morning in the sleeping bag.

He pulled up the chair next to her, and she stared at her plate, pushing her food around. 'How are you?' she asked quietly.

'I'm fine, all things considered. A bit headachy still. And you? How are you?'

'Not good,' she said, her shoulders tense. 'They couldn't find Sal.'

'I know—I heard. I'm sorry.'

Earlier in the day they'd helped Bill piece together what had happened during the blizzard. Warren observed that Dustin had downed his regulation beers in quick succession and that, being only an occasional drinker, he might not have handled them too well. Kit demurred, saying that even though Dustin had seemed relaxed and sleepy, he was otherwise coherent. Bill noted that Dustin had sounded confused and disoriented on the phone, but that this could have been due to hypothermia. Nick reported that he'd spoken to Dustin earlier in the day, and that the doc had urged Nick to come and see him in the bar as soon as he finished work.

'He told me it was important,' said Nick.

'Did he tell you what it was about?' asked Kit.

'No,' said Nick, his lips a pale line. 'He just said he had something to tell me.'

'And you didn't see him at all that night?' asked Bill.

'I didn't see him till this morning.' Nick glanced in the direction of the harbour.

After their discussion, Bill concluded it was likely that Dustin, under the influence of alcohol, had underestimated the severity of the storm and gone back to the bar to meet Nick. On his way he'd become lost and injured, so that when he arrived he was in a state of panic and distress. In an act of extremely poor judgement, Dustin had left the bar and taken a wrong turn. He had succumbed to hypothermia or a heart attack.

While the others accepted this explanation, Kit could do so only up to a point. She could understand Dustin's first bad decision, to keep the mysterious rendezvous with Nick. But she couldn't fathom why he would leave the bar a second time, to drag his injured body back out into the storm. There was also the question of how he'd received his leg wound. She kept turning his behaviour over in her mind but could make no sense of it: Dustin was bleeding, he knew help was on its way, yet he left the bar.

Now, seated next to Nick at dinner, Kit noticed scratches on the back of his hand. Instinctively, she ran a finger across the fresh red lines. Had she put those there that morning?

He looked questioningly at her, his eyes smiling, but before he could say anything, she pulled her hand away. A few minutes later, she excused herself from the table.

•

That night, Kit lay awake in her donga. At about midnight, she heard a knock at the door, but when she ignored it long enough, the person went away. If it was Nick, she didn't want to see him— not just yet. She needed time to clear her head and think about things objectively; she wouldn't be able to concentrate in his presence. He tended to have an intoxicating effect on her. She knew that she was starting to care for him, but she also knew she'd been wrong about men in the past and could no longer trust her judgement.

Kit still suspected that Nick knew more than he was letting on, while Dustin's death and Sally's disappearance had left her shaken to the core. She couldn't stop the anxious thoughts from gathering. She wondered why Sally had failed to return. She wondered if Nick had met Dustin in the bar, and if they'd argued. Had Dustin finally confronted Nick about his prolonged memory loss? Had the meeting ended badly?

She needed to proceed cautiously with Nick. But first, she needed sleep. She had to recharge her batteries so she could cope with the physical and psychological demands to come.

The next day, she would join the SAR team to look for Sally—that was her first priority. If her friend had bunkered down in a trench, then it was feasible she was still alive.

Kit might also have to perform a rudimentary autopsy on Dustin; she would know once she heard back from the telemedicine people. Bill had informed the head of the Antarctic Division about the death, and the head had then informed Dustin's closest living relative, a maternal aunt in Queensland.

To help herself sleep, Kit tried reading an article on Weddell seal distribution in winter, but still she remained awake and uneasy.

Around 2 a.m., there was movement out in the corridor: people were pacing up and down, opening doors and exchanging words. Kit became irritated. After the umpteenth disruption, she threw back the covers, cloaked herself in her dressing-gown and padded out into the hallway.

At first, it appeared no one was there. But then she could see from the shadows that someone was around the corner. She went to look.

It was Alessandra. Crouched on the floor, she was hugging her knees to her chest with her face resting against them. She was dressed in blue thermal leggings, a large shapeless T-shirt and a grubby polar-fleece jacket. This was most unlike her. Inside the shed, in the daytime at least, she was usually impeccably attired in close-fitting shirts and straight trousers.

Alessandra looked blearily up at Kit with red-rimmed eyes.

'Alessandra?' said Kit. 'Are you okay?'

The woman paused before responding, placing her left cheek back on her knees. 'I don't know. Am I?' She gave a soft chuckle.

It occurred to Kit that she might have been tranquillised. The whites of her eyes were a cloudy red haze, and there were suggestions of drool in the corners of her mouth. Kit knelt down and placed a hand on her arm.

At her touch, Alessandra looked up again. 'Where did Nick go?' she asked, her eyes closing sleepily.

'I don't know. I haven't seen him. How long have you been sitting here?'

'He was here a moment ago,' murmured Alessandra. 'So nice, so nice . . . such a nice man.'

Kit looked around the corner. There was no sign of anyone—no sound, no movement, no Nick. It occurred to her that Alessandra alone might have been responsible for all the pacing and door-slamming and murmuring out in the corridor.

Kit sighed. 'Alessandra,' she said, leaning in to speak close to her ear, 'we have to get you back to your room.' She tugged at her arm and helped her to stand up. 'Come on, come with me.'

But it was all too much for Alessandra. She fell to her knees and burst out sobbing, tears springing from her eyes. She wiped at her wet cheeks. 'I can't, I can't,' she gasped, taking great heaving breaths. 'I can't go to my room.' She cupped her face in her hands.

'Why not?' asked Kit, thinking that Alessandra might not want to see Gareth. Kit wouldn't have blamed her—she wouldn't have wanted to go back to his cold comfort either.

But the woman surprised her. 'I don't know where it is,' she whispered, peering through her fingers. 'I can't find my room.'

'You can't *find* your room . . .?' said Kit, wondering if Alessandra had taken a sleeping pill.

'No. All the doors look the same around here. I can't tell one from the other.'

Holding her by the hand like a small child, Kit led Alessandra back to her room. She spoke to Gareth at the door. 'She doesn't seem like herself,' Kit told him, shaking her head. 'I found her in the corridor. She's a bit upset, I'm afraid.'

'It was a tough day,' said Gareth, sounding surprisingly human.

'Don't worry, I'll take care of her.' He turned to his wife and patted her on the arm. 'Let's get you into bed, old girl.'

Kit said goodnight and wandered back to her donga, half-expecting to find Nick inside. She was relieved to find the room empty, and locked the door before crawling into bed.

•

In her dreams that night, Kit spoke with Alessandra again out in the hallway. This time there was a flashing light above their heads—a surreal green light, casting a ghoulish aurora-like glow over Alessandra's face.

'You don't seem like yourself,' Kit said to her. 'What's wrong?' Her voice echoed down the dream corridor.

Alessandra grimaced and laughed in fits and turns, her face contorted in despair at one moment, then covered in smiles the next. 'Can't you tell what's wrong?' she asked, madness sparkling in her eyes. 'It's written all over my face.'

Something was written on Alessandra's forehead. The letters had been carved into the skin, forming thin red lines: *Not myself.*

Kit shuddered and woke up.

26

Marion thought she saw a penguin on the outer edges of the ice. She spotted a dark shadowy blur in the distance, then heard a faint splash. She thought she caught a glimpse of flipper, but when she looked again, the thing was gone. Now she couldn't be sure she wasn't hallucinating. She'd been so hungry for so long that it was possible her mind was playing tricks on her; she hadn't been sleeping well either.

At night, the anxiety was suffocating. She would burrow deep into her sleeping bag, her bivvy companion snoring in oblivion by her side, then lie awake, her heart beating loudly and her mind fretful. She was plagued by the futility of their funereal march across the ice, their abysmal lack of food, and the uncertainty about their fate. Were they attempting the impossible? Was Thorn going to get everyone killed? The dark thoughts chased one another around her head. When she finally slept, vivid dreams came to her in a procession until the morning, leaving her fatigued.

Some nights, her mind would torment her with dreams of food. One time, she dreamt that the *Petrel* crew held a banquet on the outer edges of the ice. They were seated at a grand wooden table, the men in tuxedos and the two women in bright taffeta. At the table's centre was a roasted baby seal, glazed and trussed up like a suckling pig, surrounded by platters of fresh fruit, smoked salmon, lobster, crisp roasted potatoes, spaghetti bolognaise, creamy gnocchi, and dessert bowls full of sticky date pudding, with caramel sauce and ice-cream on top.

As the crew sat down and prepared to feast, a hunched old man appeared out of the mist. It was Tom Priestley, the dead captain. He was nothing but skin and bones, barely recognisable, raving under his breath. 'We need to find the one thing needful,' he muttered, repeating the advice he'd given to Nick on deck. 'We need to find it,' Tom warned more loudly, his wild eyes staring. 'It has to be found.' He came up behind Marion and clutched at her arm with skeletal hands.

'What do you mean?' she asked from the head of the table, annoyed by the distraction. Everyone else was ignoring the old man as they started to eat. 'Can't you see we have everything we need? We have *food*.' She shrugged the captain off and gestured at the magnificent spread with her fork. 'See.'

'No, no.' Tom shook his head. 'We need to find love and forgiveness, in our hearts, before it's too late. We need to find human warmth and comfort.'

'That's ridiculous. You can't *eat* love and forgiveness. The one thing needful is survival—we need to get through this ordeal no matter what. If a few people are offended by a dead seal, and if a little love is lost here and there, what does it matter? Nothing matters so long as we're all alive in the end. Broken relationships can be brought back to life, and broken hearts can be mended. But dead people can't be brought back, and broken bodies will die.'

Marion was dismayed to wake up before she'd had anything to eat, and she was disturbed by her little speech. She hated the sentiment, but she suspected she was right—at this point, survival was all that mattered.

She had to go and investigate that penguin sighting. It was still morning, and they hadn't yet started the day's hellish march. Hurriedly, she put the chains on her boots, then shoved the gun and a knife into her daypack. She left the half-asleep crew as they were emerging and gathering around the boiling stove. She didn't say anything in case she got their hopes up, but she would only be gone for five minutes—they would hear her if anything went wrong.

Marion headed to a splotchy grey section of ice near the outer edge where the fast ice met the sea. It looked thick and stable, but she knew that looks could be deceiving. When she got closer, she took a moment to catch her breath; her body was weak, and the meagre exercise had worn her out. She hung back from the rotting ice and looked out to sea, where several discrete floes lay still and undisturbed. The sun was shining, and only the faintest hint of breeze was in the air. Sadly, there was nothing moving in the water. Everything was calm and quiet.

After waiting ten minutes, Marion was about to head back to camp—when out of the corner of her eye, she glimpsed something on the surface. She took a few steps forward and squinted at the sea. Blinded by the glare, she pulled off her goggles and moved closer.

A penguin skin was floating a few metres away, a half-submerged mass of fat and feathers.

What the hell? At first, Marion couldn't comprehend what she was seeing. She'd expected to see a live penguin and now here were the remains of a flayed carcass. The disappointment was cruel.

But what had done the flaying? And where was it now? She looked around and felt uneasy.

Seconds later, she noticed something moving away from her beneath the water.

A shining head broke the surface, and she moved back.

She couldn't be sure what she was seeing. Was it a seal? It looked like a seal. The back of its head was brown and wide, and its thick neck was long and serpentine, with a spotted pattern on the underside. She caught a glimpse of the creature's powerful shoulders before its bulk disappeared smoothly under the water, a flipper splashing in its wake. It wasn't an ordinary seal: it was massive and intimidating.

Marion was deeply unnerved. Her survival instincts told her to move several steps back without taking her eyes off the glassy water. Then she brought the backpack around to her side and pulled out the gun. With a glance downwards, she checked that it was loaded. The weapon safely in hand, she took a further few steps back and waited.

She supposed this was how surfers felt when they saw a shadow lurking beneath their boards. Her heart was beating fast, and she was sweating despite the cold. Should she flee or stay rooted to the spot, to avoid drawing attention? She didn't want the creature to come anywhere near her, but she did want it to come onto the ice— she wanted to lure it to shore.

If it hauled out, then she could shoot it, call for help and take it back to camp. They wouldn't have to go anywhere that day; they could stay and have a feast on the ice. It would be her dream come true—albeit without the pudding.

Before she could decide what to do, something thumped beneath her feet. The soft thud-thudding shook her boots. She saw a crack appear in the grey ice. Under the thinning surface, a shadow grew, rising up from the depths.

With a cry, she flung herself back across the ice, slipping and sliding. A safe distance away, she frantically looked behind her to see if anything had emerged from the crack.

She couldn't see anything.

Marion came to a panting halt, her heart hammering, and leaned over with her hands on her knees. Once she'd calmed down, she laughed crazily to herself. She just couldn't believe that, after everything she'd been through, death was still the King of Terrors. Starvation, sleeplessness and the cold had held her in their thrall the past few weeks, and there had been times when a painless death would have been a welcome relief. But here she was, adrenalin coursing through her veins once more, giving her the energy from who-knew-where to save her miserable life. Her body's fear-producing mechanism had promptly delivered her to safety— at least, for now.

Only seconds later, she heard another thump. Dread returned to her stomach. Then it dawned on her: the creature was tracking her. With the sun shining, her moving shadow could be seen through the ice—a silhouette carrying the promise of food.

Taking a deep breath, she readied herself to flee across the surface again. Before she could move, however, the ice shattered in front of her.

A monstrous leopard seal burst through with an explosive boom, sending chunks and shards of ice into the air. The force of the eruption landed Marion flat on her back. The gun went spinning from her hand across the glass-like surface.

With one flick of a flipper the gigantic beast pivoted to face her, jaws wide.

Marion recoiled in terror.

If the creature had expected to ambush a penguin, it didn't show any surprise. It lunged for her.

With only a second to spare, she got a foothold and propelled herself away from its jaws. 'Help!' she screamed. 'Help!'

The leopard seal lunged forward again as she skidded backwards. When she kicked at its head, it grabbed her boot, tugging her towards the hole in the ice. With her free leg, she kicked viciously, scraping the sleek forehead, drawing blood. When the beast failed to loosen its grip, she aimed for its eye. But the leopard seal barely noticed—nothing was slowing its progress to the edge. Her gloves gave her no purchase on the ice.

She knew that the monster wanted to take her to the water. Once beneath the waves, it would hold her in the depths of the ocean until she ceased to struggle.

In desperation, she twisted her torso, trying to loosen her daypack and access the knife. She wrenched her back but barely noticed the pain.

As she struggled, a shot rang out.

Miraculously, the monster released her foot.

Another shot rang out, and the beast slumped onto the ice with a rumbling groan.

Marion looked up. A few metres away, Curly stood with the gun gripped tight in both hands. As soon as the creature stopped moving, he relaxed his arms to his sides.

Breathing heavily, Marion scrambled away from the beast. Its enormous body was at her feet, with a head wound bleeding out on the ice. As the pooling blood crept towards her boots, she jerked her legs away and sat up, yanking the daypack off her aching back. She reached inside and gripped the knife's handle.

Curly came up to her. He looked wrecked, as though he'd run a mile. 'Are you okay?' he panted.

'I will be.' She pulled the knife out of its sheath. On shaking knees, she crawled through the blood to the creature. Then she plunged the blade deep into its guts.

She used her weight to penetrate the outer layer of skin, then she moved the knife smoothly towards the tail end. When the belly was slit open, the fresh remains of a penguin and several half-digested fish spilled out.

Wordlessly, Marion gestured to Curly. He nodded and knelt beside her. Together, they pulled out fistfuls of the raw fish and started to gorge themselves. They held the steaming insides up to their faces and bit off pieces of flesh, swallowing them whole.

The others came to join them, shouting with excitement. They brought with them a small axe and a bag, to cut up the leopard seal and take it back to camp.

Overcome by exhaustion and shock, Marion fell into a heap not far from the carcass. Only then did she look over at the seal's head and notice that half its skull was missing. The image was eerily familiar, and her mind flashed back to Jason's body lying on the deck.

Once she'd realised he was dead, she had picked up the gun and gone searching through the passageways. Then there had only been one thought in her mind, even when she'd heard the alarm warning them to abandon ship.

I need to find Nick Coltheart.

27

Kit wanted to join the SAR team to resume the search for Sally, but Bill asked her to stay behind. The Antarctic Division had been in touch overnight: they needed to perform the preliminary autopsy on Dustin's body via video link that morning. The corpse had partially thawed out, and an inspection was required before the tissues deteriorated any further. They had already received the necessary consent form from Dustin's relative.

Thankfully, Kit wouldn't be required to perform any invasive procedures. Her job would be to guide a portable webcam over the body and take high-resolution photos for the lead pathologist back in Hobart. A full autopsy would be performed in November, once Dustin's body had been shipped to Tasmania.

In the surgery, Bill wheeled in the corpse and helped Kit remove the clothing. They used large pairs of scissors, with Kit cutting off the upper garments and Bill working on the trousers. Within fifteen minutes, they had Dustin's body undressed and laid out on the surgical table. Once the video link was established with the autopsy technician, Bill discreetly left the room.

Alone with the corpse, Kit took a moment to collect her thoughts. Under the fluorescent lights, Dustin's skin shone pale blue as if he'd caught some of the glacial brightness of the iceberg in the harbour. He was on his back with his arms reaching upwards in rigor mortis and his knees bent at odd angles above the table. She felt a tugging in her heart as she gazed upon his face and saw the slackness in his cheeks. Grey and unshaven, he looked much older than his forty-two years and much sadder than she remembered him. *Did he always look so depressed?* she wondered.

In a tinny voice, the technician instructed Kit to begin with a whole-of-body visual inspection, asking her to describe what she saw. Surveying the corpse, Kit said, 'The body appears to be intact and unharmed, apart from some minor bruising and lacerations on the right leg.' At the technician's prompting, she placed the webcam over the spot in question. She'd noticed the graze below Dustin's knee as soon as Bill removed the trousers; dried blood ran down the doctor's calf and into his woollen socks. To her mind, the injury could have been caused by a fall on the rocks alongside the road. If Dustin had sat down in the bar and inspected his leg, that would explain the blood spatters on the bar-room floor. Alternatively, she thought, the blood could have been caused on the spot as the result of a fight or a struggle. She took photos so the pathologist could examine the evidence later.

The next phase of the inspection required her to position the camera over different parts of the body. She found she could do this with some detachment, as long as she didn't think of the corpse as Dustin. The most challenging part came when the technician asked her to feel around his scalp, to check for head injuries. His hair was cold and wet, sending a chill through her. She glanced down and noticed his eyes were partly open beneath the lashes. The moment was strangely intimate. When she pulled her hands away, they were trembling.

The inspection concluded with Kit taking a few blood samples for forensic analysis. The examination had to be cut short due to an issue with the audio. When the technician logged off, Kit let out a shuddering sigh. Never had she been so pleased to experience a tech malfunction.

Afterwards, she distracted herself by looking over medical supplies. Now that Dustin was gone, Bill had told her she would have to oversee patient care on the base with telemedicine assistance from Hobart. She paced restlessly in the small confines of the surgery, trying to block out images from the autopsy and longing to hear news of Sally.

When Blondie popped his head around the door, she started with a jump.

'Blondie,' she said with a weary smile.

She was feeling bleak and unsociable, but it was hard to turn Blondie away. After their search-and-rescue experience on the *Petrel*, he'd become one of her strongest allies—the one to whom she'd confided her fears about Sally earlier that morning. His presence had been comforting. With his blunt ocker manners and down-to-earth opinions, he could be counted on as a source of calm reassurance. He felt very strongly that Sally would be okay and reminded Kit that her friend was an Antarctic veteran and a field training officer—she had the skills and the resources to survive. She would have had her survival pack, containing a sleeping bag, a bivvy, some dry clothes, food and water, a compass, and a first-aid kit.

Now, however, Kit's apprehension sat like a frozen lump in her chest.

'Any word?' asked Blondie, eyebrows raised.

'No, but I'm hoping to hear back any minute.'

'Need another pair of eyes?' He glanced at the inventory on Dustin's desk.

'Yes,' she said. 'And another brain—this one is spent.' She looked helplessly at the boxes on the counter and the floor. She'd been sorting through them in a haphazard way.

'Having a bad day?' he asked.

Kit laughed at the understatement. 'Yeah, you could say that.'

Looking down, she noticed that Blondie was clutching a vitamin D container. It was his pretext for coming to see her. 'Thought I'd get a refill,' he said, shaking the empty vial.

She glanced at the cardboard boxes out in the waiting room. They contained an assortment of medical supplies that Dustin had brought over from the Green Store—but no vitamin D.

'Oh,' she said, the last hateful memory of the pills flashing through her mind, 'we don't have any of those.'

'Oh, right.' Blondie hooked a thumb towards the sea ice. 'All gone, eh?'

Kit sighed. 'But we'll get by, won't we?' She smiled thinly. 'If seasonal affective disorder is our only other worry this winter, that'll be a good thing.'

'There are worse things, for sure.' He shuffled his feet in the doorway and took a deep breath before asking, 'So you're gonna be our new doc?'

'Not quite. I'm not a trained doctor. I don't think anyone knows what we're going to do exactly, because no one's ever lost their medical practitioner before. Bill and the medicine branch at head-quarters are coming up with a contingency plan.'

The next ship containing personnel wouldn't arrive for another seven months. In the meantime, Bill had suggested that the expeditioners would have their monthly check-ups via teleconferencing with a doctor back in Australia. They'd been given a practitioner's email address and encouraged to get in touch if they required counselling or urgent advice. On the ground at Macpherson, Kit would continue in her role as medical assistant and perform simple diagnostic tests—such as X-rays, and blood and urine checks—as well as admin in the surgery.

'Lucky we're all so disgustingly healthy here,' said Blondie, straightening his shoulders.

'Lucky for us—' Kit was going to add 'for now', but she was interrupted by a disturbance in the hallway.

It wasn't an especially loud noise, just a slight thumping against the wall and two deep masculine voices speaking to one another. But in her heightened state of anxiety, she was sensitive to emotions—and those out in the corridor seemed intense.

She frowned at Blondie as if to ask, *What's going on?*

He ducked his head out into the hall. 'Everything all right, guys?'

'What's your problem?' came a man's voice in anger. He sounded like Skelly.

With a twinge of concern, Kit joined Blondie in the doorway. The scene that greeted her reminded her of footage of Antarctic huskies who would suddenly lose it and engage in brawls out on the ice.

Nick had Skelly's back flattened against the wall, one hand clenching his shirt. The diminutive chef was almost comically dwarfed by the other man. He clawed at Nick's large hand on his chest, trying to loosen the grip on his shirt, and ended up spitting in frustration, 'Get yer fuckin' hands off me!'

Nick's face was a blank sheet of rage. 'What did you say?' he demanded with a snarl. 'What did you *say*?'

Blondie took control. 'Okay, guys,' he said, striding over and placing a tentative hand on Nick's shoulder. 'Let's break this up, shall we? Come on.' He gave Nick a quick but firm pat on the back.

Nick stared murderously at Skelly, apparently prepared to let things escalate. But then he caught sight of Kit in the doorway and seemed to think better of it. He relaxed his grip on Skelly's crumpled shirt and stepped away.

Skelly raised himself up to his full height. He glared at Nick while smoothing down his shirt and shaking his head in disbelief. 'What the *fuck* is your problem?' he growled, shouldering Nick as he edged past him and marched off down the corridor. Blondie followed.

Kit gazed steadily at Nick, who was pacing up and down with nervous energy. After a while, he pressed his forehead to the wall, then stared at the floor and exhaled loudly. There was a short silence. He cupped his face between his hands and rubbed his cheeks. 'Arghhh!' he yelled, throwing his head back.

'What happened?' asked Kit, her arms crossed.

Nick gaped at her as if he'd only just remembered she was there. He seemed shocked and incredulous. 'Skelly said something to me, in this corridor, just then.'

'What?'

'Something . . .'

She went to him and touched his arm. 'Did he jog your memory?'

'He—he . . .' Nick paused, appearing to collect himself, then continued in a calmer, more measured tone. 'He asked me if I was looking for drugs.'

'Why did that upset you?'

'I don't know.' Rubbing his neck, he looked away. 'Maybe I don't like drugs.'

Kit frowned in confusion. Something wasn't adding up. She was almost a hundred per cent sure that Skelly was the man she'd met in the darkened corridor of the *Star* that night, on her way to see the green flash. She'd later learnt he was a last-minute replacement for their scheduled chef. Given her experience on the ship, it didn't seem implausible that he'd offered Nick drugs. But why had that rattled Nick so much?

'I've got to go,' he said suddenly.

Kit scowled at his back as he walked away. She didn't know why he'd reacted so violently to Skelly, but she did know one thing: if ever Nick had lied to her, it was at that moment.

28

The Weddell seals were stupidly trusting. They sunned themselves on the rocks, basking on their backs, with their mottled grey-brown fur exposed to the air. They didn't perceive humans as a threat; they barely acknowledged their presence. When the *Petrel* crew members came up close, they turned and winked their beautiful brown eyes, seeming to smile beneath their whiskers. And when one of their number was shot dead, they didn't even seem to notice. To them, the blast of the gun was just another loud disturbance, like the roaring of the wind or the calving of an iceberg.

Marion was glad that there was no panic among the seals—it would make them easier to hunt.

Soon after the incident with the leopard seal, someone noticed a few Weddell seals up ahead on the ice. In the relentlessly white landscape, their silvery brown hides were easy to spot. After getting some sleep, the crew ventured back to the area. Curly walked right up to a seal, pointed the gun at its head and pulled the trigger. After that, two men with sacks moved in. They had to carve up the seal before it froze solid, but there was nothing like hunger to focus the mind and get the job done.

The day before, the crew had cut the leopard seal's hide into cross-sections, then laboriously removed its intestines and other guts with a serrated knife. They didn't leave a single edible scrap behind. But they knew the leopard seal would provide only so much food for twenty-one people who'd been starving for weeks. Seal flesh was salty game meat and made some people gag, but it was nutritious and provided much-needed energy. They had to take it when they could.

Marion noticed that when Curly fired the gun, he didn't hesitate. He dug his heels into the snow, his legs apart. Gripping the weapon in his hands, he aimed with precision, then pulled the trigger in one smooth motion.

She was grateful to him for his outer calm. He'd shared almost none of the crew's harrowing despair over the past few weeks. Outwardly, he seemed indifferent to their predicament. While everyone else was drowning in despair, he was observing the weather or using the compass and a map to draw up a crude trajectory along the coastline. She was pleased that at least one person was keeping it together.

The voyage leader, however, seemed intent on getting a rise out of him.

As they were cutting up the seal, Thorn asked Curly where he'd got the weapon.

'It's Jason's,' he said, ignoring Marion's surprised look.

'Jason's?' Thorn pulled his head in and frowned. 'Why do you have it?'

'He leant it to me. It was in my survival bag.'

'There are so many problems with that, I just don't know where to begin,' snapped Thorn. Personal firearms had been forbidden on the voyage. He took a moment to collect himself. 'But right now, we've got something to eat because of that revolver, and I'm prepared to let it go, so long as you keep that thing safe and never point it in my direction. Got it?'

With his head bowed and the gun hanging limply at his side, Curly nodded. When he looked up again, he caught Marion's eye.

She was relieved that he'd covered for her. She wasn't ready for an interrogation about the weapon just yet. When she'd noticed it lying next to Jason's lifeless body, she'd instantly recognised the firearm as his. He refused to travel anywhere without it.

She watched Curly smoothly tuck the gun into his daypack. *If I never see that thing again*, she thought, *it'll be too soon*.

It was the weapon Nick had used to kill Jason.

29

Kit spoke to Sally's mother, Helena, over a satellite phone in the entertainment area. In Kit's late teenage years, the Rivers' household had provided the warmth and variety that was lacking in her own home environment. A stay-at-home mum, Helena was a vibrant, contented contrast to Daphne, a single parent perpetually worn out by two jobs. Kit wanted to delay the phone call till they had positive news. But now Sally had been missing for three nights: it was time to let Helena know.

It broke Kit's heart to hear the hope and terror in the older woman's voice. 'We'll find her,' said Kit, as Helena wept. 'I promise you.'

When Kit hung up, she had a sudden thought. What if Sally had turned on one of the spare GPS transmitters for the seals? With the help of a satellite tracking system, the devices enabled them to record the long-range movements of the seal population in the surrounding area. If she were lost in the snow with her gear, then this would be one way to advertise her location. Kit would just need to look at recent data and find a pattern that didn't fit the daily movements of a seal.

But she was soon disappointed. When she pulled up the tracker on her laptop in the mess area, it seemed that all the GPS transmitters had ventured into the sea that day, before returning to one of the breeding sites on the ice. They were doing what they were meant to do: behaving like seals.

Disheartened, Kit set out a number of the gold-coloured plastic boxes on the main dining table. Each tracker was rectangular and about the size of a cigarette packet, with a bendy black antenna on top. More often than not, over the course of a year, the devices would be accidentally knocked off or become detached from the seals, and so they needed to affix as many as they could in order to get some useful results. Sally had been keen to get as many attached as possible before the winter. There were only a few weeks to go before the weather would make any outdoors work extremely difficult. Today would have been one of the few opportunities left for Sally to recruit subjects.

Kit resolved to head out to the nearby breeding site. The SAR team had returned there to look for Sally, but Kit hadn't yet revisited the area. She was tired of sitting around indoors, waiting to hear news—she was impatient to retrace Sally's last steps for herself. While she was out there, she could tag a few seals. It was the least she could do for her friend.

Grimacing with the effort, Kit used her fingernails to prise the top off one tracker and insert the long-life batteries. She then checked to see that the transmitter really did send out her location in real time; she watched the computer as it processed a position update on the screen, down to the nearest twenty-five metres or so. To assist, the screen provided a detailed high-resolution map.

Once she arrived at the breeding site, she would attach the trackers to one or two healthy-looking specimens. A few would be lying there like giant slugs, their plump bodies a mixture of gold, beige and shimmery grey-browns. Often they made a symphony of wheezing, grunting, roaring and snuffling. One by one, she would anaesthetise the creatures, inspect their teeth, then glue the trackers to the fur on top of their heads. Though they were mostly placid and compliant, sometimes she came across a cranky old beast that snapped its head and bared its teeth, making a guttural warning sound. She would immediately step out of the way—it wasn't worth the struggle.

According to the weather report, the next few days were going to be cold but glorious, with only light winds. The whiteboard in the mess bore a curt message from Prudence: *Get out, while you still can.*

When Gareth offered to come along and help with the tagging, Kit readily accepted. She didn't know him especially well, but she trusted that he wouldn't bore her with incessant talking and that he'd give her enough personal space to get on with the job. He didn't mention the incident with Alessandra in the hallway, and something in his manner stopped Kit from raising it herself. Together they went to see Bill in the station leader's office, to let him know their plans.

He was seated at his desk, staring off into space. He reeked of day-old sweat, and there were heavy dark rings under his eyes. When he said hello, his breath smelt foul and rotten, like something dead.

Kit presented him with the completed form for his final approval, while Gareth lingered in the doorway.

'You're gonna go where?' asked Bill, scratching his scruffy beard. He looked like he'd just rolled out of bed wearing the same crumpled clothes as the day before.

'To the Weddell seal breeding site, where Sal was last seen,' repeated Kit, eyeing him with concern.

'Yeah, uh, that should be fine.' He stretched and yawned, then winced in pain.

'Are you all right?' asked Kit, observing large stains in the armpits of his shirt.

'Not really,' he said with a grimace. 'Got a splitting headache.'

'That's no good. Have you taken something for it?'

'No, not yet,' he croaked. 'I was hoping to shake it off with coffee and a brisk walk. Think I slept badly—muscles in my legs were aching all night, kept me awake. Bloody nuisance. Couldn't get comfortable.' There was a short silence while he rubbed his blood-shot eyes. 'Where did you say you were going?'

Kit repeated the location.

'Have you told Blondie?'

She nodded towards the intentions form. 'Yes,' she said, thinking that Bill should go back to bed. 'His signature is on the form.'

Blondie was the official fire chief on station. In accordance with Division rules, they had to let him know that they would be away, so their spots could be filled in an emergency. Every few hours or so, they would have to radio schedule with Prudence, to let her know how things were going.

'Okay.' Bill sighed, evidently satisfied. 'Have fun. You might run into Nick on the way out—he's heading off in a Hägg for a few days by himself at Muddleroo Hut.' He referred to the isolated field hut overlooking the North Mascot mountain range.

Kit failed to hide her surprise. 'By himself?' she asked, with a hint of disapproval.

Ordinarily expeditioners weren't permitted to venture off station alone, and she was puzzled that Bill had granted Nick permission to do so—especially given that Sally was still missing. Bill's non-chalance was odd; he was usually such a stickler for the rules. She wondered if he was ill.

He grunted and muttered defensively, 'Yes, yes, weather should be fine, pretty experienced in these environs, this time of year.

Was once a field training officer himself. Said he needed some rest and relaxation—don't blame him.' Bill sniffed.

Kit looked to Gareth for his opinion, but he was gazing off in the opposite direction, apparently uninterested.

'Do you really think that's for the best?' asked Kit with some concern. After all, she wanted to say to Bill, Nick could be rather foolhardy and reckless. Instead she made a diplomatic appeal to Nick's health and wellbeing. 'This whole thing with Dustin seems to have shaken Nick quite a bit. And with Sally still—'

Bill cut her off, looking annoyed. 'That's precisely why he needs some time to himself, don't you think? We could all do with a little time for peace and reflection on recent events. I wouldn't mind some time alone myself,' he added, standing up stiffly. 'Bit sick of living on top of the same people, day in, day out.' He handed over the signed form, abruptly signalling the end of the meeting.

Kit took it without further complaint, but she was disturbed by Bill's manner. Something seemed off.

•

Kit and Gareth headed off together on the quads. An old but reliable form of transport, they were single-seater motorbikes with four wheels. The wheels on these machines had been fitted with embedded spikes to help them negotiate the terrain. Kit's quad had a light sledge at the back, loaded up with research gear, compulsory survival bags and extra food. The two of them were prepared to stay overnight if they had to, depending on the amount of tagging they managed to complete as well as the amount of wind. At minus twenty degrees, they really needed the wind to stay at an absolute minimum, otherwise the chill would be unbearable.

On the way, the quads occasionally became bogged in powdery snow. But with a bit of pushing and pulling, Kit and Gareth soon got them back up and running again. Kit found that she could usually recover her quad by herself, without Gareth's help.

They reached the breeding site in good time, then got started while the weather was still on their side.

Contrary to her expectations, Gareth wasn't a quiet companion. For a good hour or so he chatted amiably about the seals and the snow and the cloud formations, asking questions and making observations. While she was working, his soft English accent provided continuous background commentary. He'd often chuckle good-naturedly at the seals' antics and expressions, saying, 'Look at this one, he's smiling at me', or, 'Golly, he's a big 'n, isn't he?' Kit didn't mind.

But after a while, Gareth's banter turned to more personal matters. It appeared he'd been skirting around his main problem.

'So, I'm a bit worried about Alessandra,' he announced, not looking Kit in the eye as he urged a seal to leave the kennel-like enclosure in which it had been tagged. He tipped the box on its side, and the seal slid out onto the ice on its back. It righted itself and then thumped away.

'Why? What's the matter?' Panting heavily from the cold, she was standing at a short distance from Gareth, her crampons wedged into the ice to prevent her from slipping down the slope. She was checking the accuracy of the GPS transmitter and didn't want to drop the laptop. Her voice was emotionally neutral, but she sent Gareth a glance that was full of concern.

'She just hasn't been herself lately,' he mumbled, shaking his head.

Kit thought of her dream of a few nights before. She shivered at the memory of the bloodied words carved into Alessandra's forehead.

'You saw the way she was the other night, how she couldn't remember how to get back to the room.' Gareth's voice quavered.

'As you said, it was a tough day—for all of us. She seemed very upset about what had happened. I thought she might have taken something that night . . . a sedative, perhaps? To help her cope.'

'No, that's just the thing. She hasn't been taking anything, yet she's been acting like she's mad. She's been confused, she's nervy . . . she's crying all the time, making a fuss at night, not sleeping. Never knowing if she's coming or going. I don't know what's wrong, but I'm thinking I should have her committed!' He gave a cheerless laugh.

'Has she had any problems like this before? Any mental health issues?'

'Nah, she's as solid as a rock, she is.' His mouth turned down at the sides. He shook his head slowly, staring at his feet.

A disturbing thought occurred to Kit: *Alessandra is all alone.* 'Is there someone with her at the moment? Someone to look after her . . .?'

'Yes, she's sitting in on communications with Prudence,' he assured her. 'I'm going to talk with her at our three o'clock radio sked, see how she's doing.'

Kit looked quizzically at Gareth, thinking, *He's an extremely odd man.* Somehow he hadn't realised he should be at home with his wife instead of off station with her. Apparently he'd wanted to discuss Alessandra's situation with Kit in confidence, but this seemed like a rather misguided way of getting her medical advice.

There was no doubt, however, that Gareth's concern for his wife was genuine—and justified.

'Gareth, I think you should go back. I think you should leave now.' Kit took out her notepad and wrote a hurried message, in 2B pencil so that it wouldn't smudge. 'You should ask Bill to let you have some of this from the drug shelves in the surgery.' She wrote down the name of a mild barbiturate. 'Alessandra should try taking two tablets tonight. That might help her sleep. When I get back, I'll talk to the telemedicine people at headquarters, who might have other suggestions. I just think Alessandra shouldn't be alone tonight. I think she needs you there, to keep an eye on her. Go now—I'll be all right here. The job's almost done anyway.'

Less than half an hour later, Gareth was gone, leaving Kit alone in the vast white wilderness. At three o'clock, she let Prudence know that he was on his way.

'Oh, thank Christ,' breathed Prudence with relief. 'Alessandra's unwell. And I'm not feeling great either. I'm thinking of calling it a day and going to bed.'

When Kit mentioned she would be staying overnight, Prudence barely registered her change in plans. She raised no concerns about Kit being off station all alone. Like Bill, Prudence seemed preoccupied.

Something was wrong, but Kit couldn't put her finger on it. All she knew was that at a time when her colleagues should have been most concerned about safety—when one team member was dead and another missing—they were surprisingly relaxed.

•

The next morning, Kit woke inside her sleeping bag and lay listening to the wind. Unusually, so far, there had just been the occasional buffeting of the tent, a passing breeze that had blown in the walls and then pulled them out. The weather was going to be fine.

With this encouragement, she found the energy to sit up and reach for the laptop. She logged on to the GPS tracking service and began looking up real-time position data for her transmitters.

She was interested in only one tracking device: the one she had placed in Nick's Hägglunds the morning before.

While getting fuel for her quad, she'd seen the blue Hägg idling with Nick's gear inside, and she'd seized the opportunity to plant the device in the back. She told herself it would be a safety precaution in case he became lost. But what she really wanted to know was where on earth he was headed—and why.

Yesterday afternoon, shortly before she'd shut down her laptop, the transmitter had told her that he was at the base of Frost Peak, a little further out than Muddleroo Hut. Today he was already on the move—he must have woken and packed up before dawn. His trajectory suggested that he was headed for the South Mascot Ranges, a fairly remote location, she recalled Bill saying, that hadn't been visited by anyone at Macpherson for several years. The Ranges were difficult to access; there were many opportunities to get stuck along the way, and there were no welcoming huts. She was surprised.

Then she glanced at the coordinates on the left side of her screen. Realisation came like an earthquake. Her thoughts snapped to attention, and her grogginess was forgotten. She hastily kicked off the sleeping bag and reached for her polar fleece. If she was going to catch up with Nick, she'd better get moving.

30

Nick sat behind the wheel of the Hägg, twirling and rolling a piece of paper between his fingers. Occasionally, he would bring the edge to his lips, lick the paper and tug at it with his teeth. He would then rip off the dampened portion, chew it to a pulp and spit it at the dashboard.

Since the altercation with Skelly, his hankering for a cigarette had grown stronger, but he couldn't bring himself to light one just yet. He wasn't ready to settle back into his old habits so soon.

He wished he'd never spoken to Skelly that day. That he'd never walked down that corridor. Never stopped for a casual chat. Never heard Skelly speak that name out loud: *Jason.* Nick's heart had slammed into his chest. The rush of remembrance was a jet engine taking off from the tarmac, the crashing crescendo of a long piece of music, the flash flooding after a drought. It should have been the longed-for hallelujah moment—his life regained.

But there was no hallelujah. While he might have been born again, there were complications. There was something wrong with him.

Seven weeks earlier, when Nick had emerged from his coma on the *Southern Star*, he'd been disoriented. He wasn't disoriented in the sense that he'd gone into another room and forgotten what he was looking for; he was disoriented in the sense that he'd gone into another galaxy and forgotten who he was. He was a castaway on a frozen planet that had formerly been his life. He had no idea where he lived, who his loved ones were, or what had happened to him. Every biographical detail was unknown, every person a stranger, and every location unfamiliar. He had no one he could turn to, and no memory of anyone or anything that brought comfort.

Dustin had come to see Nick that first day and carried out a few preliminary tests.

There was no brain damage, the doc said, so the memory loss was likely the result of trauma. Nick would probably regain his memories in a few days or perhaps weeks, once the concussion had subsided. In the meantime, there was nothing anyone could do—they'd just have to wait and see.

Dustin looked grim as he peeked at Nick's medical chart, but then he gave a quick smile and kept on talking. 'Your basic intelligence is intact, and you're functioning normally. You can recall the meanings of words, you have your procedural memories—that means you remember how to do things like walk through a door or make a coffee—and you'll probably remember certain information as well, you just won't remember how you got it. You're going to be okay.'

His words sounded like they came from a diagnostic manual rather than the heart. The doc had then asked Nick a series of questions he couldn't answer.

'How old are you?' said Dustin, going through the list.

'Gosh, I don't know.'

'How old do you think you are?'

'Maybe about twenty . . .?' Dustin showed him a mirror, and with a start Nick saw himself staring back. 'Oh God, I'm eighty,' he joked.

'You're thirty-five.'

Nick tried to hide his alarm, but he was shocked by how worn and beaten he looked. He wasn't too worried about some of the things he'd learnt, like the fact that his parents had died years ago or that he was recently divorced—it was difficult to grieve for people he didn't remember. But he wondered if something bad had happened on the *Petrel*. He'd heard the doctor whispering about the ship to another man. He started to suspect a great mental anguish awaited him.

'How'd I get those injuries?' he asked Dustin, swallowing nervously.

'We think you fell and hit your head. Some of your back teeth were broken.'

Tentatively, Nick touched his cheek, and he became aware of a dull throbbing in his gums.

Dustin went to fetch the dentist.

•

When the woman came into the room, Nick was sitting on the bed, groggy and lost in thought. Before he looked at her, it occurred to him: 'I don't like dentists.' Then he realised he must have said it out loud, because a pleasant female voice said, 'Well, that's okay. I don't like patients.'

The levity and facetiousness of her tone were soothing. He needed a little more lightheartedness and a little less fake reassurance to forget the gravity of his situation. 'Perfect,' he said, hugging himself.

Then the two of them were alone together. The woman spoke to him again, but he must have phased out briefly, because the next thing he knew, she was leaning in front of him, trying to get his attention. She was smiling.

In that moment, Nick truly woke up. Before then, he'd still been asleep, living a kind of death. In this new life, hers was the first genuine smile he'd seen and the first real beauty he'd encountered. In a sense, she was both the first and the last woman he'd ever seen. There must have been a first kiss, a first girlfriend, even a first wife, but he couldn't recall them. Her face captivated him. To touch her skin, he thought, would be delightful; to taste her lips would be bliss.

As if sensing his thoughts, she murmured something and took his hand. The doc had taken his pulse and helped him to stand up, but Dustin hadn't touched him out of sympathy. When she rubbed his thumb, his heart started beating so fast he thought she might hear it. 'I'll be fine,' he said, smiling back at her.

Lying down on the bed and chatting, he had a moment of respite from his fear and loneliness. He felt like a normal person who could follow the usual rhythms and patterns of conversation without needing to recall the finer details of his past. He asked her a few simple, playful questions that she answered without any stiffness or artifice. He loved watching the expressions change on her face, from puzzlement and concern to ardour and thoughtfulness. He loved seeing the glow deepen in her cheeks. Every time she turned away from him, he said something to call her back.

For a while, he forgot that he was lost in space.

But the respite didn't last. Soon he became self-conscious. He noticed that he was imitating a conversation rather than having one—speaking from the manual instead of the heart. It was difficult to make a meaningful connection with someone when he had no meaningful narrative to draw on, only scraps of himself to share. He couldn't really trust himself to say the right thing, and he couldn't trust that she'd understood him.

He also knew that there was no use trying to fool himself—
the onslaught of his past was waiting for him.

•

Once he'd settled at Macpherson, something shifted. To cope with
the uncertainty, he'd busily gathered information and filed it away.
He did so in the hope that, little by little, his former self would
emerge, like a stick figure in a Heilbronner Test. To begin with, he
would have only a few branches, not the whole tree. But then the
rest would appear and he'd have a complete picture. In his conver-
sations with others, he used those branches as temporary lifelines.
He stuck fast to what he knew in the here and now, and filled in
the blanks with humour and wordplay. He kept his hands busy and
made himself useful. It was like the doc had said: he knew how to
walk through a door and make a coffee. So he ventured outside, he
mixed drinks, he did the dishes, he fetched ice, he played games, he
went for a drive, he helped at the bar.

And, of course, he sought out Kit, whenever he could.

There weren't many opportunities to talk to her; she was either
out in the field or in the surgery. But he looked forward to seeing
her at mealtimes. Amid the din and chatter, he'd study her from
across the table. She'd be talking with Sally, and her eyes would
crinkle when she laughed. With others, she was quiet and reserved,
but with her friend, she always seemed happy and at ease.

Before the meeting with Anna, he'd asked Kit in the hallway, 'Do
you think she'll like me?' He was fishing, of course—he couldn't
help himself. He was really asking: what did Kit think of him? Was
he the kind of man she might like? It mattered to him.

Later, she'd unnerved him by speaking his own thoughts: *you
should remember by now*. She was right. He was not suffering from
a brain injury, he'd had time to rest and recuperate, and he was
physically strong. The prolonged memory loss bothered him as

much as it bothered her. There'd been a few fragmented thoughts—vague and shadowy images—that had flitted across the surface of his mind. There'd also been flashes of negative emotion: anger, fear, resentment, regret, and something like guilt . . . or shame. More than once, it had occurred to him that his own mind was protecting itself: it didn't want to know who he was.

Now that the whole picture had emerged, he wanted to shove it back down. Now he knew for certain: he was not the kind of man Kit would like.

His first instinct had been to get away. With surprising ease, he logged his plans, commandeered a Hägg and headed out to the Ranges, where he spent the night alone.

He had consumed almost a whole piece of paper and was admiring the spitballs on the dash, when he heard the sewing-machine engine of a quad. He cocked his head with a frown and peered out into the void.

Someone was coming.

31

As Kit navigated the route to the Ranges, towering wind scours curled around her quad like surf waves about to crash. The arching walls cast dark blue shadows over the ground, so that she had to look even more carefully for slots—crevasses covered by only a thin layer of snow. She hoped that she wouldn't see any large holes. She was following a reasonably safe route marked out by steel drums and moraine lines, the rocks at the edge of glaciers; she was also using a hard-copy map and a GPS. But she was alone, and she didn't want to take any chances.

When she arrived at South Mascot, it was late in the afternoon and getting close to twilight. The white-brown peaks glowed and glittered in the light of the setting sun. She knew she wasn't far from Nick's last location, so she stopped the quad to get her bearings. Easing off her goggles and her blizz mask, she let the cold air burn at her cheeks and throat. Despite the pain, she was relieved to be free from the suffocating mask.

As she pulled the map from her pack, a sudden wind gust blew it out of her gloved hands and off over the ice. 'Fuckin' hell!' She looked disconsolately after the flapping piece of paper, wondering if it was worth the effort of retrieval. It would probably be blown about Antarctica for the next two hundred years. She felt bad about that, but her legs and feet were heavy and frozen from the journey.

A laconic voice called from behind her. 'What the ice gets, the ice keeps.'

Kit spun around, and there was Nick, tall and dark against the glowing apricot horizon. Her heart skipped a beat. He was grinning widely at her.

Of course, he would have heard her coming. He must have seen her quad from on high and skied down to greet her. He was dressed in a red freezer suit, his goggles pulled up, leaning casually against his ski poles.

Kit ignored the remark and wasted no time with polite greetings. 'Shouldn't eat 6753 and 6247,' she said. 'That would be sixty-seven degrees fifty-three minutes south, wouldn't it? And sixty-two degrees forty-seven minutes east, yes? The South Mascot Ranges.' She gestured at the surrounding peaks.

His smile dimmed, and he nodded.

In primary school, Kit had been taught a popular memory trick for the points on a compass: 'never eat soggy Weet-Bix'. It had helped her to remember north, east, south and west in the right order. But only when she'd seen the coordinates on her laptop screen did she realise the significance of the handwritten note in Nick's pocket. 'Never eat' had been misremembered as 'shouldn't eat', or south-east. He didn't have a food allergy. The note was a reminder of coordinates—for this location.

'So why are you here?' she asked, with a hint of impatience. 'What have you remembered about this place?'

Nick looked up at the sky. 'It's going to be too dark soon—we better get to camp,' he said, gearing up to ski further down the slope. 'I'll explain there.' He headed away from her. 'I've made us dinner,' he called over his shoulder.

Kit was ambivalent. No one knew where she was, she'd lost her map, and now she was alone with Nick in the wilderness. What on earth was she thinking?

She'd wanted to know why the coordinates were so important to him. She'd wanted to know what he remembered, and her curiosity had gotten the better of her. She hadn't thought about what would happen once she found him.

As a precaution, she pulled the radio out of her pack and called in to base. 'This is Kit. Prudence, do you read me?' She waited, but only white noise came through the speaker. She pressed the button again. 'This is Kit . . . Is anyone there?' Still, there was no response. In frustration, she threw the device back into her pack.

Casting a rueful glance at the darkening sky, she followed Nick down the slope.

•

Dinner, as it turned out, consisted of a ration pack: a meagre collection of freeze-dried meats and out-of-date chocolates from the Hägg. The meat tasted like salty smoked bread, and the chocolates were rock-hard and barely sweet. When Kit asked why they were eating emergency supplies, Nick said that after one night he was already sick of two-minute noodles. They ate in silence while watching the mist swirl about them in the sky behind the mountain peaks. His tent was set up in an area relatively protected from the wind, but it still flapped manically whenever a breeze passed through. Once it became too cold, they crawled inside and lay in companionable silence, trussed up in their sleeping bags in the dark.

After a while, Nick spoke. 'I've been here before, you know.'

'I gathered that.' Kit burrowed deeper into her bag, her feet painfully numb.

'It came back to me, after the encounter with Skelly. It was like remembering a previous life or something—a previous incarnation.

I was here three years ago, the last time I was stationed at Macpherson. I was with my workmate Jason Weathers and another guy, Curly Hollow, our team leader. We were taking ice core samples to estimate fluctuations in snowfall over the past thousand years or so.' He hesitated, and for a while Kit could hear his breath coming in halting rasps in the darkness. 'Except we weren't just taking core samples. We were also being paid to do a survey for an American oil drilling company—well paid, too, I should add.'

'An oil drilling survey?' asked Kit, frowning. 'Doesn't that contravene the Madrid Protocol?' The protocol expressly forbade any Antarctic activities related to mineral resources, other than for scientific purposes.

'Sure!' He sounded a little too cheerful. 'If you don't have the right environmental approvals, then of course it violates the protocol. But you know that there are ways around that, right? If anyone asked, we were part of a geological science program, not a commercial mineral exploration. The Antarctic Division didn't know anything about it. The company didn't want to attract an international outcry, especially after all the flak the Russians copped with Lake Vostok.' Kit recalled that some scientists had opposed the Russian drilling project because it could contaminate the lake. 'The company instructed us to fly under the radar.' He laughed bitterly, then spoke with remorse. 'Shit, it was so stupid to get involved . . . I can see that now.' He sighed. His sleeping bag rustled as he turned to face Kit. 'But I needed the cash, I needed a break,' he said. 'I had a new wife—I couldn't keep leaving her alone for months on end. We were drifting apart even before I left for the winter. I just needed a break.' He took a deep breath, and she felt a touch of sympathy as she recalled Anna on the small screen in her elegant shirt and gold jewellery.

'You wanted to save your marriage,' she said softly.

'Yes, things were pretty grim between us. We'd planned to start a family, but we had no support—my parents were dead, hers were overseas—and my job kept taking me away. I wanted to change things, to keep us together.'

'I get that.' She thought of her failed attempts to have a baby with Elliot. 'Sometimes, you can be so consumed by a goal, you'll do anything to make it happen; it can blind you to reality.'

He murmured in agreement. 'I learnt that the hard way. I only made things worse in the end.' She could hear the regret like a hollow rattle in his chest.

'It must have been painful to retrace those memories.' She paused for a moment, choosing her words with care. 'But if you can remember everything . . . what happened on board the *Petrel*? Where's the crew?'

He snapped out of his reverie. 'I don't know. I can't remember what happened on the ship. I remember arguing with Jason on deck. But everything else is just blank.'

'What were you arguing about?'

He gave a short, sharp laugh. 'That's the part I wish I *hadn't* remembered.'

There was a long silence. Now it was Kit's turn to twist around and face him. In the dim grey light, she could almost make out his features, the gleaming of his eyes and the whiteness of his teeth. But his expression was cloaked in shadow.

'We were near here, maybe five kilometres or so north,' he said. 'We were in the planning stages of setting up a borehole in a subglacial lake beneath the ice sheet. It was the site the drilling company had designated for us, based on some aerial radar surveys they'd done. We had just got started for the day, but the weather was crap. A fog was coming in, visibility was extremely poor, and the wind was wearing us down. We were about to pack it in when we got a radio call. It was a bad signal—we could hardly make out anything at first—but we knew it was a mayday call with coordinates. Someone was in trouble.

'Later we discovered a British Antarctic survey plane had gone down with five people on board. At the time, though, it was just one man's panicked voice over the radio. He said, "Mayday! Mayday! Mayday! This is Twin Otter something-or-other. We are lost in a whiteout, and our instruments are malfunctioning." He gave their last known position as a few kilometres south-east of the Ranges. We responded, but we never got a response back— just complete silence.

'After a while, Curly turned off the radio. Jason went to relay it in, but Curly grabbed the radio out of his hand. He didn't want Jason to contact the authorities. He didn't want to draw attention to the drilling site. The company had instructed us not to tell anyone our exact location or to discuss our work with anyone—our payday depended on it, you know. Curly argued that the aircraft's emergency beacon would have gone off, alerting the Macpherson and Davis crews of its GPS location. It was only afterwards that we discovered the heavy landing must have destroyed the beacon, so nobody knew where they were.

'Jason and I argued with Curly. As a compromise, we decided to Hägg out to the location and offer first aid if we could. It wasn't hard to spot the plane—it had left an oil streak about a kilometre wide. The site was a mess of twisted metal buried in snow. We searched the site but couldn't find any survivors.' He took a deep shuddering breath.

Kit could see why he'd wanted to forget about it—Dustin's psychogenic amnesia theory now sounded rather plausible. 'What happened then? What did you do?'

There was some shuffling and rustling, as Nick changed position onto his back. It was as if he'd forgotten Kit was in the tent with him, just as he'd forgotten her in the hallway. He was reliving the events in his head. 'That night,' he said, 'we agreed that we'd never

tell anyone what we'd seen and heard. You have to remember—'
he added hastily '—we thought a SAR team would respond to the
beacon. We didn't realise that the wreckage wouldn't be found.'

'Still hasn't been found,' murmured Kit. She recalled Alessandra's
discussing the lost Brits at their first meal on base.

'We wanted to get the ground survey done, otherwise it would've
all been for nothing. We would have gone there and risked our
reputations for nothing. And you have to remember, the Brits
were dead. There was nothing anyone could do for them. They were
going to stay dead whether we told the world we'd seen them or not.
Over the next few days, while we were getting the work done for the
company, it hung over our heads. I kept seeing the crash site in my
mind, and I was worried someone might have been alive and we'd
missed them. But Curly and Jason kept saying there was nothing
more we could have done.'

'But what about later, Nick?' asked Kit. 'When you came back
and heard that the plane was reported missing, why didn't you tell
someone then? Why didn't you mention you had the coordinates?'

He rolled over, turning his back to her.

She sat up in her bag and stared at his shadowy outline. Then she
touched his shoulder, pushing him gently. 'Nick?'

He remained silent and motionless for a while, then said, 'I wish
I had. It pretty much destroyed my mind—it destroyed my life.'

Kit pulled her hand away. 'And what about the British families?
Weren't their lives destroyed too, by the not-knowing, the anguish
and despair of waiting to hear news of their loved ones?'

He turned to face her again in the semi-darkness. 'You think
I don't still feel guilty about that? When it all came back to me,
it was like stepping out of a warm room into a hailstorm of guilt
and shame. It was something Skelly said—he asked me about Jason.
They used to hang out and smoke dope together in Hobart. He
asked me how Jason was going . . . Skelly just assumed I'd remember

him, God knows why. It was such a random question, but it did the trick. I remembered our last argument on the *Petrel*. Jason was so consumed by rage, I barely recognised him. He thought I was going to destroy his reputation, that he would never work again. He threatened me—he told me . . .' Nick hesitated and took a deep breath. 'That was why I had to come here, to the Ranges. It seemed like the solution to everything. I couldn't mention anything before, because it wasn't just *my* career and reputation I was putting on the line, it was also Jason's and Curly's. But I thought if I just came here and "stumbled across" the plane wreckage, I could report it—finally. Three years too late, of course. But hey, better late than never.'

'And have you found the crash site?'

'Some of it. I'll take you there—if you want to see it.'

At first, Kit didn't know how to respond.

After a while, Nick bunkered down in his bag and placed the sleeping mask over his face. They'd spent the entire night talking, and it would soon be morning.

She made up her mind. 'I want to see the wreckage. Take me there. Then we can report it together.'

•

They awoke at first light and followed the moraine lines a little further to the south. On their way through the snowfields on foot, they made quick but careful progress. As a precaution, they were roped together, with about fifteen metres or so of line between them. The area was pitted with crevasses, most of them small to medium-sized but some as cavernous as backyard swimming pools.

When they came to the spot, Nick pointed without saying anything. Kit was surprised to see obvious wreckage wedged deep into a small crevasse a few metres away. The fuselage and one grey wing were still visible, and a few numbers could be read at the side. 'I'm amazed a blizzard hasn't blown it apart,' she said.

'Oh, it's definitely moved over the years. And of course . . . the bodies aren't here anymore. I think the skuas got them.' He looked off into the distance.

They moved nearer. Up close, Kit noticed that the paintwork was scratched and the tail section was missing, but otherwise the fuselage was well-preserved; its half-submerged position in the crevasse had protected it. The sharp edges of metalwork, where a wing had been torn off, gleamed like new in the sunlight. There were even a few shards of glass in the windows.

Kit rested her ice-axe under one arm, pulled off her top layer of gloves and removed the lens cap from her digital camera. She started snapping pictures.

'There's a bit more over there.' Nick indicated a spot nested in a ridge of wind-sculpted snow known as sastrugi.

Peering over, she could see something grey sticking out only a few metres away. She sidestepped across the carved ridge, looking carefully at the ground. Then she came to a sagging patch of snow that was slightly different in colour and texture from the rest. There was a fine crack, no thicker than a pencil, down the side.

Before she could register what she was seeing, the wind picked up and blew her gloves to the ground. Without a second's thought, she stepped forward to retrieve them.

She heard the hush of her footstep—then she realised that the sound was different to the hard crunching she'd expected to hear.

With a sickening lurch of the stomach, she fell through the snow and down into open space, her arms flailing and her camera smashing against the crevasse wall.

32

Kit landed with a dull thud on a narrow ledge about halfway down the gaping pit. She fell on her hip, on her left side, with the safety rope pulled tight above her.

Her first thought wasn't one of terror or shock but of embarrassment at how stupid she'd been. Some part of her mind had known that the crack probably indicated the leeward edge of a crevasse.

When she was sure that she hadn't broken anything, she slowly placed her back to the wall. She looked up to see Nick peering at her from the lip of the crevasse, several metres above. 'Kit, are you all right?' He seemed pretty shaken.

'I'm fine,' she called. 'Just a bit bruised, I think.'

'Can you move?'

'I can probably get out of here . . . with a little help. Can you . . . can you throw down another rope, please? This one's stuck.' She tugged at the rope; it was embedded in the ice at the edge of the crevasse.

'Just give me a few minutes. I'll have to uncoil and re-anchor.'

Once he'd gone, Kit pulled her balaclava down over her face and made sure all her zips were done up. She hadn't noticed the drop in temperature yet, but she knew that a crevasse was like a freezer. If she was going to do this on her own power, she didn't want to grow too cold too soon.

Comforted by the noise that Nick was making above, panting and shuffling as he uncoiled the rope from his waist, she found the courage to look down into the crevasse. It wasn't as deep or as wide as she'd expected, just a few curved pockets of beautiful glacial-blue ice, one on top of the other, for a few metres down. She didn't feel quite so afraid then—things could have been much worse. She could have broken her hip, or been knocked unconscious, or dragged Nick down on top of her. She could have fallen forty metres and been killed by the impact. She would be okay.

Then she looked across the ledge to the other side of the crevasse. Right opposite her, wedged deep into a corner, was something large and yellow, about the size of a suitcase. Her first thought was that it was a climber's backpack. She took out her torch for a better look. When she shone the light into the corner, it was apparent that the thing wasn't a bag.

Kit couldn't help herself—she screamed.

In an instant, Nick appeared at the lip of the crevasse, knocking some loose snow into the hole. His voice brought her back to reality. 'Kit!' he yelled. 'What's wrong?'

With the snow falling in front of her face, she pointed across the ledge with a shaking hand.

She realised that from where Nick was crouched, he couldn't spot where she was pointing. 'What is it?' he repeated. 'What can you see?'

'It's a man!' she cried. 'There's a man over there, on the other side.' She waved her hand, gesturing across the divide.

A black-haired, beardless man was suspended in the ice, his face greyish-white and his blue-lipped mouth frozen open.

'Is he . . .?'

'Yes, he's dead. He's dead, he's dead, he's dead.' Her voice held a note of panic.

It wasn't that she'd thought he might be alive—that wasn't what had frightened her. It wasn't that he was obviously one of the British men killed in the plane crash—there was a Union Jack on his coat— yet he looked as though he'd died only yesterday. It was because, for one terrifying moment, when she saw the short dark hair, he looked like someone she knew.

For that brief moment, he'd looked like Sally.

Kit was desperate to be out of there. When the knotted rope came down, she snatched at it with greedy hands. Nick had attached two slings to prusik knots; she used one of those slings as a waist belt to hook herself up, and she placed the loops of the other sling under her feet. Then she took a ragged breath. 'I'm coming up,' she called, standing and placing all her weight on the foot loops.

Turning away from the dead man, Kit puffed and panted as she loosened the knots and slid them up the rope, gradually ascending. Nick had anchored padding at the top, to help her get over the last lip by herself. But when she reached the edge, he grabbed her harness and hauled her out.

Breathing heavily, they lay together on the snow a safe distance from the crevasse opening. Nick placed a reassuring hand on her back and his touch calmed her nerves, dissipating the tension in her limbs. She resisted the urge to throw herself in his arms and sob with relief. Once she'd disentangled herself from the mass of ropes, she stood up.

On shaking legs, they headed back to camp for lunch. Two-minute noodles had never tasted so good.

Later that afternoon, they arrived at Muddleroo Hut just as the sun was setting. They planned to wake before dawn and return to the station as soon as they could. They'd been unable to contact

Prudence for two days, and they didn't want to worry her any longer.

•

In the field hut that night, Kit lay awake on the top bunk, her head uncomfortably close to the ceiling. She was agitated and restless in her thoughts. Fully dressed in her polar-fleece gear, with her beanie still on, she was tucked up in her sleeping bag. The mattress was soft, the hut was warm, and after two nights in a tent it felt utterly luxurious. But she couldn't stop thinking about the events of the past few days. And about Nick.

Since their arrival at the hut, he'd been uncharacteristically silent. He seemed like a different person from the man with amnesia: less childlike, or less open and artless in his manner, more introspective and a little colder towards her, not as solicitous for her attention. In the tent he hadn't tried to move any closer or touch her; they'd slept in separate bags, and in the morning he'd had his back to her. In the hut, only hours after saving her life, he'd patted her on the arm as he said goodnight, then got straight into bed.

Now she looked dejectedly at the spot where he'd touched her. She could only assume that the memory of his stunning ex-wife had dulled any attraction she once had.

Nick was curled up in the roomier space of the bottom bunk, flicking through a two-year-old *New Scientist* magazine. The pages swished at a rate that suggested he wasn't reading anything. Eventually he flopped the magazine on the floor and switched off the light.

Saddened, she rolled over to stare at the wall. If she had ever needed the distracting comfort of another human being, it was now.

Sally, where are you?

Kit had been shocked and upset by the circumstances of Dustin's death. She felt sorry for the man himself—it was a terrible way to die. And the harsh reality of his demise, followed by her encounter with the body in the crevasse, had made her even more fearful for her oldest friend. What had happened to Sal? Was she in the ice now too? With each passing hour, Kit grew increasingly anxious.

Just when she felt like exhaustion might pull her under, a pressure in her bladder became impossible to ignore. Reluctantly, she clambered to the ground. The toilet was in a small room adjacent to the hut. She would have to put her outdoor gear on, but she wouldn't need to go far, and while the weather was unbearably cold, it was clear and windless. She would be back within minutes.

Before heading out, she glanced at Nick's outline. He looked sound asleep.

•

Upon her return, Nick was waiting at the door. Without a word, he gestured for her to turn around and helped her off with her coat. The old Nick would have greeted her and engaged in some light-hearted banter, but this one was silent.

He flicked the drift off the coat and hung it up. He then moved the few steps over to the kitchenette and leant his tall frame against the benchtop, his hands resting on the edge. As she took off her boots, she waited for him to say something. His face was in the shadows, but she could see that the buttons on his flannelette shirt were undone to the waist. In the half-light, she glimpsed a trail of dark hair leading to his navel. She recalled what it had been like to hold her naked breasts to that chest and shivered involuntarily.

'Are you okay?' he said.

'I'm fine,' she replied too quickly.

After a brief silence, he said, 'Can I ask you something?'

'Sure.'

He hesitated. 'Do you think I'm a bad person?'

The question caught her by surprise, and she waited a second too long before answering.

He chuckled mirthlessly.

'Look, I don't know,' she said in a hesitant voice.

'Well, you should know by now. You should at least have an opinion, don't you think?' He moved his arm and knocked a tin on the bench. Ignoring it, he hunched his shoulders and shook his head. 'I was paid to work for an unscrupulous oil drilling company. My work has violated the Madrid Protocol and could destroy a pristine environment. I visited the scene of a horrific plane crash, but I failed to report it. I went back to work as if nothing had happened. I left the family of those five people in an agony of suspense for years—the bodies of their loved ones have never been recovered.' He paused. 'And I left that guy—' He gestured outside, faltering as he swallowed. 'I left that poor guy,' he said, 'to freeze to death in a crevasse.'

'You don't know that for sure.'

'Yeah?' he responded sceptically. 'Well, I guess we'll never know. But that shouldn't stop you from making up your mind. You should probably think I'm a bad person anyway, just to err on the side of caution.'

He had a good point. The things he'd confided had reflected badly on him. Plus, there was no independent evidence to corroborate his version of events. The true story might be much worse. There was no reason to put her blind trust in everything he'd said.

But her thoughts flashed to his concerned expression at the top of the crevasse. He'd saved her life without even thinking about it. She knew he'd never hurt her.

'You've made mistakes—you're only human,' she replied cautiously. 'You're doing what you can to find redemption.'

'But what if I can't find it? What if the *Petrel* crew are lying dead under that ship, frozen in the ice like that British guy, and that's all because of me? Would there be any coming back from that?'

She gazed at him in horror. 'Is that what happened? Are those people *beneath* the ship?'

'No . . . I'm not sure.' He shook his head with a frown. 'I have no idea where they are.'

She moved closer to him. She could feel the heat of him and see his chest rise and fall beneath his loose shirt. 'All right,' she said, deciding to be totally honest and see what happened. 'Yes, I *did* think you were a bad person. I never understood why the others just accepted you. No one seemed to think much about why you were the only one not with the rest of the crew. When you came to base, you hypnotised the others with your laidback charm and your, your . . . charisma.'

He raised his eyebrows.

'But you should never have gotten off that easy. There's a whole lot of people missing—' She thought of Dustin as well, then caught her breath. She didn't want to accuse him of anything like that, not on a mere suspicion. Besides, if he were guilty, it would be foolhardy to voice her thoughts. She needed to proceed with care. 'You have to remember, Nick,' she said more quietly, touching his sleeve. 'You need to tell me exactly what you did. Why were you in that coolroom?'

He looked away, refusing to make eye contact. 'I don't remember what happened on the ship. I don't know what I did.'

Shaking her head, she sighed. She sensed she wasn't hearing the full story. His words had a ring of falsity.

'I have to get out of here,' he said suddenly, pulling away. 'I have to go.' He took two great strides to the back of the hut and started gathering outdoor clothes.

'Nick,' she said, following him to the bunk bed. 'Nick, don't be ridiculous.'

He threw his trousers and a thermal top on the bed, then took his shirt off. As he reached to put the thermal on, she snatched it away.

'Give it back,' he said seriously, his hands on his hips.

She hid the top behind her.

He dropped his arms to his sides. 'Kit,' he said in warning, gesturing for her to hand it over. His jaw tensed.

When she still didn't comply, he moved in, pinning her arms behind her back and pulling her to his bare chest. As he yanked at the top, she tightened her grip. He breathed heavily against her, then tugged the garment free.

Before he could step away, she leaned in and kissed him.

With a start of surprise, he pulled his head back, his eyes searching her face.

Feeling embarrassed, she broke eye contact and brought her hands up in mock surrender, conveying, *Okay, my mistake.*

When their eyes met again, he parted his lips and, with a quick breath, seized her by the waist and kissed her deeply.

The touch of his lips and tongue sent a lightning thrill down her back. She brought her hands onto his shoulders, and he pulled her in tighter, pressing his chest against hers. She responded by sinking her fingers into his hair. His lips caressed hers with greater intensity, then moved to her neckline, nuzzling her, making her heart beat faster.

Despite the fact it was minus thirty degrees outside, the hut became unbelievably warm. She was wearing too many clothes. To assist, he raised her arms and pulled her jumper over her head, followed by her thermal, leaving her hair a mess of static. As he flung the tops aside, she smiled and moved to take off her pants. The leggings got caught on her ankles, and she used one foot at a time to liberate herself, stomping them into the floor. He held her by the elbows to steady her, then dispensed with his own leggings.

Kit was left wearing only a merino singlet and a pair of knickers; Nick wore only his boxers. They took a moment to gaze at each other. She observed that his head wound was now a faded scar, and that there was some redness from the frostnip on his collarbone. She noticed a shadowy hint of hair in the middle of his chest, accentuating his muscles. When she glanced down and saw his arousal, she drew a short breath.

He reached out and whispered, 'Come here'.

They kissed again, more slowly this time, revelling in their closeness. He moved his lips across her cheek and nipped at her ear. Shivering in delight, she pressed her hips against him. With a faint murmur, he grabbed her backside in his large hands and squeezed, pulling her even closer. His touch set her on fire. As he kissed her mouth again, his right hand sought out and caressed her breasts under her singlet. He rubbed his thumb against her nipples, and her body tensed with pleasure.

At the back of her mind, she marvelled at the insanity of what she was doing. In only a few days, he had become a stranger to her again. She didn't really know him. She didn't trust his story. She couldn't understand how he made her so powerless—even if she'd wanted to resist, she couldn't have. How had she lost control?

What was it she'd said to him? That he'd hypnotised the others.

In her research before the trip, she'd read a theory that living in Antarctica made people more susceptible to hypnotic suggestion. Could Nick have hypnotised some of her colleagues? And was that what was happening to her now?

At the plane crash site, she'd known there were crevasses throughout the terrain, yet she'd walked across that snow bridge. Was she doing that again now? Was she walking across a precipice in a trance?

She couldn't stop herself. If he had held back for a second, she would have begged for more.

He edged his free hand under the waistband of her knickers. With a flattened palm, he cupped her as he kissed her. She gasped when his fingers slid between her thighs and out again. Then his fingers slid back in and lingered, moving in slow circles around her centre until she thought she'd lose her mind. When he dipped down to slip a finger inside her, she could only cling to his shoulders.

Stepping back, he gazed down at her, his lips parted. Without a word, he tugged her singlet over her head and dropped it to the floor, throwing a meaningful glance at the lower bunk. She nodded, grabbing the waistband of his underpants and raising an eyebrow. He obliged by stepping back and pulling them down, while she stripped off her own.

When they embraced again, she guided him backwards onto the mattress and straddled him. As she pressed herself to him, liking the feel of his hardness against her, he moved his hands over her back, massaging her skin, kissing her neck, her chin, her mouth.

Again, she wondered: what was she doing? It wasn't like her to leap into bed with a man; she usually took her time, to establish some trust. She tried to excuse her recklessness as an affirmation of life in the face of death—a natural response to the trauma of the day. But who was she kidding? She traced the contours of his shoulders, and leaned into his hair, revelling in the sheer power of him. She'd never wanted anyone so badly.

She tilted her hips back and forth, teasing him. He gripped her fiercely, using his legs to bring her hips against him. She could feel his breath coming in short pants, and her own breath quickened even more.

When he bent his head to take a nipple into his mouth, the buzz surged down her waist, into her pelvis and straight to her core. Moaning against his hair, she grasped the back of his head and held him to her. She could feel the heat of him straining to move within her.

He whispered, 'Kit.' And then, more desperately, '*Kit*.'

She opened her legs wider, and he entered her. Placing his hands on her sides, he guided her back and forth in a frantic rhythm. The tension mounted at her centre and built like a storm.

He seized her hips and groaned, pulsating beneath her, until he stiffened and cried out her name.

Then the storm broke within her. Her back arched as the sensation spread, saturating her with bliss. She collapsed against him and struggled to breathe.

That was like a blizzard, thought Kit. She was blinded, breathless and exhausted. And hopelessly lost.

33

The *Petrel* crew were overjoyed to discover they were not far from Macpherson. A few days earlier, they had spotted the small collection of islands known as the Robinson Group scattered along the coastline. The welcome sight indicated they were now about fifty kilometres east of the station. In fair conditions, that meant the base was only half a week's walk away, but Marion knew that it would take them longer. They had slowed their march to a weary creeping pace. Several crew members were broken, physically and mentally. Some were troubled by back pain, others were experiencing stomach cramps, and everyone seemed to be suffering from some form of headache. They were all horribly tired. Most wanted to do nothing but stay inside the bivvies, tucked up in their now dank and slimy sleeping bags.

To avoid placing everyone in danger, and to speed up their rescue, Thorn decided that an advance party of three would go on ahead to the station. They would be much quicker than the whole group, and their path could cut across the land rather than follow the coastline. If the advance party travelled light, then they could be at the station in a few days.

Thorn singled out Curly to lead the group of three. He said his decision was based on Curly's fitness and experience, but Marion suspected the voyage leader was impatient to see the back of him.

When Curly asked Marion to join him, she readily agreed. She didn't want to risk being left behind, and she would rather be in the thick of things, doing something active to change their situation. She couldn't just sit around and wait to be rescued.

Curly looked relieved by her answer, and she was pleased to receive a friendly response from him. These days he rarely spoke or showed any emotion. It had been a few days since he'd openly challenged Thorn or expressed any irritation—it was as if Curly were conserving his energy for the final push. Outwardly, he still seemed calm. But for Marion, this was disconcerting, like the calmest-looking place of a beach concealing a rip. She wondered what he was really feeling.

The third member of the advance party was one of the youngest expeditioners, Zhao, a former marathon runner.

If something went wrong, two people could stay together, while the third went back for help. They had three days' food in their packs—some frozen seal meat—and space blankets, but they would take neither sleeping bags nor bivvies: they'd march continuously until they arrived at base. Sleep would be permitted in short bursts, with someone staying awake at each nap. The person on watch would be responsible for making sure no one overslept or succumbed to the cold.

They all knew they were taking a huge risk. If a blizzard blew through their route, they would be as good as dead, so they couldn't leave until there was a clear sky and a benevolent wind.

Finally, one morning, the battered crew woke to a strangely frozen calm. The wind had lost its usual viciousness, and the bivvies had stopped their vigorous shaking and flapping. Everything was serene.

Thorn made the call: the advance party would leave that day. 'It's time to go,' he announced. He seemed defiant, as if he were daring Curly to challenge him one last time.

Curly simply nodded, looking determined to see the journey through.

At the farewell, several flagging crew members huddled together on the ice. They looked like a group of senior citizens on an aged-care excursion, the men's backs hunched and their beards whitened with drift. Each face held a conflicted expression of fragile hope and bleak despair. Everyone was eager for the trio to set off and find help, but they were also anxious about the hardships awaiting them.

For her part, Marion wanted to leave without a fuss. She said goodbye to each crew member who was present, some with a brief wave, others with a brisk one-armed hug.

Thorn said a curt goodbye to Marion and wished her well, while his eyes expressed several unspoken doubts. He nodded at Curly with a mere tilt of the head; he had nothing left to say to him.

When Beatrice clambered out of her bivvy and walked over, Marion's instincts told her that the woman wasn't coming to pat her on the back.

'Don't go,' whispered Beatrice urgently, pulling her aside while eyeing the men with fear and suspicion. 'Don't leave me here with them.'

'Why?' Marion had noticed that Beatrice still spent most of her time in her sleeping bag, but that wasn't unusual. 'Has someone been bothering you?'

'No,' said Beatrice in a lowered voice. 'But why does it have to be you? Why can't it be one of the men? There are others who are fitter than you, you know.'

Marion had to agree, but Curly had asked her to come. It wasn't fitness he was looking for, he'd said: it was mental strength and resilience.

'I'll be back soon,' said Marion, 'and we'll bring help. I promise you. You don't need to worry about anything.'

'But what happens if you don't? I'll be here alone—with them.' Beatrice glanced at the men in disgust. 'They've become a pack of animals, burping, farting and pissing out in the open. They don't care that I can hear them or see them. When you're gone, who'll look out for me?'

If burping and farting were her main concerns, thought Marion, then Beatrice would be fine. But an uncomfortable part of her knew what the woman meant. Every breach of social etiquette was a sign that everyday norms had lost their grip. Who knew what else the men might do? A few extra days could make all the difference.

'You'll be fine,' lied Marion. But before she turned to go, she gave Beatrice a fierce hug. As she pulled away, she tucked her hunting knife into the woman's open pocket.

'I can't,' said Beatrice, when she realised what Marion had done.

'No, no, go on, take it.' Marion pushed Beatrice's fingers against the knife handle. 'I'll see you soon.'

•

Once they were off, Curly set a cracking pace across the snow. They were roped together, and when the rope pulled every few minutes, Marion quickened her steps to keep up. Soon she was panting and sweating inside her layers. Mercifully, after only a short while, the men slowed their pace. The trio settled into a rhythm.

At various points, Marion and Zhao found the energy to chat as they trudged onward, eagerly anticipating what they would do once they reached the station. They fantasised about warm showers, clean clothes and dry sheets. They talked with excitement about eating a full meal at an actual table with actual chairs.

Curly said nothing. He just kept moving forward, scanning the horizon for the landmarks and drum lines that would lead them to the station.

'I wonder if they have baths at Macpherson?' enthused Zhao. 'And a muu-muu,' he added, referring to the Hawaiian dress. 'I want to have a bath and then put on a muu-muu. I never want to wear clothing against my skin ever again.'

Marion smiled. 'I'm going to burn my thermals,' she said, 'if they don't fall off me before then.'

'Oh, honey,' said Zhao, 'mine will never come off. They'll have to scrape mine off my dead body—they'll have to *peel* me like a banana.'

They both laughed in good cheer. But still Curly remained silent. When Marion glanced over at him, she noticed a flicker of resentment in his eyes. It was directed at Zhao, not her. Her smile faded.

On the second day, as the sun rose, a fog-like mist rolled in, sprinkling their heads and shoulders with a fine layer of drift. Their faces were pained as they plodded wearily through the soft snow, sometimes sinking in up to their calves.

During their night stops, they found it difficult to rest in the thick of the snow's embrace. On one watch, Marion fell asleep and then woke up suddenly, not knowing how long she'd been out. She glanced over at Curly and Zhao, only to discover that Curly was already awake and looking at her strangely. Beside him lay Zhao— pale, unconscious and motionless.

In a panic, she lunged at him and shook him, knocking Curly out of the way. 'Zhao! Zhao!'

Zhao woke in fright, crying out, 'What? What is it?'

Her heart thumping madly, she fell on her knees in the snow. 'It's okay,' she panted, patting his shoulder. 'I fell asleep. I thought— I thought—' She paused to catch her breath. 'I thought you might not wake up.'

When she looked worriedly at Curly, he was dusting the snow off his coat and frowning—at Zhao, not at her.

The incident left her unsettled. At their next few rest stops, she forced herself to remain alert whenever Curly was on watch. She dared not sleep for fear of what he might do—or what he might *not* do. She was worried about the look he'd given Zhao. She was worried that Curly might let him slumber to his death.

On the third day, she trailed behind the men in a dreamlike state. Traipsing through the mist, she felt disconnected from the ground as though her mind were set adrift from her body, floating above herself and the two men. Only the periodic tugging on her rope reminded her where she really was.

Once when she came back to earth, she could have sworn her mother was walking next to her, offering words of comfort. Marion never actually saw her mother but sensed her presence. 'Keep going,' said Mum. 'Do whatever works.'

After Curly glanced at Marion, he stopped for some reason and made them all rest. She immediately fell asleep, bolt upright, propped against a snow wall. When Curly woke her, he said she'd been asleep for an hour and that they needed to keep going. But the brief respite had only made things worse—she still craved sleep.

As they forged ahead, her mind continued to play tricks. It created images from the shadows up ahead in the snow, her brain filling in the blanks, seeing familiar patterns in the mist and clouds. She now saw a dancing figure coming towards them. She could see the silhouette of a head, then two arms and two legs appearing out of the fog. The blurry figure emerged, then submerged back into the mist. *It looks so real*, thought Marion.

She could have sworn someone was coming down the slope.

34

Kit was relieved to see the familiar boxes of Macpherson Station jutting out of the hillside. The Hägg moved towards the base, its tank-like tracks smoothly traversing the snow, leaving a powdery mist in their wake.

As they headed towards the outpost, Nick glanced at Kit. He had spoken barely two words since they'd woken in each other's arms that morning, but now they'd arrived he had something to say. 'Could you please not say anything about the drilling company?' he asked quietly. 'I'll tell them about the plane wreckage, but not the company, okay? Like I said, it's not just my career on the line . . . I have to think about the others too.' His words rang hollow in the cabin of the Hägg.

Kit shifted in her seat. She stared out the foggy window, troubled by the suggestion. She hated him for taking advantage of their closeness the night before; she didn't want to be complicit in his lie. But most of all, she hated herself for wanting him even when he was asking her to cover for him.

Her eyes searched the rocky outcrop for people and signs of life. Her colleagues were working towards the preservation of this natural environment, and they would despise Nick and his associates for what they'd done. She knew she should report him to headquarters.

But she couldn't bring herself to do it. The exposure might introduce tensions over winter—not just between herself and Nick, but between him and the other expeditioners. For better or worse, they would be spending the long dark weeks together; there would be no avoiding each other.

Besides, she didn't yet have enough facts to report. She didn't know the exact location of the borehole, she didn't know the name of the American company, and she couldn't even recall the names of Nick's workmates. It would be better to make a report once she had a few more facts up her sleeve.

'Kit?' he asked, sounding nervous.

'Sure,' she said, still looking out the window. 'I won't tell anyone.'

'Promise?' he asked, leaning forward to catch her eye.

She looked straight at him. 'I promise,' she answered, her heart skipping a beat.

Looking back out the window, her eyes scanned the station for Sally's canary-yellow Ski-Doo and the bright reds of the expeditioners' freezer suits. But there was no one around. The place seemed strangely deserted. Everything was quiet, except for the hum of the generators and the ominous clanging of a chain against a shipping container. The wind blew up some drift and sent it flying around the buildings, like tumbleweeds swirling in the streets of the Wild West.

A face appeared in a large picture window of the Red Shed, then the person ducked out of sight.

'Where is everyone?' murmured Kit, squinting at the window.

Nick was silent, his eyes scanning the other buildings. He shrugged as he turned the big wheel, heading in the direction of the parking bay.

They returned the Hägg and the quad, but no one was in the operations building to take the keys or the paperwork. With a puzzled look, Nick tucked the forms into his coat pocket.

They walked to the Red Shed, the wind whipping at their ankles.

'I don't like this,' said Kit. 'Something's wrong.'

He nodded.

Before Kit had left, Alessandra and Bill had been unwell. During her absence, Prudence had failed to pick up the radio. It now appeared the base had gone into lockdown.

They entered the mess and spied a lone woman seated at the dining table. She had her back to them, but they could see she was eating something. Her bony shoulders protruded from her shirt as she cut the food on her plate. When they approached her, she turned to face them, dark red sauce running down her mouth and chin.

It was Alessandra. She was wearing a tattered dressing-gown and ill-fitting ugg boots. 'Hi,' she said, turning back to the table. Her manner was oddly casual. With her bare hands, she used the remains of a pancake to wipe her plate clean of berries.

'Hello ...' Kit said slowly. 'Alessandra, where is everybody?' A thought occurred to her. 'Is everyone out looking for Sal?'

'No, no,' said Alessandra, her cheeks stuffed with pancake. 'Everyone's too sick.' As she chewed, her cheeks bulged. 'There's something going around,' she added, her words garbled. She took a mouthful of tea from a nearby mug and swallowed the pancake with exaggerated gulps. 'The same thing I had. You know, *nerves*. Tension, restlessness, confusion ...' She rattled off a curious list of psychological ailments.

Kit exchanged a worried look with Nick. 'I didn't know those conditions could be contagious.'

Nick snorted softly in agreement.

'Well, there's a theory going around,' said Alessandra, turning to peer out the window. 'Blondie thinks it's possible we were all contaminated by the same source. He's gone down to check the melt bell, to see if something is getting into the water supply.'

'But what could possibly get into the water?' asked Kit, a shiver going through her. She looked for signs of other people: there was discarded clothing, a half-read book and a pile of dirty dishes.

'Fungus,' said Alessandra.

'Fungus?' asked Nick.

'Fungus,' repeated Alessandra, popping another oversized portion of pancake in her mouth. 'Antarctic fungus. Hasn't been studied much. Thousands of years old and embedded deep in the ice. Thought to have hallucinogenic properties.'

'Hallucinogenic?' said Nick in disbelief.

'Sure, go and ask Blondie.' Alessandra seemed offended at Nick's tone. 'It's his theory. Go and ask him.'

Kit shot a glance at Nick, who frowned back at her. As bizarre as it sounded, they needed to investigate. If everyone was incapacitated, the station was in trouble.

'Let's find Blondie.' She led Nick out of the room.

•

On their way through the building, they passed Bill asleep in his office. He was slumped across his desk, with his head leaning on his arms. Deep snores emanated from his mouth, shaking the table. A trail of glistening drool led from his bristly chin down to a messy pile of paperwork.

Kit knocked a few times on the door, but Bill took a while to rouse from his slumber. He finally raised his head, looking confused and bleary-eyed. He appeared much worse than when Kit had seen him last.

'Bill?' she inquired, waiting for him to register her presence. 'What's going on? I hear that people are sick.'

'Yeah,' he croaked, scratching the back of his head. 'Ah . . . you could say that . . . ah . . .' Bill sounded as if he were struggling to recall her name. He looked feverish: his cheeks were red, and his face shone with sweat. The skin under his puffy eyes was a deep purple. He was wearing the same clothes as before, and a pungent odour was coming from his desk. Kit wondered if he'd soiled himself.

'What is it?' asked Nick, stepping into the room.

'It's the flu or something,' muttered Bill, barely acknowledging Nick's presence. 'Feels like the flu, at least.' He grimaced. 'All aches and pains. Can't get comfortable.'

'Do you have a temperature?' asked Kit.

'Flamin' bloody *inferno*,' complained Bill, running his hands through his hair.

'Alessandra suggested that there might have been a . . . a contamination,' said Kit. 'Is it possible you've been poisoned?'

'Poisoned?' scoffed Bill. 'Poisoned by Alessandra, bloody likely. She's the one who gave me the goddamn lurgy. Think it was all her snivelling and blowing into tissues and then leaving them everywhere, for everyone to catch her bloody germs. Should have put her into the quarantine, instead of letting her bloody roam around as she pleased. Miss Hoity-Toity, fancy-schmancy, butter wouldn't melt in her mouth, with her rancid, filthy hands, spreading germs everywhere, smearing the doorhandles and the tabletops . . . getting everybody sick.' Foamy pools of spit had gathered in the corners of his mouth.

Nick looked incredulously at Bill, his eyebrows raised. He smiled over at Kit, as though hoping to share a knowing glance, but she turned back to Bill.

'Quarantine?' she asked, an alarm sounding in her head. Bill had mentioned it as though it were a real place. 'Is there a quarantine? Here? On station?'

'Oh, yeah. We made up a makeshift one yesterday. In the Dog Room.'

'The Dog Room?'

One of the most popular parts of the Shed, it was a rec room put aside for Antarctic dog memorabilia in a tribute to a vanished world. There were photos, exhibits, logbooks and an old sled. The room had an enormous picture window that provided majestic views of the harbour and its west arm. This was the window in which Kit had seen a face peering out.

'We'll go to the Dog Room.' She looked at Nick and nodded towards the door. 'Get some rest, Bill,' she said, placing a hand on his arm.

He glanced at her, then leaned his head back on his desk. 'Poisoned!' he muttered.

•

At first, the Dog Room appeared to be empty. In one corner, Kit spotted the old rigged-up sled, complete with a first-aid kit, a tent and water containers. The sled looked bulkier than before, as if more gear had been stuffed into the undercarriage.

She heard a rustling in the corner and went to investigate, while Nick waited at the door. On the other side of the sled, she found Blondie crouched down and packing gear into a bag.

'Hello,' she said cautiously.

He started in surprise, then turned to her. 'Hey,' he said, smiling and standing up. 'I was worried about you. Where the hell have you been?' He pulled her in for a one-arm hug. Peering over her shoulder, he waved a friendly hand at Nick in the doorway.

'Didn't Bill tell you I stayed out?' she said.

Blondie shook his head. 'But then, Bill hasn't been great, you know. He's not well.' He kept shaking his head for a second.

'I know. How are you? Are you feeling okay?'

'I'm fine,' he said, shrugging.

She scrutinised his face, which appeared to confirm what he said. He was a little pale, and his cheeks weren't as ruddy as usual, but his eyes were clear and his hair was neatly combed. His clothes were crisp and clean. When he hugged her, he smelt like soap and deodorant.

'I'm so glad,' she breathed out in relief. 'Where are the others?'

'Well, they were here,' he said, gesturing to some sleeping bags strewn across the floor, 'but they've gone back to their rooms. No one is feeling great at the moment—it looks like the flu or Covid, only a lot worse. Bill thought it was a contagion. That's why he suggested using this room for quarantine purposes. But just between you and me, I don't think Bill's in a position to be making decisions.'

'So you don't think it's the flu?' called Nick. He'd been loitering in the background, inspecting an old rifle mounted on a wood-panelled wall—it was one of the guns that station leaders had used to put dogs down. Now he moved forward into Blondie's line of sight. 'What is it then?' he asked, crossing his arms casually.

Blondie hesitated. 'I think it's something in the water supply.'

'Yes, we heard about that,' said Kit. 'Alessandra thought you'd discovered a hallucinogenic fungus in the water. She said you'd been down to the melt pool.'

'Hallucinogenic fungus?' Blondie asked, taken aback. He scoffed and shook his head again, half-smiling, half-scowling. 'Is that what she said? No, no, that's a bit fanciful, isn't it?'

Kit had to agree. It seemed unlikely that the pool had been con-taminated by fungi, but she hadn't realised that till she'd said it out loud. She found his reasonableness and scepticism reassuring.

'No, that's not the problem,' he continued matter-of-factly. 'I think this is a classic prank gone wrong. Not by one of us, mind you—by some of the dickwads in the summer crew. I remember someone telling me they added green dye to the water. The colour was supposed to have appeared and then disappeared, just enough to give people a mild scare. I went looking in the tankhouse and found a bottle of the stuff. It was a pretty poor joke, if you ask me, not that funny really. And now it's polluted the water.'

'Oh shit,' said Kit.

'What's the substance exactly?' asked Nick.

'It's a pigment known as Scheele's Green,' said Blondie. 'It's got arsenic in it, and it was used in paints as well as cotton dyes back in the day. It hasn't been used since the nineteenth century because it was found to be toxic. But I reckon somebody discovered the bottle in the old huts and brought it back here. That's what the summer crew used for their prank—they thought it was harmless food dye, the bloody idiots. We need to get it out of the water supply somehow.'

Kit felt her body relax as some of the underlying tension left her muscles. Blondie seemed unaffected by the pollutant. He was still the same solid, dependable guy—always the sober responsible one, always the designated driver. Finally, here was someone who still had his wits about him.

'Jesus,' she breathed out. 'Where's this bottle? Can I take a look?'

'Sure, I've got it in my donga. I'm keeping it safe so that we can run some tests and find out what we're dealing with.' He looked at Nick. 'Wanna come see?'

'Sure,' said Nick.

Blondie led them to his donga. The bed was unmade, and filthy clothes littered the floor, but for Blondie that was nothing new—his room always looked like someone had trashed it.

He moved to the cupboard and grabbed something out of a drawer. He then held out his fist to Kit and unfurled it to reveal a vial in his palm. It was a plastic container with a lime-green cap, no bigger than a bottle of eye drops.

As Kit took the vial, she frowned and turned it over to inspect the underside. There she saw the number 1 embossed on the plastic and the imprint of a triangular recycling symbol. Her stomach dropped, and she glanced nervously at Nick, their eyes meeting. 'Blondie,' she said, 'this is just food dye.'

'That's right,' he said, 'it's Scheele's Green. It used to be used as a food dye in the nineteenth century. But it's now known to be a poison.'

'But it's in a *plastic* bottle,' she reasoned. 'With a recycling symbol on the bottom.'

'Yeah. So what?'

Studying his face again, she detected a faint sheen of sweat on his upper lip where his moustache met the skin. She noticed his left eye twitching ever so slightly. In the silence, she could hear her heart beating like a metronome. In a corner of her mind, something nagged for attention.

Nick wandered over to the drawer and pulled out a scuffed and tattered box of Queen food colouring. He read the ingredients out loud: 'water, food colours, acidity regulator, preservatives.' Then he flipped the packet over and read, 'Best before: 02/2005.'

Nick and Kit stared at Blondie. This time, something shifted in his expression—it could have been the dilation of his pupils, or the deepening of the crease between his brow, but he didn't look like the same person anymore. He was no longer solid, dependable Blondie.

Kit gaped at him. 'Blondie, are you okay?'

He turned towards her, almost in slow motion. Then, with lightning speed, he grabbed her arm and pulled her out of the room. He locked the door, trapping Nick inside.

'What are you doing?' she asked, struggling to release her arm.

'You have to stay away from him,' he said urgently. 'I'm not well. None of us are well. And *he's* the reason.'

Something slippery and black unfurled in her stomach.

Nick thumped on the door. 'Hello? Hey, Blondie, Kit, what's going on?'

Blondie's eyes were round and pleading. 'It's him!' he whispered frantically, jerking her closer to his face. 'It's him.'

'What about him?' she asked. 'What has he done?'

Blondie dragged her further down the corridor, away from the insistent thumping. He spoke in a hushed tone, so low that Kit almost couldn't hear what he said. 'Nick's infected me. He's infected all of us, every single one of us. Just think about it, Kit—' His voice had grown louder, imploring her. 'What the fuck happened to all those people on the *Petrel*? How did they get stuck in the ice? Why was the ship on fire? You saw it as well as me, Kit. Someone torched the deck. But why?' He paused for a heartbeat, his hands shaking. 'Because they had to *kill the infection*, Kit, that's why. The infection had rendered the crew powerless.'

He looked anxiously at the door to his donga. The banging had ceased.

'And now here Nick is,' whispered Blondie, trembling and tightening his grip on her arm. 'He's wormed his way onto our station, he's wormed his way into our affections, and his worms are still working. You have to look out, Kit. He'll make you forget things, make you forget your own name, if you let him. I went to check on the melt bell, to purify the water, to get the worms out. I didn't get very far—'

'Blondie, just listen to yourself. What worms? This is crazy.'

'I know! I think I *am* going crazy. That's why we need to lock him away. When I saw you from the window, I knew I needed to pretend everything was all right, to lure him back to my room. We need to keep him away from the others. He's the one who needs to be quarantined—just him—until we can think clearly again.'

'Blondie,' she said, changing tack, 'I agree that we need some time to figure out what's going on and work out what to do.' She rubbed his arm in a show of sympathy. 'Look, why don't you come and take a rest in my room? I'll make you a cup of tea, and we can talk about it there.'

•

In Kit's donga, Blondie lay on her bed and muttered unhappily to himself. With a reassuring hand on his side, she waited until she could hear his breathing become deeper and more regular. Once he was asleep, she settled back and sighed heavily.

Her thoughts vacillated between alarm and disbelief. Something was horribly wrong. She and Nick had returned to an insane asylum.

Her mind reeled from what Blondie had said about Nick. It defied belief—it was preposterous. Yet Blondie had given voice to many of her own suspicions. People liked Nick; people got along with him. Nobody wondered out loud about the *Petrel* crew or worried about why Nick had come to be locked in the coolroom. Nobody explicitly questioned Nick's continuing memory loss. Nobody raised suspicions about Nick being outside and near the bar on the night of Dustin's strange death. And now nobody was out looking for Sally. It was as if their negative thoughts had been suppressed somehow.

Again, she thought, *It's as if everyone has been hypnotised by him.*

But the reality appeared to be that Nick was now the only one at the station, apart from herself, who still had his sanity intact. He had recovered his memories, and he'd seemingly been open and honest about what he'd done and what he could remember. Right now, she needed his help. She would be a fool to listen to Blondie's ramblings about worms and mass contagion. She had to think straight.

She fetched the key from Blondie's pocket and returned to his donga to unlock the door.

Nick was lying on the unmade mattress, his long legs stretched out and his hands behind his head. 'What's going on?'

'Nick, I need you to go up to the melt bell and see if everything is okay.'

He jumped up from the bed and moved towards the door. 'What are you going to do?'

'I'll radio through to headquarters—we need assistance.'

He placed a hand on her arm as their eyes met. 'Be careful.'

'I will.' She held his gaze. 'And you be careful too. I think we're on our own here and I . . .' She lowered her eyes. 'I'd hate for anything to happen to you.'

He cupped her face in his hands. 'Don't worry, I'll be fine. Just go.'

Inside the operations building, Kit hurried down the corridor. As she got closer to the comms station, she heard a tinny female voice emanating from the radio: 'Pan-pan! Pan-pan!'

It was an urgency call with approximate coordinates not far from Macpherson.

The voice became louder the closer Kit got to the room, until finally she arrived in the doorway and the message boomed out. 'We need help,' repeated the speaker. 'We are a group of four near Macpherson, and there are eighteen people about forty kilometres from base. We are lost and cold and hungry. We are in need of urgent assistance. Over.'

Kit's heart leapt with joy and adrenalin.

It was the *Petrel* crew. And the speaker was Sally.

35

Sally had never been so happy to hear someone's voice. The response came through the radio, surprisingly clear and strong and familiar. For one brief moment, she was so overwhelmed she couldn't speak.

It had been six days since she'd become lost and at least four hours since Curly, one of her new companions, had risked his life to retrieve the radio from the Ski-Doo. From that time, she'd been relaying her plea for help continuously, her voice ruined by the effort. Now her breath was stuck in the dry walls of her throat. *Great*, she thought. Finally about to be rescued, she was going to die of suffocation.

After a few desperate gasps, she found her voice again. 'Kit! Kit, is that you?'

'Sal! It's me, it's me! Where are you?'

'I'm not sure exactly.' She was trembling as she looked at her stark surrounds: white sky, white land, white water. In the distance, she could see brown hills dotted with Adélie penguins—a colony on one of the islands, no doubt. But which island, she couldn't be sure. 'We're on the coast somewhere—I can see islands. I've set off the emergency beacon in the Ski-Doo and relayed the coordinates.

You should be able to get our exact location from the satellite. There's a large penguin rookery here. Why has nobody responded? Where's Prudence?'

'I'll explain when you get back. Let me just get in touch with headquarters. They've probably been trying to contact us. Sal, stay on air while I make the phone call, okay? I'll be only five minutes.'

Sally felt like screaming, *No! Don't go, stay with me!* But she knew that Kit needed to get the exact coordinates and get together a SAR team at the station. She forced herself to be calm, to be patient, even though she knew the effort would be in vain.

For the past six days, Sally had been spectacularly unsuccessful at staying calm.

•

In her last clear memory of calmness, Sally was out in the snow-fields trying to complete her work before the weather blew in. She noticed the Hägg only once it was a few metres away. The wind had been howling like a bereaved mother, covering the sound of the engine. When she spotted the vehicle, she stopped what she was doing and waved widely in greeting.

The driver was wearing snow goggles and a beanie, so she didn't recognise him. But when he hopped down from the driver's seat and pulled back the goggles, there was no mistaking those distinctive bulging eyes.

'Dustin,' said Sally when he came closer, shouting over the wind, 'what are you doing here?'

'Just want to have a quick chat, if you have a minute. Want to get your advice about something.'

He gestured towards the Hägg, and they hopped into the front cabin, slamming the doors against the cold and the breeze.

Out of the weather, Dustin looked steely-eyed and thoughtful, like he had something on his mind. 'It's about Nick,' he said.

'Kit would like me to make a statement about him to the federal police, in my capacity as Antarctic medical practitioner. And the truth is, I don't want to.' He paused before recounting Kit's reasons for suspecting Nick of faked memory loss.

Sally shook her head. 'I'm sorry,' she said, her brow crinkled in confusion, 'I don't understand why you've come to me. I understand why you don't want to report Nick—we have to live with him over the winter, and a formal report would make for bad blood. Plus, if Nick *is* hiding something, I'm not sure the police can do anything about it via a long-distance interrogation.' She shook her head and glanced at Dustin, who was sitting stiffly in the driver's seat. 'But surely Bill is the person you should be speaking to. He must know what procedures are in place to deal with any potential crime . . . or, or, you know, *whatever.*' Sally didn't want to say 'terrorism', because it would sound preposterous. 'Bill could advise you about proper station procedure for these things.'

'Oh, but I haven't come to ask you about "proper station procedures",' said Dustin with an edge to his voice. 'I want you to make Kit *change her mind.*'

'Oh,' said Sally, laughing involuntarily. 'Well, you should have let me know—I would have told you not to waste your time. No one changes Kit's mind, Dustin. She gets these ideas in her head and becomes rather bloody-minded about them. She gets this kind of moral outrage. Sometimes it's a really good thing—it makes her a strong person. I think it led her to find Nick on the *Petrel.* She wanted to do the right thing when everyone else just wanted to leave the ship.'

Sally was surprised to see Dustin seethe with frustration. 'That's just what I don't want to live with!' he fumed, thumping the steering wheel, his face red. 'I don't want to be *stuck* here for the winter with her second-guessing every decision, *doubting* me, making me doubt myself and undermining my standing as a medical professional.

All because she has a propensity towards … *moral outrage.*' He paused, breathing heavily, and took a moment to calm himself. 'I would like her to respect my decisions,' he said in a quieter voice. 'I would like her to respect *me*. You're her friend, Sally—she'll listen to you.'

Sally frowned. It was unlike Dustin to be so ill-tempered.

'Couldn't you talk to her and bring her around to our way of thinking about this? Couldn't you make her see reason, so that we can all live together harmoniously here for the duration of the winter?'

For a few seconds Sally just looked quizzically at Dustin, and he averted his gaze, clenching his jaw and clutching the wheel.

'No,' she said. Before he could thump the wheel again, she added, 'There's another solution. You could talk to Nick, mention the inconsistencies in his behaviour and urge him to get in touch with the police about what he knows, *if* he knows anything.'

'I doubt that's going to satisfy Kit.'

'But it's a good place to start. Open communication is the key to good relations, you know—you told us that at the pre-departure briefing. Talk to Nick, as his doctor and his friend, and urge him to come clean. Tell him you have doubts about his amnesia that might prompt you to report his bizarre behaviour to the Division—and, as a last resort, to the police. See what he says.'

Dustin sighed. The wind pushed against the side of the Hägg, rocking the vehicle to-and-fro. 'I just want . . .' he began croakily. 'I just want everyone to get along. I wanted this expedition to go smoothly this winter. I had great hopes that it would. I thought we could avoid any . . . emotions.'

Sally found the sentiment odd. In her view, emotions were a good thing, provided they were appropriate to the circumstances. A life void of emotion sounded like a bland, bloodless existence. Outwardly, she smiled at Dustin; inwardly, she was repelled.

With his mouth downturned and his jaw clenched, he was the caricature of a man who resented being challenged by women.

As he pondered her advice, his face appeared to relax, and Sally was relieved that, by the time he left, he seemed mildly cheerful. She said she might join him at the bar later that afternoon.

Once he was gone, she found it difficult to recover her momentum. She regretted sending Kit on ahead of her—she needed some extra help packing up the gear, and it took her much longer than anticipated. With the wind gusts and the snowdrifts coming in, it was tiring work.

Finally, Sally shut the boot of the trailer and hopped into the seat of the Ski-Doo. Visibility was still fair enough that she knew she could make it back to the station if she hurried. But the black clouds gathering on the horizon made her uneasy. She decided to take the short cut instead. It was an icy treacherous route, pitted with small to medium-sized crevasses, but it would cut her journey by half. She didn't like the idea of getting stuck in a blizzard out in the field; she was willing to take the risk.

Twenty minutes into the return trip, Sally realised what an idiotic decision she'd made. On the lookout for crevasses, she had to be so cautious that the journey was taking her much longer than the usual track. The Ski-Doo crawled along, and she often had to turn back up a path and start again. Traversing the crevasse field was like traversing a maze.

At one point, Sally had to get off the Ski-Doo to drag it out of a hole. The vehicle was tilted into a shallow ridge about half a metre deep. She had headed for the ridge in order to avoid a small crevasse—she hadn't realised that the ridge itself posed an obstacle.

As she stumbled in the snow, Sally's first push only wedged the Ski-Doo deeper into the divide. Her second push saw the vehicle topple over.

Then, nightmarishly, it disappeared.

One moment it was there, exposing its mechanical underbelly to her exasperated gaze. The next it was gone, swallowed into a yawning pit of snow and ice.

By the time she realised that she was standing on the weakened snow bridge of a crevasse, the trailer had gone as well, landing on top of the Ski-Doo with a dull crunch. She sprang out of the way just as the bridge crumbled beneath her feet.

Panting in shock, she used the surge of adrenalin to rush over and grab her survival bag from the jutting edge of the trailer. It was a rash move—soon after, the trailer plunged even further, taking the surrounding area along with it—but that quick snatch saved her life. The radio and the emergency beacon were in the front part of the Ski-Doo, wedged into the crevasse with the trailer on top: irretrievable.

She had no means of informing anyone of her predicament. And so she would have to spend the night out in a blizzard, alone.

Her memory of the next twelve to twenty-four hours was patchy and fragmented. She hadn't slept—she remembered that. She'd spent a terrifying night on her back with her feet and legs pushed up against the wall of the tent to stop it from coming unstuck and blowing away, sending her tumbling across the snowfield into a crevasse. All night long, the wind wailed and screamed, repeatedly coming back to vent its grief on Sally, pummelling and pushing and dragging at the tent.

In the early hours of morning, she couldn't even be sure she was inside a tent. It felt like some claustrophobic pocket of hell, a special place of torment.

She didn't notice when the wind died down. At that stage, she later reflected, she must have fallen unconscious: once her mind had registered that the danger had passed, it shut down. She couldn't be sure how long she slept, but she suspected it was for most of the day.

When she emerged, the afternoon sun was low in the sky. Her tent was covered in snowdrift, making it difficult to get out, and the landscape was scoured by the wind, a raw expanse of hard icy snow. In the hope of spotting a search party, she pulled out her compass and decided to do a quick square search of the surrounding area. Heading upwind, she slipped and stumbled as she took thirty halting steps away from the tent. Then she turned on a right angle and walked the same number of paces in the other direction, and then so on and so on, until she was safely back at the tent. She repeated the search, heading downwind this time, but still she saw nothing and no one. Until dark, she walked a number of larger squares, then she crawled back inside the tent and passed out cold.

The next day, Sally awoke to a world of panic. Her mind was a mess: she couldn't concentrate and felt like she was going mad, she was dazed and disoriented, and she couldn't stop shivering.

She cried out in terror. She pulled at her face and hair. She wept uncontrollably.

There was only one explanation, she realised: the blizzard had broken her. She had lost her mind to the wind. *What the wind gets, the wind keeps*, she thought.

•

Sally didn't find the *Petrel's* advance party—they found her. She wasn't surprised to see them, a motley band of three people coming towards her out of the morning mist. She had been doing one of her square searches when someone called out. She looked up, and there they were. She didn't wonder who they were or why they were there—she just accepted their presence, like the presence of the penguins and the icefloes. Of course they were there.

Here are more people come to join me, she thought. *Welcome, friends. Welcome to hell.*

36

Despite her own fugue state, Marion knew there was something wrong with the woman the moment she saw her. The strange figure came lurching down the slope, stumbling and limping across the wind-carved sastrugi like a zombie.

When Curly shouted, 'Hey!' the woman looked up but barely acknowledged the salutation. She did, however, make a change in direction and lurch over to the trio. 'Hey there!' Curly called again.

Marion's heart was in her throat as she lost hope that here was someone who could help them.

'Are you okay?' asked Curly.

As the stranger came closer, she pulled off her face mask and shouted something back, something apologetic. When she was only a short distance away, they could hear the shrillness in her voice. 'Sorry, but I think the wind has blown my mind,' said the woman with a lost, wretched look. 'It's gone, it's gone.'

The three of them gathered around her, and Curly made her sit down and take a few deep breaths. Zhao got her some water from his pack, while Marion fetched frozen seal meat.

She said that her name was Sally and that she was based at Macpherson. She kept babbling about a radio and an emergency beacon stuck in a crevasse. They had to walk in a square pattern, she told them, 'Keep walking in a square-shaped pattern, and you'll find it.' She made a frantic arm-waving gesture and went to stand up, but they told her to stay still, that she needed some rest— she was exhausted.

Once Sally calmed down, draped in the cold solace of Marion's space blanket, the advance party gave each other gloomy looks. It was a bitter disappointment that their first hoped-for saviour was in worse shape than themselves.

A few hours later, they found the Ski-Doo. Just as Sally had said, it was at the bottom of a large crevasse with a light trailer piled on top.

It was Curly who went down into the pit to set off the emergency beacon and retrieve the radio. He risked his life doing it, but after forty-four days in the great white, he said, he was willing to risk everything.

He looked at Marion as he said it.

•

Later, as they waited for help to arrive, the two of them sat together while Sally and Zhao slept in Sally's tent. Marion thought that Curly might have nodded off, when his voice broke in upon her thoughts. 'You know I would do anything for you, Marion.'

Unnerved by the seriousness of his tone, she remained silent, hoping he'd think she'd gone to sleep.

But he was undeterred. 'I've already done things for you. I would do more for you, if you asked me.'

Her stomach churned. This was no declaration of undying friendship: it was something more. She recalled how Curly had looked at Zhao on the trek, and the way he'd pushed back against

Thorn on the ice. Was that all for her benefit, she wondered? Had he been resentful because she'd shown them some attention?

She was glad that the darkness cloaked what must have been a look of pained confusion. Her brain scrambled to make sense of what he was saying. With a nervous laugh, she murmured, 'I never did thank you for shooting that leopard seal, Curls.'

He hesitated. 'That's not what I meant.'

Jesus. What has he done for me?

She squeezed her eyes shut, willing him to get to the point.

And then, as if Curly had heard her unspoken thought, he whispered into the darkness: 'I know what you did. I know what you did on the ship, Marion—and I don't care.'

Her stomach dropped, and her breath caught in her throat. Still, she didn't say anything as she wondered, *How much does he know?*

When he reached out, saying her name quietly, she took his gloved hand and held it in her own, her shoulders stiffening.

•

The memory of that day often came back to Marion like a half-recollected nightmare.

Still in shock from seeing Jason's body, she had desperately searched the *Petrel* for Nick. She was beside herself. It didn't occur to her to sound the alarm, or to report Jason's death, or to inform the captain. Instead, racked with gasping sobs, she had gone to hammer on Nick's cabin door.

'Nick!' she screamed. When he didn't answer, her feet carried her up and down the levels of the ship, to different corridors and sections, both inside and out.

The alarm for muster sounded as she returned to his room. She cried out in despair—she'd lost her chance! But while the crew were filing out of the mess and into the corridors, she spotted Nick.

His face stood out above the others, and she could see he was heading towards the mess, not away from it. Incongruously, she noticed, he was wearing extreme cold weather gear, a sure sign he'd just been outside.

It has to be him, she thought when she saw the clothing. *It has to be.*

She had known it, deep in her heart. Nick had killed Jason.

In the galley she found Nick washing his hands at the sink, with the top layer of his suit peeled down. He didn't notice her over the noise of the running water. Moving towards him, she grabbed a still-warm skillet from the stovetop.

He was just turning around when she hit him. She hit him once on top of the head. Then she hit him with all her might on the side of his face, and he crashed to the floor.

Right there and then, Marion had an urge to smash his head in with the frying pan till it was a bloodied gory mess.

But she couldn't do it. She didn't have the stomach.

And so she wreaked havoc in the kitchen instead, screaming and yelling, wielding the skillet like a sledgehammer. She turned over boxes of onions and potatoes, and knocked crockery and stainless-steel bowls off the benchtops. She put holes in the wall. Once her wrath was spent, she stood panting and sobbing, her face contorted with grief.

The muster alarm still sounded through the speakers, loud and incessant, calling everyone out onto the deck. The smell of kerosene and smoke could be detected in the air.

Emerging from her daze, she looked at the floor and saw that Nick was still lying there, face down. In a panic, she realised that she needed to tie him up or lock him away. If he regained con-sciousness, she'd be unable to take him on alone.

Then she noticed the coolroom door and knew what she had to do.

She rolled Nick onto his back, picked up his ankles and tucked them under her arms. It was a difficult job—he weighed a tonne—but she was strong and used her leg muscles to heave his body. She leaned her weight backwards, then pushed her feet along the ground until his body slid. At one point, she had to stop and remove an annoying slip mat beneath his head; it only made her job harder, trying to drag the mat along with him. She flung the bloodied mat into a corner of the kitchen.

Finally, with a heavy thud, she dropped Nick's legs onto the coolroom floor. She shut the door and locked it. And then, for good measure, she hit the handle with the skillet. With some satisfaction, she noticed that the handle was bent at an ugly angle. Nick couldn't get out, and nobody could get in. Her job was done.

She needed to go back to her cabin for the survival kit, and join the others outside. The smell of smoke was becoming stronger, more palpable. The alarm had ceased. She moaned and groaned as she ran through the empty mess and upstairs.

Once outside, she held her breath and tried to swallow her sobs. Curly was there at the muster site, looking keenly at her. He came over and held her hand when Jason and Nick were declared missing. Almost instantly, she was overwhelmed by guilt for what she had done. She'd intended to imprison Nick in the galley until she could tell someone about Jason's death. But then the fire had taken hold—and, she soon realised, she had effectively killed him. In a grief-stricken fit of rage, she had condemned Nick to die. Shocked by her own brutality, she couldn't tell anyone what had happened, not even Curly.

Now she realised that he must have come searching for her. Maybe he'd even seen her dragging Nick across the galley.

Seated next to Curly in the gloom, Marion looked to the heavens in dismay.

•

Early the next day, two Hägglunds appeared on the horizon, snaking along the crevasse field at a slow pace. It was the rescue party from Macpherson, come to collect them before retrieving the *Petrel* crew.

Zhao ran to greet the vehicles, his smile stretched across his face. He held out his arms as if he intended to hug the first vehicle, a blue Hägg, which stopped nearby.

When the driver stepped down from his seat, Marion recognised him straight away. He was clean-shaven with his overgrown hair flicked back, but there could be no mistake. As Zhao cheered to see a familiar face, her heart stalled in her chest. She stood staring at the man, her mouth open. She couldn't believe it.

Her rescuer, her longed-for saviour, was Nick Coltheart.

37

The *Petrel* crew were in a terribly weakened state. Despite their grateful smiles and cheerful banter, Kit's preliminary assessments revealed many problems—albeit only temporary ones. For several weeks, the group had lived from day to day in sodden clothing. During daylight hours, at sub-zero temperatures, they had never had the chance—or the inclination—to take off their clothes. At night, they had climbed fully dressed into wet sleeping bags. Although they managed to attain a kind of warmth, it was always a wet warmth. And so, when many crew members finally shed their clothing, they also shed layers of skin. It sloughed off them in pale sheets like waxed parchment. Sometimes the tissue was necrosed and black. On their torsos and legs, a number of crew members had nasty sores, red and raised and tender to the touch. All of them were ragged and thin, their faces gaunt and drawn. Many of them were suffering from frostnip or early-stage frostbite. Some of them, unable to take their usual medications, were experiencing the effects of high blood pressure or something similar.

Nevertheless, Kit was reminded of Darwin's observation about species on the frozen continent. They lived in Antarctica, he said, because they had perfected all those exquisite adaptations to the harsh conditions of life. The *Petrel* crew seemed to have adapted, while her own colleagues weren't faring so well. Nearly all the stationers were confined to their dongas: feverish, anxious and confused. Upon arrival at the base, Sally had gone straight to bed and slept for a full twenty-four hours; fretting and clinging to Kit, she hadn't seemed like herself either. Thankfully, the *Petrel* crew showed no signs of similar mental illness.

As the only expeditioners in good health, Kit and Nick held a teleconference with the Division to work out how to proceed. A flood of family members and officials wanted to speak with the *Petrel* crew as soon as possible, and journalists were seeking comments, interviews and photographs for public distribution. The Division organised a liaison team at their end to provide a formal statement, to take phone calls, and to respond to requests. Kit and Nick were tasked with the immediate care of survivors: getting them fed and hydrated, finding them warm clothing, and putting them to bed. Kit attended to the crew's physical and medical needs, while Nick prepared the dongas and gathered clean thermals and track suits. They worked tirelessly throughout the day and fell asleep next to each other on lounge chairs in the mess.

Early the next morning, Kit searched the bookshelves in the surgery, wondering what the cause of the Macpherson epidemic could be. She was about to pull a diagnostic manual off the shelf, when out in the hallway an alarm sounded from one of the speakers.

Alarms were frequent occurrences at Macpherson. During a snowstorm or even just on a high-wind day, several alarms would be accidentally triggered, calling someone out into the cold. But sometimes an alarm indicated that something was genuinely wrong.

When Kit discovered that this alarm was for the melt bell, a matching note of concern sounded in her head. Amid the excitement of Sal's radio call and the subsequent rescue effort, Nick hadn't had time to visit the location to see what Blondie had done to the water supply. Apparently there was now an issue with the melt bell water circuit, meaning that the station's supply could dry up in only a few days. Someone would have to go up to the melt lake area, just above the Red Shed, and take a look.

She found Nick alone in the mess, finishing off a makeshift breakfast.

'Could you take a look?' she asked, slipping beside him and glancing towards the loudspeaker.

'The melt bell, is it?'

'Yes.'

'I was afraid that might be it,' he said, swilling the remains of his coffee. 'Sure. I'm no tradie, but I've done some work with bore pumps. I'll go and have a look. If the problem is urgent and requires a sparkie or a plumber, I'll come back and see if I can rouse one of the others.' Blondie, Warren and their fellow tradies were still in a rather poor state in their bedrooms. The *Petrel* crew were likewise incapacitated; Kit had prescribed them some much-needed rest.

As Nick stood up to leave, Kit placed a restraining hand on his arm. Their eyes met, and her heart quickened at the look he gave her. 'Take someone with you,' she said, aware that the thin ice around the water supply area could be slippery and dangerous. It was no place to go alone.

At that point, one of the *Petrel* crew, a short bald man, appeared in the doorway. 'I'll come, Nick,' he said.

Nick glanced over and nodded in appreciation. 'Okay. Thanks, Curly.' When Kit heard the familiar name, she looked at the man with interest. She recalled he was the team leader who hadn't wanted to report the plane crash. 'Just give me half an hour to get ready,' said Nick.

As he headed out of the mess, only Kit caught the flash of annoyance on his face.

38

Marion had known Nick for more than three years but had rarely seen him without a beard or without a cigarette dangling from his mouth. When their Hägg had reached the *Petrel* crew, however, everyone had recognised him straight away. As he stepped down from the vehicle, there were thunderous cheers and cries of 'Nick!' before everyone moved forward to shake his hand and slap him on the back. He held out his arms like a windswept Jesus, a bottle of water in each palm.

On the ride back to Macpherson, they all wanted to know where Nick had been, how he'd escaped the *Petrel* and ended up at the station. He told them he'd been found in the coolroom, but he couldn't recall many details from the day of the fire. The last thing he remembered, he said, was talking with Jason on deck.

Seated at the rear of the Hägg, Marion sighed with relief. Until then, she'd hung back and held her breath, waiting for Nick to expose her. She was afraid he might have seen her before she hit him. But now she had some time to ponder her next move, and she needed to proceed with caution.

Her first instinct was to talk to Curly. She recalled their conversation of the night before. *I would do anything for you*, he'd said. She still didn't know what he'd meant, but she needed an ally— someone she could trust—and he had offered to help. She asked him to come to her room the next morning.

At the station, Marion slept a full twelve hours and could have slept another twelve, when Curly knocked at her door. He'd brought her a steaming cup of coffee. She took it gratefully with one hand and pulled him inside. 'I want to talk to you.'

'Okay, but I'm heading up to the melt bell,' he announced.

'What for?' She was surprised that he had the energy to wander about. Her own arms and legs had seized up overnight, as if her body had waited to be rescued before it fell apart.

'Nick needs someone to accompany him, to check the alarm.'

'Nick?' she replied with concern. 'You're going with *Nick*?'

Curly flicked her a questioning look. 'Do you have a problem with him?'

She laughed sadly. 'You could say that,' she said, moving away from him. She seated herself at the head of the bed, leaning her aching body against the pillows.

He shut the door. 'What is it?'

She stared into her coffee. 'Something . . . something happened . . . on the *Petrel*,' she began. 'Nick can't be trusted. He's *not* to be trusted.'

Marion looked into Curly's eyes. It had been difficult to communicate out on the ice, in balaclavas and face masks and goggles. Now that she could see the open care and concern in his eyes, it emboldened her to say more.

She took a deep breath. 'He's a killer, Curly,' she said, tears brimming in her eyes. 'He killed Jason.'

Curly's reaction resembled the sudden shutdown of an old television set. She could see his focus contract like a pinprick of light on a black backdrop: *Nick killed Jason.* Curly jerked his head back and frowned.

His next reaction was unexpected: he laughed. At first, he chuckled with irony, shaking his head and looking up at the ceiling. 'Yeah, right.' Then his laugh turned bitter, and he paced the room with his arms folded.

'It's true, Curly, you have to believe me,' she said, her chin quivering. 'When Jason didn't come to breakfast that day, the day of the fire, I went looking for him. I found his body on deck—he'd been shot in the head.' She wiped a tear away with her sleeve. 'He and Nick had been arguing about something they'd found out in the field. Nick wanted to tell the press, to report it to the public. But Jason didn't want to. And then I found him . . .'

Curly ceased his pacing and grew serious. 'What did Nick want to tell the press?' he asked, a muscle tightening in his jaw.

'I don't know,' she said, perplexed. 'Does it matter? He killed Jason.'

Curly gazed at her again. But this time, there was something else in his eyes—something black. 'Marion, I know what happened to Jason. Nick didn't kill him.'

'What?' She spilt some coffee on the bedcovers and set the cup on the bedside table. 'Who did?' she asked, wiping at the stain with her hands.

'Marion, it was you.'

Her hands stopped moving, and her shoulders tensed. After a brief pause, she managed to find her voice. 'Are you insane?' she said, scowling at him. 'I loved Jason.'

'Marion, you can stop pretending. *I know.* I heard you arguing with Jason in your cabin that night. I heard him say you didn't speak to him except to start a fight or to complain about something. I heard him say you hadn't been yourself lately.'

'What?' She reeled with confusion before she realised which conversation Curly had overheard. 'We were talking about *Nick* that night. Jason complained that *Nick* was giving him the silent treatment. You misunderstood—we weren't arguing at all.'

Some of the certainty left Curly's face. 'But I looked for you at breakfast the next morning, and Jason wasn't there. You weren't together. I followed you out on deck and saw you come out from behind the fuel tanks—you had the gun *in your hand*, Marion, I saw it. Then I went over, saw him lying there with a head wound and—'

'You're wrong,' she said, shaking her head furiously. 'You've got it all wrong. You have to believe me.' Her heart was pounding.

'Marion, it's okay, I'm here for you. I'm not going to go to the police. I know he must have threatened you. I know you're a good person, and you wouldn't hurt anyone if you weren't compelled to. But you don't need to worry—I've covered your tracks.'

She gaped at him in agonised disbelief.

'At first, I didn't know what to do,' he said. 'I contemplated hauling his body over the rail, but I could see that he'd just be exposed out on the ice. Then I saw the fuel tank close by, so I poured some over the body and set it alight. It didn't work to begin with, but then the flames stayed alive long enough to ignite his protective clothing. I got out of there fast and headed back to my cabin before anyone could see me. I thought the fire would just die out in the cold— I thought the flames would be enough to destroy any forensic evidence and protect you. But ten minutes later, the alarm went off, and we had to leave.' He hesitated, then spoke in a softer tone. 'I burnt the body to protect you, Marion. I did it for you.'

'But I didn't shoot Jason!' she said, shaking her head, tears streaming down her cheeks. A thought occurred to her. 'If I had killed him,' she gasped, 'you would have heard a gunshot. Did you hear one?'

Curly looked baffled. 'No,' he said, 'but it was noisy, and I was wearing headgear.'

'Think about it, Curly: you didn't hear a shot because *I didn't kill him*. He was dead by the time I got there.'

She could see his brain ticking over. She could see him weighing and considering the evidence, deliberating about the most probable explanation. He didn't like to jump to conclusions—it was his nature to look at every angle. As he grappled with the revelation, he stared speechless at the walls.

'You can't trust Nick out there, Curly,' pleaded Marion in a hushed voice. 'Please, don't turn your back on him at the melt bell. I think he might be unstable.' She had a sickening feeling Nick remembered what had happened that day and was only biding his time, waiting for his moment.

Curly nodded, but there was still bewilderment in his eyes.

'Better still, for the sake of everyone here,' she said, 'you should lock Nick in the tankhouse. Then we can tell everyone what he has done and why he needs to be dealt with. We need to take this opportunity, Curly—take him by surprise.'

This suggestion caught Curly's attention, because he snapped out of his trance-like state and turned to her. 'Have you told anyone else about this?'

'No, there was no time.'

'Good,' he said, gripping her by the shoulders. '*Don't* tell anyone. I'll take care of it. And you don't need to worry about me,' he added. 'I can take care of myself.'

'But, Curly, be careful.'

'I will,' he promised, kissing her on the forehead. 'I love you.'

Before she could respond, he turned away. With some relief, she watched his back disappear down the corridor. She was too conflicted to speak.

39

In the surgery, Kit wrapped the inflatable pressure bag around the frail arm of a woman named Beatrice. She was the first patient of the morning, but Kit was already running about half an hour late—she'd been unable to set up the telemedicine link with headquarters. According to her records, prior to the *Petrel* incident Beatrice had been taking medication for mild hypertension. So the first thing Kit did was a routine blood-pressure test.

'I'm sorry you had to wait, Beatrice,' said Kit, pumping the bag full of air.

'Oh, that's okay.'

Kit read out the figures from the sphygmomanometer. 'One hundred and ten over seventy-five. Your blood pressure seems to be okay. Tell me, how did you feel out on the ice without your meds?'

'Well, I've gotta say, I felt pretty anxious a lot of the time. Felt like I was going to have a heart attack or a stroke or something. I could feel the blood rushing, you know—' she gestured towards her fine-boned face '—rushing in my head, making a *swissshhing* noise.'

'I'm not surprised. It would have been a very distressing, very traumatic time for you. I'm so sorry you had to go through that. It sounds like you might have been feeling the effects of sudden withdrawal from your hypertension medication.'

'Yes, I felt all shivery and shaky, like I was sweating icicles or, or . . . coming down from something. I felt like I was going mad.'

'The good news is you seem a lot better now. You're going to be fine.'

Kit went to place the equipment back on the shelf and stopped dead in her tracks. She spun around and looked questioningly at Beatrice. She'd had a fleeting thought, but it had slipped away as quickly as it came.

'What did you say?' asked Kit, trying to bring the thought back.

'There was a swishing noise in my head . . .?'

'No, after that.'

'I felt like I was going crazy . . .?'

Yes, that was it. Kit rushed from the medical suite into Dustin's office.

That morning, when she'd spoken with the Antarctic Division doctor, Kit had told her of the mystery illness at Macpherson. The doctor had raised the possibility of the stationers suffering adverse side effects from prescription drugs. But when she checked the online records, it seemed that the Macpherson stationers were a fairly healthy bunch. While a few of them were taking prescription drugs for contraception, reflux or other minor ailments, no one appeared to be on any particularly strong medicines. And so Kit had dismissed the idea.

But now she found herself revisiting the subject from a different angle. What if *the absence of drugs* was causing the problem? What if, like Beatrice, the Macpherson crew were suffering from withdrawal?

Deep in concentration, Kit searched her mind for a substance that everyone might have taken. 'Oh my God,' she said out loud. *Vitamin D.*

It had to be the vitamin D. Averse to vitamin supplements, Kit had simply not taken her prescribed dose. But for at least twelve months prior to departure, everyone else had been taking cholecalciferol, a form of vitamin D3, on Dustin's strict orders. On base, the others had been taking the pills at breakfast every morning as part of a daily toast. The curious symptoms had started to emerge only after the supplements ran out—the day that Dustin died.

Kit was still puzzled. Surely no one experienced severe withdrawal symptoms from *vitamin D*? It wasn't a drug of dependence.

'Is everything okay?' called Beatrice.

'Yes, everything's fine.'

Kit's eyes fell upon the locked drawer in Dustin's desk. During the inventory, she hadn't been able to open it, so she'd forgotten all about it. Now she eyed it with suspicion. She went over and tugged at the handle. Still it did not open. Searching the other drawer, she found a few bent paperclips. She twisted the first one into a hook shape and poked it into the bottom of the lock. Then she folded out the second paperclip into a straight probe and wedged that into the top part. After a bit of poking and scraping, she heard a satisfying click.

Inside the drawer was an A4-sized notebook, a plastic folder, and Dustin's passport and credit cards. At first glance, nothing jumped out at her. But when she flipped through the notebook, a piece of paper fell on the desk: a spreadsheet containing the name, gender, weight and age of all the winterers at Macpherson, as well as their various medications. The final column recorded a dosage in milligrams. The spreadsheet was headed 'Vitamin D/Clonazepam'.

'Is something wrong?' asked Beatrice in the doorway.

Kit looked up, startled to see the woman was still there. 'Have you heard of clonazepam?'

'Sure, I think so. It's a party drug.'

Rushing back into the other room, Kit turned on her laptop and did a quick search. Clicking on the first website in the list, she discovered that clonazepam was a kind of benzodiazepine, a tranquilliser prescribed to help with anxiety disorders. Under the heading 'Dependence and withdrawal', the website warned that:

Severe withdrawal symptoms may occur if the dose is significantly reduced or suddenly stopped. These symptoms include seizures, irritability, nervousness, sleep disturbance, agitation, tremors, diarrhoea, abdominal cramps, vomiting, memory impairment, headache, muscle pain, extreme anxiety, tension, restlessness, and confusion. Do not suddenly stop taking this medication without consulting with your doctor.

Kit shut the laptop. 'I'm sorry, Beatrice, but I need to cut your consultation short.'

•

Kit walked aimlessly about the Red Shed, turning various black thoughts over and over in her mind. At one point, she wandered over to the nearest window and looked out at the harbour. She gazed at the spot where Dustin had been found—the spot where the vitamin D pills remained, frozen to the sea ice.

Dustin had been so desperate to get the pills back to the Shed that he'd risked his life in the storm. His behaviour had seemed bizarre. The expeditioners knew that the vitamins, together with his dietary advice and various wellbeing activities—the light therapy, the meditation sessions and the planned social events—had been a crucial part of his beloved research project. But surely they weren't worth dying for.

If his note meant what she thought it meant, however, then he'd had a hidden research agenda. For more than twelve months, he'd given the expeditioners a daily dose of anti-anxiety medication to help them cope with the rigours of isolation. He had been using them as guinea pigs. When the dosage had stopped, they'd had a severe physiological reaction.

Macpherson flu wasn't the flu: it was acute withdrawal.

Down below, Kit could see two figures struggling up the hill against the wind. Nick and Curly were heading off to the melt bell together.

Kit didn't know why—it could have been the dismay and distrust she now felt towards Dustin—but she had a sudden sense of dread.

She needed to talk to Nick. But first, she had to see her next patient.

40

At the initial triage meeting, Marion Lovall had indicated that there was nothing wrong with her—but from one look at her face, Kit was inclined to think otherwise. Marion was abnormally pale, with large blue rings beneath her eyes. She looked as though she'd been crying. During the consultation, she spoke in a barely audible voice. She gave single-word answers to nearly every question and wouldn't elaborate unless asked to.

At the end of the visit, Kit watched curiously as Marion pulled her polar-fleece jacket back on. 'Is there anything troubling you?' asked Kit.

Marion hesitated. 'No.' She sighed, slowly pushing her left arm into a bunched-up sleeve.

'It can't have been easy losing a crew member,' Kit said gently, referring to the captain. 'It takes time to recover from seeing a traumatic loss.'

Marion said something under her breath, so quietly that Kit couldn't hear.

'I beg your pardon?' she asked, leaning forward.

'Two,' said Marion.

'I'm sorry?' Kit shook her head in confusion.

'We lost two colleagues.'

'Oh, right, I'm sorry. Of course.'

The stationers had expected—or at least hoped—to find twenty-three members of the *Petrel* crew. Instead they'd found only twenty-one. One had drowned, while the other, according to some reports, had never made it off the ship. He, too, was now presumed dead.

Marion zipped up her jacket and threw Kit an apprehensive glance. 'He was my boyfriend. His name was Jason. He . . . he never made it to the muster.'

'I'm so sorry,' said Kit, starting at another familiar name. 'Do you have any idea why he didn't make it?'

Marion took a great shuddering breath. 'Because . . .' she began, then paused to take a shorter one. 'Because he was dead already,' she said, wiping her eyes.

Something unpleasant stirred deep in Kit's intestines. 'How . . . how do you know that?'

'I saw him,' said Marion. More quietly, she added, 'On the deck—I saw his body on deck. He'd been shot in the head.'

'Do you know who shot him?' Kit had a premonition about what the woman would say next.

'It was Nick—Nick Coltheart, Jason's best friend.'

Kit's blood froze as she struggled to make sense of the words. It couldn't be true—she had to be mistaken. 'Nick? How do you know it was Nick?'

'They'd had an awful fight. And after I found Jason, I saw Nick in his cold weather gear, heading to the galley. I found him there, washing the blood off his hands.'

'Why . . . why have you not told anyone till now?'

'There was no time. The alarm sounded shortly after I found the body—'

'But that was weeks ago,' Kit pointed out. 'Why haven't you told anyone since? We asked the other crew members, and they had no idea what happened to Jason.'

'I was ashamed of what I did, okay?' said Marion, her head bowed low. For a second, Kit thought she might be overwhelmed by emotion. But when she looked up, her face was dry. 'I was angry at Nick. I was so angry, it . . . it . . . it was like something evil inside me, gnawing at me, trying to get out. I had to confront him about what he'd done to Jason, taking his life and ruining everything—ruining *my* life as well. As the ship's alarm sounded, I followed him . . . I hit him . . . and I locked him away.' She paused to take a gasping breath. 'I didn't know we wouldn't be able to return. I thought the fire would be brought under control, that I'd come back with the captain and have Nick arrested. Only later did I realise that I'd condemned him to die. And then I knew I'd gone too far. I'd killed a man. And so I didn't tell anyone. I *couldn't* tell anyone about what I had done—it was too terrible to say out loud.'

'Why are you telling me now?'

Marion's face crumpled. Kit felt as though someone was squeezing her guts in their fists. 'Because I've asked Curly to lock him in the tankhouse.'

Kit rose to her feet in alarm. The woman didn't know about the drilling and the crash site—she was unaware that Curly wasn't a neutral party. If Jason had wanted Nick to keep quiet, then Curly might feel the same way.

Kit had to warn Nick.

41

Nick could feel Curly staring at his back as he made the call to station. 'Yeah, that's right,' he told Prudence on the radio, 'it was just the pump that makes the water circulate in a closed-loop system. Blondie must've turned it off. But we've switched it back on now, and everything should come right over the next twenty-four hours.'

'Might still be worth checking the melt pool, though . . .?' said Prudence with a sniffle. She'd been one of the few winter expeditioners to emerge from their dongas that morning. Though she still suffered from sleeplessness and restless legs, her symptoms weren't especially severe. She'd returned to her job as comms technician, to relay an update on the *Petrel* crew back to headquarters.

'Well, yeah,' said Nick. 'Switching off the pump could have created other problems. Me and Curly are gonna take a look now. We suspect that some water might have iced over at one of the nearby melt pools. If that's the case, then we might need to haul a tradie out of bed, get them to recommend something.'

'Okay then. Take care.'

'Thanks, Prue. Over and out.'

Nick pulled his balaclava over his chin and turned to face Curly. He wasn't surprised when the other man volunteered to help; as their team leader, Curly had always taken a special pride in his problem-solving skills. But over the past few years, their friendship had become strained. Though Curly's full expression was obscured by goggles, Nick could still see the coldness in his eyes. He bore no love for Nick, and Nick bore no love for him. There was much they could have said to one another, but so far they had exchanged few words.

'Let's get this over and done with, shall we?' said Nick, eyeing the clouds on the horizon. From where the men were standing, the sun was bright enough to cast their shadows in sharp outline over the snow. But the sky would soon be dull and grey.

They edged over to a shallow depression in the ground, where the fine white snow had turned to a patch of hardened grey ice. In the middle of the patch was an A-frame winching structure, and lying beneath that was a shiny black platform with a large rectangular opening into the ice. The opening, about the size of a manhole, had an array of wires and hoses snaking out of it. The plan was for Nick to look in the hole and dig about in the ice, to see if he could spot any water.

He pulled a harness over his head and clicked a red safety line onto it, while Curly attached himself to the other end. Then Nick gathered in his arms an array of tools, including an ice-axe and a spade. Throwing a glance over his shoulder, he stepped gingerly out onto the ice sheet. He'd taken only two steps when his feet skidded out from under him, and he landed on his backside, the tools splaying in every direction.

'Shit!' he exclaimed. 'Well,' he added with a laugh, still flailing about, 'at least we know it can hold my weight.'

Curly just dug his heels into the snow and gripped his end of the rope.

Turning onto his stomach, Nick commando-crawled over to the platform with the ice-axe in his hand. Once there, he hauled himself up and took his goggles off to peer into the hole. He began hacking away at the ice, casually throwing chunks out, then digging in further. 'That's good,' he muttered, panting. 'There's definitely water in there,' he called to Curly.

To get a better look, Nick fumbled about behind him for the spade. His hands had almost grasped the object, when Curly called out to him over the wind.

'Nick!' yelled Curly. 'Nick, I want you to do something.'

Puzzled, Nick craned his head and turned around, moving awkwardly onto his side on the ice. The glare of the sun and the snow assaulted his eyes, making him squint in pain. He shaded his face with gloved hands. Curly stood only a few metres away, but Nick couldn't see him. The tone of Curly's command rang an alarm. Something was wrong.

With some trepidation, he half sat up on his side. 'What?' he called back.

'Nick,' came Curly's voice again, steelier this time. 'Stand up and get in the hole.'

Nick's stomach muscles tightened. 'Get in the what . . .?'

Curly came closer to the ice, close enough for Nick to see the gun. Nick pulled back in surprise. 'Whoa!' he said, holding up his hands. 'What are you doing, mate?'

'I know!' shouted Curly. 'I know you killed Jason, and I know you're going to go to the press about the drilling and the British plane. Now get in the hole, or I'm going to shoot you, Nick.'

'Listen, can't we talk about this . . .?'

'You talk too much, Nick,' said Curly, shaking his head.

'I don't think I'm gonna fit in there . . .' Nick peered anxiously at the opening and then back at Curly. His hand tightened reflexively around the handle of the ice-axe.

'Get in the hole.'

Inching towards the gap, Nick looked back at Curly again, his mind ticking over. 'Hey, Curly,' he said, speaking before the man could interrupt, 'remember that story about Shackleton and the crossing of South Georgia? When his crew had just spent a year on the ice?' Desperate to distract him, Nick alluded to Curly's favourite tale of Antarctic survival. 'They'd sailed ahead to get help, but the boat landed on the wrong side of the island, so they had to climb a mountain to get help. Three of them trekked to the top and then realised the sun was about to go down.' Nick placed his boots tentatively in the opening and paused to regain his breath. His heart pounded in his ears.

Curly stared at him with blank indifference, as though daring him to make a wrong move.

'They couldn't stay where they were, because they'd die from the cold,' said Nick, shooting another wary glance at the hole. 'But they couldn't trek down the slope, it'd be too dangerous in the dark. So, after a while, Shackleton made a decision: "We can't stay here," he said. And so they sat on their backsides and slid down the precipice together—about a thousand feet in only a few minutes—all the way to the bottom. They had no choice.'

The other man sighed and rolled his eyes. 'For fuck's sake, Nick—'

'That's what happened to me, Curly. *I had no other option.*' He gasped for breath. 'After that summer, I couldn't go backwards, I couldn't go forwards, and I sure as hell couldn't stay where I was.' Curly took a menacing step towards him. 'But I haven't told anyone *anything,*' said Nick hurriedly. 'I've kept my mouth shut. I don't know what Jason told you, but you really don't have to do this. No one knows what we did—not yet.'

'But Nick, you've left *me* no choice.' Curly fired the gun at a patch of ice near the platform. The ice exploded into a riot of shards, and the shot rang out across the plateau. 'Shut the fuck up and get in the water!'

'Okay, okay!'

In a panic, Nick dropped the axe and lowered himself into the icy melt pool, catching his breath in shock. The pain was like a heart attack, a fierce stabbing to the chest. He clung to the side of the platform, with his head still out.

Curly came right up to Nick and pointed the gun at his temple. Bending down, he detached the other end of the rope from Nick's harness. 'Now let go.'

But Nick wouldn't let go. A bullet to the brain would be merciful compared to the horror of drowning. Despite the piercing cold, he held on for dear life.

'Let go!' yelled Curly, enraged.

But still Nick hung on.

For a moment, Curly seemed intent on shooting Nick then and there. But Nick's death would be easier to explain if he wasn't found with a bullet wound. So Curly contented himself with stomping on Nick's hands with his thick snow boots.

The crunching blow was too much. Finally, Nick let go.

Then Curly stepped away and kicked at the platform until it covered the gap.

As he heard Curly move away, Nick frantically trod water, the adrenalin keeping his legs pumping while his mind scrambled for solutions. His arms grappled for the cables and hoses at the side of the hole. He cried out for help, thinking of Kit in the medical suite, and the winterers and the *Petrel* crew in their dongas. But of course, they were too far away.

He was all out of options.

42

Kit heard the shot ring out as she was starting up the quad bike. At first, she couldn't be sure, but a mounting sense of unease made her fear the worst. Barely pausing to zip up her coat and pull on her ski goggles, she rode the quad out of the shed and sped up the slope. The wind pulled at her hood, making a furious noise in her ears that matched the tempest in her head.

She knew that Nick and Curly were going to the nearest melt pool, to check on the water. So she headed there, scanning the snowfields for their distinctive red coats.

On the way, she stopped the quad to pick up a small pile of rope at the side of the tankhouse steps. It looked as though it had been abandoned there recently—it was on top of the snow. Frowning, she coiled the rope around her hand and wondered if Curly might have already locked Nick in the tankhouse. She sauntered up the steps and opened the door to the big green building. 'Hello!' she called out.

The heated tanks hummed in the gloom. For one moment, she thought she heard breathing, but when she looked about, no one was there. Her anxiety grew. There was no one up the hill, there was no one in the tankhouse. Where were they?

Troubled, Kit jumped back on the quad and headed further up the slope. She made a beeline for the only human-made object in her line of sight: a flimsy-looking aluminium structure erected over an amorphous patch of ice. She assumed that this must be a melt pool, though she'd never seen one before.

As she came closer, she spotted a shiny black rectangle positioned in the middle of the ice patch. Stopping the quad a few metres away, she hopped off and moved in for a closer look. The rectangular object was a platform with a hole in the middle. Strangely, the platform was moving up and down—one moment tilting off the ice, the next settling back into place. Squatting down, she contemplated crawling out onto the ice sheet to inspect the hole, but she couldn't be sure the surface would hold her weight.

Kit was still suspended in indecision when a fist punched through the ice near the platform. The gloved hand extended its fingers.

As the platform shifted once again, it revealed an arm grappling underneath the surface. The arm pushed the platform aside.

Then a man called out. 'Help!' he cried. 'Help me!'

Kit gaped at Nick's waving arm in shock and bewilderment. Without another thought, she abandoned all her training and leapt onto the ice. She scuttled and slid clumsily towards the platform and peered into the hole.

About half a metre down, Nick was wedged between two crumbling walls of ice, with his massive legs curled up against his chest. He looked up fearfully at her. 'Kit!' he cried. From the strain on his face, it was clear that it had taken all his strength to remain in place and shift the platform—once he stopped pressing either his back or his heels against the ice walls, Kit realised, he would fall back into the water. In the meantime, the walls appeared to be breaking apart around him.

She didn't try to pull him out. 'Stay there. Don't move!' She wouldn't be any help if she fell through the surface to face her own death in the melt pool.

So she turned on her heels and went to the quad. With trembling hands, she pulled out the safety line and tied a loop in one end, then fastened the other to the quad. Back at the ice sheet, she threw the loop into the hole.

Eventually Nick's hand resurfaced again, this time with the rope looped around his wrist. With Kit acting as an anchor, he began pulling himself up and out of the hole. When he finally emerged, he lay down on the ice, looking exhausted.

'Can you stand up?' She was afraid he'd stick to the surface. 'We've got to get you moving.'

'I think so.' He scrambled onto all fours and she moved in to help him. 'It was Curly,' he panted. 'He has a gun. We need to find him.'

'I know, but first we need to get you inside.' Holding him by the arm, she guided him off the slippery ice sheet.

As they staggered towards the quad, he leaned in close to her ear. 'I thought you were trained not to do that? To come out on the ice?'

She laughed quietly. 'I forgot my training, just for you.'

'I'm glad you did.' He caught her eye. 'Thank you.'

On impulse, she turned and flung her arms about his neck, holding him tight against her. His arms encircled her back, drawing her closer. They held each other until Kit felt him shivering and saw the ice forming on his coat. With some reluctance, she let him go.

As he climbed onto the quad, she gazed at his back, impressed yet again by his strength and endurance. Somehow, despite the odds, he survived.

Her expression darkened when she recalled Marion's words from moments earlier: *I found him there, washing the blood off his hands.*

Some people, thought Kit, only survived at the expense of others. But she shook her head, telling herself Nick wasn't one of them.

43

Marion wished she could ignore the incessant knocking at her door, but she knew it would be Curly returned from the water supply area. She'd hoped to hear the report of what had happened from another expeditioner. But she had set this wheel in motion—she would have to see it full circle. She'd sent Curly up there to bring everything out in the open, once and for all. She would have to humour Curly and hear his account; she would have to speak to him at least one more time.

When Marion opened the door, however, Curly didn't want to talk. 'We have to go,' he said, bursting into the room. 'We have to leave. Quick! Grab your things.'

'What happened?' she asked, sick to her stomach.

'We have to leave.' Curly knelt down and hauled Marion's survival bag out from under the bed. He appeared sweaty and shaky, and his jaw was clenched. 'Do you have a bivvy in here?'

'Yes,' she said, watching him search her belongings. 'But why? Curly, *why*?' When he didn't respond, she spoke his name even louder. 'Curly!' Then she waited till he looked up at her. 'What happened? You have to tell me. Tell me now.'

'It didn't go to plan,' he said, breaking away from her gaze. He kept pulling things out of the bag. 'As I was leaving, I saw someone—a woman, the medical assistant. She rode up to the tankhouse, she went to the melt pool, and she pulled Nick out. I saw them coming back on the quad just then. He's alive, Marion. He's alive, and we have to leave before the whole station knows what happened.'

'*But what happened?*' shrieked Marion. Curly's words sank in, and the realisation dawned on her. Her face froze in horror. 'Curly . . . you didn't—you didn't, did you?'

He looked resigned and unrepentant.

'Please tell me you didn't try to kill Nick . . .?'

He stood up but again didn't respond. He stared at her impassively.

She pummelled his shoulders in rage. 'You idiot! Leave? Leave here? But *where* are we going to go?' she demanded, thumping him with closed fists.

'To Amundsen-Scott,' he responded, naming the closest American station, the Geographic South Pole. He grabbed her hands and held them away from him, as if she were an annoying child.

'But that—that's thousands of miles!' she cried, pulling her hands back. 'You're insane. We'll die, we'll *die* out there!'

'We haven't died yet. But we're going to need more fuel and equipment.' He shook her empty fuel bottle. 'We need to get to the Green Store. Come on.'

Marion took one long hard look at Curly. His primary reflex seemed to be an animalistic instinct for self-preservation. All his motivations and actions—his desire to help her, his concern for her wellbeing—now appeared selfish and possessive. She had thought he was calm and collected; she'd thought he had his emotions under control. But now she was struck by the notion that *there was nothing inside him.* There was nothing to control.

'No,' she said. 'I don't want to go with you. I'm going to stay here and explain what happened. You go, you go and get yourself killed.'

'Marion—'

'Just leave me alone. I don't want to be with you! I don't want to be with you out there alone in the winter darkness.' She shivered. 'I don't want to be with you here either. I don't want to be with you *anywhere*. Just go! Get away from me!'

'Marion,' he said coldly, his eyes black and ruthless, 'you have to come with me, don't you see that?'

44

Kit brought Nick back to the Red Shed and did not leave his side until he was wrapped in blankets with a hot drink in his hands. Then she hurried to the ops building and asked Prudence for her help in accessing the station webcams. The small devices were mounted on metal posts throughout the base and assisted in day-to-day operations by sending video feed to the comms station. Kit had to find Curly, and a scan of webcam images would be speedier than a ground search.

On the screen, Kit was shocked to see Curly dragging Marion by the arm across the gravel path towards the emergency vehicle shelter. The weather had turned nasty—grey clouds had darkened the sky, the wind was sending flurries of snow about the station—and the image was grainy and blurred. But it was clear that Marion was a reluctant participant in whatever Curly had planned.

Kit would have to act quickly. The man had tried to kill Nick, and now he had a potential hostage. She glanced at Prudence, who was seated next to her, frowning in concern at what the camera showed. 'Can you stay here?' asked Kit, her brain whirring at light speed. 'And radio me, straight away, if they come out of the shelter?'

Prudence nodded. 'Sure, take this.' She handed Kit a radio.

Still dressed in her freezer suit, Kit fetched the rifle from the Dog Room, the one that station leaders had used to shoot old dogs. It was unloaded, but it might look intimidating—she could use it to bluff her way through if she had to.

Hurrying out the exit, she jumped on the quad bike, which was parked where she'd left it at the side of the road. The seat was now covered in a fine layer of snow. As she headed past the Shed and up the track, the wind pelted ice at her legs.

Kit rode the quad to the side of the emergency vehicle shelter. The building was in the style of an old fire station, with two entrances at the front and two Hägglunds inside: one for search and rescue, the other for firefighting. The large overhead door to the left was wide open. She grabbed the rifle and jumped off the quad, leaving it deliberately blocking the pathway down the slope. With quiet, tentative footsteps, she headed inside—but, hearing the rumbling of the nearest Hägg engine, she darted into a corner and squatted behind a storage box, praying she hadn't been seen or heard.

The Hägg moved into Kit's line of sight but then stopped at the quad roadblock, just as she'd hoped it would. When Curly got out, she furtively circled around the back of the vehicle to the other side, where she opened the passenger door.

Marion looked down at her in alarm.

Kit placed a finger to her lips, then pulled at Marion's coat, mouthing, 'Come on.'

At that moment, the radio in Kit's pocket sounded, with Prudence's voice buzzing loud and clear: 'Someone's come out!' The comms technician had followed her instructions to the letter.

Kit winced in dismay. Marion stared back at her in naked terror, too frightened to move.

'Keep your head down,' whispered Kit, pushing the woman further inside and shutting the door.

With a deep breath and her shoulders squared, Kit walked out onto the gravel road, the empty rifle in both hands. She gripped the barrel to stop her arms from shaking.

In front of the entrance, Curly had heard the radio call and was on high alert, his eyes scanning the shelter. When she came out of the shadows, he aimed his gun at her. 'Stop right there. Drop the rifle.'

The confidence in his voice turned her bravery to water. She'd been a fool: she should've known an unloaded relic would lose to a loaded handgun any day. He'd called her bluff in an instant.

Kit raised a free hand in the air and lowered the weapon to the ground, her heart beating wildly. 'Don't shoot,' she said, straightening up. 'I'm here to help.'

'Help?' he scoffed.

To her surprise, over Curly's shoulder, she caught sight of a small figure behind the quad. Someone in a red coat had followed her to the shelter. The person scurried out of the mist and was now squatting beside the quad's back wheels. Puzzled about who it could be, Kit strove to keep her face blank and her eyes on Curly.

'You can help by moving this bike,' he snapped, without looking behind him.

'Okay, okay.' She moved forward, desperate to keep his attention on her. The red coat flickered at the corner of her eye. 'Whatever this is, we can work it out. I know you've been through hell, you must be so tired—'

'I'll teach you about hell, lady. Shut up and move it now.' With a frown, he added: 'If you don't, I'll shoot you and move it myself.'

Her stomach plunged at the icy coolness in his voice. She cast a worried look at his face, wondering if he might shoot her anyway. She took a hesitant step.

But then her heart leapt as the coated figure emerged from its hiding place. In a blur of red, the person lunged at Curly.

From where Kit stood, it looked like the figure had punched him on the back. She saw Curly stumble forward and drop the gun, clutching his shoulder. It was only when he turned around that Kit saw the hunting blade sticking out of his coat. Her eyes widened in realisation: he'd been stabbed.

Now facing his attacker, he screamed in rage, 'Beatrice! You fucking bitch!'

It was Kit's patient from earlier that day. Her face was covered, but her gait and build were unmistakable. Beatrice cowered away from him. 'Leave her alone!' the woman cried. 'I heard you drag Marion out here.' She gestured towards the Hägg. 'She doesn't want to go with you, Curly, not this time. Just leave her the fuck alone!'

Curly clutched at his shoulder, unable to reach the knife. He gasped in pain, his face contorted.

'I'm sick of you men pushing us around and doing whatever you like,' said Beatrice, a tremor in her voice.

Holding her breath, Kit rushed to kick the handgun away. It went spinning over the gravel path, coming to a stop near Beatrice's feet, only metres from Curly.

There was a long, nerve-racking silence as the man contemplated his options. He stared at the weapon next to Beatrice's boot, then turned and glanced at the rifle, before spying Marion behind the wheel of the idling Hägg. His neck stiffened when Marion revved the engine and he realised she was prepared to run him down. She stared back at him from the driver's seat, her hands gripping the wheel. He blinked several times, seemingly in disbelief. When he turned back, Beatrice had picked up the handgun.

Kit saw his confidence wane and seized her chance. She retrieved the rifle from the ground. 'You should go now, Curly,' she yelled, pointing the empty weapon at him. 'You're not welcome here. Just go.'

In frustration, he released a ragged gust of air from his lungs. Still clutching his shoulder in pain, he swivelled around until his gaze fell upon the quad. His decision was made in seconds. With the knife protruding from his back, he jumped onto the seat and started the engine. Throwing one last look at Marion, he gunned the bike down the road.

As Curly disappeared towards the west arm, Beatrice dropped the gun and collapsed to her knees. Kit went to her, while Marion climbed down from the Hägg.

The trio came together in the cold, offering words of comfort and support. 'We're going to be okay,' said Kit, placing an arm around each woman. 'He's gone now.'

She breathed easier when the roar of the engine grew faint in the distance, confirming that Curly had left the base.

45

Three weeks later Blondie and Bill stumbled across Curly's lifeless body near a drum line off station; it appeared that gale-force winds had blown the quad on top of him.

'His legs were pinned beneath the weight of the engine,' said Sally when she brought the news to Kit. 'I even feel a bit sorry for him, despite the fact he tried to kill Nick and kidnap Marion, and then threatened to shoot you.' Sally paused and looked thoughtful for a second. 'Actually, no,' she decided. 'I don't feel that sorry for him.'

Kit was pleased to hear Sally sounding more like herself. She hugged her friend, grateful that she hadn't met a similar fate out in the cold.

Shortly after Sally was found, Kit informed her about Dustin's private research project, and she had volunteered to go back on a low dose of clonazepam, to wean herself off the pills. Luckily, they had found a few spare boxes hidden away in the Green Store. Others had followed a similar course, but Sally now seemed the most laid-back of them all. She said that she barely even harboured any resentment towards Dustin—yet she was one of the few who had read his private notes and knew the extent of his disturbing thoughts.

In the notebook, Dustin had kept careful track of all his unsuspecting patients. He had recorded their drug dosages, blood and urine tests, blood-pressure results, and certain aspects of their social behaviour. His hard drive contained documents on the disharmonious social relations of extremely isolated communities. Convinced that such relations could be improved by anti-anxiety drugs, Dustin had planned to present his findings to NASA—despite his glaring lack of ethics approval.

Dustin's notes also charted his own troubling decline following the suicide of his friend Eddy, a former expeditioner. In his journal, Dustin lamented the fact that Eddy had never been properly diagnosed for depression and had resisted seeing a doctor, out of fear of being stigmatised as mentally ill. Dustin regretted that he hadn't talked to Eddy more and convinced him of the benefits of medication. This loss had weighed on his mind during his time at Macpherson, as he was continually reminded of their expedition together. His research gave him some comfort because he believed it would spare others the anguish that Eddy and his family had gone through.

Of course, the expeditioners were understandably outraged. They'd been used by their trusted doctor and polluted by drugs without their consent. But it wasn't long before Sally told Kit she'd let her anger go, as Dustin couldn't be brought back to be punished. She wanted to get on with her life instead.

Kit hoped that she could do the same.

•

Later that day, Kit sat with Nick on a couch in the library. They were alone, and he was leaning up against her with one hand lying lazily across her thigh, warm and comforting. After several nights in his arms, she'd grown used to his presence, but the touch of his fingers still sent ripples through her skin.

She had come to the library to check her email, knowing that her inbox would have a message from Elliot's lawyers. She'd finally agreed to a settlement date but was in no hurry to read their response.

She'd been surprised to enter the room and find Nick there.

As they sat together on the couch, he asked, 'And how is Marion?' He was aware that his colleague was not doing well; she'd been suffering from flashbacks and frequent bouts of crying. The doctors at head office were concerned she had severe post-traumatic stress disorder.

Kit had just sat in on a telemedicine session with Marion and a counsellor. 'She'll be okay,' said Kit, without divulging any details. She'd been relieved to find that Marion had a strong supportive family back home. Her mother had come to the session and offered to check in regularly.

Soon after Curly's dramatic departure, Nick had struck up a truce with Marion. She confessed that she'd blamed him for Jason's death and locked him in the coolroom in a thoughtless act of rage. She was genuinely sorry—she'd been overcome by grief, she said, and hadn't known what she was doing. Nick had forgiven her, and he'd explained exactly what he and Jason had been arguing about.

As he told Kit later, he'd confessed to Marion about the unauthorised drilling venture, and admitted they'd found the crash site but failed to report it. Since then, Kit had informed the proper authorities and the victims' families were notified. They planned to recover the body in the crevasse, but its retrieval would have to wait till summer. Nick would face disciplinary measures, but they were yet to be specified, and would have to wait till summer too.

He still claimed to have no memory of what had happened to Jason, and the unexplained death weighed on Marion's mind.

At the counselling session, she'd told Kit, 'I lie awake wondering if Jason took his own life. You know—' her voice trembled '—his reputation as a geophysicist was everything to him. If he couldn't work in Antarctica, if he'd been blacklisted, he couldn't have worked anywhere, really. That might have pushed him to the edge . . .'

As Kit sat with Nick on the couch, she turned the possibility over in her mind. 'Do you think Jason could have committed suicide?' she asked Nick.

Looking away, he gazed at the wall and exhaled thoughtfully. 'No.'

'But your threat to expose him might have panicked him into self-harm.'

Nick didn't speak. The silence dragged on, until finally he said, 'I know that Jason didn't kill himself.'

'How can you possibly know that?'

'I know,' he breathed out, 'because I killed him.'

Kit was stunned. His brown eyes penetrated hers as though daring her to believe him. She withdrew from his touch by sitting upright on the couch. 'But how . . .?'

'It was an accident. Jason asked me to meet him before breakfast and ambushed me. He told me to jump onto the ice sheet or he'd shoot me. I tried to wrestle the gun off him, and he squeezed the trigger. It happened so quickly, I didn't even realise why Jason had dropped to the ground. The noise sounded like the cracking of ice or the calving of a berg. I grabbed him by the chest and shook him, then I noticed his head . . . and the blood.' Nick's shoulders trembled, and he swallowed hard. Then he spoke in a clearer voice. 'I couldn't tell Marion, not after we'd made our peace. I'll let her know—and the federal police—once the supply ship comes in November. I promise.'

A hard knot formed in the pit of Kit's stomach. She knew he was telling the truth: the pain in his eyes was too intense, and his story fit with Marion's report of him washing the blood off his hands. 'How long have you known?' she whispered.

'I think I've always known. I was just in denial, classic denial. I was happy to forget who I was for a while—I was happy to be stripped back to nothing. It was like being given a second chance. I started thinking I could wipe any wrongs I'd committed. I could be a good person, a happy person, someone who did the right thing. I've always wanted to be someone who does the right thing . . . I was deluded. I can see that now.'

Blondie opened the library door and stuck his head in. 'Nick, the pool table's free—you coming?' He disappeared down the corridor.

'Sure,' called Nick, 'just give me a minute.'

Kit wanted him to stay until her shock had subsided. She wanted him to talk it through with her.

'But you *can* start again, Nick, don't you see that?' she said in a quiet voice. 'So long as you're alive, you can always keep doing better, making things better. None of us knows what ugliness we're capable of till we're placed in impossible circumstances. The bulk of human beings are never tested. But if you're tried and you fail the test, it doesn't mean your character is condemned by your actions. People can change—'

'That might be true,' said Nick, studying her face intently. 'But in the here and now I can never change what I've done. I did that work for the drilling company, and there's no getting around what I did to the families of those British men. I didn't ease their suffering when I could have. It matters what I did to Jason, even though I didn't mean to kill him—it matters to Marion, that's for sure. There are things she will never do, children she will never have, because of me. I can never erase the harm and suffering I've caused. Sometimes I wonder if I should have just let Jason kill me instead—I could have lived with that a whole lot better.' Nick gave a bitter laugh at the irony as he stood up to leave.

'No, don't go just yet,' she said, standing beside him and holding his arm. 'Nick, I know you. I know you've done things you regret and that you wish you could change. But the guy who came to this base was kind and helpful, and a great person to be around. That stripped-back, blank-slate Nick was one of the good guys. If anyone could rebuild his life and repair his wrongs, it was him. He was someone even I wanted to be around.' She paused. 'He's *still* someone I want to be around.'

Touching her tenderly on the chin, Nick tilted her face towards his. He gazed at her, stroking her skin with his thumb. 'When I met you, I thought you were the most beautiful creature I'd ever seen.' He smiled mischievously. 'Of course, I couldn't remember any other women, so you were the first and the last woman I ever knew.'

She laughed and placed her hand over his, bringing it to her cheek. 'Mate, I think you just gave me a back-handed compliment.'

'No, it isn't,' he said seriously, 'it isn't back-handed.' He leaned closer and whispered, 'You're still my first and my last.' Her heartbeat quickened as his lips brushed hers. 'You'll always be my first and last,' he murmured, deepening the kiss.

As she kissed him back, she was reminded of the green flash she had seen that day on the deck of the *Southern Star*. At the time, she had thought it was an omen of doom and disaster. But now she remembered that the portent was meant to be a blessing. Those who saw the flash would never again be deceived in matters of love. They would be able to see clearly into their own hearts and into the hearts of others.

As Nick pulled her closer, Kit knew she had been blessed, not cursed. The warmth of him seeped into her arms.

One day, she thought, her own existence—the sum total of her fears and cares and woes—would itself become a mere flash in the everlasting blackness. The world would go on without her for all eternity, as though she had never existed. No one would remember her. The whole universe would be amnesic with regard to her existence. Before then, even her own mother would be unable to recall her name. Daphne's mind would become a blank sheet.

Yet Kit had known her mother's love her entire life, had felt Sally's friendship for more than half her life, and had even known Elliot's affection for a short time. Soon, she felt, she would know Nick's love too.

During her brief flash of time, she would experience the kindness and comfort of other human beings.

And right now, that was the one thing needful—that was all she needed to know.

ACKNOWLEDGEMENTS

As a child, most of what I knew about Antarctica came from John Carpenter's *The Thing*: it's really cold there (apparently), they have alien parasites that want to kill you, and everyone's pretty terrified. So I'm grateful to the people who've ventured to the region and reported back. I'm indebted to Karen Barlow's 'Breaking the Ice' blog on the ABC News site, an account of her 2010–11 voyage on the *Aurora Australis*. I'm also indebted to Ingrid McGaughey's 'Ingrid on Ice' (1997–98) on the ABC Science website, for insights about working at Mawson Station.

I would also like to acknowledge several scientific studies of Antarctica, a few of which have made their way into the narrative. On the effects of isolation on winter expeditioners: Lawrence A. Palinkas, 'Effects of physical and social environments on the health and well-being of Antarctic winter-over personnel', *Environment and Behaviour*, 1991, 23(6): 782–99. On Weddell seal distribution in East Antarctica: Samantha Lake, Simon Wotherspoon and Harry Burton, 'Spatial utilisation of fast-ice by Weddell seals *Leptonychotes weddelli* during winter', *Ecography*, 2005, 28: 295–306. On sea ice formation: Edward Blanchard-Wrigglesworth, Ian Eisenman,

Sally Zhang, Shantong Sun and Aaron Donohoe, 'New perspectives on the enigma of expanding Antarctic Sea Ice', *Eos*, 2022, 103, doi: 10.1029/2022EO220076. The quote about the detection of malingering in cases of amnesia is paraphrased from Stefano Zago, Giuseppe Sartori and Guglielmo Scarlato, 'Malingering and retrograde amnesia: The historical case of the Collegno Amnesic', *Cortex*, 2004, 40: 519–32 (p. 525).

Finally, I would like to extend heartfelt thanks to my agent Caitlan Cooper-Trent at Curtis Brown for her unwavering support and encouragement, her generosity of spirit and her truly excellent advice; my publishers, Genevieve Buzo and Jane Palfreyman, for their kind words about the early manuscript and for taking on an unknown author; to the editorial team—Genevieve, Rebecca Starford, Angela Handley, Kate Goldsworthy and Janine Flew—for their beautifully crafted feedback and their care and attention to detail; to Charmaine Alford, for so generously sharing her first-hand knowledge of Antarctic research stations; to James Mills-Hicks, for his terrific map-making skills; and to Luke Causby for his magnificent cover. A final note of thanks goes to my family—Jeremy, Anna and Beth—for their love and their laughter.

ABOUT THE AUTHOR

Riley James lives in Melbourne, Australia, with her partner and two children. She was born and raised in north-west Tasmania and has been writing since the age of six. She trained briefly as a journalist before completing a PhD and becoming an academic. *The Chilling* is her first novel.